I0581346

Are We A Bus?

By
Jeff Agins
&
Kent Niepert

The book is a work of fiction. Names, characters, places, and incidents either are products of the authors' imaginations or are used fictitiously. Any resemblance to actual events, locales, or persons, living or dead, is entirely coincidental.

Copyright@2021 Jeff Agins and Kent Niepert

All rights reserved, including the right to print this book or portions thereof in any form whatsoever. For information on bulk orders or special discounts please contact Scaggz Publishing at scaggzpublishing@gmail.com or write to Scaggz Publishing, PO Box 1349, Queen Creek, AZ 85142

Manufactured in the United States.

ISBN: 978-1-7374027-0-1 (paperback), ISBN: 978-1-7374027-1-8 (Ebook – Kindle), ISBN: 978-1-7374027-2-5 (Ebook – EPUB)

Chapter 1

"Give me that fuckin' bass drum case!" shouted Hocker as he meticulously assembled the drum kit for rehearsal to be used by Tommy "Toupee" Thompson, better known as Triple T.

"Why are you always so mean to me?" asked Teddy Red.

"You told Jeb that you had road experience! You should already be handing me what I need before I even ask you for it."

"I told Jeb that I knew about effect pedal setups, amp setups, and guitar setups!"

"Well, with me, you're going to learn and know how to do drum setups too!"

"Well, you don't need to yell at me all the time."

"Don't be such a whining little shit! Hand me the double bass pedal box now!"

As Hocker and Teddy Red continued to set up the equipment for the rehearsal scheduled later in the day, something else was happening outside in the parking lot.

"Neusy, can you roll this cabinet and amplifier inside, then help Hocker and Teddy Red?" Jeb asked Neusy as the two of them unloaded amplifiers and speaker cabinets from the rental van parked behind Big Bang Rehearsal Studios in North Hollywood. "I see Leon over there, and I need to speak with him." He set down the amplifier head on top of the speaker cabinet that Neusy had unloaded.

"Sure, Jeb! No problem," Neusy said, rolling the speaker cabinet and head away into the building.

Across the street, a man chased a squirrel in a sparsely treed vacant lot. He caught the squirrel with his bare hands and walked back to his minivan parked next to the lot. It was a beautiful 1969 faded blue VW Combi in pristine condition. A folding chair was set up next to the sliding door, with a small telescope on a tripod next to it; small containers, utensils, and a cutting board, along with a small BBQ smoker, sat on a small folding table beside it.

He banged the squirrel on the head with the handle of his military K-bar knife, sat down in his chair, and began to skin the squirrel. He rinsed it off with white vinegar and set the skinned squirrel on the cutting board. He picked up and opened a bottle labeled *Small Animal Spice Rub*, then generously rubbed the spices all over the dead animal. He prepared the coals in the smoker and lit them. Once the fire died down and the coals were giving off a nice orange glow, he added some soaked applewood chips. It already smelled heavenly even without any meat inside yet. He wrapped the squirrel in foil, fashioned it into an origami squirrel, and put it inside the cooking chamber of the smoker.

The man went around to the driver's side door, opened it, and turned on the radio before he went back to the sliding door side of the van and opened a guitar case inside. He grabbed a powder blue Fender Stratocaster by the neck and brought it outside. He sat down in his chair and started strumming a song by guitarist Jurgen Weislangwolf.

From the radio: "Good Afternoon, heavy metal fans! This is your favorite metal DJ, Metal Mike Mayhem coming at you from 75.5 KLOD. K-L-O-D, KLLOOOOOOOOOODDDD! Next up, one of my personal favorites: 'Slap the Virgin' by the Centipedes."

The man played along with the song on the radio, matching it note for note even when it came to the intense guitar solo. However, as the song finished, the man became distracted by two men arguing on the side of the rehearsal hall.

"It's Metal Mike back at you from 75.5 KLOD. Wow! What a great song that is; I never get tired of hearing it. And here is the big announcement: the Doctor of Dynamics, Jurgen Weislangwolf from the Centipedes, is in town tomorrow night playing at the Sasquatch Club in Pasadena. So, make sure to get your tickets today, don't delay. I know I will be there!"

What was happening across the street now had the man's full attention; he turned his telescope, which he usually used to spy wild game, toward the two men arguing. One man was familiar to him; it was Jeb Acorns. The other man was unknown to him. He could hear their voices getting louder.

"You promised me six hours today and four hours tomorrow morning!"

"I have other bands coming in here that I can make more money by renting to them at better rates!"

"You promised me the hours at an agreed rate! Stick to your word!"

"I made a mistake! You can only rehearse here three hours today and three hours in the morning, for that rate!"

"You're an asshole! That's how you treat Jurgen Weislangwolf!"

"Fuck you, Jeb! Business is business; I need to make money. Jurgen Weislangwolf is a washed-up old clown anyways!"

"You should think about how you do business, Fuck Face!"

"Yeah, well fuck you too, Jeb!"

Jeb slammed the van door shut and entered the rehearsal studio's side door. The other man stayed behind to have a smoke and make a call on his cell phone.

The man watching through his telescope watched Jeb Acorns enter the building. Jeb was obviously upset about the incident. The man cautiously crossed the street. Still holding onto his powder blue Stratocaster, he ran behind the rehearsal building unnoticed. There was a maintenance ladder halfway down the side of the building leading to the roof. He strapped the guitar around his back and, jumping up to grab the lowest rung, he pulled himself up and ascended the ladder quickly to the roof. Staying low, he scurried across the roof until he laid face down on his stomach near the edge of the building right above the place the other man was smoking a cigarette and talking on his cell phone.

He watched the man on the ground pacing back and forth, clearly upsetting the person on the other side of the call as well. When the man on the ground was directly below him, he leaped down and—BAMM—struck him on the head with his Stratocaster, leaving him on the ground unconscious. He then ran back across the street and sat in his chair, strummed his guitar, and enjoyed the aroma from the smoker.

"What's wrong, Jeb? You look pissed!" Neusy asked Jeb when he entered the rehearsal room.

"It's that asshole, Leon, the manager of this place. He's trying to change the times and arrangements that I made. We don't have the budget for better rehearsal halls and are limited to using shit holes like this place."

"We'll just make the best of it, Jeb. Fuck that asshole!"

"Plus, I just read that Fishbowl's tour ended above expectations. We could have been on that tour but are stuck here on this tour, working smaller venues and dealing with pricks like this guy."

"Well, it's going to get real here this afternoon, but it always works out. You know your shit, and I'm here to help. Once the Doctor arrives, it will be abuse and confusion. But it'll be good to see old Jurgen again!" Neusy replied.

Jurgen Weislangwolf is Austria's premier neoclassical rock guitar virtuoso, famous for his part in the 1980s group the Centipedes. Jurgen was born in South Africa to Austrian parents. At the time of his birth, his father worked in the diamond business; later, the family moved back to their hometown in Austria. Their home was just doorsteps away from Mozart's birth house in Salzburg. Some say that a bit of old Wolfgang's talent rubbed off on Jurgen at a young age.

These days, the Doctor of Dynamics, or the Doctor, as he is called by his fans due to his extraordinary abilities on the guitar, tours the world playing music from his world-famous career with the Centipedes and some compositions from the years after.

Like many artists since the recorded music platform has changed over the years, he must tour to survive. His concert attendance has been down since a few years earlier when he made an error in judgment. He attempted to tour Japan at the same time he had a European tour scheduled. To his advantage, the band he was supposed to take to Japan was completely different than the band he was using in Europe. The amount of money they offered to pay for the seven shows in Japan was so high he could not refuse. He was able to take well-known musicians for his backing band and record the shows for a Blu-ray and DVD release.

At the time, he was using a band in Europe as his touring band. The band themselves were called Bus Stop. They had a moderate hit song called "Standing on the Corner" three years earlier. Instead of canceling the also well-paying Eastern European dates, the Doctor decided to let the guys from Bus Stop begin the tour while he intended to join them from Japan.

His idea, because of the time difference, was to play along from Japan using Skype. He could play both shows on the same day. The spot on the stage that he usually stood was occupied by a laptop plugged into a sixty-inch monitor showing the Doctor in a hotel room playing his guitar. After the first two shows in Poland, the fans stopped attending and demanded their money back. As per their agreement, the Doctor paid Bus Stop for the remaining canceled dates and their return to Austria. This caused a gaping hole in his finances, and he had to sell his famous Fender Telecaster guitar that he used in his days with the Centipedes.

The Doctor's North American tour was scheduled in mostly lesser-known clubs. This after Mathew Zolton, better known as Fishbowl, invited him to participate in a tour playing larger venues and some arenas. There was not one guitar magazine or guitar website that was not featuring Fishbowl regularly. Fishbowl got his name when he placed a fishbowl over his head early in his career and put sunglasses on the front before he walked into a club to perform. It caught on fast, and soon he was booked solid in local clubs and had a following. He does not have a band and plays to backing tracks but always wears the fishbowl and sunglasses.

Seven years earlier, Fishbowl auditioned for a television talent show and made the first cut. His biggest competition was a ten-year-old girl that the judges fell in love with. She not only sang Elton John songs beautifully but was also capable of playing the piano while simultaneously playing the harmonica. Fishbowl made it through the season, and it came down to just him or the little girl. Coming in second, he received multiple contract options that launched his recording career.

The tour also included Dutch guitarist Benedictus Janssen. Ben, as people call him, goes by the name Pi. Not the word Pi but the symbol π. Ben graduated from engineering school, but music was his real calling. After his parents spent a small fortune on his education, he moved to America with only his guitar. Pi landed in Los Angeles and started playing on Hollywood Boulevard. He would play his guitar hooked up to a small battery-powered amp that he had purchased from a local pawn shop. Pi would balance himself on whatever he found on the street. He became one of the most popular street performers in Hollywood. He stood on trash bins, lamp posts, parked cars, gates, a barber sign, and even on a moving bus. His balance was perfect. A local morning show discovered him and did a special on him one holiday morning. Pi's act caught the attention of a famous singer from the seventies who wanted to make a comeback. After seeing the show, she contacted Pi and hired him to tour with her. They toured together for many years. Pi would climb on top of amps and speakers, then hover over the edge playing his guitar. He claimed that his engineering degree enabled him to find the perfect balance.

Pi recorded his first solo album, and it did well. Over the next few years, he recorded two more and became a touring artist on his own, playing mid-sized clubs before opening for Fishbowl the next year. He ran into trouble when a Western Pennsylvania mathematical science school sued him for trademark infringement. They were using the pi symbol on their best-selling T-shirt and sweatshirt, and while fans of the artist Pi bought their shirts from all around the world, it was not the reputation the school was after. Ben started using the name the Artist Formerly Known as π, but he was getting too many venues that wanted to book him as a Prince tribute band. He changed his name to the symbol for square root wishing to stay with the mathematical theme. After a year and a half of litigation and touring as Square Root, it was settled, Pi could use the symbol as his name if he played one show a year for the school's students free of charge. Every March 14th, Pi day, thanks to Albert Einstein, the students get high and watch Pi perform with his band as agreed. The school's enrollment increased by thirty percent, and they embellished their new image as a party school.

The Doctor declined the tour before he even knew that Pi was also on the bill. The Doctor disliked Fishbowl immensely. In his opinion, Fishbowl was a gimmicky guitarist that he could wipe the floor with using his acoustic guitar with three broken strings. Once he found out that Pi was also on the bill, no one could talk him into doing the tour. The Doctor did not like guitarists that use symbols as a name. As far as he was concerned, if they played well, and Fishbowl didn't, they should use a proper title like the Doctor. A few years earlier, he played a benefit concert that Pi also played to raise money for an ailing guitarist. Pi had the audience going insane as he balanced on everything the stage had to offer, which included the Doctor's multi-tiered effect peddle. This caused it to short out all night, and the Doctor said that he would never play on a tour that included that moron again.

After the Doctor declined the tour, Fishbowl called his longtime friend Sideburn, whose real name was Michael Karlton. Sideburn, an old-school blues guitarist, had some success with his breakthrough album in the mid-eighties. His first drummer gave him the name Sideburn because of his bushy sideburn on the left side of his face. Since the hair on the right side of his face never fully developed, he could only grow one sideburn. Due to this, the nickname stuck.

Jeb was in a foul mood the morning of the rehearsal after he read reports that the Fishbowl and Friends tour did so well that they would be touring again the next spring in even larger venues. The thing that had him down was that, except for Cleveland, they had sold out every night on the tour and had grossed more than the Doctor had made in his entire solo career.

"We better get ready to take off," said Jeb.

"It's getting near that time, isn't it?" replied Neusy.

"Hocker… Neusy and I have to go pick up the Doctor and the band from the airport. You and Teddy Red finish the equipment setup and grab a bite to eat. I'll call you guys when we are on our way back."

"Alright, Jeb! Hey, Teddy! Wheel that bass cabinet over here, PRONTO!" yelled Hocker as if he was someone of great authority.

Teddy Red walked nervously by Hocker, pushing the Ampeg 8x10 bass cabinet along the floor to its resting place right of the drums.

"I hope Hocker doesn't rip Teddy's head off while we are gone," said Neusy.

"Nah! They'll be OK. You know Hocker is mostly bark and no bite."

Jeb and Neusy made their way out the back door of the rehearsal studio and into Neusy's BMW X5. Neusy fired it up, smiled at Jeb, and started the drive toward the on-ramp of the Five Interstate North. They were pulling out of the parking lot when Leon, the manager, stumbled in front of the BMW. Neusy had to slam on the brakes so hard to avoid hitting Leon that Jeb's sunglasses fell off his face.

"What the hell is wrong with that asshole?" asked Jeb. "He fucked us on our time, and now he's just a being dick, trying to harass us." Neither one of them noticed Leon falling back into a pile of boxes after they drove past him. The occupant of the box nearest to him stripped him of his wallet and the cash Jeb had just paid him for the rehearsal space.

"You have worked with the Doctor for some time now, hey Jeb?"

"Yeah, Neusy, it's been a while. But it is always interesting."

"Remember, I didn't even know who Jurgen Weislangwolf was when we met years ago. When you told me about him, I looked for him on YouTube. What impressed me more than his guitar playing was that guitar tech you guys had."

"Oh yeah, that guy was a trip. Johnny Scaggz, never saw anyone like him in the business."

"I remember in that one video, the Doctor broke a guitar string, then you see this guy hanging upside down from the lighting truss wheeling along on some kind of pulley contraption connected to a rope around one of his legs."

"Haha! Yeah, he hovered over and changed the Doctor's guitar string as he continued to play the melody."

"And he did all of that while hanging upside down. Never saw anything like it. Astonishing! It grabbed my attention, and because of that video I agreed to the tour."

"And you probably never will see anything like that again unless it is some Chinese group of acrobats. I think that guy added some mystery and much of the hype that surrounded Jurgen Weislangwolf at that time."

Jeb closed his eyes and nodded off as Neusy drove. The tour had just started, and he was already exhausted; after arguing with Leon, he was even more tired. As he rested his eyes, he thought back to the time that he and Neusy met.

Jeb and Neusy first met when they were hired to work for the Japanese metal band Rockiyaki. The band first hit California from Japan in 2000 with a transitional management group. The booking agent, who was concerned about the management group, contacted Jeb and Neusy. The booking agent was familiar with their previous work with mid-level rock bands. Jeb was associated with many small acts and had tour management, stage setup, minimal electronic repair, logistics, and merchandising experience.

Neusy, on the other hand, was primarily experienced with guitar setups, amplifier setups, and general stage setups. He was also a somewhat accomplished guitarist himself. Neusy had previously worked with California guitar legend Sandy Streets from the band Outrageous Silence. They were both excited at the chance to work with Rockiyaki and agreed.

Rockiyaki consisted of Hajimi Hano (vocals), Kashi Kitagawa (Guitar), Matsu Meguri (bass), and Satoshi Suzuki (drums). Each band member arrived in the USA and was assigned a handler, who took care of their needs and the translation work. That is how the band communicated with the US-based management and road crew. It was problematic because the management before Jeb and Neusy found themselves asking each handler to speak with the individual they represented. If the bass player was too loud, management would have to ask his handler to have him turn it down. If the drummer needed new sticks, he would have to ask his handler to ask the management or crew member to find him a pair.

Three days before their tour kicked off in Los Angeles, Hajimi Hano asked his handler to take him to Magic Mountain to enjoy some roller-coaster action. Unfortunately, the band had a rehearsal scheduled in Little Tokyo, and the rest of the band didn't know where he was. The manager made a call to his handler. The handler informed the manager that Mr. Hano was now on the triple-loop roller coaster Riddler's Revenge.

After three days of this, the management team quit, and Jeb and Neusy were approached to take over. The band immediately fired all the handlers. Being rich boys from Tokyo, they preferred to be pampered rather than professional. The Geisha girls they had met in Little Tokyo met their requirements and they were hired as the new handlers.

They offered the Geisha girls a handsome salary to entice them to leave their jobs. The three of them born in Japan were fans of the rock band, while one of the Geishas, Asahi Please Me, was American born to Japanese parents and could speak perfect English. She hid this fact by breaking up her speech a bit while she slurred her words.

Jeb's and Neusy's first meeting with Rockiyaki took place in a Japanese bathhouse. It was the Japanese way to conduct a first business meeting, followed by sushi and sake.

"You aren't going to get me into that human cesspool of germs and bacteria," Jeb complained to Neusy.

"Come on, bro, they said that is their way. We better do it."

"Fuck that!"

"This is a good-paying gig, and we need the work."

"No, no, no!!! I will come down with some foreign virus that there is no cure for."

Asahi Please Me walked up to Jeb and whispered in his ear as she pulled up his shirt to find his belt buckle. She unfastened it, then she unzipped his fly; his pants began to slide down his legs. "Oh, please, Jeb San, Hajimi said I am to wash you in the tub while you talk."

"You're going to whhaaatt?"

"I am going to wash your body with soft loofah and soap, head to toe. Hee!" Asahi giggled in her cute, sweet voice.

"Ahhhh! OK," replied Jeb. Neusy gave Jeb a nod that said, see, not so bad. Jeb looked down at his pants, gathered around his feet, and smiled at Neusy.

Asahi was a beautiful girl, and Jeb started getting hard. Neusy, hoping for the same treatment, asked Asahi if someone would wash him. Asahi told him that Reiko, one of the other girls, would do him. Neusy was hoping the word "do" included more than just a scrubbing. All the men undressed down to their underwear while the Geisha girls took off their kimonos to reveal barely there bikinis. The soon-to-be buddies went over to the hot tub, slipped off their underwear, and slid into the warm water. The band, Jeb and Neusy, and four Geisha girls were now seated in the giant, mineral-water hot tub.

Jeb and Neusy were getting the royal treatment of being sponge bathed by two gorgeous Japanese girls in bikinis as they held their business meeting with the band.

Hajimi Hano and Kashi Kitagawa did most of the speaking in Japanese, and Asahi Please Me translated in her practiced broken English. The other two band members just enjoyed being sponge bathed. Hajimi began to speak in Japanese.

"What did he say, Asahi?" asked Jeb.

"He ask if you are happy?" replied Asahi.

"Oh yeah, I am great! You tell him that."

"He happy that you happy."

"Tell him that I like to keep a tight ship on the road, and when I say for something to be done or to be somewhere on time, I mean it."

"He understand. Japanese people very punctual. The band, certain stage setup they require. Kashi Kitagawa give printed diagrams later, for the equipment setups."

"OK, I understand," said Jeb.

The rest of the time in the hot tub was very relaxing, and the conversation kept to a minimum as the men relaxed in hot water. At the end of the bathing session, all the men stood naked, waiting to be dried off by one of the Geisha girls. Neusy was dried off first by Reiko and stood wearing a towel around his waist. Jeb, standing naked with a hard penis, was dried off by Asahi. The Japanese men were staring at Jeb's penis. Hajimi spoke in Japanese.

"What did he say?" Jeb asked Asahi.

"He said it true about American man's penis. Your is big and fat like soup can."

"Please tell him thank you for me," said Jeb.

Jeb woke up just as they were nearing the airport. Barely forty-five minutes had passed, but Jeb remembered a lifetime ago worth of good memories.

The Doctor and his accompanying musicians had already arrived at LAX on their flight in from Austria. Jeb had arranged the pickup an hour after their 4:30 landing, giving time for clearing immigration and customs.

Jeb's phone rang. "Hello," Jeb said into his cell phone.

"Jeb, this is Bobby! We are at the airport driving around. We stopped at the terminal, but the police made us move. Where are you?"

"Just pulling into the airport, see you soon," he replied. "You know which terminal, right?"

"Yeah, I know!" assured Bobby, and he hung up.

Along with the band and small crew on this early part of the tour were the Doctor's old friends, Bobby Santos and his wife Sadie. Both were mild-mannered Philippine Islanders with long black hair past their waists. They looked like brother and sister. They took care of the Doctor's food preparations and comfort necessities while the tour was in California. Whatever personal comforts the Doctor needed, Bobby and Sadie were happy to please.

Jeb and Neusy pulled past the big letters LAX and entered the airport. After circling for ten minutes, Jeb's phone rang again. This time it was the Doctor.

"Achhh! Jeb, where are you? We are standing on the curb outside the terminal. You should not leave us waiting."

"Just pulling up to your terminal now."

"We haven't all day," snapped the Doctor.

Jeb and Neusy saw the travelers and pulled right in front of them. The two men jumped out of the car. The Doctor was shaking his head, showing that he was frustrated. There were handshakes and hugs all around as the Santoses pulled up and jumped out. Sadie had two brown shopping bags, approaching them all with a huge smile.

"You are late," the Doctor said to Neusy.

"Yeah, it's rush hour here in L.A. and traffic sucks. But everything is being set up at the rehearsal studio as you requested. Hocker and Teddy Red are there now, just finishing with the equipment."

"Bobby and Sadie, how are you guys?" The Doctor asked as he embraced his two friends.

"Good, we brought you a salad and some rolls from Whole Foods. Also, some red wine for your hotel room. Are you hungry?" Bobby asked.

Sadie was so pleased with this gesture she held up the bags one at a time. As she was lifting the second bag, the bottom tore open and two bottles of red wine fell to the pavement and shattered.

"Achhh, yah, that wine does me no good now!" exclaimed the Doctor.

Sadie looked dejected; she held up the second bag again and said, "Well, are you hungry?"

"Yah! That I am."

Jeb opened the rear of Neusy's BMW and started putting in the equipment and luggage. After putting in the band's luggage and trying to fit in the Universe Guitar, bass, and Nathan's guitar, he realized that there were too many things, so he took everything back out and started reorganizing.

"Who wants to ride with us?" asked Bobby.

"Why don't you take the Doctor and Heinz and Neusy and we will take Torsten and Nathan," replied Jeb.

"Yeah, no problem, Jeb."

"OK, listen up! The first order of business is to get you all checked into your hotel rooms. After that, we will head to the rehearsal studios and get cracking. The rehearsal hall manager is giving me problems, so the sooner we get there and start rehearsing, the better," said Jeb.

As they were pulling out of the airport, Jeb's phone rang once again. "Jeb, It's Teddy, don't get mad, but there is a lot of smoke coming out of the Doctor's main amp."

"That's just fucking great!" yelled Jeb. "Put Hocker on the phone."

"Yeah, fucking Teddy blew up the amp."

"How?" asked Jeb.

"He didn't change the voltage switch on the transformer from 220V to 110V."

"There is another amp in the van; go grab that one and set it up yourself. We have the Doctor and the band now and are heading to the hotel to get them all checked in. I'll call you when we are on the way to the studio."

"OK, boss!"

Hocker closed the phone and sent Teddy Red out to the van to get the other amplifier head. Teddy Red returned from the van and nervously handed Hocker the head.

Hocker, a large muscular man complete with a beer gut that took years to perfect along with his gruesome face and bald head, looked menacing to Theodore "Teddy Red" Redwood, who was a tall twig of a man. With a whining nasally voice, Teddy Red was disliked by Hocker from day one with his rag-mop hair and colossal nose.

Teddy Red had been looking forward to going out on the road with his childhood guitar hero. Over the years, he had managed to get close to the inner circle and workings of this guitarist's management and crew. He even took college music courses to sound more intelligent when talking with musicians to get closer to the guitarist.

Teddy Red approached management regarding touring with the Doctor as a guitar tech. Promising that he knew what he was doing and offering to tour without being paid, he told them just the honor of touring with the Doctor would be enough!

Management accepted—Holy shit! It was too good to be true! Teddy Red would be touring the States with his guitar hero! Now all of this could be in jeopardy with him frying the Doctor's amp.

Chapter 2

The first leg of the Doctor's North American tour was spent mostly in California. Jeb decided to save the high cost of a tour bus by using Neusy's, Teddy Red's, and the Santoses' cars to travel in for this leg. The equipment and merchandise were hauled in a rental van from Enterprise.

Both band and crew members rode in one of these four vehicles. Except for the band's drummer, Triple T, he would drive himself to most California shows in one of his classic sports cars. His constant worry was that his wig would be blown off if the air conditioning was too high or when someone opened a car window while driving at high speed. To ensure this didn't happen, he preferred driving himself. Since California was his home state, he would drive alone before joining the band on the tour bus portion of the tour, later on.

The dates on this tour were booked mostly in clubs through a booking agency called Burger Musical Bookings International. They operated out of a small two-room office in Beverly Hills, CA that carried a prestigious address. Spud Burger ran the agency. Even though Spud ran the business mostly by himself, he thought the operation would seem more significant and more important to clients if it had a prestigious address and a two-room office. Spud had been booking tours for thirty years and formed his agency eighteen years ago with the help of his friend, Brian Wallack, the silent partner who would work a few hours a week when needed. The state of California requires that every licensed talent agency carry a bond to protect the artists they are booking. Since Spud's credit was slightly above being a deadbeat, he could not get the bond on his own. No bond, no license, no business. Spud needed Brian, and Brian liked only working part time. The business, bond, and bank account were all in Brian's name. After five years, Spud convinced Brian to add his name as a signer on the bank account. Brian liked this idea as it meant that his part-time hours would consist of even fewer hours.

Spud specialized in eighties music, more specifically eighties metal. He had a roster that seemed always to change. This was the third tour that he had booked for the Doctor. While Spud was able to book a tour that initially looked decent as far as the offers, the truth is that Spud was one of the worst booking agents of all time. Spud was notorious for creating fictitious expenses to charge artists or hold back money from the deposits. The artists, including the Doctor, all knew this. Both Jeb and the Doctor knew they would be shorted on the total deposits from Spud but continued to use him to book shows. The only other alternative was not to tour since no other agency was interested in booking the shows.

It was a fine line that Spud walked. Artists could easily file a grievance with the State of California against Burger Musical Bookings International and collect against their bond. Their license would be revoked, and Spud would be out of business. There would then be no one willing to book artists like the Doctor. Artists accepted what Spud sent them, which was better than the alternative of not touring.

The next day after the rehearsal, the mood was upbeat. It was the first show of the tour, and there was a buzz. Fans started arriving early, and for the most part, the crew that the tour hadn't beaten up yet were also in a good mood.

Using the backup amp meant they now needed to use extra caution. Jeb took Teddy Red to the side. "Hey, Teddy, we need some amp fuses, extra guitar strings, and two more power cables; why don't you find a store and go get those things before the show starts." He made sure to write down the gauge of guitar strings that the Doctor seemed to break regularly, having little faith that Teddy Red would remember. Teddy Red was more than happy to get away from under Hocker's thumb for a while.

Jeb found dealing with Teddy Red exhausting but couldn't afford the time of anyone else in the crew to be off their job. The whole setup of the stage—drums, guitar amps, and various effects for the Doctor and band—needed to be executed perfectly on a nightly basis.

Hocker Flemming, the main roadie, had been working with the Doctor for only a short time. Before landing this job, he worked with various no-name, obscure acts throughout his whole career. A few years back, he had landed this job when the band he was touring with shared a bill with the Doctor. Hocker, Jeb, and Neusy met at the bar before the show and had a few beers. A few weeks later, the Doctor's last roadie and stage manager, Johnny Scaggz, was fired. Jeb called Hocker. It was a stroke of luck to find Hocker. It is still unknown if that is his actual name or one that he earned due to his habit of chewing tobacco and continuously hocking loogies. Teddy Red detested working alongside Hocker. However, he tried to tolerate him and hoped one day he would be in the Doctor's most inner circle and be enlightened musically by this position.

Load-in was supposed to happen mid-afternoon at 3:00, but in reality, it would usually occur somewhere around 4:00 due to whatever the day's issue happened to be. Almost every night, Jeb would hear the same thing from the venue's manager. "Thought you were arriving at three. My guys have been sitting around waiting!" Jeb would just ignore them and start the load-in process. This always led to everyone being pissed off at one another until the load-in was complete.

"Neusy, now that Teddy Red is gone, I need some real help in getting this fuckin' stage set up right!" snipped Hocker.

"No problem, bro," said Neusy.

Neusy and Hocker had always worked well together in getting the stage set up. The effect pedals had particular importance to being lined up and wired in the proper order, along with paying close attention to the mismatched 220V European power and 110V American power requirements of each stompbox effect unit.

"After we get these cymbals in place, we're finished," said Hocker.

"Then we can go to the bar and get a cold one," said Neusy.

"You got that fuckin' right!" said Hocker. Neusy thought he saw Hocker drool at the mention of beer.

Jeb was sitting on a barstool at the old varnished oak bar about thirty paces from the stage. He talked on his cell phone, trying to make some last-minute arrangements for the next day's hotel. "We can only get four rooms tomorrow," remarked Jeb to Neusy and Hocker as they grabbed two barstools next to him.

"Where's Teddy Red gonna sleep? Not with me!" stated Hocker. "Let that cocksucker sleep in his car! I don't know what smells worse, his weed or his farts."

"Definitely his farts," said Jeb. "Or his fucking breath!"

The three of them laughed at the expense of Teddy Red as they sat sipping their ice-cold, thick-foamed Hefeweizens from their frosty beer mugs. Yes, this was a perk of being part of the road crew: the free beer!

It was at this time that soundcheck would typically happen. The Doctor despised soundchecks. While most professional musicians appreciated the formalities of soundcheck, the Doctor just preferred to show up at the performance and make his amp louder than everyone else's.

The Doctor had been skipping the soundcheck more and more often. It worked for him. However, his band saw it differently. Triple T used this time to completely rearrange his drum kit, which Hocker seemed never to set up the same on any given night. One night on the last tour, he set up the kit for a left-handed drummer, which was problematic since Triple T was right-handed. Triple T had grown used to this, though it was a far cry from where he used to be; he was still gigging, so that's what counted.

Tommy Thompson was nicknamed Triple T after he had a wig mishap on stage. His toupee got caught on one of his cymbal stands during the opening song on the first night of a rebooted seventies band's comeback tour that he was hired to tour with. For the remainder of the song, he constantly tried to grab the toupee between beats but failed as it was just a bit out of reach. After the song was finished, he placed the wig back on his head as the guitarist announced to the audience, "Ladies and Gentleman, let's hear it for our drummer Tommy 'Toupee' Thomson."

A native Californian, he was hired to play drums on this tour and the tour last year. Triple T was medium height with shoulder-length black hair and was slightly out of shape. No one knew much about him other than he showed up for a soundcheck, played the gig, and then disappeared. The one thing that everyone did know was that no matter how hard he banged on those drums, his hair stayed perfect. It was never wet from sweat, never out of place. No one had ever seen him without his toupee. The crew had many times tried to knock it off accidentally, but Triple T was always one step ahead of them. Like he had eyes camouflaged in that mop of hair.

The other band members consisted of Austrians—Nathan Lieber on rhythm guitar and vocals, Torsten the Viking on keyboards, and Heinz Beckenschultz on bass. Nathan Lieber was unquestionably the most handsome man in the band at 6'1" tall, along with his medium-length blonde hair, blue eyes, and bright smile. A young Austrian of twenty-nine years, he began playing guitar at ten years old. The Doctor chose him in a local talent contest to be the second guitarist in the band. He has played with the Doctor for five years and was just happy to be in the band. It got him away from his hometown, and he was able to see the world. He thought himself to be very good and felt that he could play on equal grounds with the Doctor. The Doctor liked him because he was that good. Nathan traded leads with the Doctor at times and felt that he would be the "New Doctor" one day. Then the whole roadshow would be his own.

The only problem was nobody cared. The audience barely noticed him as they were focused on the Doctor all night, which led to Nathan's biggest problem: he hadn't gotten laid since he joined this rock band and, in his mind, became a rock star. Twenty-nine years old and in a rock band, you'd think it would be easy. The groupies seemed to like him enough. The women smiled at him, but other than just a hello, he was invisible. Amazingly, all Teddy Red had to do was open his mouth and the girls would dig him. But the guitarist in the band can't get one girl? Yeah, Nathan tried all sorts of stage antics to stand out. But nothing seemed to work. Not even the muscle tee he now wore on stage. He thought that would have done it. The American girls are especially tough. Nathan was far from being a virgin, but the curse started when he joined this band. It had been five years and nothing! Not even at home. The curse was now his.

Torsten the Viking on the keyboards was a different story. The half-Danish, half-Austrian musician was always occupied with his laptop and mostly kept to himself. His four-feet-long straight red hair was often braided, along with a bushy red beard. He had a semi-muscular body, but no one noticed with the loose-fitting clothes he always wore. He lived for music and came alive on stage.

He also was twenty-nine years old and got his solo each night. Every night he got to be on stage, just him and his keyboard, playing what he loved: classical music. He already knew what he would play for that night's solo—an improvisational piece based loosely on Beethoven's 5th Piano Concerto. Yeah, Torsten could get the girls. He was tall and handsome, and the girls loved him. He did not care! His music was his life. This was a quality about him that Nathan did not understand, and he became infuriated when he witnessed the girls coming on to him.

The last band member was the Austrian-born bass player Heinz Bekenschultz. This would be Heinz's second tour; he had been with the band for just over a year. Heinz lived in America for ten years before moving back to Austria and landing this job. He stood 6'3" tall, had long curly black hair, a cleanly shaven face, and a fit muscular body. Heinz liked to exercise and eat healthy foods constantly. He learned the songs quickly. His one problem was that sometimes he would stand too close to the Doctor and bang his head when the Doctor was soloing. This annoyed the Doctor.

Heinz had a slight accent, but his English was perfect. This made the crew especially happy as not one of the crew could speak or understand German, and it made them uncomfortable when the Doctor spoke German to his band. This was happening less now that the drummer was also an American. Things were looking up!

The band tuned up and went through the motions of a soundcheck with the house sound engineer. Each night, it was someone new as it was in the band's rider that the venue provided a sound engineer. "What about the Doctor?" the sound engineer inquired. "When will he arrive so that I can get his level set up?"

"He won't be here until about a half-hour before he goes on. You will have to adjust him on the fly," replied Jeb.

The sound engineer walked away, mumbling something Jeb couldn't understand, and Jeb returned to drinking his beer. Similar conversations happened every night. The Doctor would always comment to Jeb after each show how bad the sound was. Jeb reminded him daily that if he would show up and actually be part of the soundcheck, the sound would be better. The Doctor would always reiterate, "Achhh! You know I hate soundchecks!"

Chapter 3

The band finished their soundcheck and disappeared into the backstage area where they had dinner waiting. Another point on the rider supplied to each promoter and venue. The three crew members at the bar continued to drink their beers until the doors opened and the fans filled the venue. It was time to get to work. The three men quickly finished their drinks then headed over to the merchandising area to help set up. Six different T-shirt designs were unpacked and hung for the fans to view, depicting the Doctor with his guitar in hand from every angle possible.

Bobby and Sadie Santos walked in. Bobby walked off backstage, and Sadie walked over to the merchandise booth. "Hi guys, we just dropped off a salad at the hotel for the Doctor," she said as she immediately started to make signs to display prices of the shirts. Sadie looked great behind the booth, and the fans loved talking with her. Jeb had noticed that the nights she was behind the booth, more shirts seemed to sell. So, the crew left Sadie to finish up on her own. Neusy and Hocker returned to the bar, and Jeb walked outside to call Teddy Red, being that he had left on his errands a while ago.

This west coast leg of the tour was a short run of nine dates, all traveled by cars and a van, opposed to the more expensive and much more comfortable alternative of renting a tour bus. The only reason Teddy Red was allowed to stay on tour after blowing up the amp was that he was driving band members in his own vehicle: a 2017 Dodge Caravan. Jeb spotted the Caravan as soon as he hit the parking lot.

That's odd, he thought. He approached the van and saw Teddy Red reclined in the driver's seat. Jeb thought he must be asleep or dead; if he was lucky, he would be dead. Jeb opened the door and the smell of weed surrounded him. "WHAT THE FUCK!" screamed Jeb. Teddy Red jumped. "Did you go to the store already and not tell us you're back? What if we needed that shit right away?"

"Oh shit!" cried Teddy Red. "I must have fallen asleep."

"Where are the strings?" inquired Jeb.

"Oh shit… Haaaahaaaaa… This weed is fucking amazing," exclaimed Teddy Red. "Do you smell it…? Haaaahaaa… It is in the bag still in my pocket… Haaaaahaaa. I smoked a little and must have fallen asleep. Don't worry, bro, I am on it; I'll go now and get that stuff for the Doctor."

"Why bother now? We can pick it up tomorrow; the doors are open and the Doctor will be here soon. Thanks a lot for fucking nothing!" replied Jeb. "You couldn't just get the things we needed. Fucking asleep for an hour and a half!"

"Dude, don't talk like that. I thought we were buddies, are you mad at me? I am starting to feel like you are taking advantage of me."

"Look, just pick up the shit tomorrow on the way out of town." Then, after a deep breath, "Taking advantage…? What are you, fucked in the head? We all were fucking working our asses off in there. You wanted to come on tour with us, well this is what it takes, and not sitting in your car feeling sorry for yourself," Jeb said as he walked back towards the door to the venue. *Fucking useless*.

It was starting to fill up inside. People were at the merch booth, and Sadie was doing her thing. Hocker was now behind the booth as well, trying to look important. He wanted everyone to know that he was with the band. He was leaning on a wall with a shirt not long enough to cover his oversized beer belly, with the chew in his mouth using an empty beer bottle to hock in. *Lovely sight*, thought Jeb.

As the opening band was setting up their gear, Neusy was on stage doing a once-over to ensure everything was set up for the show. Neusy wanted to make sure that they did not mess up the backline of equipment they set up earlier. On several occasions, the opening band moved or bumped the Doctor's equipment and caused problems. It would be a nightmare when the Doctor hit the stage and started the evening with an amp that crackled or, even worse, did not work at all. Neusy would have to fumble around on the stage in the dark while the Doctor screamed at him; with the audience's noise, Neusy couldn't understand what he was trying to tell him. He understood that several hundred people expected to watch a show, but instead, they watched him connect and reconnect cables until he found the culprit. It was not enjoyable, and as long as Neusy watched the fucking opening acts that didn't give a shit, it would not happen again.

The opening act this time was the Kinks Jr. This was the first time they had opened for the Doctor. They were stoked as the Doctor was the guitarist, Little Eddie's favorite, and he had petitioned hard to get on the bill. The Kinks Jr. were quite an unusual act. First, they were a Kinks tribute band, and there were not many tribute bands dedicated to the Kinks, and second, they were all dwarfs. Not one of them was over forty-five inches tall.

After ordering another beer, Jeb walked toward the stage. Neusy was looking down and talking. It appeared he was talking to himself. Perhaps the tour was getting to him already on day one. But as he arrived at the steps leading to the stage, he could see that Neusy was talking with one of the opening band members. Seeing that all was going well, Jeb headed backstage to get a bite to eat. Just as he was about to go back, Teddy Red tapped him on the shoulder.

"Hey can we talk?" he asked.

Oh shit, now what is with this fucking moron, thought Jeb. "Sure," he said and regretted it the moment the words left his mouth.

"Yo, dude, I think that I am going to go home after this show. You guys don't need me, and I feel as if you are all talking about me behind my back; it makes me feel uncomfortable."

Jeb took a moment before answering. *You've got to be kidding; this guy is a fucking little bitch.* He reworked a few things in his mind. Rent another vehicle in the morning, talk with the band, ask Heinz to drive. "OK, if that is what you want to do," he finally said, "that is fine."

Teddy Red had a puzzled look on his face. *That easy?* "Yo, bro… I just want us to be able to be friends still…" He was starting to get close to Jeb's face. The stench of his breath, a combination of weed, cigarettes, garlic from lunch, and just naturally bad breath, was starting to make Jeb sick.

"Fine, we'll still be friends, now do me a favor. Go to the hotel and get the Doctor," he said before he walked off backstage.

Teddy Red turned away, feeling good about himself. He could not wait to get into his car and take another hit of the joint he started just before confronting Jeb. "Can't fall asleep," he kept mumbling to himself as he walked outside. He lit a cigarette and walked to his car. He opened the car door. A glow on the floor caught his attention. "Fuck!" he screamed and picked up the still-lit joint. He took a hit and sat in the seat of the Caravan. No worries… Only a tiny burn hole in the carpet, and the joint was still good. *That was close. I wouldn't want to waste any of the weed; there is not much left… So gooooooohooooood!* Stoned out of his mind, he drove away to go pick up the Doctor.

The venue was like most of the venues that the Doctor played these days. It was a larger club with a capacity of one thousand but was a little better than other clubs he had performed in. There were three bars total, one on each side of the stage and one in the back. The concert area was mostly standing room with a few high bar tables in the back. Behind the tables was a curtain, and on the other side were a half dozen billiard tables. During the concert, the curtain was closed, dividing the club in two.

Neusy was chatting with the guitarist, Little Eddie. "Can't believe we are playing on the same stage as Jurgen Weislangwolf!" Little Eddie said in his high-pitched voice. Little Eddie could not stand still because he was so excited. "How is it on the road with him?" he inquired.

"It is an experience…never know what is going to happen each day. Hey, aren't you guys worried that people standing after the first row won't be able to see you?"

"We get up above the heads of the people when we are playing."

"No shit, how do you guys do that?"

"We stand on step stools when we are playing. We have step stools that were modified for us to give us each a three-foot square platform to stand on—gives us each another fifteen inches and a little bit of space to move around."

"Right on, I'll check out your set; got to go backstage now." *That is fucked up*, thought Neusy. "Good gig, man!"

"Nice talking to you," said the little voice as Neusy walked away. Neusy entered the backstage dressing room area consisting of one twenty-by-twenty room that was dimly lit with three couches and two tables with a small buffet of salad and sandwiches. Hocker was hovering over the buffet table, picking at whatever he could find.

Neusy said, "What's going on?"

"'Ey Neusthy," Hocker mumbled as food fell out of his overstuffed mouth. Jeb nodded at Hocker, and Neusy shook his head.

"Fucking Teddy Red said he is going home after the show tonight." Jeb filled the pair in on what happened with Teddy Red and how he fell asleep in his car.

"Big fucking baby!" commented Neusy. "Fucker needs to grow up!"

From the buffet table, "Fthuck thim!" as more food fell out of Hocker's mouth.

"Yeah, exactly. Now we have to rent another fucking car in the morning," Jeb said. "I just sent him out to pick up the Doctor."

"Uh-oh, hope he can do this without fucking up," said Neusy.

From the stage, you could hear some drums, then guitar to "You Really Got Me." Neusy motioned to the door—"This you gotta see!"—and the three of them walked out to the side of the stage. The Kinks Jr were going at it full force. The two guitarists and bass player stood on exactly what Little Eddie said: a three-by-three-foot platform each, fifteen inches off the stage floor. Little Eddie was at the microphone center stage singing. Behind him was the bass player on his left and another guitar player on his right. The drummer was on his platform, or mini drum riser, with a smaller-than-standard drum kit. The audience seemed to like it, or at least were intrigued by what they were watching.

The three crew members looked around the stage and then at each other, then at the stage and each other another half dozen times. Hocker, with a sandwich in each hand, did not miss a step. Neusy motioned to the back where another twenty or so dwarfs were standing on tables wearing black the Kinks Jr. shirts, with some wearing the matching cap but all with their fists pumping in the air. Hocker dropped one of his sandwiches; Jeb took a step back in complete awe and stepped on the sandwich. The three of them were mesmerized.

The song ended, and the audience applauded. The dwarfs on the tables screamed and howled. The band started playing "Lola." The dwarfs in the back were high fiving each other and screaming.

The three men stood still for the forty minutes the band played. They watched it all. The dwarfs at the back screamed for an encore that turned to boos once the lights came back on. As the Kinks Jr. exited the stage, they all gave the three crew members pats on their asses.

"That was fucked up… Man!" said Neusy, and the three of them went about their jobs. Once the Kinks Jr. had their equipment out of the way, it was just a final check to ensure that nothing got moved or disconnected. All was good; the band was back in the dressing room awaiting the arrival of the Doctor. Jeb's phone rang, the display showing it was Teddy Red. With a shake of his head, he answered, "Yes, Teddy."

"I just wanted to let you know we will be leaving the hotel in about fifteen minutes. The Doctor was sleeping when I arrived, he told me to go away, so I sat in my car. I just checked on him, and he is taking a shower; he said it will be another fifteen minutes."

Jeb managed a sarcastic, "Great! That means we will be starting late again… Just hurry up."

Chapter 4

After about forty minutes, Teddy Red showed up carrying the Doctor's guitars. He always walked with a swagger that encouraged people to watch him while carrying these guitars. He felt special, and the joint he just finished smoking didn't hurt either. The Doctor was about ten paces behind, surveying the venue.

Teddy Red arrived in the dressing room like he just saved the world. "I got the Doctor; he wants to go right on," he said. The band and crew eyeballed him as he set the guitars down and opened one of the cases. He turned to Jeb and said, "Duuuude…we have to talk—I'm not going home. The Doctor and I had a nice chat."

"What are you talking about?" said Jeb surprised.

"It's all good dude, you and I just operate on different wavelengths."

The Doctor walked in, saw Teddy Red with one of his guitars, and said, "Why is this guy touching my guitar?"

Neusy grabbed the guitar that Teddy Red had in his hands and said, "Why are you touching the Doctor's guitars? Go bring some bottled water out onto the stage for the guys!" Neusy opened the other case before walking out of the room with Teddy Red, who was doing his best not to drop any of the dozen bottles of water that he was carrying.

"Teddy, what the fuck, what the fuck? What the triple fuck are we talking about with these wavelengths?" asked Jeb as they were leaving the room. Teddy Red dropped a bottle; when he bent down to pick it up, he dropped the rest of them. The plastic bottles bounced in every direction when they hit the floor. Neusy turned and smiled at Jeb, stepped over the bottles, and then walked on stage with the guitars.

The Doctor grabbed a Red Bull off the table and said to Jeb, "I'm ready; I want to go on now."

Jeb said, "I'll let them know," and walked out of the room.

The Doctor picked up his Universe Guitar, a marvelous creation of his own, one that only he could play to the fullest; some say beyond the universe is where his playing takes them. After years of playing Chapman Sticks and his Fender telecaster, he developed the first Universe Guitar. The instrument consisted of nine strings and thirty-four frets. It could cover every note on the piano and then some. It could even play notes that only dogs could hear. Sometimes dogs would be let into venues so that people could see his guitar's effect on our canine friends.

The smallest string was a .003 gauge that was so small that it took an exact, delicate pressure that only the Doctor could execute; anyone else would break the string because it was so fragile. The guitar had a specially designed pick-up system that was so dynamic nothing else could compare to its sound. The scalloped white-maple neck had abalone planet fret markers. The scalloping of the guitar neck was important to the Doctor; he liked the notes to sound fuller without the string making contact with the wood of the neck.

The Universe Guitar has a unique shape of a comet with a long tail for a neck, encircling a central planet-shaped body with the pick-ups and bridge attached. The tail and the body looked like two different pieces, and no one knew how they were attached. Some speculated they were held together by a magnetic field, but only the Doctor knew for sure. The color of this wondrous creation was cosmic purple with airbrushed white stars gleaming in the background, with the body a brighter bluish-white. The guitar also featured a tremolo arm that was twenty-two inches long. This tremolo arm, when fully depressed, would rumble the building with subsonic waves of a 6.8 earthquake.

Every time the Doctor donned the Universe Guitar on stage, there was a standing ovation. The crowd would lose their minds. As he played his first notes, their screams would grow even louder and louder. On occasion, some individuals would pass out and faint from the excitement of the sight of this unique instrument.

The Universe Guitar almost had a life of its own. People would always want to see it. Wherever Jurgen Weislangwolf would make an appearance, people would always ask to see the guitar. The guitar had become just as famous, if not more famous, than the man playing it.

Neusy and Teddy Red returned from the stage, the house lights went off, and the band was on the stage. The audience was utterly awestruck at the magnificent image that stood before them.

The Doctor was wearing a purple coat with many buttons from an earlier time. One that the composers of the 1700s might have worn. The front had constellations hand-set into the fabric. Underneath, he wore a black shirt with Mozart's image done in sequins, along with black spandex pants from the 1980s featuring a jewel-encrusted silver-and-leather belt from India. On his feet, he wore handmade clogs also with the same jewels. Bracelets made of silver and embedded with many different colored stones covered both of his wrists. On his head, he wore his favorite white Mozart wig with a braided ponytail adorned with a purple bow from a previous century, tying it at the end. The Doctor's grandfather obtained the wig in Austria at an auction when he learned it was actually Mozart's wig. The Doctor liked these types of wigs from the past. Among his favorites were ones that looked like J.S. Bach's hair. Since he wore the wigs all the time, everyone was left guessing his actual hair color. However, since his eyebrows were brownish, it was assumed his hair was also brown.

The band looked at the Doctor, waiting for their cue, which was the Doctor raising the guitar in the air and then lowering it abruptly and nodding his head. He did so, and the band began to play "Universal Delusions," a classic composed by the Doctor. And with the opening notes, the crowd was lulled into a delusional state. In the song's midsection, the Doctor hit an ear-splitting high C note that brought some of the listeners down to their knees in brain-shattering pain. When he played in the high range of the Universe Guitar, the club owner's, Blind Melon Nixon's, seeing-eye dog started yelping and whimpering while trying to climb the walls. The song came to its climax, and then he brought everyone back into a state of delusion.

"How did you all like that little number? It has always been one of my favorites." The Doctor looked at Triple T tuning his drums and said, "Everyone, please give applause for our drummer, Tommy Thompson. He is doing a wunderbar job, yah?"

Triple T just looked up from behind his drum set and smiled. His hair wasn't wet at all after the ten-minute-long first song that they had just wrenched out. He finished tuning his snare drum and was ready to rock once more.

"Here is one you all may know, 'Potato Gravy!'"

YAAAAAAAAAAAAAAAHHHHHHHH!!!! The crowd sounded like an angry Roman Colosseum mob. And with the twenty-two-inch-long tremolo bar depressed down to the body of the guitar, and his 900-watt custom Galactic tube head, the Doctor rumbled the house. Beer bottles fell off tables, bottles fell off shelves behind the bars, men in the restroom couldn't pee straight into the urinals, women couldn't pee straight in the toilets sitting down as the low-wavering sound shattered two bar mirrors hanging on the back wall. It was tearing into the very souls of the people, and they loved it. Then Nathan belted out the lyrics.

Sitting around the dinner table, waiting to spice up my spuds
Hungry, hungry
Sitting around the dinner table, waiting to pour on some mud
Potatoes, plain potatoes
PLAAAAAINNNN POTATOES
I need some sauce
PLAAAAAINNNN POTATOES
They need brown sauce
POTATO GRAVYYYYYYYYY!

It was just incredible, just like the old Centipedes song was supposed to sound: fantastic. A strange piece but meaningful to the Doctor because he was a vegetarian.

It was unknown whether it was the excitement or the volume, but people would black out regularly at the Doctor's performances. The blackouts were interesting because, usually, vocalists were the ones to woo the audience or make them go crazy. But when Jurgen Weislangwolf played his Universe Guitar, it was just out of this world; people went nuts for it. The song ended, and the Doctor approached the microphone.

"Achhh! How about a Deep Purple song, yah?"

"Please welcome our guest singer, Michael Marvel, yah!"

YEEEEEEEEAAAAAAAAAHHHHHHHHHHHHHH! The crowd roared. Michael Marvel came out in black leathers and a blue handkerchief headband. He stood 5'8" tall and was known for his extraordinary high voice, which could also produce pitches that only dogs could hear. Marvel had previously toured with the Doctor on a recent album tour, but that proved to be difficult for the Doctor and the rest of the band. Marvel would talk to himself while traveling on the tour bus. He would crawl into his bunk and start a conversation with himself, annoying everyone wanting to sleep. When he began having arguments with himself that turned violent, he was asked to leave the tour, and that is when Nathan took over the vocal duties.

Marvel always needed his supply of liquid on stage. Most of the band just wanted water, but Marvel would not even walk on stage until his water bottle, filled with baby formula, was waiting for him.

Right before Marvel walked out, he asked Neusy, "Where is my drink?"

"On the drum riser," replied Neusy.

"Three scoops of powder, not any more or any less, right?"

"Yes, I mixed it myself," sighed Neusy.

"Good, it helps me hit those notes!" he said and walked on stage. Neusy gave him a thumbs up that turned into a fuck you as Marvel's back was to him.

It was weird shit, and the Doctor, being a tolerant person, only tolerated Marvel for a month on the road. Now Marvel would only do guest appearances with the Doctor. And when it came to Deep Purple, Michael Marvel could sing Ian Gillan better than Ian Gillan, no shit! The band began to play, and Marvel began to sing.

"Nobody's gonna take my car. I'm gonna race it to the ground..." Then he did the screams. "WAAAAAOOAWWWWWWWWHH!"

Girls took off their panties and bras and threw them at him; it made him sing even better. He stuffed the panties in his pocket and saved them so he could sniff them later.

During the Deep Purple tune, the Doctor looked at Heinz Bekenschultz in frustration. He thought, *Ach! This guy isn't getting the groove right.* He gave Heinz the Austrian Glare of Death, which was like the sign for the "Evil Eye" used in Transylvania. Heinz knew he better tighten up his playing, or the Doctor might give him the ax and replace him. The Doctor was quickly frustrated by poor musicianship and was known to replace more musicians than Ritchie Blackmore. Bass players got the ax quite regularly.

The Doctor announced, "Here is another oldie, 'Bitchy Wife.'"

YYAAAAAHHHHHHHHHH!!! arose once more.

People couldn't help noticing that Triple T's face looked like he was trying to take a painful shit. He had a grimace of sheer displeasure on his face, and after an hour of playing, his hair still wasn't wet. The Doctor wondered if he should call a break after this song to let Triple T go to the bathroom. He finally realized that is how Triple T always looked when he played the drums; that was just how he got into the music by looking as if he was about to take a shit on stage.

On this particular night, the Doctor pulled a few surprises out. He played songs off the Centipedes' *Poisoned Virtue* album. This concert was the first time since touring with the Centipedes that he played these songs, including the hit "Life's Like a Dagger." The audience loved it. The band played on for three hours until the power got cut off due to the curfew. The venue was not allowed to have bands play after midnight due to complaints from residents, who lived behind the club. The Doctor instructed the band to finish playing with no power. Nobody could hear a thing except for drums in the background. Nothing unusual; nobody in the band or crew thought anything of this. Neusy looked at Jeb, and Jeb just gave him the nothing-I-can-do look.

Neusy and Hocker broke the stage down. Jeb settled up with the venue. Cash is king and is how Jeb liked to be paid. Hocker was carrying equipment out the stage doors and was loading up the van.

The Doctor stopped Neusy. "I have to get back to the hotel. I'm tired! No meet und greet tonight!"

Neusy looked over at Teddy Red, who was sitting on a speaker cabinet. "What are you doing, Teddy? That's fucked up! We are breaking down and you are just sitting on your ass. Why don't you take the Doctor back to the hotel before Jeb sees you."

"It's all good, bro… He and I work on different wavelengths." Teddy Red then turned to the Doctor and said, "No problem… I'll take you back…ready?" And with that, the two left the venue. Most of the crew would not see the Doctor until he arrived at the next gig. Same story every night with no bus—and the crew preferred it that way.

Chapter 5

The day after the show in Pasadena was the day that many long awaited. It was a day that Jurgen Weislangwolf, the Doctor, spoke to 100 handpicked musicians that had paid in advance to hear him talk about his music, inspiration, and life. The venue remained closed during the day as these 100 guys and gals shelled out $1,000 a piece just to be in the same room with him as he spoke words that they yearned to hear. Many of these people were just Jurgen Weislangwolf fans that were in awe to be in his presence. Others were serious musicians who aspired to play as well as the Doctor. Neusy noticed that there were Egos with a capital E. Guitarists could take the stage during the "play their own piece" part of the seminar; many had swelled heads, leading the way.

The preparations for the seminar started early. One key ingredient to the seminar was twelve lollipop flavors, one for each musical note. There was an immense laptop projector as he used visual aids along with audible music. The projection screen needed to be hung somewhere on a wall, or from water pipes or ceiling beams, since it was discovered that the poles and stand for the screen were still back in Austria.

Neusy duct taped the screen to wherever he felt he could hang it where the class could see it, and it would not fall. The screen was twenty feet wide and twelve feet tall, made from heavy vinyl. The laptop was set on a card table far enough away to get the proper aspect ratio. The Doctor liked it to be perfect and spent an hour after he walked in before the seminar adjusting the distance from the projector and the screen. A keyboard and guitar amp also had to be set up for the Doctor to play notes as he spoke to the class. A second amp was set up for the students to come up and demo.

One of the most important things that had to be available when the Doctor walked in was coffee and plenty of it. During the seminar, it was Neusy's job to constantly fill the Doctor's cup with coffee as he spoke all day. Sadie Santos would make sure that the coffee pot was continually brewing fresh coffee. With everything in place, the classroom venue was set for the Doctor to begin his teachings.

"Guten Morgen!" he said as he walked in and greeted the class. "I am going to speak of things that you have never heard of in your meager, little lives, nor have your puny brains ever conceived of such things," the Doctor said. "Now, close your eyes and don't speak; just listen," he ordered. "Can anyone tell me what a root note is?" Many people raised their hands and suggested answers; however, none of their answers were what the Doctor was looking for. "You have all answered incorrectly!" he said in a somewhat annoyed manner. "It has taken me all of my life to answer this question, and you all have failed miserably."

Neusy sat in the background, chuckling to himself. *This is great,* he thought, how funny the Doctor's voice sounded. When he was away from the Doctor with the crew, Neusy would always mimic the Doctor's voice for a comical response. "Neusy," the Doctor called out. "It is now time to close the lights." Neusy went into the hallway behind the club's kitchen area and dimmed the lights.

While in the hallway, he bumped into Jeb. "Hey, Neusy, I need you to do me a favor today," said Jeb.

"What do you need?" Neusy said.

"I have to leave now with Hocker and go set up the equipment by ourselves at the Brassiere Club for tonight's gig. I need you to make sure that the seminar is over by 4:00 p.m. Get Jurgen in your car and drive out of here by 4:15. I need Jurgen to be in Redondo Beach at the Brassiere Club by 5:30 for a soundcheck." The Brassiere Club was not available for the seminar, so they decided to hold the seminar at the venue from the previous night since it was available. This made the day difficult, being at two separate locations.

"All right, Jeb, I'll handle it," said Neusy, but knew that this task would not be easy. The Doctor's long-winded speeches could take forever to get through. The Doctor would often make a statement and then re-explain it four or five different ways. A five-minute statement could be repeated and reworded over a twenty-five minute period.

"Neusy, where is my coffee?" the Doctor cried out.

Oh shit, Neusy thought and rushed back to the coffee pot to refill the Doctor's cup; he would have to find where the Doctor sat his special stainless steel coffee cup.

All morning, Neusy and the Santos couple took care of the Doctor, ensuring that the seminar ran smoothly. Teddy Red was of no help. With Jeb and Hocker already gone and on their way to the next venue, he was free to do as he pleased. So Teddy Red decided he would be a non-paying class attendee for the day. Why not? He had been working hard and deserved to absorb some of the Doctor's teachings. He pulled up a chair and joined the rest of the class.

It was now getting close to the lunch break. Sadie Santos ran out to get salad lunches for the Doctor, Bobby, Neusy, and herself. The Doctor, being a vegetarian, limited the choices for lunch. When the Doctor called a quick break, Neusy and the Santoses discussed whether to start the lunch break now or in a little while. Before they decided, the Doctor returned to his place in front of the crowd and began speaking again.

Neusy had already started to eat his salad, quietly and non-obtrusively behind the giant, elongated, wooden bar where alcoholic delights were served the night before. Unfortunately for Neusy, the Doctor always was in perfect unison musically with his environment. If 100/100 hearing was possible, the Doctor had it. He heard Neusy take a bite of lettuce fifty feet away. "Achhh! I hope we are not disturbing your lunch, Herr Neustadt," the Doctor blurted out sarcastically.

"Sorry, I thought this was the lunch break," answered back Neusy.

"Nein, it is not lunchtime. There is a time to eat and a time to listen and learn. This is the time to listen and learn. Yah!" retorted the Doctor. Neusy suddenly felt that he descended to the level of Teddy Red. Now the Doctor had ridiculed him in front of the class. Being called out in front of everybody would bother Neusy for a long time to come.

Thirty minutes later, the actual lunch break began, and the students had a chance to eat and think about what the Doctor taught during the morning session. the Doctor and the Santoses sat on barstools around the outer side of the massive bar and ate their salads. Neusy, not wanting to socialize after his scolding, ate his lunch in the kitchen hallway. After the lunch break, the Doctor had a special treat designed to expand the puny minds of everyone in attendance. Something so unorthodox, as far as teaching music and philosophy, no one would ever have conceived of it; no one except Jurgen Weislangwolf. "OK, Neusy, it is time to dim the lights!" commanded the Doctor. Neusy dimmed the lights as instructed, and the image on the screen was now visible. It looked like a recipe for fruit salad.

"Und now it is time to pass out the lollipops," instructed the Doctor. Bobby, Sadie, and Neusy grabbed the specially prepared plastic bags, each bag with twelve lollipops, each lollipop a different flavor. There were 110 plastic bags in all, one bag for each attendee and a few extra. Teddy Red was happy to get a bag unnoticed. "Yes," he said to himself, *perfect for cottonmouth*, and he slipped a lollipop into his mouth.

"Now, everyone has the lollipops?" the Doctor asked. And when everyone answered him back with a headshake or a grunt, it was time to begin. "It is possible to compare music and notes to flavors and taste," stated the Doctor. "I want everyone to take out the cherry lollipop und put it in your mouth. Now, can you taste an A note?" he asked the class. "Und now put the lemon lollipop into your mouth. Can you taste C sharp?" he asked. "Suck on the note…feel the note…be the note!" the Doctor exclaimed.

Wow, what a concept: notes with the same value as a flavor. Neusy chuckled to himself, wondering if this was Willy Wonka giving a class on candy making, or was this a great composer discussing music and its elements?

Teddy Red, being stoned, didn't care; he was busy shoving different flavors into his mouth. The full-flavor spectrum of musical notes was pleasing to him. The spectators were in total awe of this kind of instruction. The Doctor was right: none of their puny little minds could have ever thought of these things. The Doctor went through all the notes and flavors over the next few hours, and the students wholly opened their minds to new things.

Grape would be remembered as G Sharp, Raspberry as E, and coconut remembered as B.

Teddy Red started to experiment. He was putting the lollipops one by one in his mouth, trying to put runs together to see what certain songs tasted like. He started with "Jingle Bells" and, before long, was trying to taste the Centipedes classics. He was moving lollipops quickly in and out of his mouth, simulating notes of what he thought he was tasting, that the people around him were starting to stare as he hummed ever so quietly the songs he was tasting.

The Doctor took notice. "Teddy, what are you doing? That is quite disturbing to the class!"

Teddy Red looked up; the class looked at him. "I was just operating in the zone—this concept is amazing!" There was red saliva on the left side of his mouth, blue on the right, and his chin had the remnants of all the flavors.

The Doctor walked over to Teddy Red. He had sucked his lollipops down to the sticks; only two lollipops remained, each a quarter of their original size. The Doctor smelled the weed, eyed Teddy Red, and said, "We must talk later, Teddy! Neusy, give him another bag of pops. Now stay with the class!" The Doctor returned to the front of the class.

Neusy handed Teddy Red another bag. The Doctor smiled and said, "Now you see the power of the lollipop, yah? I think that Mr. Redwood understands. Isn't that right, my friend?" Teddy Red felt great. The Doctor used him as an example of something good, something that was right. *Fuck Jeb and the crew*, he thought. *The Doctor understands me. We operate in much closer frequencies than Jeb and his band of assholes.*

The Doctor started up again, explaining how each note was relevant. He instructed the class to open their minds, explaining that everything in the universe was connected in this same manner. He told them to remember these flavors when they played and composed music, and to use these ways to think of how to play a run of notes.

Teddy Red again started humming a song in a low voice and, with each note, popped a different lollipop into his mouth. *WOW*... he thought, *this is too cool! Jurgen is truly the Doctor.* The Doctor was in full swing now. He eyed Teddy Red as he was speaking. He knew Teddy Red was fragile after his conversation from the previous evening. Teddy Red was tapping his foot, moving lollipops in and out of his mouth at record speed. Fellow students were looking at him, and the Doctor stopped talking. The Doctor nodded at Neusy, and he turned on the lights.

Teddy Red didn't notice the lights come on as his eyes were closed; he was in full jam mode. His humming became louder, and his foot pounded the time on the floor. Lollipops were flying in and out of his mouth. Everyone in the room stared at him. Neusy flashed the lights on and off, hoping to get Teddy Red's attention. Several of the students near him whispered things like, "Dude!" "Bro, what is wrong with you?" and "Stop that stupid shit!" But nothing was bringing Teddy Red out of his trance. The Doctor looked at Neusy and then towards Teddy Red. Neusy started towards Teddy Red, not knowing what he would do.

As Neusy approached Teddy Red, he could see that Teddy Red's face was wet and streaky with the different colors of the lollipops. *Disgusting,* he thought, *I am not going to touch him. Kick him, yes, but not touch him.* Teddy Red's humming was getting louder, and the lollipops were moving faster, as if performing the finale to his new composition. Neusy approached Teddy Red as the humming became even louder. Some of the lollipops were now just sticks again. Neusy lifted his foot, and Teddy Red screamed right before Neusy moved his foot. The scream, more like an orgasmic scream, made Teddy Red throw his head back with his eyes still closed. With a content look on his face, he remained motionless. The room went silent. Everyone looked at Teddy Red then back and forth at Neusy, waiting. Neusy, after a moment, put his foot down and walked over to the light switch and the room went dark.

It was approaching 3:45 p.m. Bobby Santos reminded Neusy that they would have to finish soon as he had promised Jeb. Bobby told Neusy to gradually dim the lights to let the Doctor know they were getting close to the end of the class. The Doctor was deeply involved in a subject and was going through his many different explanations of the same thought. Neusy was in the kitchen hallway, with his finger on the dimmer switch raising the lights little by little, when a screeching voice yelled out from the other room.

"Neusy!" the Doctor shouted, "Turn off the lights, you Dummkopf!"

Oh, shit, thought Neusy, *I am really like Teddy Red now.*

Teddy Red was sitting in his chair with the other students, laughing at the Doctor's scolding of Neusy. "Ha, ha ha ha ha ha haaaaaa!" he laughed out loud. "Fucking Neusy got it now!"

Bobby looked at Sadie. "Oh shit, did I get him in trouble or what?" he asked his wife. They kind of just shrugged their shoulders and listened on.

Jeb called Neusy on his cell phone. "Do you have him in your car yet? Are you guys driving to Redondo Beach?"

"No, I'm trying, but he just keeps talking; I just got reamed out for turning the lights on," replied Neusy.

"Let me talk to him," said Jeb.

The Doctor was standing in the center of the class, talking away while Neusy stood next to him, waving his cell phone. He didn't dare to say a word. After this had gone on for a few minutes, the Doctor looked at Neusy waving the cell phone and said, "What is it now? Is that Jeb on the phone? Let me guess, he wants me at the Brassiere Club for the soundcheck, right?" Neusy felt about two feet tall. "You tell Jeb we will leave when I am ready to leave."

Jeb heard everything through the cell phone and hung up. "Do all of you see what just happened here?" asked the Doctor. "Neusy has ruined the mood of what I was saying. There is a right time to interrupt and a wrong time to interrupt, und this was the wrong time, Neusy," the Doctor scolded him again in front of the class. "There is a valuable lesson in this."

Neusy felt so small and wanted to crawl into a mouse hole he saw in the baseboard earlier. Being belittled in public by his favorite rock guitarist was more than he could take. But Neusy wasn't a weakling like Teddy Red; he stood there with a perplexed look on his face and withstood the Doctor's verbal abuse.

After the verbal whipping, the Doctor announced it was time for all students to go outside in the parking lot for the annual class photo. Neusy knew after the picture was taken he could finally get the Doctor in his car. He would fulfill his responsibility of getting the Doctor to the next venue for the soundcheck that the Doctor despised.

Neusy could hardly wait to get the Doctor into his car for a more detailed look in retrospect on how he fucked up. The time came, and the Doctor was finally in Neusy's car. He asked if Neusy had learned what to do and what not to do. Neusy said he understood, but he was responsible to Jeb to get him to Redondo Beach in time. They both civilly agreed, and they were on their way.

The Doctor asked, "Neusy, don't you have a GPS?" Neusy gestured that he didn't as he missed the freeway on-ramp to Redondo Beach.

"Do you see why you need a GPS?" the Doctor asked. "Everyone in Austria has a GPS; that way, these things don't happen." Neusy kept quiet, pulled a fancy hairpin illegal U-turn under the freeway overpass, and got onto the correct freeway on-ramp.

Chapter 6

Jeb and Hocker pulled the lucky duty of loading in and setting up the stage at the Brassiere Club. The famous club was located underground, right on the beach. Once inside, it looked like a classy joint. The place resembled a well up-kept 1940s dinner club that was right out of a movie set. This club was well known, and many movies taking place in the thirties or forties had used this club for interior shots of dinner and dance clubs. It was so well preserved that it has become a tourist attraction for people visiting the L.A. area.

Above the club sat a restaurant and a surfboard shop. Jeb and Hocker carried all the equipment down the two flights of stairs. Among the equipment were three guitar amps and speaker cabinets custom-made for the Doctor and his rhythm guitarist by world-famous German amp company Galactic Amps. They also had to haul in drums, cymbal stands, cymbals, the Hammond B3 organ, and bass amp and speaker cabinet. Being right on the water made it extra humid, and the pair were in foul moods while setting up the stage. After spending as much time cursing and arguing with one another as hauling in equipment, the job finally got done.

The Santoses arrived first from Anaheim and filled Jeb in on the events of the day. Jeb found the Doctor's actions of the day to be quite annoying but was used to this, so he had grown immune to these actions. The Santoses always made being on the road a little easier, and both immediately got to work. Sadie busied herself with the merchandise while Bobby made sure the backstage area was stocked properly for the Doctor.

The merchandise on this tour included T-shirts with a picture of the Doctor and Jurgen Weislangwolf's name; each shirt had a slightly different picture. One shirt had the Doctor on the front and his signature Universe Guitar on the back. Another had the Universe Guitar on the front, and the tour dates with the Doctor's on-stage image on the back. All the shirts carried the same themes. The Doctor insisted on having a variety of similar-looking shirts.

Also sold at the merchandise booth, which was just a couple of tables set up in the back of the venue, were various CDs and DVDs by the Doctor. The Doctor would frequently sit after the performance by the booth and sign the merchandise, which always was welcomed by Jeb. People bought more merchandise while the Doctor was in signing.

Where the hell are they? thought Jeb when neither the band nor the Doctor had shown up. Hocker had already taken his seat at the bar and was finishing his second beer, talking to Michelle. She was the bass player in the opening band who was waiting around with her bandmates for the delayed soundcheck to end so they could set up their gear. An all-girl band and Hocker couldn't believe his luck: the hottest one of them was pounding beers with him! The bartender handed them each a third beer, and Michelle finished half before the bottle hit the bar. Hocker thought this chick was incredible, and as the beer hit his system, he began to fall in love.

Jeb left Hocker alone, figuring the big guy might get lucky. Hocker would have a habit of over exaggerating every circumstance to boost his image. He would take credit for just about anything. "The tour would never have gotten off the ground if I didn't book additional tour dates, because the booking agency isn't worth shit." Or "See the T-shirts, what do you think? I designed them." Or even "You know about the Doctor's guitar, right? When he had it built, he would consult me every day to make sure it was done right."

The opening band was an all-girl Kiss/Iron Maiden tribute band that called themselves the Kissing Maidens. Jeb was standing at the entrance of the club, looking at a poster of the night's show, waiting for the Doctor to arrive. *Jurgen Weislangwolf, legendary guitarist of the Centipedes,* the poster stated with a current picture of the Doctor. On the poster was also a picture of the opening band.

These ladies wore Kiss makeup and played a set of Kiss and Iron Maiden songs. A four-piece band, what the poster did not mention was that the bass player was named Michael Erickson. That's right, a man, in fact not only a man but a gay transvestite. He was the hottest girl in the band! Unsuspecting guys hit on him before, after, and during the shows. Which he, of course, did not mind since he was addicted to sex.

Occasionally Michael would get his ass kicked by a guy who thought he was kissing a woman and ended up with another guy's junk in his hand. Michael was careful and tried not to let that happen. But on most nights, the unsuspecting man would go home with a smile after the show. Michael loved giving blowjobs and had no problems finding willing takers. After all, Michelle, as he called himself, was a beautiful woman.

By the time Teddy Red, the Doctor, Neusy, and the band showed up, Hocker was feeling pretty good about himself. Jeb saw them and walked with them to the stage, where Triple T was waiting behind his drum kit. The sound engineer was reading a newspaper and commented how late it was for a soundcheck.

The Doctor responded, "Don't worry, this will be the quickest soundcheck ever!"

And so it was. Ten minutes and they were done. The Kissing Maidens started to set up their equipment. Michelle kissed Hocker hard and deep and said, "See you later."

"Yes, you will," Hocker responded. He finished his beer, grinning from ear to ear. Everyone in the room noticed the bulge in his pants as he could not stop touching it.

The opening band set up their gear, no soundcheck, and the doors opened. After an hour, The Kissing Maidens began their set. They were in full Kiss makeup and attire. They opened with "Detroit Rock City." They were good; the audience liked them quite a bit. Hocker was in love. He spent the whole hour watching from stage right. He could not keep his eyes off Michelle. She was hot! Hocker felt like he was in heaven every time she smiled at him. So what if she had on goofy Kiss makeup? That would come off after the show. Otherwise, it would be like kissing Gene Simmons… Yuk, that was a horrible thought!

Jeb was sucking on some cold suds with Neusy. Hocker gave Neusy and Jeb the thumbs up with a boyish grin on his face, standing in front of the stage now. Neusy returned a thumbs-up sign, and Hocker raised his beer high in salute. Hocker was happy! Neusy looked around the stage to make sure that none of their backline was moved. Satisfied that all looked good, he returned to his beer.

The Kissing Maidens finished their set, and the audience called them back for more. Iron Maiden's "Number of the Beast" finished off their set. Hocker was pumping his fist. He had a fully throbbing hard-on that was moving to the beat. *Holy shit*, he thought, *this chick is awesome!* The Kissing Maidens finished their set; they walked off stage with the audience applauding. Michelle stopped by Hocker and kissed him. *Weird*, he thought, *but she is really hot in that makeup!*

After a half hour, the Doctor walked out on stage. People were screaming and pointing at the amazing Universe Guitar. The Doctor said, "Hallo Redondo. We played here last year. Who was here?" They started shouting. The Doctor continued, "I was here too! We are going to start with something different tonight." Then to the band, "You guys don't know this, just try and keep up." The Doctor played the first few notes of the Centipedes' classic "Smelly Cat!" The audience ate it up!

Hocker was waiting for Michelle to change and join him for another beer. Jeb and Neusy were resting in the back. Teddy Red was sleeping in the dressing room.

Finally, Michelle came out in what she was wearing before the show: jeans and a T-shirt. She had her woman makeup on now. Hocker could not stand still; she waved to him working up on the stage. The show continued with many Centipedes classics. They followed up with songs from the Doctor's solo career. The show was short, only two and a half hours, as far as Jurgen Weislangwolf standards. He played three encores.

The show ended, and the crew jumped into their routine. Tonight would be different for Hocker; he had a date! He rushed around the stage, picking up drums, dropping drums, picking up drums again, moving faster than he ever had.

Neusy said, "Cool it, big guy. She's waiting for you."

"Can't stop thinking of her. Have you seen her? She said she would be waiting for me around the stage."

"I'm sure she's around."

Jeb collected the money and joined the crew on stage. Teddy Red was doing his usual post-concert job, which consisted of trying to do nothing. He was following the Doctor around while he was signing autographs. The Doctor was in great spirits tonight after the show. He went backstage, changed clothes, and emerged with a bottle of red wine. Perhaps the wine was the reason for his good mood.

The crew had the stage broken down. Now to haul it all up the stairs. Hocker was pushing the other two. "C'mon, guys, let's get this done. Haul this shit up those steps… Fuck, this place has the worst load-in!"

The crew managed to get everything up the steps and loaded in the van. Teddy Red was smoking a cigarette outside. "Those steps are fucked up," he commented to Hocker as he emerged with an amp in each hand. Hocker was going to beat on him but was in such a hurry to meet up with his date, he walked past without stopping. The crew finished up and headed back inside. The few remaining people were all crowded around the door to the dressing room.

Jeb said, "What the hell is going on?"

Neusy responded, "Something happened."

The three headed to investigate; as they approached the group of onlookers, Jeb asked, "What's going on?"

"Someone strangled the bass player from the Kissing Maidens," said one of the onlookers.

"NOOOO!" shouted Hocker.

"Yeah," the onlooker continued, "with a guitar string. Stabbed her in the neck and pulled it halfway through and then wrapped the string around her neck."

"NO, NO, NO, NO!" shouted Hocker again even louder.

The Doctor joined them, looking on. "What's this?" he said. "The girl has a Schwanz?"

The three crew members looked in the room. Michael was laid out on the floor, blood puddled around his neck and pants pulled down, exposing his penis.

"Oh shit!" said Jeb.

"That's fucked up," said Neusy.

Hocker violently vomited all over the floor.

The police were summoned but found that the band and crew were all busy with their respective jobs and all had alibis. Most of the patrons that were left in the bar had alibis too. After an hour, all were cleared to leave.

At the end of a long night, Neusy and the Santoses drove to their hotel across town. The Worst Eastern Redondo Beach Hotel was where they would stay the night. Neusy and the Santoses shared a room to conserve money. They all got along fine, and Sadie Santos was always a good sport with the off-color male humor of her husband, Bobby, and Neusy. Especially when they competitively farted in the room at night, which was almost always guaranteed to happen.

They parked their car, grabbed their luggage, and proceeded to the lobby. Neusy had the Doctor's small little polka-dot travel pillow he had left in the car earlier. Neusy was now plastered; he had been drinking beers all night to pacify his feelings after the Doctor hurt them earlier at the seminar. As they walked in the lobby, Neusy was mimicking the Doctor's voice to the Santoses.

"Neusy, turn off the lights, you Dummkopf!" Neusy said, laughing a bit. "I hope we are not disturbing your lunch, Herr Neustadt… Neusy has just ruined the mood of what I was just saying." The three roommates were hysterically laughing as they rode up to the third floor. "What is this, an elevator? Blah, ha, ha, ha… Neusy, you fool! Bring me some more wine!" Neusy was on a roll as he imitated the Doctor's voice.

Before the elevator reached the third floor, Neusy felt the ever-familiar bubble sinking to the bottom of his anal canal. He quickly held the Doctor's travel pillow behind him and farted out a trumpet blast. FFRRRRRIIPPPP! "Ahhh, how do you like that, huh? Fuck with Neusy, huh!? Who's laughing now, Fucker!?" Neusy blurted out.

The Santoses and Neusy rolled out of the elevator door, laughing intensely with red faces. "That was fucked up!" said Bobby. Neusy fell in the hallway near the room door in an uncontrollable fit of laughter, his face turning red and bordering on getting a headache. They entered the room, noting the beautiful décor. This was a nice room for a hotel that thought they would have fun with their name. Very nice compared to some of the joints they had stayed in together. It was painted in gray and white, had circular architectural design on the ceilings and walls, complete with modern furnishings, and a separate living room and kitchenette. After separately taking showers in the massive standup shower, it was time for bed. Neusy laid down on his bed and grasped the Doctor's pillow as if it were his own. He had a smile on his face as he started to nod off. Sadie Santos took a picture of him holding the pillow as if she wanted to keep it for future blackmail. With Neusy sleeping, Sadie turned to Bobby in bed and said, "That was a terrible thing that happened tonight at the club, wasn't it?"

"Yeah, I don't know what is worse: the murder itself or that Hocker was going to get some Schwanz instead of some pie," responded Bobby.

"Hey, don't knock it," said Sadie with a smile on her face. The two kissed and fell asleep.

Chapter 7

The following day, the crew, minus Teddy Red, checked out of the hotel and climbed into Neusy's BMW and the rented Chevy van. They got on the road to drive to the next venue, which was about 230 miles away. Excrement, CA was near the giant redwood forests, at the foot of the high Sierra Mountain range. Once they arrived there, they would have to load-in and set up.

Teddy Red had escaped humping equipment and setting up once again by volunteering to use his car to drive the Doctor to the redwood forest earlier that morning. So, it would just be Jeb, Hocker, and Neusy handling all of the preparations for the evening's show.

They arrived in Excrement at 2:45 p.m. They all enjoyed the drive to the venue; being out of the large metro area was refreshing. It took them ten minutes more to reach their destination, and they arrived right on time. The night's venue was an old barn that had been converted into a restaurant/club. It had post and beam construction. The room had a warm feeling to it, with all the exposed wood, and a large balcony area over the entrance. The food served was top notch and a highlight for the band and crew while in CA. The club's name was Sierra Pinecone Dinner Club, situated among rolling hills of avocado farms.

Dirk McNulty was a big intimidating-looking man, standing 6'11", 400 plus pounds, and white hair that was never brushed and hung down to his mid-back. Once he started speaking, he was not intimidating in the least. His soft voice and appreciation of the bands that play his venue were a refreshing break from the normal club owners that Jeb had to deal with. He was arriving himself as the boys showed up. He got out of his car with a guitar case in his hand. "Hey Jeb, great to see you!" he said as the two shook hands.

Jeb had known Dirk for a half dozen years already. Being a huge fan of the Doctor, Dirk always welcomed them and made them feel at home. "Dirk, it's always a highlight of the tour to be at your beautiful venue."

"Thanks, Jeb; I have an amazing meal for you guys planned. My chef has been here since early this morning, prepping for you guys. We have a full house tonight, and he has his hands full—230 people for dinner plus you guys. Dinner and a rock show, what can be better?"

"Nothing Dirk, your place rocks," said Jeb. "We better get started. What's with the guitar?"

"Do you think that the Doctor will sign it for me? I am a big fan, as you know. I want to hang it in the club."

"Yeah, no problem. Same set up inside? We roll through those barn doors in the back?"

"Yes, you still remember."

The crew got to work, and soon the setup was complete. When Teddy Red wasn't helping, it usually didn't take as long. At this venue, the merchandise booth would be set up behind a five-foot-long counter in a little recess in a wooden wall about thirty feet from the entrance to the club. Hocker stood behind the counter to get a feel for the space as Neusy and Jeb brought in the brown cardboard boxes of Jurgen Weislangwolf T-shirts.

Jeb brought his first box to Hocker, and after he left the small merchandise alcove, he let off a foul-smelling fart for Hocker to enjoy. "Oh, you mother-fuckin' swine!" Hocker yelled in anguish. "What the fuck is wrong with you!" he cried. Jeb, amused with himself, just laughed as he walked away to get another box from the van. Neusy came up with a box of T-shirts to leave behind the merch counter. As he set it on the floor, he did the same thing as Jeb and let out some gas. Neusy had his timed right. He farted as he walked away, and just as Jeb was returning with another box. As Jeb put his box down, Hocker finally got a whiff of Neusy's little present that he left behind. Since Neusy had already left the scene, he naturally blamed Jeb. "Fuck man, what's wrong with you, letting off those shit cannons? Why don't you go and fart outside? Why keep farting on me?" Jeb scratched his head, wondering but still chuckling to himself.

Meanwhile, Neusy was down the corridor laughing. He found great levity in his little prank. Those are the little things that he got great pleasure from. When Neusy returned with another box, he looked Hocker straight in the eye; with a huge smile on his face, he pinched off another one. When the stench reached Hocker's nostrils, he yelled, "You fuckin' nozoole, you too? You mother fuckers are horrible!" He exhaled and then took in a quick breath. The bombardment from Jeb and Neusy continued for another ten minutes, with the pair timing their appearance with the gas they needed to pass. Finally, Hocker became silent and took the silent punishment.

The three had become quite the team. They could get setup and breakdown done in record time. They sat at the bar while the sound engineer set up the mics. The band and crew had been looking forward to playing at this club. The hospitality was excellent. A beautiful 100-year-old building, lots of wood all around, with gourmet food and good beers.

The sound engineer finished up, the crew finished their beers, and the band arrived with the Santoses. The Doctor was still in the mountains with Teddy Red. Soundcheck happened, then band and crew ate a meal that could not be beaten: choice of chicken, fish, or steak. Four courses and many beers, they were stuffed but content. The Doctor still hadn't returned from the mountains with Teddy Red. This was a good thing. Jeb and Hocker took a nap in the van. Neusy drank another beer with the band, enjoying the break!

After three hours, the Doctor showed up—there was no opening band tonight. The Doctor remarked how amazing and inspirational the redwoods were and immediately went on stage. Even though it was a lovely intimate setting, the volume was ear piercing.

Teddy Red was outside talking with Neusy and Jeb. "Dude…you should have come with us to the redwoods…it was awesome. The Doctor said he was inspired, and I was too… There was one tree that they had hollowed out… Heehehheh… I smoked a joint inside that tree…how cool is that…brotheees, fucking things are huge."

Teddy Red seemed pleased with himself, and Jeb mumbled, "Well, someone had to load-in and set up."

Hocker was nowhere around; Jeb and Neusy figured the big guy was sleeping again somewhere. The crew would often take time to rest before the show was on and, being an easy gig, Jeb decided to let him be wherever he was while Neusy watched the stage. Hocker had been working hard and Neusy could handle any issues on the stage.

After the show, the Doctor was in a great mood and signed autographs, or Doctor's prescriptions, as his fans called it, for the next hour. Jeb took this time to settle up with Dirk and get paid. He then joined the crew in breaking down and loading out the equipment.

After, the crew found the Doctor with Dirk. Dirk's guitar was on the table. It was a beautiful green Les Paul, with the freshly signed prescription on the front. They had just opened their second bottle of red wine, and the crew joined them. The Doctor was saying, "Those redwoods are incredible! I haven't been so inspired since I was in the dark forest in Austria. Do you go there often?" he asked Dirk.

"Don, the chef, goes up there often," Dirk replied. "By the way, where is that S-O-B? He enjoyed the show a lot. I thought he would have been out here by now. Let me go look for him."

Jeb asked Nathan Lieber, "How was it tonight?"

He replied, "I drank three beers in record time to give me an edge. Still, not one woman talked with me." Jeb was referring to the concert but smiled to entertain Nathan. "Amerrrikaner bitches!"

The rest of the band walked in. The Doctor said, "Tommy, why, is it that you cannot come in on time when we do 'In Your Pants'?"

Triple T did not look happy, but he smiled and said, "I…"

Dirk came screaming into the room as fast as his huge frame would allow. "Someone gassed my chef, Don."

"WHAT?" shouted Jeb.

Neusy looked suspiciously at everyone in the room while Dirk ran over to the bar and called 911 on the bar phone.

"That's right," he said. "I smelled gas and opened the large oven; there was Don, arms tied behind his back, his feet and legs duct taped, and his freakin' mouth duct taped with this black tape. Gas was fully on."

Jeb, Neusy, and Hocker looked at each other; black duct tape is what they used on the stage. After about ten minutes, the police arrived.

Police questioned everyone.

Jurgen Weislangwolf: "I was playing my concert. After that, I was signing autographs, and the Santoses were with me selling T-shirts."

Sadie Santos: "My husband spent the whole show on the side of the stage to help Jurgen Weislangwolf, and I was behind the T-shirt booth selling merch."

Teddy Red sat, twitching nervously: "I…fuck…helped break down the stage for a few minutes… This is so fucked up… Then went outside to smoke a joint… Oh shit…is that cool…you guys don't mind that I smoke a little weed… Then I was sitting here at the bar…the band…they…can verify that."

Nathan represented the band: "We were all at the bar, winding down after the show. Yah, I saw Teddy Red there. There were girls with us too, but none of them were talking to me. Bitches!"

Dirk: "Hey, he is or was my chef; I needed him around. I was with Jeb, then I sat in here; all the guys saw me."

Neusy: "I was with Jeb the whole show, then I was breaking the stage down with Hocker, and later Jeb joined us." Neusy thought about how Hocker was missing for a while but made no mention of it to the police.

Jeb: "I settled up with Dirk and helped load-out. I was never alone; during the show, I was with Neusy." He, too, thought about how Hocker was nowhere around during the show.

Hocker: "Right on… What Neusy said, plus during the show, I took a dump that lasted for an eternity and should have won me a medal, and that was it!"

The mystery of Hocker's whereabouts was solved. Jeb gave Neusy a nod of assurance and received one back. They were both relieved and felt a little more confident that the murder of the chef had nothing to do with the tour.

The police excused everyone after they took down phone numbers and checked IDs and passports. The cars and van left the parking lot in a hurry.

Chapter 8

Johnny Scaggz worked with the Doctor for twenty-two years as his guitar tech and was later promoted to stage manager. He was not only the perfect guitar tech for the Doctor, but flawless at his work. It took great patience to work closely with the Doctor as he would constantly change his setup; if there was a new gadget or guitar effect that he would come across, he would find a way to obtain it and use it live. He would have various products that did the same thing. Whether they were flangers, distortion units, delays, fuzz boxes, wah-wah pedals, or whatever was new, he could have a half dozen of each in his setup at any given time. Of course, they would each have a task. Different manufacturers, different sounds, or same units set different to create the sound the Doctor wanted at that moment.

It got to the point where a custom pedalboard was needed to house all the special guitar effects. Scaggz welded together steel square tubes that were completely adaptable. When the Doctor obtained additional effects, Scaggz would weld a new section to the pedalboard. Once it started to get too large to move comfortably, he built sections that snapped together. The idea was great, and when reps from the effect companies saw this, they wanted to create a commercially available version. Scaggz patented his design, and the Doctor stood to make a fortune on this endorsed product. With multiple bids, Scaggz counted the money in his mind, thinking that he would finally make some real money working for this idiot.

As time went on, bids got higher and the pedalboard got longer. It got to a ridiculous fourteen feet long and stretched almost across the stage. The other members in the band would inadvertently step on one of the effects and change the Doctor's sound. He insisted that the band not move towards the front of the stage because of this and stay near the back. His onstage performance was talked about throughout the industry. Some clubs did not have large enough stages to accommodate this massive beast. Shows had to be canceled as time moved on since the Doctor refused to use less than his 132 effects. For the shows that they were able to perform, he was up front on the stage, running back and forth throughout the show, trying to keep up with the effect he wanted in his mind. The spectacle was not rock and roll and the offers stopped when the Doctor doubled over from exhaustion after every song.

Scaggz came up with design two. He dismantled the entire board and developed a multi-level version. It was three levels and made it so that the Doctor could reach all the pedals without running back and forth. Scaggz talked the Doctor into reducing his pedals to half, so the new design worked. The Doctor agreed, and for a year all was good. The Doctor started creeping some of the old pedals back into his routine, and Scaggz had to add another level and then another level. Soon, the Doctor could not lift his leg high enough to reach the top row of pedal effects and insisted he have a step stool on stage to use all his pedals.

When Jeb came on board as tour manager, he told the Doctor that the pedalboard was gone. He told him to choose twenty effects, or no one, including himself, would work with him. Somehow after a month of trying to convince the Doctor, he agreed to this, and Jeb was hired.

Johnny Scaggz stood only 5'6". His dark blonde hair, braided in a ponytail, extended to his mid-back. He had a mustache that looked more like whiskers. He came from a family of circus high-wire performers; he was light on his feet and had perfect balance, like a cat! People would marvel at how cat-like Scaggz was. Scaggz could fix any problem during a concert, reach any part of the stage or lighting rigs at any time. Any problem that would arise during a show, Scaggz was always asked to take care of it.

The promoter of the largest festival in the Czech Republic invited the Doctor to play the festival. It was a week-long celebration of music with a different artist headlining each night on the main stage erected in a park. It was determined, once constructed, that the stage was too small for the multi-band event. There was not enough space along the front of the stage for the monitors or speakers the bands use to hear themselves play, so they were put on smaller platforms in front of the stage. The ten-foot-high stage and these smaller platforms were separated by about three feet. These smaller platforms were four feet wide and anchored to the stage with cables. It worked well, and they installed five of them across the front of the stage.

The Doctor at this time had a vocalist by the name of Kasper Von Kelp, who was known for his incredible vocal range. He was fired after only one album and four months of touring. Von Kelp was a maniac on stage. He would swing his microphone stand, hitting everything in its way. He knocked over drums and keyboards regularly and, on several occasions, hit people in the front row. He was fired right on the stage during a show after knocking the Doctor's amp over, causing the custom amp to stop working. During the festival in the Czech Republic, he was swinging his stand around, trying to avoid hitting the Doctor, when he fell over and hit a monitor on one of the platforms right in front of the Doctor. The cable disconnected, and the Doctor could not hear anything.

Scaggz saw the whole thing happen. He jumped up and scaled the PA speaker. He came down in front of the Doctor, walked across the support cable, and balanced himself on the monitor platform. He leaned over and repaired the broken connection. Everyone was relieved, and Scaggz was the hero once again.

Scaggz had it all down. He knew and could predict what the Doctor needed before the Doctor would even speak. The Doctor went through a phase that used six channels to play through six different amps at once. It was Scaggz who built the splitter box, and it worked perfectly. "The wall with balls," as the Doctor called it. It was the life that Scaggz always wanted. Growing up a huge Centipedes fan and now working closely with his idol, For twenty-two years, he worked every single concert! He was there for the

Doctor at every recording session. It was all going perfect until it came to an abrupt end at what is referred to as the Munich Incident.

It was a rough time in Scaggz's life. He was spending increasingly less time at home. In anticipation of a six-month tour, he sold everything he owned, except his Volkswagen Kombi stored at a friend's house. Scaggz spent the three years leading up to the Munich Incident on the road. When there was a small break, while the rest of the band and crew would go home, he chose to camp in whatever city the tour ended. Touring and recording with the Doctor all the time, he failed to see the importance of having his own space. He could not tell what day it was anymore. He started becoming confused and lost his temper very quickly.

The Doctor had just begun a huge European tour that kicked off in Zurich. Jurgen Weislangwolf and eighties metal legends the Hurricanes, who had reunited and started their worldwide reunion tour, were a double bill. The Doctor was on fire that first night; this would be a great tour!

They agreed that the Hurricanes would play first, and the Doctor would close the show due to his popularity in Europe at that time. The Hurricanes played for about an hour and twenty minutes. Their lead guitarist accidentally stepped on one of the Doctor's cables during the second show, causing the thin wires to break inside the insulation. Scaggz had all the Doctor's gear set up behind the Hurricanes' gear, as was normally the practice. It would simply take too long to set up the complex web of wires needed to connect the vast amount of equipment during intermission. It took Scaggz twenty minutes to figure out what was wrong with the gear. The Doctor took the stage late and was behind the amps yelling the entire twenty minutes, while all eyes were on Scaggz.

Scaggz swore that type of accident would not happen again. The next night they were in Munich. It was a beautiful 3,000-seat theater with a large stage area. There were catwalks above, with various curtains that were used to block off parts of the stage so the size could be adjusted. After setting up the gear, Scaggz informed the Doctor that everything was set up. He guaranteed him there would be no trouble before he disappeared.

The Hurricanes took the stage. Scaggz stalked the guitarist like a cat on the prowl. He started behind the amps, crouching low so that no one would see him. After the first song, he climbed up to one of the catwalks above the stage. He paced back and forth, keeping his eyes on what was happening below. The lighting truss partially blocked his vision. He moved to the adjacent catwalk, but still, he did not have an unobstructed view of the guitarist. He crouched, stood up, then paced and did the same thing on the other side of the catwalk. Still, the fucking lighting truss was in the way. He made his way to where the truss crossed close to the catwalk and very lightly climbed on board. The truss shimmied, but no one noticed.

Scaggz made his way on the lighting truss until he was directly above the guitarist; he could now see perfectly. Like a panther in a tree, stalking a small animal, he watched for another twenty minutes. Then it all happened so fast. The Hurricanes launched into their biggest hit, "Hurricane at Midnight." The audience went crazy, and the band's adrenaline kicked in. They were jumping and moving about the stage; the guitarist jumped in the air and landed extremely close to the Doctor's gear. Scaggz cocked his head and moved into an attack position as he arched his back. The song was coming to an end with another jump, and this time the cable that had made him look so bad the night before was grazed. The song ended, and Scaggz dove out of the lighting truss headfirst right onto the guitarist, whose legs buckled under the impact. Scaggz grabbed him by the collar and said, "Keep off the gear, asshole!" Various roadies, security, and the promoter rushed onto the stage and removed Scaggz from the guitarist, who lay collapsed on the ground.

That was the end of the Hurricanes for the night and the tour. The guitarist suffered a broken leg, broken collarbone, and three broken ribs. They have never returned to the stage since, and their future remains uncertain. The tour was canceled after the Doctor played his portion of that gig. Scaggz was told to leave and not come back by the Doctor, and no one had seen nor heard from him for years.

Four years later, Scaggz had a whole new outlook on life. He was now a Jehovah's Witness but still followed the Doctor's career closely. Since that day, Scaggz couldn't sleep inside. He felt too constrained and claustrophobic. He spent as much time outside as he could. He had been living at various Jehovah's Witnesses' Kingdom Halls, mainly in California. Well, not actually inside these places of worship, but they did allow him to set up a tent on their property.

For food, Scaggz would use his cat-like reflexes for hunting small animals. Squirrels were his favorite. He created the perfect spice blend for all his captured meals. For squirrels, it was salt, pepper, paprika, brown sugar, garlic powder, onion powder, and thyme. He would slow cook the animal over a fire. Sometimes it would be rabbit or possum. He had been seen chasing raccoons, pigeons, chipmunks, even a badger. Although raccoon no longer was on his menu. The last time Scaggz came upon a raccoon, he had stalked the animal for two hours. Every time he wanted to make a move, the animal seemed to have a sixth sense.

The raccoon knew Scaggz was there and took him on a tour of this beach town until they ended up in a park. The raccoon knew what he was doing and got Scaggz right where he wanted him. In this park, with people all around, so many trees to climb, perfect for the raccoon. The raccoon led Scaggz up and down trees. He would get Scaggz up in a tree and then scale down the opposite side and run. Scaggz was equal to the task with his reflexes and would scale down the tree just as fast. Four trees, the raccoon took Scaggz up and down.

Scaggz started thinking that this was not your average raccoon. The raccoon thought that Scaggz was not your average human. Of course, this was in raccoon thinking and not rational thought. The raccoon envisioned all humans in a group, and this particular human was not part of the group. Sure, the raccoon has had kids throw rocks at him or yell at him. But never one to chase him. He liked humans; they always put food outside their homes for him covered in the large containers so other animals could not get at his food. The humans encouraged him to eat more with their reaction of fists in the air, screaming, and jumping up and down. What a regular celebration for the enjoyable meals.

The raccoon knew this would not stop. On the fifth tree, he climbed up and waited for Scaggz to begin climbing. Once Scaggz was on the tree, the raccoon slid around to the side of the tree that Scaggz was on. He jumped down on Scaggz's head, and Scaggz immediately had visions of when he jumped out of the light trellis onto the guitarist's head. But the raccoon had nails, and they hurt. The blood from Scaggz's scalp was running down his face when he let go of the tree with the raccoon still holding on.

A slew of onlookers had their phones out recording the two as they rolled around on the ground. They were moving so fast that no one could tell who was winning the fight. First Scaggz was on top, then the raccoon, then Scaggz. This fight went on for fifteen minutes. Scaggz was exhausted; the raccoon never gave up his fight for life. Scaggz bit the raccoon; the people watching gasped. The raccoon then bit him on the shoulder. Scaggz let go, but the raccoon did not and looked Scaggz right in the eye. What he must have seen was the despair and let go. The raccoon walked away and, after eight steps, turned around and looked at Scaggz lying on the ground, beaten. The video online went viral. Over three million hits worldwide. *Man Loses Fight With Raccoon* was the headline.

Scaggz started concentrating on smaller animals. Although he never admitted to eating dogs or cats, there had been some reports of suspicious disappearances of people's loved pets when Scaggz had been in the area. Scaggz now preferred to do his hunting in the middle of the night when there were no people around to witness his struggles.

Scaggz set up near beaches where he sold artwork out of the back of his VW for money. Most of his paintings were of the Doctor wearing his wig in various stage poses, holding the Universe Guitar. His paintings of Mozart and the strange guitar were in demand, providing him with a steady income.

Chapter 9

Scaggz woke up refreshed under the trees next to the parking lot of another place of worship. The embers of his fire were almost out. His stomach was content with the previous night's meal. He was lucky enough to catch a gopher snake. He stood up and pissed on the embers; they sizzled. He checked the Doctor's schedule and saw that his next booking was a seminar and concert in Arizona. He packed up his tent, loaded it into his VW, and started the drive.

In his mind, that day in Munich kept replaying. *If it weren't for that guitarist in the fucking Hurricanes!* Who cares? He belonged on the road with the Doctor!

The caravan of vehicles headed to Tempe, Arizona for a seminar scheduled at 10:00 a.m. the next morning and a concert at night at a club called the Venue. (The name came about when the owners were building out the remnants of a grocery store and always referred to the space as the venue. When it came time to order the signage, neither of the partners could think of an appropriate name, and the Venue was born.) They drove on the off day, which made it easier. They made it without any significant incidents, other than the Doctor, who went missing for a half hour before Jeb found him behind a restroom at a desert rest area where he was trying to friend a rattlesnake. Fascinated by the snake, it took Jeb fifteen minutes to convince the Doctor it was in everyone's best interest to leave the snake alone.

During the time at the rest area waiting, Jeb and Neusy discussed the possibility of replacing Teddy Red. They decided that once they no longer required the extra vehicle that it would be time for Teddy Red to go home. If Triple T had not refused driving other band members, then Teddy Red would have been long gone. But Triple T said that he preferred to drive alone. Jeb figured it was because of wig privacy but later found out he liked to drive wearing only a bathrobe and his tight whites.

Jeb remembered a guy that he once met that was a trombone player and worked in a small music store in Arizona. He was giving horn lessons during the day and wanted to go out on the road. Neusy agreed that this guy should be contacted.

Marlon Jiggs' band performed several nights a week in the Phoenix area. Iron Cauldron was their name. They were a self-proclaimed, seven-piece, dark-metal swing band. Consisting of vocals, drums, trumpet, French horn, saxophone, tuba, and Marlon Jiggs on trombone, they were hardly metal. The only thing they had in common with dark metal was their singer, who was a guttural, deep-from-within, all-out grunter. The combination of the horns and the vocals started out being a band people would see as a gag. Some went because of the name: they thought that they would see a death metal band. It didn't matter why people were coming out, they were getting the gigs.

Their fans were the typical death metal fans sprinkled in with many older people coming for the swing portion. There was a lot of denim and leather in the crowd, along with sweaters of all types. But the band had something, and it was working. People would come back, time and time again. In the beginning, the fans started to mosh. The smooth sounds the band created with the horns mimicked bands of the yesteryear swing era. The moshers developed a whole new style that was much less violent and more like dancing at a lovefest. Iron Cauldron was bringing people together.

Marlon Jiggs was having a blast. He walked around town with his head high. He told everyone that was not a musician, "we musicians see life differently." He started wearing chains and a bandana, trying to be more spiritual. Believing that he was, he would walk the store where he worked with an extra spring in his step and always say what was on his mind. Whether he was in a conversation or not, he would yell out random things. People that worked with him would laugh, customers in the store would look at him strangely, and his boss hated him.

Marlon wanted to go out and experience life on the road. The real-life. Marlon Jiggs was thin, wiry, and reckless. He was average height, with short, straight black hair, and baby faced with large brown eyes. He was a frantic man who moved about like a baby, bouncing off objects and changing directions. He had similar personality traits to Teddy Red, meaning he smoked a lot of weed and did stupid shit, and was more focused, but would lose his mind if he did not smoke any weed. He was interested in giving the road life a try.

What an opportunity, he thought when Jeb called him and asked if he was interested in joining the tour. "What?" yelled Marlon into the phone so loud that Jeb had to move the phone away from his ear. "Are you joking? Yes… Yes… Yesssssssssss… I am in! Shit, I never have been out of Arizona. I can't wait to see the country. Holy shit. I am going to see it all!"

He told his pregnant wife, "I received the calling." His three kids were crying when Dad said goodbye. His wife thought it was an excellent opportunity, not really for Marlon but herself, to not have to listen to his ramblings and stoned conversations. Since the tour was about to go through the Tempe area for a seminar and concert, this would be the perfect time. Jeb told Marlon to meet them at the Venue, and then he could ride back to CA with the band in their cars.

Teddy Red would be let go when the tour-bus portion of the tour began. After dinner and several beers later at a local brewery, it was time to go to sleep. It was a nice change to have no show. The next day was going to be an early day with the seminar scheduled at the Venue. That is where Marlon was told to be during the day.

Chapter 10

The crew arrived at the Venue and set up the stage for the 10:00 a.m. seminar and the show in the evening. All they would need for the seminar would be guitar amps and a keyboard. The students were waiting outside when they arrived, excited to get this time with the Doctor. The Doctor arrived late with Teddy Red. Finally, at 10:30 a.m., the students were allowed in.

It was time for another seminar and the opportunity to hear the Doctor's teachings and hopefully gain some encouragement from them. Some might receive praise, but it was certain that others would go down in flames. Forty-five students filled the music hall, all sitting around with their guitars on their legs, tinkling away unplugged at scales or songs as they chatted with each other. They all wondered who would get the first chance to play something for the Doctor. What would he say? The first thing that the Doctor did say was, "Hallo! Achtung! We are now ready to begin our seminar. The first thing I want everyone to do is to stop tinkling on your guitars! I can't stand this tinkling around on the guitars while I am speaking. So, stop it now!"

Everyone immediately stopped noodling on their guitars out of fear of the famous scolding they had all heard about and the punishment of not being allowed to showcase their piece. "Dankeschön! Und now, who would like to play first?"

The first two students to take the stage were Alexandro Dante and Louis Le Fleur. The Doctor had written both pieces that were chosen to be performed by the first two seasoned players. Who would play better? There seemed to be a minor problem as both players had forgotten to bring their guitar straps and would have to perform sitting. So, the two grabbed some stools sitting off the side of the stage and placed them on the stage. Then Le Fleur said, "I don't want to sit too close to Dante, it might look gay."

To that, the Doctor said, "That is your problem!" To which the whole group burst out in laughter.

Le Fleur placed his stool at a moderate distance, and then he played first. He had a highly evolved skill, and the onlookers were enjoying his performance. Afterward, the Doctor commented, "Le Fleur, you play very well, but you lack the essence of the piece. You are not in the zone!"

Then it was Dante's turn to play the piece. He played beautifully, and the audience was entranced. He had the right feel and the proper techniques to play the piece as written. When he finished, the Doctor said, "Aha, very nice, Alexandro. You have good techniques und the right feelings to play this piece. However, there is one problem! You play like a ninety-pound weakling, like a sissy-boy girly-man, no power!"

Dante bent his head down and said, "Thank you," and shuffled off the stage.

Next up was Bobby Santos. He would also attempt a song that the Doctor featured on his second solo album. Bobby Santos was a strong player, and his picking hand didn't miss a lick. He played the song note for note and with the right feeling and tempo. And then the critique. "You have played the song well, Bobby. However, your attack is too hard, Bobby. You are like Bruce Lee karate chopping the strings. You must balance the hard and the soft, like the yin und the yang."

Neusy, a guitarist, worked out a classical piece by Mozart and wanted to give it a shot. He raised his hand after Bobby Santos was finished and the Doctor called him up to the stage. Neusy had prepared a backing track with the orchestra playing, and he would play electric guitar along with the orchestra. "What do you have for us today, Neusy?"

"I am going to play *Eine kleine Nachtmusik* by Wolfgang Amadeus Mozart."

The sound engineer started the backing track, and the orchestral music flowed out of the monitors. Neusy began to play along. His was not a flashy show of skills. He intended to give the listeners more of a relaxing and comforting feeling. Plus, this piece was well known to all. After about three minutes, the song came to an end. "Achhh, that is a very nice piece! Mozart is my all-time favorite composer of the great masters. Not too bad, Neusy! However, I must point out some basic music theory here. What key is the song in?"

"Well, it is in G major."

"Yah! Correct! But you are not emphasizing the proper timing of the notes. For example, what are the notes of the G major chord?"

"G, B, and D," said Neusy.

"Yah, und when you play the main theme, the first note G is held for a half note, und the next note D is only a quarter note, und when you play G again, it is a quarter note. The spacing und timing of the notes are critical things. Don't forget what I tell you, yah?"

"OK, thank you very much!" said Neusy as he exited the stage.

Neusy felt quite pleased with his critique from the Doctor. The Doctor didn't say anything that bad or harsh about his performance. It gave him confidence, and it meant that he was progressing as a musician.

A player who called himself Watered Mouse took the stage. His outfit was a zebra-striped vest over a bare chest with tight, pink spandex pants hugging his skinny ass and legs and standing in white boots. His brown, curly hair was matted down like he slept for a week and never brushed it when he awoke. The guy smelled like a goat; he never used deodorant when it was clear that he would greatly benefit from the practice. He performed a song from the Centipedes called "The Moon on My Feet." The backing track played through the PA, and he began to perform.

What a performance, mostly posing in-between riffs and chords. He played the main riff, kicked his right leg over his head, and then planted it in an Elvis-style karate side stance. Then came another phase, and he got down in a full split on the stage with the guitar playing behind his head. He turned into a belly dancer during the guitar solo section, snaking his waist around and around, floating backward into another stance to play the solo. The Doctor's jaw dropped to the ground in utter disbelief.

"Mama mia! I don't know what to say," said the Doctor. "As for your playing, it isn't happening! Und what is with this dancing stuff? I sense that there is something dark in your soul, und maybe you need an exorcism."

Falcon was the next person that took to the stage. The famous guitar player from Detroit, who considered himself a genius, was ready to perform his piece. His backing track was all ready to go as he took center stage. The backing track began, and so did Falcon. His solo piece opened with some diatonic sweep arpeggios and then some more. He liked to play many arpeggios to show everyone that he could play them better than anyone else in the room. The arpeggio section lasted about five minutes, a tad too long for anyone's liking. Then finally, a melody, haunting and strange, seemed to capture everyone's attention. Then Falcon displayed his tapping method, a method of using the picking hand's fingers to tap out notes on the upper neck while the fretting hand fingered triple notes or something like that. The tapping section of his piece went about eight minutes and then more arpeggios.

Finally, after thirty minutes, the piece ended. The Doctor drank three cups of coffee to stay awake as he struggled to watch and then said, "Achtung! Wake up, everyone!" As people started to revive and wake up, one guy in the back of the room did not move. The Doctor raised his voice. "Hallo, is anyone home?" The man did not move. Bobby walked back to the fan slanted sideways in his chair and gave him a nudge. The man fell over on the floor. The Doctor said, "Is he alright?"

Bobby replied, "I think he's dead!" The room was filled with anxiety and fear. Was it another murder, or did Falcon's composition drive him to commit suicide?

The seminar was over, cut short by the death of the Doctor's fan that came to get a life lesson on guitar and paid for it with his life. The Doctor cried, "What is with all of this death? Why are people dying all around this year?"

Neusy called the police as Jeb replied, "This is now more than a coincidence. We need to be on alert all day."

The Doctor just sighed, "Yah, that we will do."

The local police came, and so did the coroner. No one could see any foul play and the police felt that natural causes were the cause of death so everyone was free to go.

Scaggz, on the roof of the Venue, was looking down at the body as it was loaded into the back of the coroner van. He smiled and said to himself, "It's great to be back. What a tour!" He climbed down to a lower roof on the side of the building, then to the ground, and disappeared to his VW parked around the corner, throwing a syringe into nearby bushes.

67

Chapter 11

The Venue in Tempe had about thirty-five of the Doctor's fans milling about, some at the bar and some standing in front of the stage waiting for their chance to see the Doctor in action. The show was still a half hour off and, with no opening band, would end early and give the boys an easy night. Arizona was never a hot spot for the Doctor but usually drew more than a hundred people. Perhaps the death of a fan earlier in the day was to blame for the light attendance.

The bar was in the center of the room, with an oval island bar situated halfway back from the stage. The usual suspects were standing there drinking a cold one. Jeb was scanning the room with a beer in his hand; Neusy looked at the stage, studying every detail to ensure a smooth show. Jeb noticed in the dark back corner of the room were two men. They clearly looked different from everyone else in the rock club; they had to be some type of law enforcement. He said to Neusy, "Take a look. We have guests tonight. Guess they are thinking that dude's death this afternoon was somewhat unnatural."

"Damn, I barely can see those guys hiding there. They look like the Blues Brothers! Should we speak with them? I would normally say that they are the opening band, but we have none. You're thinking cops…huh?"

The boys watched the pair in the corner. They indeed looked like the Blues Brothers. Both wore cheap suits and sunglasses, even though the room was lit by minimal overhead lights and dim blue LED stage lights. A short, squat man with black hair and a prominent nose seemed to be fumbling with something in his hand while the other, a tall thin man with black hair and what looked like a drawn-on mustache, was trying to grab it from him. "I'm not sure what I am watching, but I will say they are entertaining," said Jeb.

Neusy chugged his beer and said, "Yeah, let's go and talk with them."

The pair walked past the merch table where Sadie Santos talked with one of the fans, holding up a T-shirt. She eyed the two as they walked by; Jeb motioned with his head at the two men in the corner. Sadie watched as Jeb and Neusy walked away towards the men.

As Neusy and Jeb approached the men, they immediately stopped their dispute over the cell phone; they stood erect with as much authority as possible. Jeb was first to speak and said, "Good evening, guys. I am the Doctor's tour manager; my name is Jeb Acorns."

Neusy added, "I'm Kurt Neustadt, but call me Neusy."

They shook hands with the two men. The shorter one spoke first. "I am Agent Jathan Sparrow, and this is Agent Crow, Jester Crow." They both produced their badges as if on cue.

Neusy looked at Jeb, who shot him the I-know-what-you're-thinking-but-can't-say-it look. They both smiled slightly.

"Jason," Jeb said, "what's up? Can we help you with something?"

The shorter agent replied, "It's Jathan, with a T-H, but you can call me Agent Sparrow."

The taller one added, "And you can refer to me as Agent Crow. It seems there have been a few murders on your tour. Now there is one in Arizona as well. The FBI is taking over. We will be following your tour for a while. Although local police have cleared you all in the different cities, we have not. You are all suspects. We will be talking with everyone involved in the tour. I want you to provide me with a list of everyone involved. We will be watching all of you, every step you take, every move all of you make. We will notice everything you do, and if one of you touring, gypsy assholes did these killings, we will come down on you like a hoard of flies on a pile of shit."

Sparrow, shaking his head in agreement and staring at Neusy, added, "Sparrow and Crow will not take any shit from you motherfuckers. We have seen it all, and we don't like you heavy metal people. You people are always up to no good. With that shit blasting, that loud bullshit you call music… We don't want to be here anymore than I am sure you want us here. We are the guys that get the cases that no one else wants. The shit cases… Now we have to listen to this shit."

Neusy and Jeb stood there in disbelief that these "agents" were tough-talking them. But it is true, Sparrow and Crow do get the cases that no one wants. They are the last agents to be assigned a case. The confidence in their abilities to solve a crime was the subject of many conversations at their field office. Other agents would make bets with one another regarding the outcomes of their cases. There were always side bets about which one would get hurt first, or on what day they would crash their vehicle, or the amount of expenses the two would submit. Sparrow and Crow submit more expenses than any other agents that work twice as many cases. Massages, strip clubs, shoeshines, expensive dinners or hotels with separate rooms, and late-night clubbing were always on their expense reports. They would always insist they had a lead or were following a person of interest, and that is where they would end up. And if they did not spend money, it would stand out.

The agents could not believe their luck in this case, being in clubs with fans and groupies. Easy to get laid, they thought, and easy to stretch into more massages and strip clubs. It just seemed natural. They looked at the touring schedule given to them and were smiling ear to ear when they left their field office. Their supervisor watched them leave the building on the security monitor. When the two high-fived each other, he summoned his assistant and instructed him to limit their corporate credit cards to $150 a day.

Neusy couldn't contain himself. "Well, my foul friends, the show will be starting soon. Why don't you stand on the stage to the side so you can get a good bird's eye view of the venue." Jeb looked shocked at Neusy and smiled. The agents did not think those remarks were funny. They heard things like that from other agents nonstop. They pulled foam earplugs out of their suits and put them in their ears. They abruptly walked past Jeb and Neusy, with the smaller agent brushing into Neusy and the taller one elbowing Jeb in the back.

Jeb said to Neusy, "I know, you couldn't help yourself. I almost burst out laughing. Well, this will be fun having these two with us. I bet they don't know that we are heading to the West Coast Guitar Summit after this gig. Good luck getting in there, boys."

Marlon Jiggs walked into the Venue right before the Doctor arrived with Teddy Red from his hotel. He made a beeline to where Jeb was standing with Neusy and Hocker near the merch booth. He had a suitcase with him. The introductions were made all around between Bobby, Sadie, Neusy, Jeb, and Hocker.

Marlon pulled Jeb aside and said, "I don't know about this. It was so hard saying goodbye to my kids. I have never been away from my family. This will be the first time I leave the state. I started crying when they said goodbye."

"Oh, OK, will you be alright?" replied Jeb. "It will get easier as we move along. I know it is tough, but tonight grab a beer and enjoy the show. Here is an all-access tour badge that you will need to get around the venues. Don't lose it as we need these every night. This tells security you are the band or crew, and you are allowed to be backstage. There are some beers and some food there. Watch the show from the side or out front here. Tonight, don't worry about anything. Tomorrow you will start working. Your job will be loading in and out and then working the merchandise table as Bobby and Sadie will only be with us on this first leg of the tour. They took the week off from work to be with us, so check out the booth, and if you have any questions, ask Sadie."

"Wow," exclaimed Marlon as he looked at the laminated tour badge given to him. This year's badge had a photo of the Universe Guitar with the words *Jurgen Weislangwolf World Tour—All Access* around the guitar. He felt important and was already feeling better.

Marlon immediately wanted to try out the badge and walked out the backstage door past the security guard, who nodded at him. He pulled a joint out of his cigarette pack and lit up. "Yes," *this is the life! The tour will be OK—I can call the family every day.* With each toke, he felt better. He finished his joint and walked back to the door, which was locked. He knocked, and the security guard opened the door. Marlon lifted the badge hanging around his neck to show the guard. The guard nodded once again and Marlon walked in, found the beers backstage, and chugged four of them in ten minutes. "Yes," *for sure, this is going to be OK.*

The Doctor walked past him with Teddy Red, which left Marlon star struck. *Holy Shit! That was the Doctor! Wow…that weed was terrific.* Stoned and drunk, he walked to the stage.

"Hey, Arizona! Are you ready?" the Doctor said into the mic. The thirty-five people shouted, and the Doctor began to play. Marlon started screaming himself. Then he realized, *Shit… I am part of the tour and not a fan.* He yelled so loud that the agents standing next to him were startled. *Wow!* thought Marlon, *this weed is sooooo good.*

Hocker, who the agents just interrogated, was standing there as well. "Yeah, this guy won't last long. By the way, he was not with us until just this evening. He starts tomorrow. So he had nothing to do with these deaths, just like the rest of us. You're wasting all of our time. The killer is out there, and yet you are here watching a concert and bothering me while I work," he said to the agents as he spit into an empty beer bottle. The agents fumbled with their earplugs, trying to hear what was being said over the loud guitar. "Fucking idiots," Hocker said.

Marlon turned around to get another beer in the dressing room and, as he was opening the beer, he looked at the agents thinking, *Wow! The Blues Brothers?*

The show ended, and the meet and greet went quickly as only about a third of the fans paid the $55 fee to meet the Doctor, take pictures with him, and have him sign their merchandise. Marlon watched this from behind the table while Sadie explained to him what his new position would be. He liked this. This job put him out in front of the fans, and people would notice him. He had already engaged in conversation with about a half dozen fans, telling each one that he was with the Doctor on tour. He loved the attention.

The meet and greet ended. Load out was quick, and all went back to the hotel. Marlon smoked another joint and went inside his room, which he shared with Neusy and Jeb.

At 3:00 a.m, Jeb and Neusy were suddenly woken up from the light being turned on and Marlon hyperventilating. Jeb shouted, "What the hell, Marlon?"

"I can't do this! I can't. I just can't! I have never been away from my family. I just can't!" He was sweating and now shouting between breaths. "I have to leave. I am going to call a cab and go home!"

"Marlon, you accepted this job. Get your shit together and go back to sleep!" Jeb said from his bed.

"I just can't. ...I...ca...nnnnnn't...breea...tthhhhhe... I need to leave," Marlon whimpered.

Neusy stood up and walked over. He sat next to Marlon and, in his calm manner, put his arm around him. "Marlon... I know it is tough. Just relax. Tomorrow we'll drive to California. They have killer weed in California. You can get some, and it will calm you down. It will get easier. Please give it a couple of days. All you need to do is concentrate on the next couple of days. You can phone your family in the morning, but we are still in Arizona. Just give it a day or two. I promise you that I will be here for you to talk. OK?"

"I... I... I... I... I... I don't know if I can do that! I don't. Oh shit!... I should never have agreed to this... Oh, shit!"

"Marlon," Neusy continued in his calm demeanor, "it's the first night. In a few hours, we will be driving to California. I will be there for you all the time. Please give it a try. One day, then the next day. You will get through this, and if you feel this way like I said, you can go home. It will only be a few days, and maybe you will feel more comfortable by then. Trust me."

"Neusy, you are a good guy, thanks. Please can I drive in your car tomorrow?"

"Well, I have a few of the guys with me, but I think we can fit you in. Right, Jeb?" Neusy said.

"Yes, I think we can make it work out for you, buddy." Jeb stated, "Neusy, don't forget that you have that amp to get fixed once we are in the L.A. area tomorrow. The one that Teddy Red blew up."

"Yes, that's right." Neusy said to Marlon, "You will enjoy tomorrow; it will be interesting."

"OK, Neusy, I am sorry guys, I will try," Marlon said. He then picked up his cigarette pack and left the room to have a smoke.

After Marlon walked out, Jeb said, "Always something. I never had this happen with anyone I have hired.".

"Good thing old Neusy was here. Right?"

"Yes, that is a good thing; I do not have your patience," agreed Jeb, and Marlon walked back in.

"I am OK now; I will think *one day at a time*. You are right, Neusy. Thanks," Marlon said. He then rolled over and was immediately asleep. Jeb turned off the lights, let off a goodnight fart for everyone to enjoy, and the three were sleeping.

Chapter 12

The West Coast Guitar Summit, or WCGS as it is known throughout the industry, was being held in Costa Mesa, CA. WCGS is an annual gathering of the world's greatest guitarists and all guitar, instrument, amplification, and effect companies wanting to show the industry their new products and who is playing them. The entire music industry focuses on this four-day weekend in California.

This conference is also where new products are introduced. Many guitarists are endorsed by one of these companies and are showcased playing or using their products. The convention consists of three different events. The trade show itself occurs at the convention center. Meetings between the manufacturers and either the media or buyers are held in both the convention hall and several hotel ballrooms in the area. But the highlight of the convention is the WCGS concert.

The concert takes place at a local venue large enough to hold the event. This year was the largest and was at the arena in Anaheim. Sixteen thousand people for three nights. Tickets were tough to obtain. They were free for those attending. But just like the entrance to the WCGS trade show, you had to be in the industry to gain admission. At the trade show, all the exhibitors receive a certain number of tickets to the concert based on the size of their display space. If you know someone, you are in; if you are a buyer for a chain of stores, no problem, you are in. But if you are just a fan, good luck. So there is a lot of mystery to these concerts as the average fan cannot attend.

The band and crew were scheduled to arrive in Costa Mesa, CA, where they had to engage in a day and a half of rehearsals for the WCGS concert. The Doctor was closing the evening of the first night with a scheduled one-hour slot in the large arena. Everything had to go exactly as planned. If it didn't go perfectly with everyone firing on all cylinders, it would be a disaster.

The band and crew headed out at 7:00 a.m., which was very early for the band, and no one was in a good mood, especially Hocker, who was rarely awake before noon. Hocker and Jeb were driving the van. Bobby and Sadie had their vehicle and had already left an hour earlier with Heinz. Neusy had the other two Austrians and Marlon packed in with him. All suitcases and baggage were with Hocker and Jeb in the van.

The Doctor was getting seriously angry about the non-working Galactic Amplifier and complained about the situation all morning. "How stupid is this guy to blow up my amp? You have to be a moron not to change the voltage switch!" Changing the voltage was a simple but serious chore. Teddy Red was supposed to have set up the amp and changed the voltage input for 110 volts upon returning from Europe, where it had been set to 220.

Neusy remembered that he knew a guy that fixed amps in Monrovia, CA, a shop called Ramp Amp. The amp repair shop was next to the freeway exit ramp of Myrtle Avenue and the 210 Fwy. The only problem was that the whole tour was in Tempe, AZ and they had to be in Santa Ana, CA for rehearsal at 5:00 p.m. Jeb had to be in Santa Ana one hour before that with Hocker and the equipment van to set up for the rehearsal.

Teddy Red reluctantly accepted to drive the Doctor to Santa Ana. This meant it would be Neusy's job to drive the custom 900-watt Galactic head forty miles out of their way to the Ramp Amp in Monrovia before he took Nathan and Torsten the Viking to rehearsal. Neusy knew if he got the Doctor's Galactic head fixed, it would score massive brownie points with the Doctor and he would be the hero, a far cry from the verbal lashing he endured during the first seminar.

Neusy asked if either of the two Austrian bandmates cared to drive his White BMW X5 while he rested in the back seat. Torsten the Viking volunteered to drive first, and the journey began. Neusy warned Torsten not to drive too fast for the first hour or so because Interstate 10 in Arizona was full of cops, so Torsten took it easy.

"I love driving! It makes me feel free!" shouted Torsten with the most excitement he had shown so far on tour.

"Yeah, me too!" replied Nathan.

"Tell me, in Austria, do you drive fast over there?" Neusy asked.

"Oh yah, much faster than here," said Nathan.

"Und it is not crazy hot like here in Arizona!" added Torsten.

Nathan had his laptop open, engaged in music studies. Neusy inquired, "What are you doing there, Nate?"

"Oh, I have a test when I return to Austria."

"What kind of test?" Neusy said as he looked over with a puzzled look on his face.

"I am taking a music course. I must learn fifty songs for my test," said Nathan.

"So, tell me, Nate, how are the chicks back home? Are they hot?"

"Well, some are hot, und some are not," sighed Nathan.

"You must get laid a lot, being on the road playing rock music?" Neusy inquired.

"Nein, nein, once in a while, I get some, but not recently. Not since touring with the Doctor. Now shush! I have to study," snapped Nathan, whose irritation to being asked such questions reached a new height of intolerance as his drought continued.

Neusy sat back in his gray, leather, high-back seat in the rear of the BMW X5. Torsten opened his window and the moon roof and happily drove down the highway, being careful not to break the speed limit. Torsten's forty-eight-inch-long hair was blowing behind him, nipping Neusy in the face with the air rushing through the vehicle. Marlon, sitting in the back of the car with Neusy, still managed to light up a joint. Neusy gave him a look that it was in his best interest to put out the joint.

"Oh, sorry, dude," said Marlon. Neusy didn't like people smoking in his car.

About an hour and a half later, Neusy woke up. He rose in his seat to see where they were. He saw a white Chevy SUV, a highway patrol vehicle, parked along the highway. "Fuckin Nazis!" he remarked.

"Who, us?" said Torsten.

"No, the police here in Arizona; I have never seen so many police cars along the highway in the US."

"Yeah, I guess they want their revenues," said Nathan.

"Yeah, those fuckers always want to screw us! That's what it is all about—money!"

"Neusy, I am getting tired of driving. Can you take over for a while?"

Neusy, who was starting to get bored in the back seat, said, "Yeah, sure, why not—aaagggggght!" spitting Torsten's hair out of his mouth.

They pulled the car into the next rest stop and rotated seats. Neusy would now drive; Torsten was in the back seat. Nathan was still looking at his laptop. Marlon jumped out and lit up his joint, looked at Neusy, and raised his joint in the air with a smile.

After they were all seated, Neusy pulled back out onto the interstate and asked if they wanted to hear some tunes. They all agreed, so he popped in a CD of the Doctor's works and listened as they drove west on Interstate 10. They were coming up on the California border where Neusy could finally speed up a bit; he was anxious to get to Monrovia. As they passed Blythe, California, he remembered back to the days when he and his pals would camp at Blythe and go waterskiing or parasailing, getting drunk, enjoying the Colorado River. He remembered humping his first girlfriend on top of a farmer's twenty-foot-tall haystack near the river.

Blythe was now in the distance. They were driving through Palm Desert when Neusy noticed the car calling for gas. "I'm going to get some gas, guys," he said as he looked for the next off-ramp showing a gas station.

"Und I have to take a leak," said the primarily silent Nathan.

"Me too! And get something to eat!" added Marlon.

"Maybe get some snacks?" said Nathan.

"Und some coffee!" added Torsten.

"Yeah, I could use some coffee or some Redbull," said Neusy as he yawned.

"Und some pussy would be nice, but nothing comes my way," said Nathan.

"Well, I don't think you will find any at a station in the desert unless she is missing a bunch of teeth," said Neusy in a tone of concern.

Neusy maneuvered next to the gas pump, swiped his credit card, pulled out the nozzle, inserted it, and started the pump. The four road mates headed into the store and looked for the restroom. Neusy grabbed a few Starbucks Double Shot Mocha cans. Nathan spotted some bottles of Becks. "How funny you Amerikaners have Beck's here at the petrol station. I must buy one of these as a souvenir."

"Whatever!" said Neusy with very little interest.

"Nein, nein, this is cool!"

Neusy scratched his head as they went to the register to pay. The broad-shouldered girl behind the counter asked Nathan for his ID. He had left it in the car, so Neusy offered to pay for the Beck's, but the girl insisted on seeing Nathan's ID. He went out to the BMW and retrieved his passport to show the girl. After that, the three got into the vehicle, this time with Nathan behind the wheel.

"Shit, where is Marlon?" asked Neusy.

"Here he is!" answered Torsten.

Neusy turned around to see Marlon getting into the car with three large bags of snacks. "Are you a little hungry, Mr. Stoner?" he asked. "Hahaha… Must be good stuff you're smoking. Good to see you doing better today."

Marlon laughed and said, "Yeah…I need my medication or I freak out. But damn, I am hungry!"

"How embarrassing to be questioned for my ID," Nathan said.

"Well, here in California, if you don't look thirty or older…" Neusy informed the Austrians.

"I am twenty-nine… In Austria, I wouldn't have these problems."

"What is that smell?" shouted Neusy.

"Ach, sorry, I made, how do you say, fart?" said Nathan apologetically.

"Yeah, it is fart, Nate. How do you call that in German?"

"We say poopzen when we are with Herr Doctor; that is the nice way."

"And the other way?"

"Furz or fuchsen."

"Well, I think that was a furz. If not, you shit your pants. What do you call that kind of person?" laughed Neusy.

"Hosenscheisser!" Nathan and Torsten said in unison with a slight chuckle.

"Well, roll down your window, Nate, that's fuckin' sick!" Neusy instructed.

"You Amerikaners are so funny, yah? Making a big deal with this. Back home, we do not care who farts."

Marlon used this moment with the window open to take another drag on his joint unnoticed as he was eating potato chips. "Well guys, we are almost at the Ramp Amp… And Marlon, I can fucking see you dropping shit out of your mouth, clean it up!" Neusy said. "I'm going to make you sweep out my car later!"

"Sorry dude…but they're chips… I'll clean up," replied Marlon.

"What is the Ramp Amp like?" asked Nathan.

"Oh, you'll dig on it; they have old tube amps and classic effects pedals," answered Neusy as he eyed Torsten, asleep in the back.

"Sounds interesting," Nathan said as they pulled up to the Ramp Amp. They exited the car, walked up the path, and rang the bell. Marlon stayed by the car and secretly took another hit.

The Ramp Amp was located in the garage behind the house of the proprietor, Dude Danner. Dude welcomed the three into his shop. Being the Doctor's guitar player, Nathan was most interested; he liked all of the gadgets he saw. Torsten the Viking was less interested, being a keyboardist, but he did like some of the vintage sound effect boxes. Bringing in the 900-watt Galactic head, Neusy sat it on the workbench. Dude unscrewed the outer shell and started inspecting for damage. He found some burnt capacitors and a few other issues. "Can you get it fixed, Dude?"

"Yeah, Neusy, I can do it, but it is fucked up," he replied as he looked through his lighted magnifying lens.

"Dude, I love your place. Dude…this place is very cool," said Marlon as he walked in, not having any idea what this person's name was.

"Thanks, my friend," said Dude. "Dude Danner," he said and stuck out his hand.

Marlon shook Dude's hand and said, "Whatever, why does everyone make fun of me." Dude didn't understand and went back to the amp.

"How much is it going to cost?" Neusy inquired.

"I don't know yet; you will have to call me later. But someone has been working on this before and has fucked up some other things in here. Look at the bypass filter; it isn't original. How did this amp get fried?"

"A guy named Theodore Redwood had the voltage switch on the power converter on 220V, and the amp was set to 110V."

"What a Dummkopf," said Nathan. He was mesmerized by the bench with all of the old effect units and stompboxes—DOD, MXR, Boss, Kent, Colorsound, Fuzzface, and so many others—a guitarist's dream of vintage sound devices. "Wow, look at this Univibe, a real one! Und looks at this original Maestro Echoplex? Und look at these old Marshalls. Ach du lieber!"

"Yep, one is 1967, and the other is 1964, all original, my friend," explained Dude.

"What wunderbar treasures you have here!" said Nathan.

Torsten reminded Neusy, "We must get to rehearsal."

"Don't forget to call me later for the price, and I will tell you when you can pick up the amp," Dude said as they walked down the driveway to the car.

Back in the car, they headed across town to the 210 Fwy eastbound. Torsten asked in perfect English, "How long would it take to get to this place?"

Neusy, amazed at this, asked, "How can you speak perfect English now, and normally I hear you speaking with a German accent?"

Torsten replied, "Well, my dad is Danish, but my mom is Austrian. Most Danes speak perfect English, but around the Doctor and the others, I speak as my mom does. How much longer until we arrive at the rehearsal hall?"

Neusy replied, "Maybe forty-five minutes or so." The four men sat back and listened to some music. Neusy discovered that the two Austrians dug Seals and Croft and knew every word to every song. *How weird,* he thought. Soon they were in Santa Ana and were minutes from the rehearsal hall.

Neusy's phone rang; it was Jeb. "Hey, how is it going?"

"It's going good! Dude is working on the amp. He will let us know the cost."

"That's great; at least I have one guy I can depend on," said Jeb. "I'll have some nice cold suds here ready for you when you get here."

"That's great. I need some now; I'm beat. It's been like eight hours of sitting in the car," Neusy said.

An hour later Neusy pulled up to the multi-room rehearsal hall in Santa Ana, where Jeb had reserved the largest room for two days. They would rehearse into the night and then again in the morning to prepare for the most important performance of the WCGS.

It was 6:00 p.m. when Neusy and the boys arrived. Heinz and the Doctor were already there with Jeb and Hocker. Old familiar faces greeted Neusy, who had just received the good news the amp would be ready to pick up in the morning, with a $300 fee and no surcharge for the rush job. *Yippee*, thought Neusy. Then he felt a hand tapping him on the shoulder in perfect 120 bpm metronomic time. He turned around, and there was the Doctor.

"Hallo, Neusy. Did you have any luck with the amplifier?"

"Yes, it will be ready in the morning," said Neusy, proud of his actions.

"Ahhh, das ist gut, you have done well! You will receive serious brownie points for this!"

"No problem, happy to help out," said Neusy.

"You have done more than help out; you have saved the day!"

Neusy thought to himself, *I would gladly trade my new brownie points for one of those three new MXR Carbon Copy Delay stompboxes that the Doctor had just received for free from Dunlop.* Surely, he wouldn't mind letting Neusy have one. But unfortunately, he was wrong.

Chapter 13

Trenton Towers, a young genius from the UK, invented a special device and guitar system that could play the guitar through thought waves. The science behind this was called Teleguitarism (guitarkinesis), and his invention was named the Metal Mind Melder (MMM). The reading device, called Thought Reader Module (TRM), was mounted on a microphone stand with a flexible wand that could bend toward the user's head. It is connected to a specially built guitar (Thought Transference Guitar or TTG) mounted on another stand via a special cable. Protruding from the back of the body of the TTG were two mechanical arms with robotic hands and fingers that would either strum, fingerpick, or fret the notes on the neck. It kind of looked like the Terminator Guitar. The principle itself, in theory, was quite simple: the user could imagine a melody, and the TRM would read it from their brain and transfer it to the special guitar. The guitar would play itself without the guitarist touching it. Kind of like a player-piano, but worked by thoughts.

For years, Trenton had many players try out his system, but it failed or malfunctioned. In one instance, a musician testing it was thinking of a song from Hair's musical play. The TTG went crazy, with the mechanical arms ripping out the hair of the user. Another occurrence early on happened when the user thought of the song "That Smell" by Lynyrd Skynyrd. At the moment of the solo, the TTG's mechanical arms went through the motion of mixing cocktails, rolling joints, then chopping lines.

Three years ago, Trenton was frustrated with his device and ready to abandon it when he read in a music magazine of the Doctor's attempt to play the European shows from Japan. He already knew the Doctor from years back and reached out to the Doctor, who liked hearing about new technology and agreed to give the system a try in the lab.

The Doctor immediately flew from Vienna to London to meet with Trenton, who was at the airport to pick him up. The two had a friendly embrace at the airport and then took off in Trenton's car, a white 1968 Austin-Healey. The Doctor liked driving other people's vehicles in foreign lands and asked if he could drive Trenton's car. Trenton said OK and handed him the keys.

Trenton's car was equipped with a GPS, so everything was in happy accordance. They left the airport parking lot like a bat out of hell, screeching the tires as they made a forty-five mph right turn onto the main street. Trenton buckled up his seat belt. The Doctor made it on the main highway to Trenton's factory, Imagemusik. He was driving over 100 mph with his window down and his long hair flapping behind him. The sound of the wind was quite loud, so they both had to shout in conversation. He kept asking Trenton the same question every few miles.

"What is the speed limit here in England?" asked the Doctor.

"Well, it is seventy mph," replied Trenton Towers.

"Ach du lieber! That is too slow! In Germany, there is no speed limit. And in Austria, I drive this way too!"

"Maybe you should slow down a bit, mate!" shouted Trenton. The Doctor noticed he was grabbing onto the dashboard. He smiled and increased his speed.

"Nein, nein. We will be fine, Trenton!"

Another twenty miles, the same question came up again.

"What is the speed limit here in England?"

"It's seventy mph," Trenton answered back, seemingly annoyed.

After another hour, they arrived in Bath, England, where Imagemusik was located. They entered the parking lot the same way he left the airport: a screeching forty-five mph left turn and then entering perfectly into a lined parking space.

Trenton and the Doctor approached the outer black-glass-door entrance to the building. Trenton then tapped in the passcode on the keypad to enter the facility. The Doctor recognized the sounds of the passcode as it was the first six notes of a very famous Centipedes song. He had a smirk on his face as they entered the building. The building was graveyard silent; being a Sunday, all the employees were at home. Trenton led him down the black-glass-walled corridor to the laboratory.

The door at the end of the corridor read, "Thought Transference Technology Laboratory." Again, Trenton entered a passcode on the keypad, and once again, the smirking Doctor recognized the song: it was the first six notes to "Air on the G String" by J.S. Bach.

Trenton whistled the melody and the lights turned on. Curiously, the Doctor looked around and saw many mechanical devices and inventions; it was a robotics laboratory. Trenton led the Doctor to the TRM set up in a black-glass booth, five feet square. He was fascinated by the first sight of the TTG. It resembled a guitar spider with two arms instead of eight.

"This is fantastic! I have never seen such a device, Trenton!" remarked the Doctor with much excitement in his voice. "What do I do?"

"Stand with your head close to the device mounted on the wand," said Trenton. Trenton pushed the on button, and the device emitted red and green lights onto Jurgen's forehead.

"What do I do now?"

"Close your eyes and think of a short melody," instructed Trenton. "Put your arms down to your sides; the device doesn't like any additional body movements."

The Doctor closed his eyes and stood motionless in thought in front of the TRM. Miraculously, the TTG's mechanical arms began to play. It began to play Mendelssohn's "Spring Song." Trenton was overjoyed with tears. After years of disappointment and failure, now with the help of the Doctor of Dynamics, the device functioned as he always had imagined.

The Doctor remained motionless and continued in thought. The TTG continued to play. However, it began to slow down in tempo at around the one-and-a-half-minute mark, and then at two minutes, the two mechanical arms dropped lifelessly downwards. Jurgen inquired what had happened.

Trenton replied, "I am not sure… Try it again."

Jurgen agreed and again stood motionlessly in front of the TRM. The green and red lights blazed onto the Doctor's forehead.

After a minute, the arms raised to their proper positions on the TTG and began to play. This time it played *Eine kleine Nachtmusik* by W.A. Mozart. Trenton again was pleased that the device was working correctly. But then, at the same time sequence, the machine slowed down and eventually stopped.

Jurgen said, "Yah, what is this? Why did it stop?"

Trenton replied, "I think the device can only support about one and a half minutes of thoughts per session…" And with that, they both decided it was a successful test, and it was time for a lunch break.

Over the next three years, Trenton would make upgrades to the TRM. First, he increased the system memory. He discovered that when the Doctor activated the system, his thoughts were far quicker and at a higher level than the system could handle.

The TTG could also not keep up with the Doctor's playing. He finally got it to play five minutes, then ten, and finally up to an hour. But the problem was the Doctor could only get it to play simple songs like "London Bridge" or "Mary had a Little Lamb."

Finally, after two and a half years and flying his new best friend to England twenty-eight times, Trenton figured it out. He had completely redesigned the entire system a little at a time, with eighty terabytes of memory and a twenty-four core processor that he designed. It landed him on several cable news shows. It was not only the design, but the speed at which he did all this.

Finally, his invention was ready. This was the year Trenton would show the world what he had invented. Trenton applied for membership to the WCGS and received it. He bought a double booth with a small stage. However, no one would see more than a video of the device in action until after the Doctor wowed the crowd at the WCGS concert.

Chapter 14

Agents Sparrow and Crow were driving around in an ever-growing circumference around Santa Ana and looking for a hotel. They had been doing this for the last three hours. Neither of them called in advance to book a hotel, and this being the one weekend a year when Santa Ana hosts the West Coast Guitar Summit, all the hotels were full.

"Fuck, this is ridiculous, Jath!" said Agent Crow. Neither one knew much about the music industry, much less about the guitarist they were following. "Bullshit, we get put onto this case, and it could have been explained to us a little better what the fuck this guitar show was all about."

"What is on that schedule this afternoon that the tour manager gave you?" asked Agent Sparrow, who was driving the FBI-issued SUV with blacked-out windows.

"Rehearsal in Santa Ana. Shit, that starts in a half-hour! What's that over there? It says vacancy." They turned into the parking lot of the Purple Rose Motel, a small fifteen-room white building that stretched the entire length of the parking lot, with purple doors that all exited onto the parking lot. "Well, this is better than nothing."

They exited the vehicle, went into the lobby, and showed the manager their badges. Crow said, "We need a room. Agents Sparrow and Crow—FBI."

The manager said, "Very nice fellas, for the hour?"

"Very fucking funny!" Sparrow said, "for the fucking night. Two beds!"

"Well, in case you haven't noticed, gentlemen, we ain't exactly a resort over here. We do not have nightly room rates; we rent by the hour… And as the sign says, it's nineteen bucks an hour, two hours minimum. Oh, and we do not have rooms with two beds. However, I do have a nice room with a waterbed, king size, of course," said the manager with a grin on his face that exposed large gaps in his teeth.

"Fuck you… Well, we need the room for the night, and you're the only place that has vacancies with this dumb-ass guitar bullshit event!" explained Sparrow.

"Well, if you can wake up and leave the hotel by 5:00 a.m., then I will charge you for only ten hours. That is a bargain."

"Bargain?" exclaimed Crow. "It's robbery, for this shit hole!"

"Gentleman, I am busy. Take it or leave it. My rooms fill up every night."

"Yes, yes, OK, we will take it," said Crow as he handed him the corporate card.

The manager ran the card and said, "Declined."

"What?" said Crow. "Jath, give him your card."

The same result. "Declined."

Sparrow and Crow locked eyes, and Sparrow said, "What the hell is up with the cards?" Crow shrugged, and Sparrow handed the manager his personal credit card.

"OK gentlemen, you are set, room fourteen, out the door to the left."

Sparrow grabbed the key and, as they left the office, said, "Your card next time, Jester, I am not using my card all the time. What is up with the agency-issued cards? Let's put our bags in the room, then head down to rehearsal."

Crow nodded as they parked towards the rear of the property, retrieved their bags from the trunk, and opened the room door. Better than expected, the room was not terrible. It had incense burning that smelled like a rose, fresh paint, pink with purple towels hanging on the wall outside the bathroom, a king-size bed with nightstands on either side and lamps on both. One was dimly lit, illuminating the complimentary earplugs and custom condoms with the hotel's logo on the packaging.

The agents left their room in a hurry and headed for the rehearsal hall forty-five minutes from their love nest. The next day, they tried to find a hotel closer to the WCGS but failed in their attempt and had to pay a second night, by the hourly rate, at the Purple Rose.

The Doctor hated rehearsals, and learning new songs fell upon the individual musicians to learn themselves on their own time. However, the Doctor insisted on any harmony parts of the songs that involved Nathan, Heinz, or Torsten the Viking be worked on as a group. And it was the Doctor's grand scheme of things to use the Metal Mind Melding Device at the concert at WCGS. The debut would be tomorrow night in front of sixteen thousand industry people. This had to be perfect! The Doctor and band began the special rehearsals.

"Guten Abend, boys!"

"Guten Abend!" the lads playfully replied.

"Today we will rehearse the songs for tomorrow's concert. Then once again in the morning. I will stand here and concentrate on the notes und you will play normally."

The Doctor approached the wand and put his head close to the TRM device. The green and red lights shined on his forehead, indicating it was ready for transmission. They would first play the Centipedes classic "Soar into the Sun." The Doctor explained that the solo sections couldn't be longer than a minute and thirty seconds. This wasn't a problem for most songs because the original tracks didn't have extensively long solos. Although Trenton did figure out the initial limiting issue, the Doctor wanted to take no chances on stage. However, the time limit did bother him greatly in using it in his standard, free-flowing long solos he was known for in a live performance.

The band began to play only the solo section with the harmony parts. The Doctor concentrated, and the mechanical arms started to play the proper notes on the TTG. All seemed to be going well. They all paused at the end of the solo, and the Doctor spoke with them.

"Nathan, don't forget on the fourth bar, you don't play the third, you play the fifth. Torsten, at the same section, you play the third. Und you, Heinz, you play the root note on bass with me. Understand? Verstehen Sie?" The bandmates all nodded their heads in silent accord. No one dared to question the Doctor's advanced knowledge of musical theory and the application thereof.

The agents opened the door to the rehearsal room, and the Doctor just put his fingers to his lips and motioned to the agents to have a seat on the couch in the corner. The agents noticed that everyone in the room had earplugs, and they sat for the next two hours with their fingers in their ears.

The band once again played "Soar into the Sun." Crow said to Sparrow, "Tomorrow, bring those earplugs from the motel."

Sparrow responded, "WHAT?"

Crow repeated himself, and so did Sparrow. They went on like this another five times, and then the music stopped. Crow quickly pulled out his cell phone and texted the message to Sparrow just as the band started up again. Sparrow texted back a thumbs up.

The band started playing the song "Life's Like a Dagger." This song was a bit more complicated as it had three sections with harmony parts. The Doctor would have to back away from the TRM wand device each time he finished a section so the machine could reset.

The band began to play the song. They made it through the first solo section and then paused. The Doctor spoke. "Nathan, you do not have the right feeling here. You are too stiff. You must loosen up und get into the zone!"

"I understand! Ich Verstehe!" said Nathan.

They started again. Upon finishing the segment, the band paused and waited for the Doctor's response. "Heinz, you are playing with an erratic tempo. This is not tempo rubato here! Tighten it up!"

Heinz nodded in silence. He was not used to being criticized and took pride in his playing. They tried again. This time the Doctor had no complaints. He told them that they would proceed to the next section.

They began to play the second section of "Life's Like a Dagger." Everyone was in the zone; everything was going perfectly. Nathan, in the moment, stood next to the Doctor and posed as they played together at the eighth bar. Nathan thought of tapping out his part of the solo on the fretboard, à la Edward Van Halen, to change it up. The TRM device began reading Nathan's thoughts and tapped out what he was thinking on the TTG.

He had gotten too close to the MMM, and it played what he thought. The Doctor shouted, "STOP! What are you doing, Nathan? Do not get too close to me when I am using the TRM. Und we don't tap here on my songs!"

Nathan's head sunk in embarrassment. He said it wouldn't happen again. The band continued for another hour on the remaining two songs that needed harmony work, and then they broke for a late lunch.

After, they continued. The Doctor, at midnight, said, "That is it for today. Now go to the hotel and get some rest, then tomorrow at 10:00 a.m. we will start again."

To ensure they did as they were told, Jeb insisted everyone was driven back to the hotel. He then went to the lobby and set up a wake-up call for all rooms at 8:00 a.m. He made his way back to his room and found Neusy, Hocker, and Marlon drinking beer. Marlon declared, "That was sick as fuck at rehearsal. I scored some excellent weed here. Man, I bought from three different dispensaries. I have enough to last me for a while. I also am doing much better than yesterday. I spoke to my wife and spoke to my kids. It broke my heart. I cried, but now I am OK. I am ready for this tour, and that MMM fucking device is the coolest thing I ever have seen."

"Good!" said Jeb. "Tomorrow, I need you to be on top of your game!" Marlon nodded and lit up a joint. After another beer, the crew went to sleep.

The next day, the rehearsal started at noon. First, the Doctor wanted to buy new stage clothes for the show. Jeb drove him to the mall, where he shopped all the women's stores. The Doctor only wore women's blouses, mimicking rockers like Robert Plant and Mick Jagger. He declared that "These women, yeah…they have all of the good clothes. Men's clothes have no personality!" He bought several bags of clothes. He bought some new pants and even a pair of jeans.

After two hours, Jeb was exhausted. The Doctor was paying for his jeans and said, "Yah… Jeb, tonight is crucial. You must make sure all is OK. Do not let anyone touch the MMM machine, yah?"

"Yes, of course, no one will touch it."

"Und!" the Doctor continued, "I think for this special occasion, I will wear these jeans." And then to the clerk, "Can I pay in Euros? I have no US dollars."

While tapping on her cell phone, the young woman behind the counter said, "Huh?"

"Yah, maybe you should stop with the handi-phone and do your job!"

"Huh?"

"Yah… Can I use these Euros to pay?"

"Dude!" the clerk replied, "I am not following. I cannot understand your words."

"Dummkopf!" said the Doctor as he put his other bags on the counter.

Jeb pulled out his credit card and handed it to the clerk, saying, "Here, use this card." She then rang up the jeans and the shirt. The Doctor picked up the new bag, leaving his previous purchases on the counter. Jeb grabbed the bags and sprinted to catch up to the Doctor. "Here, you left your blouses on the counter."

Two hours later on the way to rehearsal, Jeb looked at his phone. Neusy, Hocker, and Marlon all called him multiple times. He called Neusy and gave the update. The Doctor reminded Jeb to bring the Metal Mind Melding system to the arena no later than 4:00 p.m., as Trenton wanted.

Everyone was waiting for Jeb and the Doctor to arrive; even the agents were there on time. The rehearsal was on another level. Everybody played perfectly and the Doctor was pleased.

The rehearsal was going full force at 4:00 p.m. Jeb tried several times to get the Doctor to stop rehearsing with no luck. He then had the power cut to the room at 4:30. "What is this, Acorns? Why do you disturb my rehearsal?"

"It's now 4:30. You went over time. We need to go and bring the equipment to the arena."

"Yah, you go do that. Und later, when the show is on, I will go over time there too. One hour they give me. Never enough time!"

Jeb laughed as he knew this routine and regularly saw it when he worked at festivals or multi-act concerts with the Doctor.

Usually, the stage manager just cut the power to get him to stop playing. That's what gave Jeb the idea.

Jeb instructed Neusy and Hocker to collect the TTG and TRM wand and bring it to the arena. Marlon fit right in, unplugging amps and cabinets and loading them into the van. He was stoked to be working on the road with a real rock band. Off to the arena, life on the road never stops.

"What a crazy device, Hocker!" Neusy said as he drove.

"Yeah, crazy man!" He spit his chew out the window. "I hope the fuckin' thing works. You know how many times these things Herr Doctor uses don't work!"

"Yeah, I know. We also can't try it out at the arena and test it," Neusy said.

"Why not?"

"Because supposedly it only works for the Doctor… but we will see," said Neusy.

They pulled into the arena parking lot, then into the loading area under the arena. They took the device components from the back of the SUV. Jeb and Marlon arrived with the van containing the rest of the equipment.

Hocker said he wanted to hurry and set it up so they could have a couple of beers and a burger. After checking in with the stage manager coordinating the event, they all agreed and set it up in record time.

They placed the two components behind the Doctor's amps since two other bands were also playing the event. Later, they would set it up in the area of the Doctor's pedalboard, just a little to the right, so when he didn't need to use the system, it wouldn't be in his way for the other songs.

After having a couple of beers and eating burgers that could not be beaten, the crew returned to the arena just after the second band finished. The Doctor's band was all assembled in the green room. They would be going on in thirty minutes. Everyone laughed and joked around, making Doctor jokes, as they often did when he was not present. The arena was packed with about half the people in their seats as the other half wandered around during the intermission. The crew moved the MMM to the stage. They set the unit in place, checked the lines, and made sure that their equipment was not disturbed.

Marlon wandered around, stoned as usual, and thought about what he could do. Standing at the front of the stage, he thought about the extraordinary things he had heard about the Metal Mind Melder system. The curtain was drawn, and he was standing there by himself. It looked remarkable, very futuristic. The guitar was purple and fashioned after a Fender Stratocaster but had these two mechanical arms with robotic hands that presently stretched down towards the floor. He approached the TRM device and, on the wand, pushed on the button. He put his head close to the TRM device and closed his eyes. Not expecting anything to happen, he thought of *Do-Re-Mi-Fa-So-La-Ti-Do,* and it played the notes for him. Tickled with himself, he thought of "Jingle Bells," and it began to play it for him. He then thought, *man, I'm losing my buzz, better roll up a few joints for later.* One of the robotic arms reached toward his front left pants pocket and pulled out a pack of rolling papers that he had. The other robotic arm then went toward his other pocket, removed a green plastic container and opened it. Then the one hand poured the weed into a rolling paper that the other hand was holding. The hand with the rolling paper rolled a perfectly cylindrical joint. Marlon thought he would like a few more, and the machine continued to roll two more for him.

Jeb saw him up on the stage and walked over to him. "What the fuck are you doing, Marlon?"

"Umm, well, I thought I would try the MMM."

"No, no, no!!! No one can touch that thing but the Doctor!" yelled Jeb. "That thing is worth tens of thousands of dollars; if you fuck it up, you are off the tour. Plus, it only works for the Doctor."

"I'm sorry, dude," said Marlon as he put the perfectly rolled joints into his pocket and smiled.

"Get your ass down from here. Wait for Teddy Red to arrive with the Doctor in the loading area. Call him and say we are ready."

"OK, Jeb. I'm sorry, I'm sorry."

"OK, shut up! We'll keep it between the two of us. I hope to God it works tonight and you didn't fuck it up."

The audience had mostly returned to their seats. They were anticipating the Doctor's arrival. Many of the people were fans of the Doctor, wearing shirts from previous tours. Looking out into the audience, Jeb thought this was good.

There were fans waiting outside the loading area to get an autograph, or a Doctor's prescription. The fans knew that is where he would enter the venue. Among these fans trying to get into the show were the agents, who were having no luck, even after flashing their badges to the security guard multiple times. "Agents Sparrow and Crow," said Sparrow. "We need to get into the arena!"

"Guys!" said the security guard. "I see all sorts of badges all night. You will need more than that to get in there. No exceptions. This is a show everybody wants to get into, but it's a private event."

After getting declined at every entrance, they decided that they would have to sit this night out and wait at the conveniently close strip club across the street. They were relieved that their corporate cards worked at the entrance for the $25 cover and figured it was a glitch at the motel. However, they were soon disappointed when their cards failed to gain approval for the $187 bar tab at the end of the evening.

Teddy Red pulled up in the back of the arena with the Doctor, and they were waived in by security after Marlon stated who was in the vehicle. Four fans ran in simultaneously to try and get an autograph and a few words. The Doctor didn't deny them and signed some of their memorabilia. Then he politely excused himself and entered the back door. The Doctor could be surprisingly polite to fans, but he could be incredibly rude and condescending to the crew and the band. One of the bouncers stared down the fans, and they dispersed as he entered the backstage area.

The Doctor walked into the dressing room, sat down for a minute, and guzzled a coffee. Jeb, Marlon, Neusy, and Hocker were on both sides of the stage watching the equipment, making sure no one would touch any of it. Theft was always a concern on a show like this. On the last tour, a fan stole one of the Doctor's stompboxes right off the stage after a show. Of course, Neusy got bitched at by the Doctor for it and had to buy a new pedal out of his wages. The Doctor called Jeb on his cell phone and told him to make the introduction. Jeb looked at Marlon and said, "Do you think you can handle a simple task?"

"Sure man, anything."

"Go up on the stage and announce the Doctor."

"OK, boss!" said Marlon, very excited.

Marlon ran with glee up on the stage and spoke into the microphone on the Doctor's side of the stage. "Testing, testing, can you hear me out there?"

The audience screamed in unison, "Yeeeessssssss!!!"

"Good evening!" The curtains opened, and there was an enormous roar. "Are you guys ready for the best part of the night?" The crowd was all focused on the MMM. "Well, without further delay, let me introduce to you the man you have all been waiting for, the man who needs no introduction but will get one anyway. Here he is, the Doctor of Dynamics and my best friend and mentor, Jurgen Weislangwolf."

"WAAAAAAHHHHHHH! Fuck yeah! Bring it!" The crowd went crazy.

A deafening sound rang out from the Universe Guitar and the 900-watt Galactic Amp. The building shook, and the fans responded with screams. "Guten Tag, my friends! It's been a long time since I was here last in the arena. It's time to rock! Here is 'Peter's Limping!'"

The Doctor depressed the twenty-two-inch tremolo bar on the Universe Guitar and it created a 5.2 on the Richter scale. The first twenty rows of seats started sliding across the floor, back and forth like a rocking ship. The arena came alive. Everyone was screaming—they had their hands in the air like they were riding a roller coaster, screaming and laughing—a couple of them threw up.

"Und now we will play 'Stuck in the Mire.'" Again, the fans came unglued, screaming, jumping, singing every word. The song ended with a crash of stomping, yelling, and applause.

"Now we have a special surprise. We will play 'Soar in the Sun,' und I will use this new EFX, the Metal Mind Melder."

The crowd got very loud and then suddenly silent. The band began to play, Nathan began to sing, the crowd started to sing. Everything was in complete harmony. As Nathan sang, he scanned the audience for possible after-show pickups. Several hot candidates in leather and other sexy apparel stood in close vicinity of his stage position. He continued to sing, and the band continued to play.

> *One day, we'll fly away and soar into the sun*
> *I always yearn for when we'll burn together*
> *It'll be a bash when we turn to ash together*
> *Soar into the Sun*

We will feel the heat when we roast our meat
Soar into the Sun

The whole room was in unison and harmony. The Doctor was extremely pleased and grinned at the audience, kind of like a platypus if it could grin. The band had approached the solo; everyone was ready to play the harmonies together with the Doctor. He stood in front of the TRM wand; the green and red lights beamed on his head. He closed his eyes and put his arms down at his sides. The crowd was digging it; they couldn't comprehend what they would see next. The Doctor, Nathan, Heinz, and Torsten all began in perfect harmony. He smiled with his eyes closed; everything was going as well as he wanted. As they were in the middle of the solo, Nathan, out of habit, moved closer to the Doctor and posed as he played. The Doctor didn't notice as his eyes were closed in concentration. As they played, Nathan saw a blonde hottie with a low-cut, pink, tight-fitting top with her C cups bouncing left and right in motion with the music. He had his mind made up: this was his girl tonight after the show and the curse would end! He smiled at her, and she smiled back. She purposely shook her tits at him, pulling her shirt to the side to show more skin. Nathan got hard; everyone from as far back as row forty-eight could see the bulge in his pants.

Suddenly, one of the mechanical arms reached over, zipped down Nathan's fly, and pulled out his Schwanz. The other robotic arm reached over and handed him a condom from his back pocket. Nathan embarrassedly turned, hurried away, and zipped up his fly. The Doctor didn't know what had happened; he opened his eyes and looked around. He saw the TTG's robotic hands making sexual gestures. The one hand made an OK sign, and the other hand made a middle finger and thrust it in and out of the circle of the OK sign in the other hand. The Doctor thought the machine had malfunctioned. He looked at Neusy and gestured to him to retrieve the Universe Guitar. Neusy readily handed it to him and plugged it in.

Fortunately, the mistake lasted only a short moment in time, and they were able to get through it with Torsten's tight keyboard riffs along with Heinz's bass parts. Nathan played it off cool and began to sing the next verse as they transitioned into it. They finished the song, and even though the machine went haywire over Nathan's sexual thoughts, the crowd enjoyed it and made it known.

Nathan thought he would have a smorgasbord of women after the show, only later he out that he was like the kid in school that was caught masturbating in the boys' room.

"Well, I don't know what happened with the MMM, but sometimes these things happen with the new technology. Und now we will play 'Bitchy Wife.'"

The crowd continued to roar with approval as the band played as if nothing had happened, until the show abruptly ended fifteen minutes late when the stage manager cut the power. Jeb just nodded at him like it was the proper thing to do. The Doctor looked at the audience and attempted to say something into the mic, but no one heard what he said since there was no power.

No one noticed Johnny Scaggz driving past the rehearsal studio every half hour, and nobody saw him the whole evening in the rafters up top of the arena. He lay up there for the entire night, waiting for his moment. When he used to work for the Doctor, they called this improvising. From his vantage point, he could easily drop the Fender Stratocaster he had strung over his shoulder. It would kill anyone under it, falling 200 feet down to the floor.

He found his mark: the man in the fourth row not impressed with the Doctor's playing, flipping him off several times during the solo of "Stuck in the Mire." But Scaggz could not keep his eyes off the MMM. He became so mesmerized by the machine that he forgot to drop the guitar at the end of the show. He did not move from his position until the crew removed the MMM from the stage. His mind was racing as he thought of the things he could do with this unit.

Chapter 15

The following day was the official opening day at the WCGS show.

The Doctor sat in the fancy, upscale restaurant in the lobby of the Morton Hotel, having breakfast with Trenton Towers and Svetlana, his blonde, giggly, curvaceous, big-boobed wife. Trenton's invention was an overnight success and had everyone talking about last night's show. There were smiles all around the table.

Svetlana was born and raised in Russia. Her family was a well-known circus act, and she was a high-wire artist and a dancing bear trainer. One day during her high-wire act, she leaned over too far and the weight of her EE-sized breasts caused her to have a terrible fall. Trenton, at the time, was designing electronic medical instruments and was delivering a product to a hospital. He was connecting the device when he saw Svetlana lying in her hospital bed with a broken leg. It was love at first sight.

The Doctor had his usual meatless breakfast of eggs Florentine with three slices of apples and a sprig of parsley. Trenton and Svetlana both had the farmer's plate, heaped full of bacon, sausages, ham, scrambled eggs, hash browns, and two chocolate shakes to boot. Trenton and Svetlana always ordered the same things, wore similar clothes, and did the same activities together; it was true love.

The Doctor looked onward at the heaping plates of animal flesh and said, "My God! All that meat will give you a heart attack.

I can't stand to put animal flesh into my mouth. I find it nauseating!"

Trenton and Svetlana grinned, looked at each other, and continued to shovel the food into their mouths. After Trenton swallowed, he looked at the Doctor and said, "Tonight's show is gonna be great, Jurgen! You know who will be here, don't you?"

Jurgen replied, "Yeah, I think so!"

And they uttered together at the same time exactly, "DEEP GERBEL!"

The Doctor said, "Jinx! Trenton, und now you must buy me a milkshake."

The world-famous Australian Deep Purple tribute band, DEEP GERBEL would be playing the WCGS evening concert, which was very special. Something even more special was that both the current guitarist Steve Remorse and the original guitarist Bitchie Makemore had agreed to share the stage with the rest of the band, I'm-a Villain, John Bored, Anger Glovemaker, and Ivan Set-the-Pace.

"Maybe you can get up there on stage with them, Jurgen!" Trenton said.

"Yeah, that would be wunderbar! I will show those boys how to play!"

After Trenton paid the check, the three friends finalized their schedule for the day at the WCGS. As they stood up to leave the restaurant, one of Svetlana's enormous breasts squirmed its way loose from her already loose-fitting, low-cut top. The Doctor saw her perky nipple staring him in the eye and said, "My dear, you have one of your titties winking at me!"

Svetlana said, "Oh, silly me," and slapped the side of her breast. It immediately found its way back home behind the fabric, as if trained to do so.

This show would be a special WCGS trade show for the Doctor. It was the year that a major guitar manufacturer was to produce the Doctor's very own design, the Universe Guitar. It would be available to only a limited number of guitarists around the entire world. The world-famous Malfeasant Guitars were the only company authorized by him to produce his unique instrument.

The threesome excitedly proceeded toward the convention center entrance to gain access to the WCGS and witness the showing of the Universe Guitar.

The tension mounted as many famous artists from around the world lined up at the gates. They would be the first ones allowed inside the convention halls before the public could enter. The doors opened like the gates at a horse racing track, and they were among the thoroughbreds that sprinted through the doors. The threesome's finish line was the grand Malfeasant Guitars booth. The booth consisted of a whopping 5,000 square feet of guitars in various shapes, sizes, and colors. As always, the booth featured the Malfeasant Girls. These scantily dressed fashion models wandered about, displaying their wares to allure customers away from other booths.

The display of the Universe Guitar was unique as well. The guitar was suspended fifty feet in the air, above the Malfeasant Guitars booth, by a twenty-five-foot-long electric guitar G string specially designed for this purpose. One end of the string was attached to the guitar headstock and the other end tied around a ceiling water pipe above the crowd's heads. Many marveled at the spectacle of it all, the lone instrument suspended in a heavenly fashion for the world to see, as spotlights changing colors highlighted the guitar. The Doctor would have to appear at selected times to sign autographs, and of course, demonstrate the Universe Guitar in the Malfeasant Guitars booth.

The cost to purchase one of these guitars was quite astronomical. The Doctor, heavily into astronomy, set the price at a solid $150,000 per instrument. Why would it be so expensive, people would ask. One reason was no other instrument like the Universe Guitar existed in the world, or anywhere in the universe for that matter. Another reason was Jurgen Weislangwolf's name was attached to it. The third and most important reason: it was the Doctor's retirement plan.

After the first showing of the Universe Guitar and autograph session, the three friends had some time to look around at products and then jammed with others. Jurgen said, "Trenton, I heard that Jorge Cantina is playing over at the PMS Guitar booth."

Trenton replied, "Let's go there and check him out!"

The three friends made their way across the center of the convention hall to PMS Guitars, occasionally being stopped by fans for autographs.

Wow, the Doctor was excited to meet Jorge Cantina, the famous Mexican guitarist, gold album winner, and owner of over 100 cantinas throughout Mexico. Jorge also admired the Doctor, but they had never crossed paths in all of their international touring.

Madame Mary Jane Prescott founded the PMS Guitar Company, as an inspiring young guitarist; she accidentally menstruated on her white electric guitar, and a new art form was born. Now Madame Prescott personally signs all PMS guitars by squatting over the freshly manufactured white guitars at that particular time of the month. After drying, it is covered with a transparent lacquer. Each instrument is individual and unique; no two are alike. Jorge is, of course, endorsed by the company.

The Doctor and his pals reached the PMS Guitar booth. There was a swarm of fans blocking all entrances to get a glimpse of their favorite guitarist, Jorge Cantina. Trenton, being charismatic, approached a security guard and told him that the Doctor was there to meet Jorge; minutes later, the three were allowed through the back door to have an intimate meeting with the Mexican guitar master. The two masters fell into a strange, destined embrace and began complimenting each other. Moments later, Jorge Cantina was paged to the PMS central stage for the first jam of the day.

Jorge said, "Jurgen, mi amigo, do you want to play the first song with me on stage?"

Jurgen replied, "Yeah, that would be a great honor!"

The two played one of Jorge's world-famous songs, "Puchi, Smell the Bra," written about his first obese, extremely unclean wife, Alejandra. The two traded licks back and forth in perfection and harmony, as if they had rehearsed the songs over and over for a month. The crowd roared and threw hats up in the air. They did the Mexican hat dance and drank margaritas. When the song was done, the two embraced once more, said goodbye, and the Doctor hurried along with his two friends to see more wonders of the WCGS.

As they took to the aisles, they noticed an electronic effects company. The sign read Puketronics. All of the little metal stompboxes were colored and textured in, vomit brown or puke green. Some had the image of peas and corn floating in the simulated vomit brown colors. But they boasted new sounds not found in other effects boxes. One of their most unique stompboxes, called the *Barfbox*, when activated, made the sound of someone ralphing in whichever musical key was played through it. Puketronics claimed it would hypnotically win over angry drunks in any bar gig. Another device displayed was the *Homovibe*, which made an interesting vibrating, swirling sound with echo. It came with an external dildo head on a cord that inserted in the stompbox. The Doctor read the box, which stated, *The only limit is your imagination.*

The salesman told the Doctor that when he plays that special guitar solo with the *Homovibe* activated, "it will lift you to new heights and give you a buzz you can't get any other way." The Doctor thought about it for a moment, then exhaled the sound of a whale's blowhole and said no thanks, and the threesome continued on.

Another interesting booth was Wriggles Guitar Picks. They made spearmint, peppermint, and wintergreen guitar picks that you can suck to any thickness you desire. And because they are a special kind of real candy, they are sticky and stick to your thumb, so you never lose or drop a pick during a performance. The Doctor was utterly enthralled with the idea and immediately asked for a complimentary bulk package.

As they ventured through the convention halls, they found MinstrelMan Guitars. Reddy Von Headache was on the stage doing his famous guitar solo.

The Doctor said to Trenton, "I want to jam with Reddy Von Headache!"

Trenton said, "Go for it, you madman!"

The Doctor grabbed a guitar, plugged it into an amp, and played Rainbow's song "Kill the King." When it came to the solo, the Doctor was standing on stage in a wide stance. Reddy, standing on his head, started playing a tapping solo on the Doctor's guitar with his bare toes. The onlookers shouted with ear-deafening screams, which could not be heard over the loud amplifiers that were already destroying hearing. Reddy Von Headache was well known for playing so loud as to give one a headache.

Something else that was on the Doctor's mind was to find the loudest guitar amplifier manufacturer at the show. And that company was the German amplifier company Arschloch Amps.

Arschloch in German, simply put, means asshole, and you have to be a giant asshole to play louder than everyone else in the band, or arena, or in the whole universe. And you'd have to be a giant asshole to want to give people permanent ear damage. But that is what the Arschloch Amps Company made: 1,000-watt tube amplifiers. The Doctor wanted them to make him a 2,000-watt model, which no one could ever compete with. The three walked back to Malfeasant Guitars for another signing feeling depressed that a new amp would not be in the Doctor's near future.

The band had the day off and had decided that they would spend it at the hotel pool, which they often did whenever possible. This type of activity would soon be coming to an end once the tour bus portion of the tour started. There would be very few hotel rooms while sleeping on the bus. The band and crew would soon make their way up to Walnut Grove, CA, where the tour would resume and the next show was to take place.

But for now, sitting at the pool drinking beer was heaven. The crew, at the same hotel, sat in the hotel bar. Jeb hated pools, thinking of them disgusting and equating them to community bathtubs. Just the thought of being in one with other people's sweat, stench, asses, and privates all soaking in the water made him want to puke! So, he stayed away. Hocker felt the same way. However, Hocker was precisely the type of person that made Jeb feel this way. So they all sat in the bar, minus Teddy Red, who no one knew where he was, and no one cared.

The Doctor was still out with Trenton and had plans to join the band and crew at the hotel. Everyone at the hotel was anxiously anticipating the arrival of the Doctor's good friend Cowboy Cal Crabs. They knew he should arrive at any time, but no one was sure of when it might happen.

Chapter 16

The desert night was silent, still, and empty. In the distance, you could hear the howling of a lone coyote. A mom and pop gas station sat alone about two miles off Interstate 10 in Arizona near the California state line. Funny enough, the station was called Mom and Pop's Gas. The name came about after Mom and Pop had too much refried beans for dinner while discussing their new investment in the gas station. There was a light on in the office where an elderly man sat reading a Penthouse magazine, sipping on a Budweiser with his feet up on an old wooden desk.

Suddenly, the shining of a big rig's headlights cut through the blackness of the night. The truck was blazing toward the gas station at nearly 100 miles an hour. Once the big rig was 300 feet from the station, the driver hit the brakes. The trailer fishtailed radically left and then again right, but the trailer and the cab became perfectly symmetrical as the truck came to a complete stop. Not a thing could be seen through the cloud of dust caused by this little maneuver, engulfing the entire gas station. As the cloud finally dissipated, the giant truck was in perfect alignment with the gas pump. The truck itself was a midnight pearl blue Peterbilt beauty with Texas plates, complete with a sleeper compartment and a handsomely matched trailer that stood tall and proud amid Mom and Pop's Gas station. The truck driver turned off the engine and the lights, but you could hear its massive sound system pumping sonic waves of music through the steel body of the cab. The sounds were familiar to most hard rock fans: the Centipedes song "Slap the Virgin."

The man peered out of the office window to see if anyone was getting out of the truck as it sat there motionless with its lights off and its music blaring. He grabbed his double-barreled shotgun, proceeded out toward the gas pumps, and began cursing at the truck. "What the hell are you doing in there? Are you fucking crazy coming barreling in here like that?" cried out the old man. "If you want gas, you better get it and get the fuck outta here; I'm not a patient man!"

The door creaked open, and a giant cloud of smoke—not as big as the braking incident but nonetheless a vast billowy cloud—came out of the cab. The old man slowly approached the cab with his shotgun ready in his hands. The smoke from the cab of the truck hit him in the face, and he became a little dizzy. A single rattlesnake-skin boot proceeded out of the cab and steadied itself on the chrome-stamped steel running board, and then the next boot came down to the ground. There stood a 6'5" man with a thin muscular body, long stringy brown hair, bulbous eyes like Marty Feldman, hemp-woven cowboy hat, and a blue denim sleeveless shirt. He wore Levi button-ups and a cigar was hanging out of his mouth.

"Howdy partner, fill 'er up!" the intimidating figure said.

"Who in the hell are you, and what the fuck are you doing coming in here raising all hell like that?"

"Who am I? Why, I'm Cowboy Cal Crabs! Professional driver, big rigs, buses. Hell…three years ago, I was driving the monster truck circuit. And I always drive one way, and that is precise, the only way to keep my blood pressure down."

"Well, you raised my blood pressure about fifty points with that asinine stunt you just pulled."

"Well, sorry about that, old man. I'm just excited, and I'm trying to get to the L.A. area before my tour leaves without me. See, I am getting ready to park this beast for the next six weeks and drive a tour bus full of crazy cats."

"What show, the rodeo?" said the old man, now showing interest in this massive figure standing in front of him.

"Naw, an old friend of mine is here from Europe. A guitarist. I am going to be driving around a bunch of crazy, brilliant musicians from Austria," replied Cal.

"What the hell is that music blaring out of your cab? Turn it down so I can hear you better!" begged the old man.

"That blaring, as you put it, is my buddy's song, 'Slap the Virgin.' He is the cat I'm telling you about that I will be driving. World's greatest guitarist."

"Well, turn it off before I slap you on the side of the head with this here shotgun!"

"All right, calm down, old man, I'll turn it down," said Cal.

"And stop calling me old man, my name is Jim! What the hell was all of that smoke that came out of your cab and made me dizzy?"

"That's a Monte Cristo."

"Is that a cigar, boy?" asked Jim.

"You got that right, ol—ehem—Jim. Now can I get that gas? I'm in a hurry."

"Alright, just keep your pants on there, young whippersnapper."

Jim inserted the gas nozzle into the truck's gas tank. A long, bare, feminine leg stepped out of the cab and finally made it down to the ground with the other matching leg. A second pair of feminine legs also appeared and made their way to the ground and stood next to the first set of legs. As old Jim looked up from the feet to the waistlines of these two shapely bodies, he found them both clothed in purple see-through negligees. When his old, tired, angry eyes made it past the double set of perfect milky white breasts, they became affixed upon the two angelic faces of twin sisters, with blonde hair, dimples, and pearly white teeth.

"I must have died and gone to heaven," said Jim as his attitude suddenly changed. "Twins, dirty fucking little twins," he mumbled to himself, then louder, "Well, my friend, now I see why you took so long to get out of that there cab."

"Cal…baby…are we there yet?" one of the girls asked.

"Naw, honey, we have another two to three hours to go. I'm shootin' for two, but with these drivers…who knows. Hell, I can make it to Costa Mesa in an hour and a half with this big beast if it weren't for all those assholes on the road."

"We're getting lonely up in the cab without you, baby."

"Just keep your panties on until I get the gas, and we'll be on our way."

They both climbed back into the cab one after the other in the same long-drawn-out fashion; Cal patted the second one on her ass as she disappeared into the cab.

"Boy, you sure know how to live; you're one lucky fucker," said Jim. "Well, all filled up, that will be $328."

Cal took out a large wad of cash held together by a rubber band. He peeled off four one hundred dollar bills and handed them to Jim. "Here ya go, old timer, and it was nice talking to you."

Jim's eyes nearly bulged out of his head as Cal climbed up into his cab and turned over the engine once more to begin his approach to Tarzana. He slowly pulled out of Mom and Pop's Gas and headed toward Interstate 10.

Jim put the extra tip into a plastic container under the counter where he kept his extra money that Mom didn't know anything about. He picked up the Penthouse and thought he would get a massage with this secret stash next time in the city.

Chapter 17

Agents Sparrow and Crow arrived first in Walnut Grove and were ahead of the game: hotel booked last night and traveled early enough. Crow said, "Jath, I think that guy Jeb is correct. We interviewed everyone involved with this tour, and everyone has alibis for all the murders. Jurgen Weislangwolf has no enemies that we can tell. It seems everyone involved in the tour is quite open and would say something if any of them suspected they had some idea who could be involved."

"Well, yes, I agree. Now, they are not the brightest bunch, but I do feel we need to concentrate elsewhere, in my professional opinion. Do me a favor, though, let's remember to speak with the tour manager and see if we can get on that bus. We can never drive like that bus will. We would have to fly to each city. But better we are on the bus. Then we can observe all, plus, I must say, this is almost going to be like a vacation. There have to be girls hanging out on that bus."

"Yes, we will do this. We also have to call in to see what is up with our credit cards; we already spent over $500 from our own pockets."

At last, everyone in the band and crew arrived to set up for the Walnut Grove, CA show at a small, old-style, tavern-type venue with a decent sound system, small stage, and a calm, serene atmosphere with beautiful green trees decorating the quiet Northern California town. The crew was already setting up the equipment. Hocker, Neusy, and Marlon first humped Torsten the Viking's massive, heavy, Hammond B3 organ upon stage right. The

Doctor's equipment would be set up on stage left, as it always was. Soon the crew could indulge in some tasty Northern California micro-brewed suds at the bar. With the small stage, it took less time to get things in order. Jeb handled connecting the effect units while Hocker set up Triple T's drums, which Triple T later reconfigured.

The Doctor sat outside in the equipment van, restringing one of the Universe Guitars with a broken .003-gauge string. "When will they make strings that don't break?" he exclaimed as he turned the machine head to wind up the new string.

The Doctor stayed in the van until showtime since this venue had no green room. The Doctor entered through the back door. People began to line up for autographs, wanting to touch him or say hello. Jeb tried to keep things moving forward and yelled out, "Let the Doctor through; no autographs until later, make way." Jeb, Hocker, and Neusy had the people form a human parting of the Red Sea as the Doctor proceeded through to the stage.

There was no backstage area at this venue. The Doctor and his band had to enter the stage from the left side of the two-foot-tall stage, behind the seven-foot-high PA columns, and carefully walk through a three-foot-wide space; the stage was narrow, only seven feet deep. They had to maneuver themselves around the Doctor's effects pedals, without treading on any of the devices that were wired painstakingly and lined up parallel with the front edge of the stage. After the band was all in place, the Doctor spoke into his microphone. "Guten Abend, Walnut Grove!"

The crowd, consisting of the weirdest assembly of trolls, fairies, derelicts, dopers, and drunks Jeb had ever seen, chanted at the top of their lungs, "Jurgen, Jurgen, Jurgen!!!"

Jeb was up on stage behind the PA tower, looking over the crowd. From his vantage point, he could see Agent Crow out front directly in front of the Doctor's amp. He saw Sparrow at the side where the merch was set up. Hocker was at the bar, and Neusy was with him making his way back to the stage with a couple of beers in his hand. He watched Marlon sell a couple of T-shirts with Sadie looking on, but no sign of Teddy Red. He was amazed that they were able to have this challenging venue setup without any problems. Neusy handed Jeb a beer as the Doctor started his show.

"Und now here is a song from a long time ago, 'Life Makes Me Shiver.'"

"YAAAAAHHHHHHHHHHHHH!!!!" the drunken crowd roared again.

The Doctor hadn't played this song since he was with the Centipedes twenty-five years ago. The Doctor and Nathan played the opening licks in perfect harmony, just as recorded those twenty-five years earlier.

"YAAAAAAAAAHHHHHHHHH!!" the crowd shouted in a crazy, uncontrollable manner.

After "Life Makes Me Shiver," the Doctor pulled another hit out of his bag of tricks. "Und now here is another one of my favorites, 'The Nails in My Coffin.'"

"YAAAAHHHHHHHHHHH!!" The crowd could not settle down; it was just too much for them to hear all of the Doctor's greatest songs, one after the next. "Nails in My Coffin" had the greatest guitar solo ever conceived in rock music. They pushed up closer to the stage and wedged Agent Crow up against it where he would be blasted with the full 900-watt Galactic Amp onslaught. The crew calls this area the doom zone. It would not be uncommon for people in this first row to grab their chests thinking they were having a heart attack when, in reality, it was just their chests vibrating like a speaker cone.

"YAAAAAAHHHHHHHHHH!!!!!" they roared once more. Agent Crow could not move. One hand was on his face, and the other on his chest. His teeth rattled as if they were about to fall out, and his nose, he was afraid, would end up on his forehead. He could not think; all thoughts had been zapped out of his mind. For the remainder of the show, he stood motionless in the same pose.

A strange woman next to him, dressed like a witch from *The Wizard of Oz*, complete with ruby red slippers, was banging her head on the stage and dancing like a banshee set on fire. She kept staring at Nathan in hopes that he might give her some of his Austrian summer sausage. Nathan tried not to give her any glances so as not to encourage this.

During the next song, the strange woman walked up next to Neusy, standing off stage to the left, and yelled in his ear, "He is just great, isn't he?"

"Yeah, he is," replied Neusy.

"Do you work for him?" she inquired.

Neusy said, "Yeah!"

"It must be the greatest experience working with a man that brilliant and talented," the woman shouted once more. "I think you're cute!"

"That's great," Neusy said, uninterested; this woman did nothing for him and seemed very strange.

"Some men find that I come on too strong, but I don't think so; I just like to talk and get to know people and maybe get laid," she shouted, slobbering her beer drool in his right ear.

Neusy looked at this chick through the corner of his eye and thought, *Ugh, to sleep with her and wake up next to her in the morning would be a horrible nightmare.* She had Julie Haggerty black, straw hair, an anorexic-looking twig body, and next to her mouth that wouldn't stop talking were two unattractive moles. Neusy eyed Jeb with eyes that indicated he hoped she would go away soon and find someone else to talk to. Jeb saw this and walked over to merch. Eventually, Teddy Red appeared out of nowhere and, to Neusy's relief, she started following him around. With her not bothering him, Neusy could now refocus on the stage.

After the show, a line of a hundred people formed on the side of the bar near the pool tables to get an autograph and a few words in with the Doctor. *This is going to be a long night,* thought Jeb as he looked at all of the trolls, fairies, freaks, dopers, and drunks. Agent Crow was in the men's room staring into the mirror to make sure every part of his face was where it had been prior the show.

Hocker, Teddy Red, and Neusy started tearing down the stage. There wasn't much room to break the equipment down with all of the people in the way, so the guys had to set cases on top of cases, stack cabinets, and wait until there was an exit route back out to the van parked behind the building. The Hammond B3 was taking up too much room for the guys to work. Hocker said, "Let's put this fuckin' thing up on the drum hardware case for a while so we can make some space up here."

Neusy gave Hocker a hand and they lifted the musical boat anchor onto the drum hardware case. Over in the back by the pool tables, the Doctor stood with his back against the wall near the merch booth, sipping his red wine and talking with the next fan in line. "Did you like the show?" he asked the man.

"Yeah, it was great. I wish you came up here more often. Can you sign my *Slap the Virgin* album?" asked the man.

"Yah," said the Doctor.

The next person in line was a thin woman dressed in black, wearing ruby red slippers, and had black straw Julie Haggerty type hair. Oh no, could it be? Yes, it was Cathy Klackenzinger, the woman who slobbered in Neusy's ear. From a distance, Neusy looked in horror as she told the Doctor her whole life story. She took up the time of four fans as she blabbed away about her droll history. The Doctor appeared to be calm and understanding. She was getting closer to the Doctor, as if she wanted to kiss him, but the Doctor applied a tai chi push hands technique gently against her arms to keep her at a distance as she spoke.

Jeb made a motion toward the Doctor to remove her from his presence. The Doctor glared at Jeb with a look that told Jeb to back off; the Doctor could handle this. After Cathy Klackenzinger finally strolled away, the Doctor said, "Please excuse me, but I have to pee."

The Doctor left to reset his mind after the pounding that the last fan had exposed him to. The place was emptying and had about fifty people left speaking about the night's performance and praising the Doctor. The Doctor returned to continue talking to the last few fans left in the house.

Jeb spoke with Neusy. "God, that chick wouldn't stop."

"Yeah, I know, she was hitting on me up at the stage earlier, fuckin' annoying the shit out of me," said Neusy.

"I saw that. Later, over at merch, she tried to stick her tongue down my throat and brushed my dick through my Levi's with the backside of her hand," said Jeb in disgust. "She gave me her business card: Cathy Klackenzinger, artist."

They both looked at her card in Jeb's hand. "Lucky, you gonna call her later?" asked Neusy.

"Fuck no!" said Jeb as he threw her card under a bar stool.

Teddy, Hocker. Neusy, Marlon, and Jeb returned to the stage to finish up so they could get out of there and get some sleep. It was going to be another long drive in the morning. Teddy Red reached the stage first and noticed the Hammond B3 organ lying on its side, toppled off the drum hardware case. The Doctor was winding down. It was 2:00 a.m. with only a handful of people remaining.

"What the fuck, Teddy? What did you do to the organ?" screamed Hocker.

"I didn't do anything, don't blame me!" Teddy shouted back.

They inspected the Hammond organ to make sure nothing was broken, but something was definitely out of place. On the backside of the organ protruded a pair of ankles, with ruby red slippers. As the five of them lifted the organ, they discovered the lifeless body of Cathy Klackenzinger. The organ made the body look flattened, like when the Coyote got hit with a rock in a Roadrunner cartoon.

"I guess she couldn't take life anymore and she pulled the organ onto herself," said Neusy.

"How could she do that, she is lying face down?" said Jeb. The five scratched their heads and wondered what could have happened.

The agents were hanging around the signing unsuccessfully, attempting to score with some of the few women fans left. Their appearance always seemed to be identical: dark suits, dark sunglasses, hair perfect. Fans thought they were Blue Brothers impersonators and tried to take selfies with them, who tried to avoid this at all costs. The selfies always had the agents moving, or with a hand up over their faces, or turning away. The fans thought it was part of their routine, which caused more fans to take selfies with them until discovering the body. At this point, they walked up to the stage, not sure what they should do. Sparrow said, "No one touch anything," then called his supervisor, who called in the CSI team.

After three hours, they told the crew they could finish doing the load-out as the body was carried out of the venue.

Chapter 18

The caravan arrived at the club where they were headed in Tarzana, CA. Waiting for the release of the equipment the night before made it a long night. The agents, with a reserved hotel waiting for them, were in the rear of the caravan. It's not often that every car on the tour leaves together, but since they all slept in a little, it was so. The agents reserved a more modest motel room for their stay in Tarzana after being informed that their credit cards had a new daily limit not there in the past. They were now learning basic economics, with a budget to work within for each day.

They arrived in Tarzana a little later than they wanted. The crew loaded in quickly after Jeb had to deal with the house manager. "Thought you guys were arriving two hours ago. Your driver has been here for three."

"Driver?" Jeb said to the manager, and then saw him standing at the bar.

"Weeeeelllll, the Doctor and company!" said Cal Crabs.

"Craaaabsss!" said the Doctor. "My good friend."

"You boys sure took your time now, didn't ya?"

"Well, you know how these things go, Cal. You have been a good friend for a long time."

"Well, I am glad you guys made it. Hey, Jeb, what's up, my man?"

"The usual tour bullshit and some murders," said Jeb.

"MURDERS?" shouted Cal Crabs. "What the hell are you talking about?" After Jeb filled Cal in on the happenings, with Marlon always trying to add words out of context, Cal said,

"Damn, boys. That shit won't fly on the bus. I have my man going over the bus now. I parked it down in San Diego last month, and he should have the maintenance complete by tomorrow. So we will be ready to go." Jeb was pleased, and Cal added, "Boys, wait till you see my buddies; I got them on the bill when I heard you guys were playing here in Tarzana. Fucking awesome bunch of guys going to be opening the show tonight. You will be left speechless, I promise." With that, he disappeared, as he so often did. One minute they would be talking with Cal Crabs, and the next, he was gone. No one was sure where he goes anymore. When he was smoking weed, it could be explained, but ever since he "forgot" to stop at the Canadian border several years back, he quit smoking cold turkey, and now it's nine-hour energy drinks and coffee all the time.

The truth of what happened at the Canadian border was Cal fell asleep at the wheel about 1,000 feet from the border, slowing down but still going fifty miles an hour. He went right through the border patrol booths perfectly. Not a scratch on the bus or any damage to the booths. The border agent had to go through therapy for the next two years after seeing the bus coming at high speed right for him, and then past, leaving him unscathed.

This led to a chase about five miles into Canada. And while the authorities in several vehicles chased him, Cal hit a bump, which caused him to jolt forward and his foot to depress the accelerator. As his speed increased, the authorities thought they had a runaway border crasher and called for backup helicopters and additional autos. All at once, Cal was woken by Jeb tapping him on the shoulder, saying, "Crabs, shouldn't you have stopped back there at the border?" With that, the bus came to a screeching halt. Lucky for Cal Crabs, he always has a camera recording what goes on in the bus for insurance purposes. He spent a night in jail and was released the next day. A hefty fine, which he is still paying off to this day, was the verdict handed to him. One show on the tour was canceled, and no one ever spoke of this incident again.

It can be agreed in most circles that Led Zeppelin is by far one of the most beloved rock groups that ever was. Millions recognize the voice, the guitar, the drums, the bass, and the songs of Led Zeppelin. Even groups like Dread Zeppelin that made a parody of the great group's songs have found a place in many people's hearts. So, when the boys heard about a Zeppelin tribute band opening up for the Doctor, everyone was excited. Even if they were only so-so, at least people could get into it a little and rock out, right?

The crew—Jeb, Neusy, Hocker, Marlon, Bobby Santos, and Teddy Red—were hanging out in the club waiting to see this Led Zeppelin tribute band. The guys were fond of Led Zeppelin music and were anxious to hear some of their favorite tunes. Are they in for a BIG treat! Unfortunately, the crew would have to start setting up after the tribute band's show because the Club's management wouldn't allow them to set up equipment until after this act. Management said they could not be responsible for any damage to the Doctor's equipment. What the hell did that mean?

The stage was set up with the band's equipment, the drum set was even a clear Ludwig Vistalite set like John Bonham used. The Marshall amps were set up like Jimmy Page, and the Ampeg bass stack was on the other side. It looked like Led Zeppelin was going to play here. Their road crew set up an eight-foot-by-four-foot table in front of the drum riser. The crew looked at this with great interest. "Never seen that before," Neusy said as he motioned to the table. The crew agreed with shakes of their heads almost in sync.

Two guys dressed in tuxedos with tails set the table with candles and cups, but no silverware or napkins. Then the butlers brought out four giant baked turkeys, mashed potatoes, cornbread stuffing, cranberries, beets, pumpkin pies, cream pies, Krispy Kreme donuts, ten Subway sandwiches, six pizzas, buffalo wings, and the list goes on.

"That's something you don't usually see," said Bobby Santos.

"I have no idea," said Jeb.

"I'm getting hungry," said Hocker. He was thinking of jumping up on stage to lend a hand so that he could get a little snack off the table.

Drool was dripping out the side of Marlon's mouth. "Damn, boys, I got the munchies. Is that for us?"

Neusy returned from the bar with an ice-cold beer. "I love Zeppelin; I grew up with their music."

"Me too," said Bobby Santos.

"BOYS!!" shouted Cal as he walked over to the crew. "Get ready; these guys will blow your mind!"

The house lights went down; the stage was dark. The two butlers came back out on stage. Each struck a match and lit the two candles on the table. Then a voice spoke over the PA. "Alright, all of you Zeppelin fans, give it up for Led Dumplin." Then in complete blackness, the sound of the guitar shot through the air. It was "Whole Lotta Love." Bum-ba-ba-ba-bum-bum-ba-bum-bum-ba-bum. Yeah, the crowd went wild, it sounded just like Page. Soon the rest of the band came in together, just as they should; the whole audience bounced their heads with the beat.

"This is fuckin' cool," said Jeb.

"You bet your ass! Cowboy Crabs never lies," said Cal, and then screamed, "WHEEEEEW!!"

"Fuck yeah," said Hocker as he bopped his head in furor.

"When are they going to raise the lights?" asked Neusy.

"Yeah, let's get a look at these guys," said Hocker.

"I'm soooo…stoned!" said Teddy Red.

"Yeah, me too!" shouted Marlon as he and Teddy Red high fived.

"Come on, let's see the band!" shouted Hocker.

"Boys, get ready," said Cal. "It's coming."

The lights came on for a second and then went off. A fraction of a second, then the cycle again, then again, the lights went on and off so rapidly all the people could see were silhouettes and then nothing. Then with a loud BOOM, the lights on the stage came on with an explosion.

The singer had the blonde, curly, golden locks of Robert Plant, but he was 400 pounds. He even wore a pink, girly, ruffled blouse as Plant did, but his fat hairy stomach hung over his blue jeans down to the bottom of his zipper. He had three belts attached end to buckle to hold up his size 132" Levi's. His six chins were on display for all to see. The guitarist had black curly hair and wore a black suit embroidered with orange dragons. But he had a weight problem too. Not as bad as the singer, he only had four chins, and his pants hosted only two belts. He wasn't missing any licks on his Tobacco Sunburst Les Paul. The bass player looked like Augustus Gloop from *Willy Wonka*, but had John Paul Jones' weird English hairstyle. He had many stuffed heart ornaments hanging from his clothes, which looked like a custom white silk moo-moo, like a Polynesian woman might wear. The drummer had black hair and a black beard and was wearing no shirt; you could see all of his excess draping down around his drum stool. Except his drum stool was custom made with a sitting area of thirty-two inches across, set on a hydraulic system to support his 350 pounds. One of his floor toms had a hole in the head and was filled with donuts. While playing, he could reach through the hole and grab a donut to munch on. Then the singer started singing.

You need coolin', baby I've been droolin'
Way down inside, my tummy, you know I really need it
Gonna get me some lunch, gonna get me some lunch
OHH! Wanna Whole Lotta Lunch, A Whole Lotta Lunch

And with that, he pulled a leg off one of the roast turkeys and started munching on it! The song just went like that; it was about food. And during the drum solo part of "Whole Lotta Lunch," the guitarist grabbed a slice of pizza with one hand and waved his other hand in front of the antennae of the theremin to make that cosmic wave sound. Once the song ended, the audience, although mesmerized and confused, burst into applause; they had to because the songs were good, except for the singer singing with food in his mouth.

Then came another familiar tune from the *Presence* album. Na-na na-na na-naaaaah, Na-na na-na na-naaaaa.

"Yeah, I know this one," shouted Cal.

"I'm not sure we know this version?" asked Neusy.

Nobody's fat but mine, said it's nobody's fat but mine
Yeaheh, got to change my crazy life, nobody's fat but mine

The singer grabbed a handful of mashed potatoes and stuffing, no utensils, and crammed it in his mouth. Particles of food were flying out of his mouth all over the stage, and he was mumbling his words. After the song ended, the singer introduced the next song and spoke a bit. The drummer reached over the bass drum and grabbed a whole cream pie and down it went. The bass player reached out to grab a subway sandwich. Then the singer started.

Ahhhhhohhh, I can't quit eating, babe
So I guess I'll have to put it down for a while
I said I can't quit eating, babe
I guess I'll have to diet for a while

Every song was about food, and these guys couldn't stop eating. The more they ate, the better they played, and the bigger the mess all over the stage.

"What the fuck is this shit?" said Hocker.

"It's disgusting, isn't it?" said Santos.

"Yeah, but it's making me hungry," said Marlon.

"But the crazy thing is, it sounds like Zeppelin," said Neusy.

Hocker turned to Jeb, "I'm not cleaning that shit up!"

Teddy Red, with excitement, said, "Do you think they will leave some of that food for us?"

Hocker said, "I don't know about you, but I am not waiting." He spotted a whole slice of pizza on the stage floor near his side. He looked from side to side, then darted for it and stuffed it in his mouth. "Wow, Numero Uno, my favorite!"

"Why don't you help them tear down later?" said Neusy.

"Yeah…will have all types of leftovers," said Cal.

The agents walked in and up to the stage where the crew was. They were arguing, and Jeb noticed a lot of hand gestures. He could not hear what they were saying.

"Interesting band, I love Zeppelin," said Sparrow. "Is this normal to run into bands like this on tour?"

"Hardly," responded Jeb.

"Anything happen? We would have been here sooner if Crow booked the correct hotel."

"Nothing…unusual," replied Jeb. As he turned around, out of the corner of his eye, he thought he saw Scaggz in the back of the club. He turned to get a better look but could not see the person he thought he saw.

Led Dumplin played hit after hit but substituted their own words. "In My Time of Dieting," "When the Levi's Break," "The Lemon Pie Song," "Ram it Down," "Glazed and Infused," "Achilles Last Meal," "Hot Dogs," "Jelly Roll," "Houses of the Wholesome," and "Good Times, Fat Times," just to name a few. Then came the haunting theme, the song every wanna-be guitar player ever learns, ringing out into the crowd. The singer grabbed a Subway sandwich, crammed it down his throat, then poured down a beer. He helped himself to some pumpkin pie, without knife or fork, just with his hands eating right out of the pie tin. He picked up the pie and ate it during the guitar intro and, within seconds, was ready to sing. With orange pumpkin stains around his mouth and crumbs falling out onto the stage, he began to croon.

There's a fat pig that's sure, all that glistens is food
And he's climbing a stairway to 7-Eleven
When he gets there he knows all the prices are low
So he grabs all he can get for thirty dollars
Ohhoohh, and he's buying at 7-Eleven

Standing there watching this was getting too much for the crew. Other than Hocker, who would grab scraps off the floor, the guys were getting disgusted. The only reason the audience didn't walk out is that they really did sound like Zeppelin. Some people laughed, some cried, some screamed, and some vomited, but most people liked the music and its comedy. Just when it was almost over, the Doctor joined the boys standing in the crowd to see what was going on. "What is this? Who are these guys?"

"Led Dumplin. They are a Zeppelin tribute band," said Cal. "High school buddies of mine."

"Are they any good?"

"Yeah, they are good at the music part, but…" said Neusy.

"What is this mess all over the stage?"

"Oh, that's the funny part—they eat while they play," said Cal.

"Ach! That is disgusting! Und look at their disgusting fat bodies, my word! They better sweep und mop up there before we go on, Neusy. It is like a swine pen up there!"

The Doctor was right; the stage was covered with crumbs, particles, stains, beer spills, empty pie tins, and turkey bones. Hocker eagerly waited for the band to stop playing, hoping that there would be morsels of food left for him. The singer approached the mic for the last number, donut in hand. The drums, bass, and guitar started on a hit off of *Zeppelin IV*, the song that John Bonham used four drumsticks to play the piece. But this drummer was using real drumsticks—four turkey legs—to play the song. This group was just crazy! The guitarist and the singer were jumping up and down on the stage. The floorboards were flexing and bending with their jumping. Food on the stage floor was shooting all over as they jumped. The guitarist's effects pedals also jumped up and down off the stage as it flexed. The drum set even bounced up and down to the groove. Food particles and crumbs were bouncing, and something hit the Doctor right in his mouth. He stared at the scene in front of him.

"Ach, that is a piece of dead animal! Nauseating!" he said and ran off to rinse his mouth out.

As the drummer played the song, he would take a bite of one of the four drumsticks, and at the end of the song, there were just four bones left in his greasy hands. At the end of the fury, the singer ripped a hole in the back of his 132" jeans as he said thank you and took a bow. He walked off the stage backward as the stage lights went down and the house lights came up. They had to wait until the mess on stage was cleaned before they could hit the stage. The Doctor came back and said, "Yah, that is no good. I will not play on that stage tonight. I will play an acoustic set on the floor in front of the stage."

Jeb thought this was a good move, and it would get them out early tonight. There was no load-out to mention, other than the acoustic guitar and the merch, which Sadie Santos had under control. She would be missed after the next show when she and Bobby would return home. Jeb instructed the crew to load all the equipment back out into the van, and they did. They walked back in, talking about how they saw a man with a keg scale a wall, running full speed.

Scaggz, hiding now in the beer cooler with the kegs of beer, was happy it was intermission. That was close; that disgusting band caught him off guard. This slight pause as he looked at the stage was enough for him to get noticed. He wasn't sure if anyone saw him, but his instincts kicked in and he immediately dropped to the floor in such a sudden move that no one saw him drop. Same as no one saw or felt him as he slithered like a snake to the beer cooler. He opened the door and quickly jumped inside, where he waited for his moment.

Now that it was intermission, he needed to get out of there. He would head to San Diego, abort today. *Why does the Doctor have the Blues Brothers hanging around with him these days*, he wondered as he grabbed an empty keg of beer and put it up on his shoulder to hide his face. He made a swift move towards the rear doors. Crow noticed this and said to Sparrow, "Wow, these metal guys sure drink a lot of beer. There goes another keg."

Sparrow saw this as well and noted, "Yeah, that guy sure moves fast carrying that thing. Technically we are not working, right? We are here to observe the show; I don't see why we can't grab a beer. I'll ask him when he comes back in with the new keg if he could hook us up with a deal." Sparrow waited twenty minutes by the back door for the man changing the keg to come back in. The man never did.

Chapter 19

Another great show was over, and it was exactly 1:00 a.m. The Doctor finished the meet and greet, and it was time to get out of the venue and go back to Howard Johnson's Motor Lodge to collect his suitcases from his room and hit the road for San Diego. Neusy was again the chauffeur for the Doctor. They loaded the Universe Guitars into the rear of the X5 once again and pulled out onto Sepulveda Blvd toward Howard Johnson's.

"That was a great show! I was inspired by the acoustic. I will do more of this," said the Doctor.

They arrived at Howard Johnson's, parked the car, and entered the lobby. The Doctor's room was on the right-hand side down the corridor. The Doctor swiped his room's electronic keycard on the sensor repeatedly, but the room would not open. The Doctor started getting impatient. "What is going on here?" he squawked. The two of them proceeded to the front desk in the lobby. They spoke with the night manager.

"Why doesn't my room key work?"

The manager replied, "I'm not sure, show me your ID and I can make you a new room key."

The Doctor looked for his passport and could not find it. He checked his pockets, his fanny pack: nothing. He checked the pockets of his pants, shirt, and hoodie: again, nothing. "Yah, it must be in my room; I am Jurgen Weislangwolf, please check the computer, this is me." He handed the manager one of the CDs that he had in the fanny pack.

"Sorry, there is no Jurgen Weislangwolf registered here."

"What do you mean? I checked in at 3:00. I have already slept in the room!" the Doctor snapped angrily at the manager.

"Sorry, you are not in the computer," said the night manager.

"This is just ridiculous! Is the room booked under Jeb Acorns?" asked the Doctor.

"No." Neusy and the Doctor looked at each other, wondering what was going on as they leaned on the front desk.

"Is it under Theodore Redwood?" asked Neusy.

"Yes, there is a Theodore Redwood." That was the answer to the riddle.

"OK, now can I get into my room? We have to leave for San Diego, right now!" said the Doctor to the manager.

"Sorry, I will have to see an ID for Theodore Redwood!"

"You've fuckin' got to be kidding us, right?" Neusy asked the manager.

"Redwood already checked out hours ago; there is no Theodore Redwood here."

"Look, I will make it simple for you, take us to my room; I will describe the room to you before you open the door, yah?" said the Doctor. The manager, the Doctor, and Neusy returned to the room and stood outside the door.

The Doctor said, "On the left side of the room, I have two suitcases; one of them is open. I have some red shirts und some turquoise jewelry in this suitcase. On the right side of the room, there is a table lamp with the lampshade removed from the TV interview that I did earlier." The manager opened the door, and sure enough, the room was exactly how the Doctor described before the manager opened the door.

"The people in this country are so stupid!" said the Doctor.

"Thanks a lot," said Neusy. The manager left, and the two started collecting the Doctor's things before they had to meet Jeb in the lobby and leave on their long night-time journey to San Diego. Jeb had the night off driving the van; Marlon, who was waiting for the luggage in the hotel parking lot, would be at the wheel. He was going to follow Teddy Red, which Jeb thought would be OK, and the two could keep each other in line, maybe smoke a lot of weed, but he had faith in them. Torsten the Viking was riding along with Teddy Red, Triple T drove himself, and Heinz and Nathan were stoked to ride with Cal in the big rig. The agents decided to spend the night in Tarzana.

"I just love to drive cars!" said the Doctor as he hot footed it out of the parking lot of the hotel towards the southbound interstate to San Diego as Neusy and Jeb were hanging on tight. The Doctor had to keep asking Neusy for directions because there was no GPS.

"What is the speed limit here in California?"

"It's sixty-five mph."

"Ach, that is too slow. I will drive ninety."

"OK, watch your mirrors for the CHP, and if you get a ticket, you're paying for it yourself. How about some music?" asked Neusy.

"Alright, how about some classical music?"

Neusy found a classical music station for the Doctor, and they were playing some Mozart. "Ahhh, Mozart's *Symphony No. 40*, one of my favorites!" said the Doctor as Jeb in the back thought how nice it is that he does not have to drive right before he fell asleep.

"Do we have any Red Bulls?"

Neusy looked over into the back seat where there was a red-and-white ice chest, and he opened it. He saw three Red Bulls and two bottles of red wine that were not in there earlier. The Doctor must have taken these from the venue. He grabbed a Red Bull, popped the tab, and handed it to him.

Twenty minutes later, the Doctor announced, "I have to pee!" as he made an abrupt turn onto the off-ramp from the far left lane. Jeb was jolted awake.

"What the hell?" shouted Jeb, then saw who was driving and said, "Oh…"

The Doctor chose a lonely exit that the road ran parallel along the coast. After they drove down the deserted road, they stopped the car and both got out to urinate. Jeb, feeling drowsy, also got out.

"Aaahh, this feels great, hum?" said Neusy.

"Yaaahhh, there is nothing more pleasing than a nice piss," answered the Doctor.

Jeb walked away from the two and found his spot behind a tree out of sight. He finished and could still hear the Doctor's voice. *No getting away from him. What is he rambling on about now? I should have stayed with the van away from this circus.* He took his time, stared at the stars for a minute, and slowly walked back to the car where the Doctor was in the back seat with a bottle of wine in his hand.

The Doctor took one last sip of the bottle and threw the bottle out the open door. "Yah, that is very good wine. I sit back here; Jeb, you can sit up there with Neusy. I am too tired to drive."

Jeb picked up the bottle and handed it to Neusy and asked why the Doctor was drinking. Neusy's return look indicated he could not do anything to stop what just happened.

Neusy was the driver now, and they sat in the car a moment so that Neusy, who was also very tired, could drink a couple of the energy drinks. He then headed south down the dark, deserted road in hopes of finding a freeway on-ramp as they heard the Doctor open the second bottle of wine.

From the back seat, "Are you sure you shouldn't have made a U-turn to get back on the ramp?"

"I'm not sure, but there might be another on-ramp down here by the nuclear facility," said Neusy.

"GPS, always bring GPS…yah, yah!!" After realizing his mistake, Neusy made a U-turn and headed back north to the original off-ramp. They re-entered the Interstate 5 South toward San Diego. "Yah, you see what just happened? You know that I am always right," said the Doctor.

Jeb was starting to get to that point that the Doctor pushes him every once and a while as they approached the bend near San Juan Capistrano. Jurgen saw a venue that he played at once. "Achhh, I remember that place!" said the Doctor. "Yah, I was a guest of the guitarist, Steve Remorse. Do you remember this, Jeb?"

"Yeah, he's phenomenal," said Jeb, starting to get annoyed at the Doctor, who, when he drank, got very chatty and eventually would start picking at people's attributes. Jeb found this tedious and embarrassing.

"Well, when I arrived at Steve Remorse's concert, I didn't have my passport, und they wouldn't let me in."

"Shit, what did you do?" inquired Neusy, who was curious.

"Well, I had some of my CDs in my fanny pack, und I showed one to the doorman. I said, 'see, this is my picture.' Still, he wouldn't let me in."

"Then what happened?" said Neusy, who was starting to see a pattern with the CDs and wondered if the Doctor kept the CDs in his fanny pack only as identification.

"Well, I was really fuming, und I said, 'look you, Steve Remorse is my good friend, you send someone inside und tell him that I am outside.' Finally, the manager told the stupid doorman man to let me in. He was a Dummkopf!"

"Yeah, sounds like that for sure!" agreed Neusy.

As the Doctor reclined in the back bench seat, he lifted the wine bottle to his mouth and took a gulp. "This is some goooood wine!" he said, slobbering, as he now spoke a slurred speech that was more like he was singing a song.

Jeb, now officially pissed, replied, "Look at the great maestro, a fucking drunk!"

"Yah, yooou don't know meeee that well, Jeb… Don't fuuuck with meee."

"Don't know you that well? How long have we been working together? I'm always making you money that you just fuck off with. I know you all too well, look at you, you're a fucking mess; you need to get a handle on yourself!" Jeb retorted.

The Doctor took another long sip from the bottle. As they drove past the San Onofre giant nuclear reactors, which resembled two gigantic concrete breasts with red lights on top for nipples, Neusy said, "You know we used to go surfing down here when we were young, and we always thought those things were giant tits."

"Yaaaaah, that isss how you Amerikanerrrs think; yooou have a warped sense of humorrr," replied the Doctor. "Weee Austrians are much morrre refined."

Neusy and Jeb started to laugh at the Doctor's comment. "Oh, God, you are funny!" said Neusy.

"Stooooopp caaalling meeee thaaaaat!" said the drunken Doctor as Neusy kept chuckling.

"No, he is drunk!" added Jeb.

"Ach duuuuu lieeeeeber, I'm soooo fiiiiiine, I'm iiiiin complete contrrrooool!" replied the Doctor in a calm voice.

"You are not fine nor in control! Look at yourself, drinking out of a wine bottle like a skid row bum!" Jeb yelled as he became more infuriated. "I am supposed to be your manager, and you right now are unmanageable!" snapped Jeb. "What if…important people saw you like this?" asked Jeb.

"Aaaach, leeeeave meeee alone, I want to sleeeeep now." The Doctor then drained the second bottle.

The whole time this was going on, Neusy was driving the SUV along the highway. He was trying not to burst into laughter. Although it was a desperate scene, he found humor in it. He saw something that no fan, nor anyone outside the inner circle, would ever see: a drunken Jurgen. A very talented expert, a world-renowned musician who had an internal conflict within his soul. A man involved in a love-hexagon with six women around the globe and paid all of their living expenses.

This was one reason he had no money all the time, or six of the reasons, to be more precise. How none of the six women knew of each other bewildered Jeb. Sure, the ones in different countries were easy, as the Doctor would be traveling so often, adding days to his schedules and spending time with these women could be managed if one's heart was in it. Having two women in his hometown in Austria took some precise maneuvering, especially when one is his long-time girlfriend, with whom he's had eleven children: ten girls and one boy, who now, at the age of twenty, wished he was born a girl. Jeb had tried to help the Doctor manage his expenses on the side; however, it was a fool's errand.

They approached a rest stop. "Hey, Jeb, I'm going to stop; I need to take a piss, you know those energy drinks."

The Doctor, in his drunken stupor, mumbled, "Ahh, pee-pee, Hahaha."

Jeb said, "Go back to sleep, drunk!" Jeb and Neusy scuttled out of the car and headed to the men's room. Aaahh, what a relief, the simple pleasure a man enjoys. Neusy spotted the snack machine on the way out. "Hey, Jeb, do you want some chips or some chocolate?" asked Neusy.

At the exact moment, the Doctor, with his supersonic hearing, yelled out of the window, "You know…I woould like some chocolatesssss!"

Jeb, who was still aggravated with him, said, "Sorry, they don't have any liquor-filled chocolates!"

They were getting closer to San Diego. Neusy needed to get the Doctor to his hotel room to sleep off the drunk. Then Neusy and Jeb could relax and unwind. The tour bus would arrive in the morning at the hotel.

"Where is the hotel? Where are we supposed to go?" asked Neusy.

"Did you see Sea World Drive yet?" said Jeb, who was getting sleepy.

"The sign says two miles ahead."

"OK, get off there and make a left under the freeway, go about three miles east, when you get to Pancho Villa Drive, make a right and go two more miles. When you get to Town Center Blvd, make a left. The hotel is called the Juan Ramirez Inn, and the address is 12355 Town Center Drive. Here is the confirmation." Jeb put the confirmation on the dashboard, then said in a mocking tone, thinking the Doctor was asleep, "Now I must get some sleep," to which Neusy laughed.

From the back seat, "Yah, everyone tries to do my voice, none of youuu can get iiittt correeect."

"We probably won't arrive until another twenty minutes," said Neusy, once again trying to control his laughter. Twenty minutes later, they arrived at the hotel. Jeb checked them in, and then he and Neusy steadied the Doctor up to his room. Jeb led him to his bed, pulled the covers down, and covered him up once the Doctor had lain down.

"See, you can never be mad at him for long," said Neusy in the hall after Jeb closed the room door.

"No, I guess you are right. We are too good of friends for me to stay mad at him. I just wish he would be more responsible. He is his own enemy."

"Well, Jeb," said Neusy, "we made it through another day. Tomorrow, once we get the bus loaded, your life will become easier. Let's get to our room and see what's in the mini-bar." The two walked to their rooms, feeling a sensation of accomplishment by completing the tour's driving portion.

Chapter 20

Jeb and Cal Crabs were finishing up breakfast together, discussing the remainder of the tour. The bus driver and the tour manager must be in sync. These are the two that will keep the tour running and moving forward. They have to know every detail together, and when all hell is breaking loose, the tour proceeds as planned because of these two. Jeb had instructed the crew to go to the club, load everything into the venue, and return the van.

After the show, everything would be loaded into the trailer that the bus would be towing. Not very large, just twelve feet long. But large enough to accommodate the equipment and the merch. Then on to San Francisco and north up to Canada. After this show, Teddy Red, Bobby, and Sadie all leave the tour. There would be fewer hands to help out. Jeb and Marlon would also have to work the merch table in addition to the rest of their duties.

However, being on the bus would make it easier for Jeb as they would all be in one location together. Neusy would make one more drive back to San Francisco, where he would leave his car with a friend till the end of the tour. Tomorrow would be the last night that they would all sleep in hotel rooms. They would be sleeping on the bus and saving money with only a couple of hotel rooms a day to shower in and for Cal Crabs to sleep when not driving. Cal insisted on the hotel to rest and get the sleep needed as he had the responsibility to bring everyone home safe.

The next day was San Francisco, and Cal wanted to give everyone a little extra rest before the two-day drive up to Portland. He informed Jeb, "635 miles. In a car, perhaps possible in one day, but in a tour bus, it is not happening. The bus cannot drive like a car; we need to stop several times. Plus, I am not supposed to be behind the wheel for more than ten hours. This is something that will be checked. So, we have to be careful." Jeb had no choice but to agree with Cal. After breakfast, the two had Neusy drive them to pick up the bus from where Cal had it parked and maintenance had been performed.

Some people think traveling on a tour bus might be glamorous and exciting. But from the perspective of those who travel on one, there is a different point of view. Living in such tight quarters for long periods requires rules. Jeb posts these rules on every tour right on day one. The band and crew have fun changing the rules on the posted sheets as a joke, but everyone has to obey, or Jeb comes down hard. While Cal drove the bus back to the venue, Jeb completed the list to hang in the lounge of the bus:

1 - Clean up after yourself; your mother is not on the bus to clean up after you.

2 - Be quiet in the sleeping quarters regardless of the time of the day. Anyone not obeying will have their bunk moved under the bus.

3 - Do not eat other people's food in the fridge, especially mine. There will be bait food in the fridge with surprises in them; trust me, you do not want to eat what I put in these items.

4 - Do not distract the driver while driving, and *NO*, he will not open the window for you to smoke *ANYTHING*!

5 - The front table is called the tour manager's station for a reason. If you are not the tour manager, then get up when the tour manager enters the lounge. He has a lot of work to do!

6 - Do not go into the Doctor's rear suite unless he permits you. Universe Guitars bite!

7 - *MOST IMPORTANT* - No shitting on the bus. Hold it…we will eventually stop. Make the most of these stops!

Jeb printed four copies with his mobile printer. He hung one up front by the bus's door, one in the front of the lounge, and another in the kitchenette. The final one he hung in the bathroom at eye level while using the toilet.

Marlon Jiggs approached the ominous silver tour bus and stared at the shiny metal door. What would he see once it opened? He had no idea whatsoever. He had ridden on a city bus a few times and knew what those were like. People crowded into the seats, and if there were no seats, then you grabbed onto a hand strap or a pole and stood on your journey. Marlon was reasonably sure there were no poles or hand straps inside the tour bus. If there were, he must make sure to get a seat. Standing would suck on long rides. As he examined the door, he wondered where on the bus he could smoke weed. He approached the door and noticed the keypad and handle. He remembered that Jeb had given him a code to open the door, 567477.

Marlon's task was to fetch Jeb's laptop that he had left in the dining area of the tour bus. He entered the code and grabbed the handle to pull the door open. As he entered the bus and began to take his first step, he was startled by the large figure reclined in the chair behind the steering wheel.

There sat the same 6'5" man that was driving the semi-truck to the last gig. He was reading a newspaper and listening to rock music on the bus's stereo. Marlon perused his thin muscular body, long stringy brown hair, bulbous eyes, hemp-woven cowboy hat, and blue denim sleeveless shirt. He had on Levi button-ups and beautiful tan-and-black rattlesnake skin boots.

Cal turned his head to Marlon and, in a deep gravelly voice, said, "Who are you? What do you want?"

Marlon stuttered, "I-I'm Jiggs; I'm supposed to fetch Jeb's laptop."

"Well, go look for it then; what the hell are you staring at?" said Cal Crabs. Marlon was terrified by the man and inched by him slowly. Cal smelled the weed on Marlon right away as he passed by.

Marlon noticed that the man wasn't seated in a regular bus driver's seat. It was a 1920s barber's chair from an old barber's shop in Brooklyn, New York. Marlon thought that was pretty cool. As Marlon entered the bus, he noticed the lounge where all of the band members would be at different times of the day. There was a giant TV screen on the wall to watch movies or play video games. What looked like comfortable seats lined both sides, with a small table up front and a seat on either side of this table.

In the rear of the lounge, there was a small kitchen area for cooking simple meals. Just a microwave, sink, and fridge, with a small counter connecting them all and a trash bin built into the counter; lots of drawers everywhere. Across from the kitchenette was another small table with a bench.

Behind that, he saw the corridor that led back to the Doctor's suite. He saw sleeping bays cut into the walls, where all of the band and crew would sleep on both sides: twelve bunks, three high with two bays on each side of the corridor. In front of the bunk area was the toilet. As his eyes continued to scan the room, he saw Jeb's laptop sitting on the bench seat next to the dining table. He grabbed it and turned back toward the front of the bus to exit. He caught sight of one of Jeb's lists and read it, thinking it was a joke. *That Jeb is a funny guy, jokes on day one!*

He again carefully inched by the driver to go outside. The bus driver said, "Close the door next time! Don't ever leave it open like that again, son. Don't let any flies in here!"

Marlon said, "Yes, sir!" as he exited.

"Jiggs," Cal said before Marlon closed the door. "Do you know what flies are?"

"Of course!"

"We call the fans that try and get on the bus, flies… Got it?" informed Cal.

"Yes," said Marlon. "Cool… I got it, close the door." Marlon walked away thinking, *this is great! Learning all sorts of new things, seems like they all have a sense of humor.* He hurried back to the venue, all proud of himself, just having been on the bus.

As he entered the club, Jeb said, "What took you so long?"

Jiggs said, "That tall, scary man sitting in a barber's chair inside."

Jeb said, "Oh, that's just Cowboy Cal Crabs, pay no mind to him. Didn't you see him at the last show? He has been the Doctor's good friend and driver for years."

"I was so stoned yesterday… That crazy band with the food… I saw someone tall but didn't pay attention."

Chapter 21

The agents had a plan and executed it perfectly. They woke up early, then exited their hotel to travel down to San Diego. They were adjusting to the rock tour life and wanted to make the most of each day. They knew that other agents might handle this gig differently and watch the band every second, never leaving the band's sight. However, they figured that their day didn't need to start any earlier than load-in at the venue, or possibly even later. There had been no murders early on in the day, except in Arizona, but that was during a seminar and kind of like a concert.

They woke up at 4:30 a.m to be out of their hotel by 5:00 and drove to San Diego before too much traffic was on the road. They did not figure on one thing, and the reason the band and crew left last night after the show: driving through Los Angeles was not like any other city. Unless it was the middle of the night, and even then, a lot of the time, there was always traffic in Los Angeles. So, when the agents arrived at Mission Beach, it was already after 11:00; they were both exhausted with only three and a half hours of sleep and the long drive.

"Now, this is why we made the drive early," said Sparrow as they were parking the car at the beach.

"Yes, a few hours here to unwind, then we will meet up with the tour after lunch. What is the name of the club?"

"Block by Block," answered Sparrow.

"Strange name, wonder why they call it that?"

"Well, we will find out soon enough, I am sure. Grab that cooler, and let's go get some sun."

And so, they did—two and a half hours on the beach. After spreading the bedsheets they had stolen from the hotel, the two men laid down. Both laid face down, and neither one had thought about bringing sunblock. They got woken up by the park ranger, who informed them that they should seek medical attention as their backs radiated heat that he could feel from three feet away. The agents packed up their sheets, walked painfully back to the car, and drove to their hotel to shower and get ready for work.

The Doctor's band had played the Block by Block club a year before and had pulled in a decent crowd. Jeb remembered that the club manager was somewhat of an asshole. He bounced a check to the group, and it took a lot of time and effort to get paid after the fact. The club manager, an Englishman named Dick Noggin, was a short, bald, stocky man with a quick temper who had a habit of changing contracts, saying one thing, and implying another. His reputation was notorious in the tour industry.

The contract agreed upon by Block by Block contained the pay for the show, along with other agreements for the evening, such as hotels, crew, dinner for the band, or a per diem. Dick Noggin negotiated the booking in good faith and signed a fair contract.

Dick Noggin believed he could still negotiate and change the deal on show night. With all of Jeb's touring, Dick Noggin was the only one who practiced this method.

Jeb had called Noggin weeks before to make sure they agreed to the amount on the contract and to ensure an all-cash transaction. Noggin had agreed; however, tonight, Noggin greeted Jeb with, "Hey, Jeb, we need to talk."

Jeb could feel his pulse rising. "Dick, what is it?"

"Pre-sale tickets are low; I am going to lose my ass. We have to renegotiate the guarantee."

"Dick, we have a contract, and if we don't get paid what's in the contract, we are leaving."

"Awe, come on Jeb, we both know that the contract doesn't mean shit and it's just a place for us to start negotiations. I have to shave one thousand dollars off the guarantee."

"WHAT?" screamed Jeb. "A contract is a contract, and if you do not honor it, I am leaving!" Jeb turned to Neusy and Hocker as they were rolling in equipment and said, "Guys, roll it back onto the bus, just pull the van next to the trailer, put it all in the trailer, no show tonight." Then to Noggin, "Fuck you, I am out of here!"

"Fuck me? Noooooo, fuck you, goodbye!" said Noggin as Jeb walked out to the bus.

Jeb opened the door to the bus. Cal, sitting on his throne, said, "Bro, a little trouble, I see… Hehe, usual bullshit, huh?"

"Yup, that asshole Dick Noggin, when he knocks, don't open the door. I will walk out and talk with him. Keep him waiting a minute. Every fucking time with this guy!"

As Jeb predicted, Dick Noggin knocked on the door, and Cal looked down at him, not saying a word. Noggin waited a minute and knocked much harder. Jeb said to Cal, "Just another minute or so should do it."

Noggin looked at Cal through the bus door. Even though Cal could see him, the driver just stared at him. Noggin knocked with both fists. Jeb walked up and then walked out.

"Jeb, look, let us come to an understanding. I am losing my ass tonight. I like you guys, and we have known each other for years."

"I'll knock $500 off the deal, and that's it," Jeb said. He had expected not to get the total amount, but by canceling the show, they would lose more money, plus there were the added expenses of bus, food, and hotel. Jeb had already inputted the guarantee for this show minus the $500 in his budget, but had to play it out. He became pissed off at going through this every tour with Noggin.

"Does this fuckin' douche nozzle ever stick to an agreement? Now he wants part of the merch money?" Jeb asked Hocker.

"You know this asshole, Jeb, he never sticks to nothing, that cocksucker!" replied Hocker. He spit a slimy, red wad of chew on the ground.

"Sadie will have to hide half the sales so he does not know what we sell; tell the boys to load on in."

Hocker, Neusy, and Marlon started to set up the stage. Teddy Red had driven the Doctor to the beach in the morning, and they were just getting to the venue. Teddy Red felt pretty good about himself and was happy that this would be his last day on tour. He would not have to put up with Hocker's harsh attitude anymore.

"Fuckin' Teddy, put this bass pedal…thrown in this drum case this way. I told him at least ten times about this!" said Hocker out loud to anyone listening. "Where is that fucker?" Then, as he spotted Teddy Red walking in, "You're a fuckin' nimrod!" Hocker yelled. "It's because you're stoned on weed all the time, isn't it?" Hocker shouted again. Marlon heard weed and looked up, but then saw Hocker yelling at Teddy and pretended not to listen.

"Yeah, I know it's always my fucking fault; I always fuck up everything!" Teddy cried out in sorrow and then smiled, knowing he would not have to put up with Hocker's bullshit after tonight.

Jeb attended to the guitar effects and stompboxes. He couldn't take chances with Teddy Red hooking things up wrong or blowing up transformers. Neusy hooked up all of the guitar and bass amps to their respective cabinets.

Neusy and Jeb sat outside in a quiet patio area of Jake's BBQ Restaurant just behind the Block by Block club. While the guys were setting up, the smoky aroma of BBQ ribs from Jake's permeated the air; it smelled so good they just had to try it. Another great thing about Jake's was that they had Jonas Schultz beer on tap, one of Jeb's favorite brands. The two decided on the BBQ beef sandwiches on big, white, sourdough rolls, with sides of homemade coleslaw sprinkled with slivered almonds. As the two awaited their food, they enjoyed their beers and talked about their adventures on this trip.

"Wow, this one has been one hell of a time on the road, hasn't it, Neusy?" asked Jeb.

"Yeah, you can say that again. Man, am I beat. I'm glad this is the last show before the bus, this driving sucks. I know it saves the Doctor money…but damn it is tiring." Neusy sighed. After a short time, their BBQ beef sandwiches were delivered to their outside patio table. "Mmm! It smells good!" said Neusy, his mouth watering. They both sunk their teeth into the tender, finely smoked beef sandwiches on the white sourdough rolls.

The Doctor strolled out through a small iron gate between the club and the patio and sat down next to Neusy and Jeb. "Ach! I see that you both are poisoning yourselves with that poor animal flesh und that bread!" exclaimed the Doctor.

"Yeah, but the poison tastes sooooo good! Do you want to try?" said Jeb.

"Yah, you are not so funny. I am getting hungry, though… I wonder if they have anything that I could eat here?" asked the Doctor.

"They probably have nice salads here," said Neusy. He asked the waiter to bring the menu back to the table. The Doctor looked it over and decided on a Greek salad, and then he saw they had onion rings.

"Aaahh, I love these onion rings, especially homemade ones!" he said. They sipped the remainder of their beers. The Doctor didn't like his crew to be drunk before the show. Neusy signaled the waiter, and he walked over.

"Onion rings and a Greek salad, please, and another pitcher. The Old Town Hobo Red was good, but I think we will switch it up and have another Jonas Schultz beer pitcher. How about the Smoking Seagull IPA?" Jeb nodded, and the waiter went off.

The Doctor said, "So you boys are having a good time, no? I hope you do not get plastered before the show, yah."

Jeb said, "We'll be fine."

Almost as if called by Neusy's beer selection, pigeons were scooting around their table, looking for morsels to eat. The Doctor said, "Neusy, why don't you break off some of your bread and give it to the birds?"

"So you want me to poison the birds, hum?" Jeb looked up at Neusy and smiled. The Doctor also smiled; Neusy raised his left eyebrow.

Teddy Red walked up to Jeb. "OK, what is it?" and the two went to another table to converse.

"My house is flooded, and I need to get home to check on it."

"Why don't you have your wife check on it? She is working, right, but she is only twenty minutes from home and not five hours like you."

"Yeah…you're right," said a dejected Teddy Red as he walked away from the table.

Jeb resumed drinking his beer with the boys and finished off some of the best BBQ he had ever tasted. He thought about the conversation with Teddy Red and pawned it off as typical Teddy Red. Another beer, last show, things were looking up. Teddy Red walked past the patio on his cell phone. He started pacing and screaming so all could hear him. "Fuck… Fuck… Shit!"

Everyone at the table turned and laughed. Teddy Red then appeared at the table again. "Dude!" he said to Jeb, and this time everyone was listening. "I have to go home; the police just called and said my alarm went off. I think someone burglarized my house."

Jeb looked at Neusy. He raised his eyebrows, Neusy shrugged his shoulders. Jeb said, "Have the cops check your house and call you back. It is going to take you five hours just to get there." Neusy nodded in agreement.

Teddy Red walked away and mumbled, "OK!"

"What's up with that?" asked Neusy.

"He is trying to pull some shit. He wants to go home and is thinking of all sorts of excuses, is what I think. What the fuck? Tonight is his last night. Why leave before the show?"

"Seems kind of weird to want to drive all that way at this time, but what the fuck! It's Teddy Red."

Neusy went out to his car to find his cell phone. Jeb went back into the club to do a final check on everything before soundcheck. There was a small line waiting for the doors to open. Jeb was pleased that people were already lining up, as the doors were still an hour and a half from opening.

Scaggz was watching this all unfold from his secure place on the roof of the club. No one noticed him as he watched. Jeb was close to him when he walked into the club, just under the roof where Scaggz was hiding. Jeb disappeared inside and then returned to the patio.

Teddy Red was all serious when he caught up to Jeb as he walked out of the club. "Jeb, dude… I am sorry… I have to leave… Something is going on at home…with my wife… We are having trouble… I have to check on something…sorry!"

"OK, go then. What is happening with her?"

"I don't know. Bro…I have to check on her. I want us to be friends still… I don't want this to mess up our friendship, OK Jeb?"

"OK, no problem, just go!" said Jeb as he thought, *this guy is nuts. Friends, we are not.*

Teddy Red came out to the parking lot and stood next to Neusy. As he was finishing up his phone call, he sat on the tailgate of the X5. Teddy Red started whining, "I have had enough of this shit... Jeb and Hocker are taking advantage of me... Do you think they are taking advantage of you?"

Neusy responded, "Maybe so, but I agreed to this job; I am in till the end."

Teddy Red then remarked, "I'm going home. That's it, I'm through... I'll see you later." He started up his Caravan and pulled out of the parking lot.

Scaggz saw it all and was now making his way into the club. *Perfect*, he thought, *nobody inside but a few bartenders, and they are too busy to watch me.*

Chapter 22

The band entered the club from the bus and began soundcheck, except for the Doctor, of course, who was busy eating his onion rings and feeding the birds. Triple T, Torsten the Viking, Heinz Beckenshultz, and Nathan Lieber all took to the stage and manned their instruments. With the bus now parked next to the building, the band and crew had a place to go and get away, opposed to being stuck in the venue all night.

Five minutes into soundcheck, there was a power outage and the club became pitch black. Everyone inside barreled out of the dark through the front and side doors into the still-sunlit world. The sound man ventured back into the club with a flashlight. He found the main breaker had popped and he re-engaged it to the on position. All the band members, club employees, and crew members returned inside the club after the lights and power were back on. The band resumed the stage and finished the soundcheck. Jeb and Neusy joined Hocker up on the stage to inspect that all the wires were out of the way and not getting stepped on.

During the power outage, Sparrow and Crow arrived at the venue. As they struggled to get their sunburned bodies out of the car, Crow said, "This does not look good."

"Nope, not good," replied Sparrow.

"We cannot let this case slip away from us; there better not be a murder! We could never explain why we are only now pulling up; we need to be a little more careful."

"Yes, I agree. It is going to be tough after this since that tour manager, Jeb, does not have room on the bus for us. Although he did say he would see what he can do, we are still on our own for the next couple of days," said Sparrow, as the agents were finally successful in exiting their vehicle. Their backs and the back of their legs and arms were sunburned, but they looked normal from the front. At least no one would know that they were at the beach, sleeping.

Entering Block by Block, the agents saw that the club was more of an upper-scale venue. The entrance area was large, and once inside, there was a huge bar right by the entrance. Past the bar was the main room: the concert room. The agents walked into the room while the band was in the middle of soundcheck. When they looked at the stage, it became apparent to them where the venue got its name. The stage looked like it was sitting on blocks— alphabet blocks, like a little child would have, but much larger versions. Each block was two feet squared and painted, just like the children's blocks. The high stage made it so the agents had to look up at the band. Behind the band on the stage was a wall, approximately ten feet high, made of the same blocks. The agents thought they were standing in a very cool venue.

Jeb walked up to the two and said, "I saw you guys getting out of the car, rough night, guys?" Laughing, he slapped Crow on the back.

Crow screamed, "OOOWWW!!!"

Walking away, Jeb said, "I thought you agents were a little tougher than that. I barely touched you." *Pussy*, he thought.

Crow said, "It's not that, you see, we were in the sun too long." But Jeb was already far enough away and, with the music, he did not hear the response. Crow turned to Sparrow and said, "Everything looks OK. Must have just tripped a circuit breaker; let's look around." So they did and were satisfied that nothing abnormal happened while the power was off and took seats at the second bar in the back of the venue.

The Doctor showed up fashionably late as usual and asked, "How is the sound?"

Jeb replied, "It would sound better if you came here earlier to soundcheck with the band."

"Yah, I know."

The room filled up and did not look empty, not a large crowd, but not embarrassingly empty. After the Doctor drank his energy drink, he was ready to strap on the Universe Guitar to start the show. The show started with a few of his classic tunes. The audience was dazzled at the Doctor's hand moving up and down the neck, doing finger gymnastics and back flips. Song after song, hit after hit, was played unto the blissful onlookers.

"We are going do one off the *Slap the Virgin* album; this one is called 'Mellow Craven,'" the Doctor announced as the crowd screamed. They sang the chorus with the band.

Come to me, my asthmatic breather
Go grab your inhaler
So that you can breathe…
Come to me, my asthmatic breather
There you are, there you are…

Another famous guitar hero took the stage with the Doctor. "Would you please welcome Norman Vintouchi! We will now play 'Wine in My Liver!'" Norman remembered this song from his childhood and played it well on stage with the Doctor. The crowd's excitement was unbridled as it was too much for most people to have two guitar greats on the same stage.

The agents thought this was cool; with everyone singing, they pulled out their phones and added the Centipedes to their Spotify accounts. The second time the chorus came around, Sparrow and Crow were singing just as loud as everyone else.

Triple T was displeased with his bass drum sound. He constantly adjusted the drum head with his drum key between songs, but couldn't get the sound right. He figured Hocker had done something to the head, always something with Hocker. It would just produce a resounding thud with no inner resonance. After the show, the satisfied crowd finished their drinks and lined up to meet the Doctor. The road crew began to disassemble the stage. Hocker and Neusy began their usual duties of taking apart the drums, unplugging wires, etc.

The club's soundman also was up on stage to collect his microphones. "What the hell is this?" he said as he looked at the hole cut into the bass drum head and saw a human nose sticking out. Triple T came up with his drum key, and they removed the outer bass drum head.

They found the club manager, Dick Noggin, bent into a pretzel shape and stuffed into the huge twenty-eight-inch bass drum. They would never have seen him through the black Evans hydraulic drum heads had it not been for the sound man detecting his nose popping through the forward hole used to put the microphone in. Hocker pulled the dead club manager's body out of the bass drum and set him in the middle of the stage, surrounded by wires, cabinets, and drum cases. A drumstick sharpened on the tip side was thrust through one ear and out the other, with blood encircling both ears and dripping down his neck.

The bartender called the police, unaware that the FBI was already in house. After twenty minutes, four squad cars, one unmarked car, and CSI arrived on the scene. The agents, who were now up on the stage and taking photos, wondered how they could not have noticed this themselves. But the stage is high, and they could not see up there while the band was playing. Or at least that's what they would tell the guys at the field office. The police stood there wondering why they were called when the FBI was already there. Sparrow and Crow introduced themselves to the police. "Lieutenant, I am Jathan Sparrow, and this is my partner, Jester Crow."

Lieutenant Wilson replied, "Really? Sparrow and Crow? My officers are here to help. We already have shut the venue down; no one is entering or leaving. Do you want us to take statements from all here?"

The agents thought this was a good idea and realized they should not have allowed anyone to enter or leave themselves. Sparrow said, "Yes, that would be helpful."

"Get everyone's contact info," interjected Crow.

The Lieutenant said, "Believe it or not, we have done this before."

Eight uniformed officers began a barrage of questions of all the people inside the nightclub. Patrons were questioned. Employees were questioned. The band, especially Triple T, was questioned, because the body had shown up in his drum. Being always calm and cool, he answered all their questions. He seemed to have an airtight alibi. They went outside when the power went off. The police couldn't get any information that would give them any clues to who would have committed this heinous act, so they took people's phone numbers and addresses.

Since all the fans were locked inside the venue until being cleared by the police, merchandise sales were through the roof. Bobby and Sadie were selling more than they ever had. Jeb was happy about this, and since he would not have to pay anything on the merch sales to Noggin, he smiled. He would have to call the owner in the morning to inquire how he would get paid for the gig. The bartender walked up to him just at that moment and handed him an envelope that stated it was for Jeb, Jurgen Weislangwolf's tour manager. Inside was a check for the amount agreed upon before the show. The bartender said, "I found that in the office, that is you, isn't it? Jeb, tour manager?"

"Yes, my friend, I appreciate it," said Jeb, hoping that check would clear.

Cal Crabs, who was in his hotel room sleeping, arrived at the club just at this moment. Jeb heard him from across the room. "Son, I am the bus driver; I need to get inside. I suggest that you get out of my way!" He was outside trying to get in, but an officer half his size was standing in his way.

Jeb ran to the door and said to the officer, as he showed his tour badge, "Yes, he is with us. Can you please let him in? He was in his hotel room sleeping all night." The officer stepped aside, and Cal walked in, looking down on the officer as he passed.

"Bro…what the hell happened? Murder?"

"Yup, looks like we will be a little late getting out of here," replied Jeb.

They needed to get this moving along, or at least see if they could load-out. Jeb asked Sparrow, "Can we start loading out?"

Sparrow said, "All the amps were examined, along with all the drums. That organ is good to go. Just leave the big drum. We want more time with that."

"Yes, OK, we will leave the big drum. It's called a bass drum, for your report." Jeb said to Marlon, Neusy, and Hocker, "OK boys, everything can get loaded out other than the bass drum." No one missed Teddy Red.

Cal Crabs had casually walked up on stage and began to examine things on his own. He asked the crew before loading everything up and moving it all down from the high stage to look at the equipment quickly. He walked around the stage, then backstage. He did not notice anything strange. Then back up on stage just as the crime lab boys had finished with the bass drum.

Fiddling with the bass drum, he noticed a single brown hair that did not appear to belong to the victim caught around the bass drum support leg. The hair was not visible until he extended the leg. He looked around to see if the police or FBI observed him, and then carefully used one of his roach clips to pick up the hair and place it into a Ziploc bag that he always had an abundant supply of from his days as a pot dealer. He claimed he still sells only occasionally to help a buddy out. Cal didn't think the hair belonged to anyone in the band or crew since it had a kink and appeared to have been braided.

Chapter 23

The bus left Block by Block in San Diego later than they had expected, with the events that unfolded after the show. Cal turned to Jeb as they sat in the parking lot of the club. "How are we looking, bro, we are two hours later than I wanted to leave. I figure a ten-hour drive. Can we leave in the next ten minutes?"

"Yes, I can make it happen. Give me a minute, the Doctor is still inside talking with some people." Jeb left the bus and walked back to the club. About fifty feet away from the bus was the stage door. Jeb found the back door locked; he walked around the building to the front. There the Doctor was, standing with the agents. Sparrow was smoking a cigarette, talking with the Doctor and Agent Crow.

Jeb approached as he heard Crow saying, "This is quite the production you have here. I've never been part of anything like this."

"Yeah," said Sparrow. "It's quite amazing. The bus looks nice. Hopefully, Jeb can make room for us."

"Yah, this is what we do," said the Doctor. "I have been on these tours for forty years. First, of course, with the Centipedes, then with my next band, Darkened Moon." He stopped talking and looked at the cigarette in Sparrow's hand, then said, "You know I don't smoke. It is very bad for your health." Then to Jeb, "Can we not make room for these agents on the bus?"

"Well," said Jeb, "the bus is full. We have nine people sleeping on there, and you know that the guys need the space in the spare bunks for their instruments and personal things. Bus is leaving now; we need to go."

"What!" exclaimed the Doctor. "We leave when I say we do!"

"We are leaving. You can sit here and say when you will leave, but at that point, you will be driving with these guys in their car. I know that I would rather be on the bus," Jeb said, being stern with the Doctor. He is the one guy on the road, other than Cal, that can talk this way to the Doctor.

Jeb turned and said, "See you guys up in San Fran. Are you coming, Jurgen?"

"Yah, see you guys later; I must go!" The Doctor followed Jeb back to the bus. Jeb opened the door and informed Cal, "He was busy bonding with those agents."

"Those guys are trippy," said Cal. "Check the bus. Make sure we are a bus."

Jeb checked the bunks. Hocker on the bottom bunk, first on the right. Check. Torsten was up on top of the same bank, with Neusy in the middle. Check on both, as Neusy was up front in the lounge. Nathan watched a tennis match on his tablet in the middle bunk across, and right under him was Triple T. *Great*, thought Jeb, *all here so far*. Top bunk empty. The second set of bunks on the right, Jeb was top bunk with Marlon right under him in the middle—he could smell the THC vape coming from Marlon's bunk. The bottom bunk was an empty spare bunk. Then across from them, that bottom was also a spare bunk, with the middle occupied by Heinz, who was also up front drinking a beer with Neusy. The Doctor had a small suite in the back that contained a seating area and a bed.

Jeb walked up front and spotted the Doctor talking with Cal. Neusy handed him a beer as he walked past and then said to Cal, "My bro, we are a bus. Let's get the fuck out of here!" and they did.

As they rolled to the front of the parking lot, Marlon came running out from the back yelling, "Crabs, please stop! I hope the club is still open; I gotta run in for a minute."

"Son, we are rolling; what is so important?"

"Dude, I have to take a shit. PLEASE!" Cal stopped the bus. Marlon ran out, the Doctor retreated to his suite, and Jeb stayed up front with Heinz and Neusy and opened another beer.

Neusy said as he watched Marlon running toward the entrance of the club, "Amateur. I'm going to lay down." Heinz finished his beer and retired to his bunk; Jeb moved up front and sat in the shotgun seat next to Cal.

Marlon opened the door and stepped on board. Jeb said, "Crabs, we are once again a bus." Cal pulled out of the parking lot and headed toward Interstate 5 North.

Neusy felt the bus moving. His eyes opened and then closed hard again. He finally forced his eyes to open. Then it sounded a bell in his head, and he jumped awake. Oh, shit, he forgot his BMW in the parking lot. Worriedly, he hurried out of the sleeping bay and shuffled toward the front of the bus.

"Hey, Jeb, can we stop?" said Neusy.

"Why? What's the matter?" said Jeb.

"I left my BMW back there," replied Neusy.

"Great," said Jeb, "and I even knew that you are supposed to be driving up there. Hey, Crabs, we have to go back!" said Jeb.

"What the fuck for now? I'm rolling," said the pissed-off driver.

"Well, somebody forgot his car in the parking lot."

"Your first night on the bus is not going well. We are going to risk me now having an overdrive day, and you will owe me two days' salary. It is going to be over ten hours." Jeb threw up his hands.

Cal exited the next off-ramp, made a U-turn under the freeway, and entered the on-ramp back to San Diego. Thirty-five minutes later, they were back at the club. Neusy told the guys that he would drive the BMW to San Francisco and meet them there. The Doctor was jolted awake by all this maneuvering and came up front to investigate what was going on. When he found out that Neusy needed to drive the BMW up to San Francisco, he said, "Achhh, Neusy, I would like to go with you!"

"Alright."

"Do you mind if I drive? I like driving German cars."

"OK, if you like."

The two exited the bus together. The Doctor hopped in the driver's side, and Neusy sat in the passenger seat. The Doctor wasted no time in barreling out of the parking lot and onto the freeway. The bus followed them at a more moderate speed. In a way, the guys liked that the Doctor decided to go separately. That way, they wouldn't have to listen to his snide or sarcastic comments.

After four hours, the sun was up. The guys were starting to stir. Jeb was up front first, sitting at his table working the books from the night before. An hour later, Heinz immediately put on a pot of coffee. Slowly, all the faces were up front, other than Hocker, who was still sleeping. Marlon said, "Ooohh, coffee!" then helped himself to a cup.

Jeb wanted to have some fun and started mimicking the Doctor's voice. "Nathan, you missed some notes last night! Und Heinz, you are playing at an erratic tempo. I will not stand for this! Verstehen Sie?"

"You are so crazy, Jeb," said Nathan. "We always make fun of Herr Doctor too, but we are afraid that you would say something to him. This is Great!"

"There is nothing wrong with my tempo!" said Heinz.

Triple T walked out in his tight whites and no shirt. "Tommy, I thought I heard you make a poopzen on stage last night," said Nathan.

"Shove it up your ass, Doctor, without a glove!" said Triple T, laughing. "I never get this criticizing with anyone else I play with. The Doctor always has something to say."

Torsten also got into the act. "Jeb, you have set up my pedals all wrong! You Dummkopf! Und my fan was pointing the wrong way. It was blowing Nathan's hair, not mine. You fool!"

Cal Crabs was chuckling as he drove the bus. He thought these guys were hilarious. Even though he was the Doctor's old friend, he wouldn't betray the guys. He somewhat felt he was one of them. Cracking jokes about the Doctor could go on for hours, and it made the travel time to San Francisco go by fast.

"Marlon, where is my coffee? I can barely keep my eyes open, you Dummkopf!" said Jeb.

"Did he call me a Dummkopf?" asked Marlon.

"No, just fucking with you," said Jeb.

"Marlon, why are your eyes always red? Are you smoking the marijuana?" said Jeb.

"Come on, dude!" snapped Marlon. "That's getting kind of personal!"

"Lighten up, Jiggsy!" said Jeb.

"Hey, Torsten, are you going to wear your Viking helmet with the horns at the San Francisco show?" asked Marlon.

"Yah, I think so," said Torsten.

"I think that's the coolest helmet I have ever seen."

"Thanks, I like it too."

They made it up to San Francisco laughing. The camaraderie on the bus happened fast. When you stick ten people traveling long distances in a small tube with the only private space being a seven-foot-long, two-and-a-half-foot-wide, two-foot-high bunk, they seem to get to know one another quite well.

Jeb managed to reserve a hotel right next to the venue. This was convenient but rarely happened. There were three rooms available, and the contract for the show allowed for it. Jeb would get reimbursed for them up to $100 a room. Two rooms for the guys to shower and one for Cal Crabs to sleep in while they were in town.

Cal went along with Jeb; the rest of the guys split up and walked in different directions, looking for food and a bathroom. Neusy pulled up in front of the two and opened his window. "Wow, what a great morning. We walked along the water and had a great breakfast," he said before parking the BMW and following Jeb and Cal into the hotel. The hotel was called the West Northern Hotel.

"Hi, I reserved three rooms for tonight; when I called, I was told we could check in early."

"What's the name?" said the clerk.

"Jeb Acorns."

"OK, I see it here."

"What type of discount can you give me?"

"Well, I don't know if I can…"

Jeb surmised the man might be a rocker, as he had long hair and was listening to AC/DC on his radio.

"I can give you a free ticket to the show tonight."

"Are you in a band?"

"No, but I am the tour manager for the former Centipedes guitarist, the Doctor of Dynamics, Jurgen Weislangwolf," replied Jeb.

"You're shitting me?"

"Yes, really."

"Well, I can give you a twenty percent discount for a concert ticket."

"Done!"

"Is the Doctor on that tour bus outside?"

"No, he is in that white BMW."

"Man, do you think he would sign a prescription for me?"

"I don't see why not." The deal was sealed.

The band now had a bathroom they could use. Marlon grabbed a key from Jeb and ran away. "Oh boy! Oh boy! I hope I make it," he said as he disappeared.

Scaggz was waiting behind the club, leaning against the wall, crouching, as the bus arrived. He saw the bus, pulled up his pants, and was careful not to step in the pile he just dropped as he ran around the corner behind the supermarket and into the adjacent parking lot where his VW was parked. *What took them so long?* he wondered. *Boy, is being back on tour exciting.*

Scaggz, in his VW, with his twin-blade razor, shave cream, and a bottle of water shaved off his beard and mustache. He put on a green polo shirt and then tucked his hair under a black baseball cap. He bought a pair of reading glasses with heavy frames from the local store. Everyone knew that Scaggz hated the color green, so no one would suspect a thing. Other than not being able to see distance with the glasses, and the fact that they made his eyes appear huge, he felt safe that no one would recognize him. He looked in the small mirror he had on a shelf in the van and said, "You, my friend, are a genius!"

Chapter 24

San Francisco's famous Anti-Social Club was precisely what its name implied. Everyone that worked there, as well as guests, were antisocial. It was a well-known club, and it was expected that when you entered the club, you too would be antisocial. The bouncers that admitted people to the club would point at a sign posted by the entrance. In white letters on a black background, a three-foot-high sign said, *Anyone caught being social will be thrown out!* The larger of the two bouncers always said to the newly arriving patron, "Take this sign literally."

People passing by would stop and wait as, almost every ten minutes, someone would get thrown out. Four bouncers or bartenders would each grab a limb, open the door, and throw out the socially outgoing patron. It has become well known around the world and always draws a large crowd. Unfortunately, not all of them went inside for the Doctor's performance but waited out in the street to take pictures, videos, and selfies of the incidents. The bouncers would charge twenty dollars a selfie if someone wanted to take a picture with them. It would not be uncommon for a bouncer that worked at the Anti-Social Club to bring home an extra $300-$500 a night. So the hiring pool for bouncers was never in short supply.

The interior had rotting, wood-paneled walls. The back wall was red brick with graffiti all over. The place was trashed; there were broken beer bottles on the floor and posters of many famous punk bands hung crooked on the walls. In one corner, there were a couple of heroin needles under a table. The whole place smelled like rotten shit. You could even find dried human turds on the floor. Homeless people would relieve themselves up along the exterior walls, and unknowing patrons carried it in on their feet.

The management were a bunch of derelicts and street trash. The head manager, a withering, limp-wristed, foul-mouthed, grey, greasy-haired, unshaven guy, goes by the name of Rude Ralph. Sara, his hostess, had blonde frizzy hair and a tattoo across her chest that read Sex Pistols. She was missing both front teeth. Two of the bouncers, Bill and Rick, sat in the back playing gin rummy on a table. Ralph spoke with Jeb as the load-in proceeded. "It's about time you assholes arrived. I have to get to the bank!" said Rude Ralph.

"Well, we would have been here sooner if three of the one-way streets we took to get here didn't have road construction on them," replied Jeb.

"I don't want to hear your fucking hard-luck stories. 3:00 p.m. means 3:00 p.m." said Ralph.

"What's with the attitude, buddy? We're gonna make you some money tonight!" stated Jeb.

"That's the way we are around here: antisocial. We expect it, it's our thing. Go outside and take a look at the sign by the front door," said Ralph.

"OK then, fuck wad! Hope you had a shitty morning and develop diarrhea as the evening carries on!" said Jeb, and then he shouldered the guy in the chest, walking past him to take a look at the stage area. Rude Ralph smiled.

Hocker and Neusy carried a Marshall cabinet in and walked toward the stage with it. Marlon followed them in with sections of the Doctor's pedalboard. "Boy, look at this guy, a big mistake of Mother Nature!" said Ralph.

"Are you talking about me?" asked Marlon.

"Yeah, nobody else here that looks so stupid!" said Ralph.

"That's pretty rude, sir; I never said anything to you."

"Fuck you, fart breath."

Hocker and Neusy walked toward the door to grab some more gear; Hocker noticed that the manager spoke harshly to Marlon. "Hey, little buddy, is this guy fucking with you?" he said to Marlon.

"Yeah, he insulted me for no reason."

"What's up, dick nose? Why are you fucking with my little buddy?"

"Fuck you, you big fucking ape," said Ralph. Hocker stuck out his arm and clothes-lined Ralph to the ground, then spit some chew on his forehead. They walked outside with Neusy to continue the load-in. The bouncers looked over and laughed as they pointed to Ralph on the ground. They all expected this kind of behavior and didn't give it too much mind.

After the load-in, the guys decided to go somewhere else to eat and drink. They really didn't like the vibe in the Anti-Social Club. Down the street, they found a fast food Chinese restaurant and decided to eat there. Jeb, Neusy, Hocker, and Marlon entered the restaurant. Nothing extraordinary about the interior of the restaurant with its white walls, grey floor, and red curtains. There were twelve tables with four chairs at each. Since it was fast food, they stood around the counter and looked at the menu.

Jeb said, "Why don't I order a bunch of stuff, and we can just share?"

"OK!" said Neusy.

"Get to it, I'm hungry!" said Hocker.

An elderly Chinese woman asked them what they wanted.

Jeb started the order. "Let me have an order of pork chow mein and twelve egg rolls. And let me have a large bowl of hot and sour soup, an order of kung pao chicken with four bowls of white rice."

"And to drink, sir?"

"What kind of beer do you have?"

"We have Hong Kong Kung Fu Brew!"

"Alright, give me four of those."

After about ten minutes, the lady set all of their food on four orange plastic trays, and the guys each grabbed a tray and a beer and walked over to a table. They all sat down and began to eat. "How's the food? Hock?" Jeb asked.

"Not too bad… It's decent," he remarked. Some noodles fell out of his mouth that he grabbed with a swoop of his tongue before they managed to drop too far.

"I've had better in Hong Kong!" said Neusy.

"Well, this isn't fucking Hong Kong, is it?" said Hocker. Food flew out of his mouth onto Marlon's fork without anyone noticing but Jeb, who turned away before the fork entered Marlon's mouth.

"No, I guess not." said Neusy as he drank his beer.

"Man, what I like most about this weed I bought is that the food tastes so good. But I still miss my wife and kids," said Marlon as a tear rolled down his cheek.

After a dry heave and clearing his throat, Jeb looked straight down into his plate and said, "I thought we were past that by now." No one said a word for the rest of the meal.

While the guys were finishing up their meal, a crowd began to line up outside the venue, along with the regulars that hung out waiting for the next person to get the boot. Green-haired people with buzz cuts. Pink-haired people with Mohawks. Bald bikers with scraggly beards and tattoos. A few were sitting on the sidewalk shooting heroin into their veins. Several shabbily dressed homeless were shitting by a wire fence next to the venue. A few old, discarded sofas were next to the venue, with people sleeping on them. And about twenty people were standing in line in front of the door of the Anti-Social Club.

Walking slowly back to the club, they scanned the different types of people outside. "Look at all of those stinking, smelly people!" shouted Marlon.

"Oh! Oh! Look at that guy shitting on the side of the building! That fucking pig!" said Hocker.

"Wow! Look, his girlfriend is shitting next to him," said Marlon.

They now all noticed the pink-haired girl with tattoos on her arms squatting next to the blue-haired man with both of their pants down around their ankles, shitting away, crouched with their backs leaning against the building. They held hands as they did it, looking into each other's eyes. True love.

"I ain't never seen anything like that before," said Neusy.

"Me either!" said Jeb. "Although I did once step in a pile of human shit under the elevated trains behind that club out in Chicago. I thought that was pretty gross, but this?"

The opening band for this evening's performance was the Hormones, a bunch of bums, a collection of street trash that played on the sidewalks during the day. Two of the guys were drunks, and the other two were heroin addicts, and all of them publicly shit on the street prior to the show with no thought of being embarrassed. They covered the Ramones' music as parodies and wore black wigs. The lead singer, named Hamlet Hormone, acted like Sid Vicious.

The guitarist, Henry Hormone, was reckless on stage and often kicked at people in the audience. Joey Hormone, the bassist, spun his head around and around the entire show. His long ponytail, with a feathered weight tied to the end, spun like the propeller of a helicopter. If you got too close to him, the feather might slice an eyeball out, if not certainly leave a scar. Joey was the only one who had long black hair. Melvin Hormone played the drums hard and destroyed his drum set at the end of the performance.

"Please welcome, the Hormones!"

"Fuck those pieces of shit!" shouted someone in the crowd.

"Fuck you, ass face!" Hamlet kicked that guy in the face from the stage and he fell backward. "Alright, you gutter rats, here is our song, 'Impregnated!'"

I want to be a pervert twenty-four hours a day
I want to get impregnated
I want to suck dick until you say
I want to get impregnated
So give me, give me, give me some more of your cum
I'm rather drinking your load more than a shot of rum
When I'm through drinking, I'll show you my bum
I want to take your loving home
Now, now, now, now, now, now, now, now, now
I want to get impregnated

It was a very disgusting song. But at the Anti-Social Club, anything goes. The crowd couldn't care less about this band. They had seen them playing the same songs on the sidewalk during the day several times in the past week.

"Fuck you, assholes! Bring on the Doctor!"

"Fuck you, Hamlet, you piece of shit!"

"Boooooooo!!!"

If you cheered in the Anti-Social Club, it would be considered social, and out you would go.

Their last song was called "Shit on you!" During the song, Hamlet and Henry dropped their pants and did exactly what the song stated on the stage. When they finished the song, they picked up their creations and threw them at people in the audience. Then they ran as fast as they could out the back door. The people that got hit by shit ran to the restroom to wash it off.

The crowd was getting impatient. Rude Ralph and his bartenders were slinging the beers as fast as they could. "Where's my fucking beer, asshole?"

"Fuck you! You'll get it when I'm ready!"

"Hurry up, dick!"

"Here's your beer, fuck nose!" Ralph spat in it when the biker wasn't looking. "A little extra foam for you on the house."

"Come on! Bring on the Doctor!"

"Stop fucking around!"

"We want the Doctor! We want the Doctor!"

The Doctor and the band were listening to the crowd from the green room. "The people sound very violent! This place is scary! After the show, we will leave immediately. No meet und greet tonight!" The Doctor instructed Marlon to get some bleach and scrub the stage where the Hormones had shit on it.

It would be one of the fastest sets the Doctor ever played. He played all the solos precisely as they were on the original albums. There were no extended solos, no encores. He just wanted to get out of this place and escape to the tour bus.

They received the typical Anti-Social Club welcome.

"BOOOOOO!"

"Fuck you, Doctor!"

"We are going to sue you for malpractice, you asshole!"

"Can I get a prescription so I can flush it down the toilet!"

The Doctor only played half his set and did not say a word to the crowd. Marlon and Jeb were trying to sell the merch; people were spilling beer on everything. Someone took a couple of CDs and threw them towards the stage. Jeb saw someone spit at Marlon. "Marlon, let's roll all this shit back to the trailer. No more, and no meet and greet."

After the Doctor finished the set, he said good night and he and the band made their way quickly out the back door and onto the tour bus. The crowd started throwing bottles and anything they could find. The bouncers carried a barrier fence up the stage to protect the crew as they broke down the equipment and carried it out.

Scaggz spent the show in the first row. He looked very clean-cut and not very antisocial in his outfit, but after he beat the crap out of the biker that was calling him a "preppie asshole that is in our world now," no one bothered him for the rest of the night.

After the show, he talked with the agents, who spent the entire show with their guns in their hands. "I loved *The Blues Brothers* movie," he said.

"Yeah, it was pretty cool," said Sparrow. Crow hit Sparrow in the arm; he was tired of hearing that comment. It was just who they were. They were not trying to look like anyone, and he hated when Sparrow ate up the reference.

"I'm one of the Doctor's biggest fans. I have seen him hundreds of times. Isn't he amazing?" said Scaggz. "Have a good evening, guys. It smells like shit in here, so I'm leaving. I'm sure I'll see you at other shows. I am going to a few on this tour."

"OK," said Crow, "let's go out back. I'm going to throw up if I have to spend another moment in here." The two agents walked out back as the crew carried the last of the equipment out to the trailer.

From the bus, one by one, they all walked to the hotel to shower and get the smell of the club off of them. Jeb said, "Hurry up! We are leaving in an hour."

They were drinking beer and whiskey, the Doctor red wine. Cal came on board a half hour later. "What a crazy place. Did they boo you? I have been here with other tours, and some like it and some don't."

"Yah, we did not like this place," said the Doctor as the last three, Nathan, Marlon, and Heinz, walked off the bus to the showers.

Cal asked, "How many more need to shower?"

"That's it; those three are the last. Then go right away. Get away from this place," answered Jeb.

Two fans were outside the bus trying to open the door. They were hitting the door with bottles. Cal stood up and opened the small slide window in the door. "Boys, I need you to stop that. The Doctor is not coming out."

"Fuck you!" said one of the overweight bikers.

"Yeah, you overgrown cowboy-looking mutha fucker," said the other, and they both started banging on the door again.

Cal turned to Hocker and said, "Hocks, can you come here a second?"

Hocker replied, "Yeah, Crabs, what do you need?"

"Hocks, remember last year in Houston?"

Hocker nodded and said, "Yup, same deal?"

Cal Crabs pressed the door button and the door opened. The two bikers took a step up on the bus. They were screaming and pumping their fists right before a foot caught each one of them between the eyes. They both fell backward off the first step of the bus. Marlon and the two musicians returned; Marlon screeched in a high pitch, "OOOHHH GOD, OOHHHH MY GOD!"

Heinz, staying calm, said, "Yah, jump over them quick," and they did. Up the steps, they ran. Cal pressed the door button once more, and as the door closed, the bus drove away.

"Well, that's how that is done," said Hocker.

"WHOOOOHHOOOO! This tour is starting to get interesting," said Cal.

Neusy said, "Wow, that was intense. Do you think that they are the guys killing people?"

"I don't know, but those agents were what, twenty feet away? I saw them go out back, and they could not come over to assist us?" said Jeb.

The door to the bunks opened, and the two agents walked out to a full lounge. Sparrow said, "Wow, this bus rides smooth. A little tight up here; can you guys make us a little space?" The band and crew were shocked. Now there were two more on the bus—a total of eleven and the driver.

"I thought we already discussed this," said Jeb.

"Yah," said the Doctor. "I told them it is OK, Jeb, just relax!"

"Are you joking? Look how tight we are up here."

"Yah, now Jeb…they can't drive all this way. We need them; there have been murders."

"OK, but guys, here is the deal, and I will not allow any conversation that says otherwise. You can ride until Seattle. Then we go to Canada. This is always a time-consuming border crossing with the bus. It has to be perfect, or they will hold us. We are scheduled to cross at the border crossing in Blaine, Washington. That is where our papers were sent, and if we deviate from what is on those papers, we will be held up. You guys will have paperwork to submit, and they will make calls. It could take hours."

From the driver's seat, "Yes, Jeb, they must go before the border, but up till then, this is one big rolling party. Welcome aboard, fellas, to the ride of your life."

Jeb continued, "You guys are the FBI, so I am sure they can buy flights for you while we are in Canada. Plus you don't have jurisdiction up there. So, you fly, and then you can join us once we are back in the States. If we were to be pulled over, or the police wanted to check our papers along the way, the same issues would occur, and we would lose time. That is my offer."

Crow said, "That is fair. Sparrow, we need to call the field office in the morning and have them book for us. I'm not sure our cards will be able to handle that extra purchase every day."

"Good call," agreed Sparrow.

"Read the rules; they are serious. Number one is there are no number twos allowed." The agents read the list, looked at each other, and shook their heads in agreement.

Torsten got up and made a tea, then disappeared to the bunks. The rest of the band and Marlon followed. The agents were thrilled to be on the bus. Neusy cracked another beer and gave one to Hocker and another to Jeb as he poured the Doctor a glass of wine.

"Yah, so that is settled then, this is good," the Doctor said. And then to Hocker, "Well, that certainly was not good tonight. Why did my sound always change und cut in und out?"

Hocker, feeling tired as well, stood up and hugged his beer, then said, "It was that fucker with the green shirt and baseball cap. He kept fucking with things. I kicked his hand a couple of times, but he kept on fucking with shit. That is a horrid club. That asshole threw a matchbook from the club at me. Shit, I think I still have it!" Hocker reached into his pocket and pulled out the matchbook. His beer dropped from his hand. He showed Jeb.

Handwritten on the inside was, ***You big fat fuck, I should kill you next.***

Chapter 25

Jeb, as usual, was the first one awake as the bus traveled north to Portland. Early in the morning is the time that he got most of his tour manager's work done. He had a backlog of emails to return, calls to make regarding upcoming shows, and yesterday's income and expenses to reconcile. All sorts of sounds were coming out of the bunks as he walked in sweatpants and his sleep tee into the lounge. He saw that he was actually not the first one awake. Agents Sparrow and Crow were fully dressed in their suits, their faces planted up against the front windshield. Cal saw Jeb in the mirror positioned over the windshield and said, "Good morning, my bro. We are making excellent time and should be there in about two hours, maybe a little longer depending on traffic in Portland. We got ourselves a couple of excited first timers here," nodding at the agents.

"Yeah, I see that," said Jeb, hoping they would leave him alone so he could get his work done.

Crow stepped back. "Hey, I am going to make more coffee. This is great, I can't believe this. Amazing driving, Mr. Crabs. Anyone want coffee? Boy, this is great! Even a coffee maker on board."

Cal said, "Son, call me Crabs, or Cal, if you want. Most people call me Crabs. Take this and fill 'er up with coffee." Crow looked at the oversized metal travel mug. Cal added, "But this takes a whole pot, so you will have to make two."

It went on like this for the next hour and a half. Jeb, at his table, was working, taking care of the business end of the tour. He was putting money aside for bus expenses and Cal's salary, then the rest in a cash bag to be deposited when they were near a bank. Rude Ralph got his last laugh. In the envelope with the cash was a handwritten note that appeared to have shit stains on it and the words *Cock Sucker*. Jeb washed his hands, then made his phone calls. He set up the coming shows with the venues, so they knew what to expect, and sent them the rider with the different requests from the band members. The agents could not sit still and were just happy to be riding on the bus, although Crow did manage to call their field office and straighten out their travel plans.

One by one, the rest of the crew and then the band members came up front, waiting for the bus to stop so they could use the facilities and buy food. The agents watched everything, taking it all in to look like they belonged, and so the band and crew would accept them. It would be embarrassing to tell their supervisor that they were asked to leave the bus. Crow had to almost beg for the plane tickets, but he managed to convince his superiors since they were saving money by riding on the bus. But if that went away, they would be mocked and laughed at again by their peers. When the bus stopped, they sat and watched what everyone did and followed along.

They were at a Walmart, and after an hour, everyone was back on the bus. They were smiling and feeling good after eating at one of the fast food restaurants in the parking lot. The Doctor was last to arrive at the bus with a shopping cart full of primarily useless items for his room. They all watched him carry a large mirror, three lamps, and bags full of new blouses, candles, stuffed animals, throw rugs, and curtains back to the room. After ten minutes of this, the bus was rolling again.

Cal finished his coffee and said, "Boys, I need a refill." Crow jumped up and turned on the coffee pot.

Jeb said to Neusy, "Maybe not so bad having these two here; we can put them to work."

"I am way ahead of you," replied Neusy, then they both went back to their bunks.

The night's show was at the El Diablo Club, one of Portland's oldest rock venues—anybody who has toured through Portland knows of this club. At first look from the street, the club looks like an ordinary bar. But once inside, it's anything but. The bus made good time, and they arrived at the club at 2:30 p.m.

The club was split into two sections, each with a street entrance. The first side they called the local side. It was more like a bar than a rock club. There was a bar, and they served bar food, mostly fried items. There was a small triangle-shaped stage opposite the bar that local bands would play on Friday and Saturday nights. They would play for three hours and receive minimal pay. It was a favorite among the locals; with a large dance floor, it had become a hot singles venue on these nights over the years. Anyone looking for a hookup, this was the place, and, until pot became legal in Oregon, the place to go to score weed as well.

The other side can be accessed through two large sliding doors, which allow the two sides to be opened into one for large events. The national side, this side was where the acts that toured nationally performed, such as the Doctor. The national side of El Diablo had a large floor area in front of the stage where people would stand and enjoy the music. In the back were booths elevated five feet above the floor on a platform accessed by stairs.

The stage was different than most. The stage was twenty feet across and fifteen feet deep. The PA speakers, which hung on both sides of the stage, sometimes become an obstacle with only seven feet under them from the top of the stage. A very challenging venue for the band and sound engineer. The stage was four feet high, which the band liked as they get up high, and people can see them from all parts of the venue. At the center of the stage towards the front, which is the exact center of the building, was an eighteen-inch square support pillar for the ceiling and the apartments above. The drums sat at the back of the stage on a platform mostly obscured by the pillar. The Doctor does not like this venue, but it's a paying gig, and they all count.

In the past, the Doctor had scratched one of his Universe Guitars on the concrete pillar, so now he insists on setting up as far from it as he can. One has to watch themselves on stage as many times, guitarists moving around, nodding their heads to full-on head banging, have collided with the pillar. In the thirty-seven-year history of El Diablo, eighty-nine guitarists had knocked themselves out by banging their heads into the pillar in a moment of passion on the guitar. The tally for the number of guitarists rendered unconscious on the stage of El Diablo is notched into the concrete of the pillar with a grinder. Eighty-nine marks on the upper half of the pillar are visible from the audience's side. It is one of the most photographed sites in the entire city. Bands are asked to sign the pillar by management when an incident occurs.

Marlon could not contain his excitement. From the first day he had joined the group, he repeatedly mentioned that he couldn't wait to see this venue. He immediately jumped out of the bus and took a selfie with the pillar. Standing in front of it, then on stage, and then leaning up against it while standing on his hands. Jeb awoke from a nap in his bunk to his phone notifying him that a friend has posted a new photo. He climbed down out of his top bunk, walked to the front lounge, where the band and crew had gathered, to witness everyone looking at their phones. There were comments such as *asshole*, *imbecile*, *moron*, and *Dummkopf*.

Jeb said, "What's up?"

Neusy said, "Look at your phone."

Jeb looked. "Putz."

Neusy said to Jeb, "So this is that place?"

"Yup!"

"With the…" Neusy continued.

"Yup!"

"Marlon is quite enthusiastic, better than San Diego…"

"Yup!"

Neusy warned the crew and band, "Well, at least he is not crying… Just don't ask him how his family is doing!"

Everyone knows the drill. Load-in is at 3:00 p.m. and hopefully, by 5:00 there would be a soundcheck. This gave everyone a little time, the crew a half hour and the band a little longer. Jeb, Neusy, and Hocker walked off to see what was around. The guys in the band wanted to go to a music store, and Marlon went looking for a dispensary to purchase more weed. The agents hung around the bus, trying to look important.

The club was on a street below an overpass. The bus parked right on the side of the building and the trailer parked perfectly adjacent to the stage door. Cal Crabs made one swift parallel park with the bus and trailer to get it perfect. Cal then went to his hotel after Jeb handed him an envelope with his salary for the first three days. Cal remarked, "Thanks, smells like shit. Did you give me only money from yesterday?" Jeb smiled as he thought that was funny and was exactly what he did.

At 3:00 p.m., right on time, as if they were professionals, Jeb met the crew at the trailer. As he waited, Jeb pulled out his key to open the trailer; he immediately noticed the two long padlocks were already open. He remembered that he did lock it the night before. Only he and Neusy had the keys; perhaps Neusy opened it earlier and went to take a piss. But that would be careless; Neusy knew better than to leave the trailer unlocked with all that expensive equipment and merchandise inside. When Neusy arrived, Jeb asked, "Bro, did you unlock the trailer? I found the locks opened."

Neusy answered, "You know that I am cautious with this. Too many valuable things inside."

"Someone's playing a joke? We need to buy new locks," instructed Jeb.

"I'll send Marlon later to a hardware store," Neusy said. "Bizarre joke, though. I have a bad feeling about this with all that has been going on." Scaggz watched all this go on from the overpass, then got in his VW and drove away.

The crew loaded in quick; they were now in the groove. Neusy even had the agents load-in the merch, and they were happy to be part of the tour. Marlon, stoned as usual, had so much weed with him he decided to put one of the bags in a spare box in the trailer where it would be safe. The box he chose was the MMM machine box.

Chapter 26

Marlon returned to the El Diablo Club with the locks and, with a smile, handed them to Neusy, who took a look and said, "They should be long throw locks, so they are easier for us to remove. Go take a look at what is on there, then go back and buy the proper locks." Marlon, feeling shunned, did as he was told. After another half hour, he returned. Out of breath, he showed Neusy the locks. Neusy praised Marlon, "Great locks, good job. We will put these on the trailer tonight after we load-out."

Marlon said, "Dude... Shit... I ran the last half block... Dude, something is up with Tommy...he was walking in traffic; his toupee was all fucked up sideways on his head."

"What? He is supposed to be in here; the guys are waiting on him to soundcheck."

"Yeah, dude... I brought him over and sat him on the curb next to the bus."

Neusy ran outside, Marlon followed, and there was Triple T in his tight whites back out in traffic. His toupee was covering one of his eyes, and he had a weird collar around his neck. "Tommy, come on, let's get out of traffic. Marlon, go get Jeb and the agents."

Marlon ran in, and out came Jeb and the agents, with Marlon trailing behind. Triple T was back on the curb; Neusy handed him a bottle of water. "What happened, Tommy?"

"Shit, I'm all dizzy; I fell...banged my head. Shit... Fuck... My head hurts."

"Tommy, how did you fall?" asked Neusy.

Agent Crow said, "Wow, I couldn't tell you wore a wig." Sparrow slapped him. "What…it's a compliment."

Sparrow slapped Crow again and said, "Tommy, easy now, tell us what happened."

"I… I… I… I was napping as I always do before soundcheck… My alarm set in an app on my phone as always… I don't know… I don't know. My bunk is on the bottom… I… I…fell… The…alarm…it went off… I crawled out of my bunk… I… I… I…was on top…fell…head first to floor… My…head… I was in my bottom…bunk… I…fell…from the top."

"Are you telling me that you fell asleep in the wrong bunk, up top, and not your bottom bunk?" asked Sparrow.

"Noooo…I… I…was in my bunk… I was always…in my bunk…on the bottom."

"So, you went to take your nap in your bunk?" asked Jeb. "Then when you woke up, you were in the top bunk? Someone moved you?"

"Is that even possible?" Neusy added, "How can that be? Wouldn't you wake up?"

"Ye…ye…yes… I mean…yes, I was…was moved… But I… I am a deep sleeper. I can sleep through annn…anything… I can never get up… My…wife…she can never get me…up. She…she bought me a modified dog training collar… It…it is paired with…the app on my phone…and it shocks…me… It startles me awake."

This was something that none of them knew or ever heard of. Marlon was the only one that could say anything. "Wow," he said, "that is crazy, dude. You were shocked awake and then tried to crawl out of your bunk and fell the six feet from the top… Wow, dude, that is some messed up shit."

Crow said, "How is that possible? You are, how can I say, not exactly a small man." Sparrow once again slapped him. "I mean, look at him. Do you think you could move him from the bottom bunk to the top? I can barely climb up to my top bunk."

"That is a good point," said Sparrow. "Who has that kind of strength?"

Neusy looked at Jeb and said, "The bus was empty, so it was the perfect opportunity to play a joke like this. But who would do something like this? It's dangerous. None of the guys here have that kind of strength, maybe Hocker, but he would not do that, plus I saw him on stage, waiting for the soundcheck. One of the bouncers could do that, I think; they are big guys, but there were two that I saw, and they were both standing near me."

"There are people out there that have exceptional strength. I can think of two right now. That one woman in Cleveland several years ago. That stage manager there. She was carrying two amps and cabinets with each arm," said Jeb.

"Yes, I remember her," replied Neusy. "Byth was her name, like Beth but with a Y. All night she would say that. Fucking annoying, but a damn good worker. Remember, Scaggz was so into her, they climbed up the lighting trellis like a half dozen times, racing each other… Shit… Scaggz, that's the other guy you are thinking about, isn't it?"

"Yup, Johnny Scaggz, that guy was incredible. He could do it all."

"Who is this Scaggz guy?" asked Sparrow.

Jeb replied, "He used to work with some of us years ago. He was the Doctor's guitar and stage tech. He was quite incredible, I must say."

"Do you think he did this to Tommy?" asked Crow.

"Nah, not a chance; he is living off the grid. He came out the last tour and had dinner with us. What do you think, Neusy?"

"No way. Although, he did have that incident in Munich, but no, he is content living like he is. The touring after all those years was enough for him. Remember at dinner last year, he was so calm, like I have never seen before. Seemed happy, said he could never tour again like he did in the past. Said he was working on a cookbook."

"Yeah, that's right. He even brought us some old guitar effects he had lying around from previous tours. Didn't see him this year, but that's normal with him," said Jeb as Sparrow and Crow took notes.

Neusy asked Triple T, "So do you think you can do soundcheck?"

"I'll give it a try," said Triple T, and they helped him up. He fixed his toupee, removed the collar, put on pants, and they all went inside where the Doctor was waiting and talking with the band.

"Yah, why is it I must wait like this? The one time I want to soundcheck. I want to rehearse an old song that we will try to play tonight. Und what is wrong with Tommy? He doesn't look well."

"He had a little accident, but he thinks he can play," said Jeb.

They helped Triple T back behind the drums, and they warmed up with the classic Centipedes song "Freeze the Sea." The Doctor said, "Yah, just like yesterday, Nathan, you are skipping notes on the harmony, but that is what I am used to. Tommy, yah, this is what I was afraid of, you are way behind the beat. This is no good!"

"I…I…I will try; I am still in a daze from hitting my head."

"Yah, well then. Let's try it again."

Neusy was in the back helping Jeb and Marlon set up the merch. He asked Jeb, "Why does he want to rehearse? It does not seem to be going well on this song for Tommy. What if he cannot play tonight?"

Jurgen was talking about bringing in another song, "The Day the Doctor Visited."

"I have never heard that," said Marlon.

"Yes," Neusy said, "it was on the fourth and final album from Darkened Moon. That was his band after the Centipedes; check it out, you have it to sell there with the CDs. The album is called *In Front of the Stellar Mud*." Marlon found it with the CDs and put it aside to listen to later.

From up on the stage, the Doctor called out, "Jeb, come here!" When Jeb arrived; he said, "Yah, Jeb, this is no good. Tommy cannot play tonight, he is way behind the beat."

"Well, I don't know, do the acoustic show again?"

"Yah, we could do this. But I am thinking of something else. Bring the MMM in here at once!"

"Marlon!" yelled Jeb from up on the stage, "go get the MMM and bring it up here." Marlon took Neusy's key, entered the trailer, moved his bag of weed to another box that never seems to be loaded in each night, and brought the MMM into the club. Everyone stopped what they were doing. Neusy stopped setting up the merch, the band stopped tuning their instruments, Triple T stopped adjusting his toupee, Hocker stopped chewing, and the agents stopped playing Virtual Police Dept on their phones. They all watched Marlon walk the box up to the stage.

"Yah, now you will witness something. Marlon, take that TTG und set it up behind the drums. Put some drumsticks in the hands. Tommy, you cannot play tonight; it is no good. You must rest. Hocker, you take a long cord und you connect it up here next to me." The boys did what they were told. No one else moved and just watched what was going on. The agents had no idea what that machine was and now were up front trying to get a better look.

When it was all set up, the Doctor said, "Yah, you see, most people's puny, little brains cannot do what I will be doing. I always play each part of the song in my mind. I will be playing the drums in my head; Trenton designed this with me to make it better. Now, I need quiet!"

They all watched the Doctor, who was standing in front of the drums, studying the kit and notating the spacing of the drums and cymbals. He made a couple of adjustments to the positioning of the kit and then said, "Okie dokie, now we will try it again."

The Doctor started playing the first chords of "Freeze the Sea." On the fifth chord, he leaned into the TRM, and the machine came to life. The intro was magnificent. The band played along and the crew stood there on stage with the agents in front, all with shocked expressions to what they were witnessing. If it weren't for the stupid pillar, they could see it better. But it sounded amazing. The Doctor was in the zone and blazed through the song on the guitar. He played the high notes in such an arrangement that it created the perfect resonant frequency with the drums that caused the building to sway with the music. The security guards ran out into the street, thinking it was an earthquake.

"Whooowww!" Marlon said. "That is insane!"

When the song ended, the band just stood and looked at each other for a while. The agents were applauding. Neusy looked at Jeb, as they so often do, without saying a word. They had developed a way of relaying thoughts without words. Hocker was just nodding his head on the side of the stage in agreement with what he just witnessed. The Doctor then went right into the rehearsal for the song "The Day the Doctor Visited." He blew through that song with ease. MMM was going in full mode with the TTG playing fills that seemed impossible to play. After rehearsing the song just once, the Doctor took off the Universe Guitar and said, "Yah, OK, that will work for the show tonight," and walked out of the club.

No one moved for the next five minutes until the bouncers, who returned after realizing the building was not falling down, said, "Five minutes till doors open. You guys went way over on the soundcheck." The sound engineer started making phone calls, telling his friends that they had to come down tonight and see this.

The El Diablo proudly welcomed Portland's own Harold and David, with their *Bagging with the Eagles* show. Harold and David had been visible in the Portland music scene for the last ten years. David, a singer-songwriter at thirty-seven years old, had been playing guitar since he was ten. He had released several CDs locally and had a decent and loyal following. Five years ago, Harold, the self-proclaimed West Coast premiere bagpipe player, was on the same bill as David. Harold, at twenty-nine years old, had mastered the bagpipes. After the evening and many drinks, they decided they would try and work together. Just like that, three weeks later, they played their first gig, and that's when the *Bagging With* series began.

Their first show brought in each of their local following, and with the club heavily advertising these two musicians, drew a large crowd. At first, they were not sure what they were watching. But once David, with his golden voice, started singing, it was pure magic. They played two hours of music from the band Bread. *Bagging with Bread* was the show. Then the next year, *Bagging with Billie Joel* was also a hit. They continued with *Bagging with the Allman Brothers* that showcased the pair's skills at the improvised jam. They would change licks, first David on his guitar, and then effortlessly into the bagpipe talent of Harold. The audiences loved it, and the reviews were off the charts. It was an idea that worked. People came out to see them. David, with his shoulder-length blonde hair, along with his blonde beard and blue eyes, was eye candy for the ladies. The women came out for him, and he made the most of this. It would not be uncommon for him to walk into a venue with one woman and leave with another. Harold, just the opposite, had black hair cropped short with eyes no one could see because he was constantly squinting. He would play the gig and then get drunk. No one wanted to talk with him. After all, he was just the bagpipe player. He drank every night and would get angry at his mother for the bagpipe lessons when he was eight years old when he wanted a guitar.

After two years of *Bagging with the Allman Brothers*, they felt the need for change. *Bagging with the Beatles* was their most critically acclaimed show. They were guaranteed to sell tickets and people started referring to them as the Fabulous Duo. They recorded their performance, and the CD reached number seven in Portland. On average, they were drawing twice what the Doctor would. They started getting requests to play in other cities. They were touring up and down the West Coast and up to Vancouver. So, when the El Diablo booked the Doctor, they knew adding David and Harold with their *Bagging with the Eagles* show would assure them of a great crowd.

David and Harold set up their merchandise table full of T-shirts, CDs, and now even a DVD, next to Marlon and Jeb. They had patches and posters and mini bagpipe key chains. Jeb looked around the room and at least half the people were wearing some form of *Bagging With* T-shirt. This was very strange. Hocker, standing on stage, eyed the crowd and then the stage. One acoustic guitar on a stand and a set of bagpipes on what he had never seen: a bagpipe stand. Both were sitting there just waiting to be played.

Neusy walked over to the merch girl from *Bagging With*. She was dressed in a *Bagging With* T-shirt and a mini skirt, with eyelashes so long that when she blinked, she brushed her bangs to the side. Her makeup was so thick that Neusy wondered what her face looked like. "Sooo…these guys draw pretty well. This should be interesting. How long have you been touring with these guys?"

She replied, "I met David last night; he played by himself at a coffee shop near my house. This morning, when we woke, he asked me if I could sell the T-shirts for him. I said yes, of course."

OK, thought Neusy. He looked over at Jeb, who instructed Marlon on how to get the fans to buy them beers. Marlon was listening intently, as he was all for the free beers.

Hocker walked over. "I fucking hate bagpipes. I think I may wait this one out on the bus. Do you see the fucking agents over there in the first row? Imbeciles, That fucking Crow sleeping up top keeps snoring all night. This tour is making me drink more than I normally do."

The lights went out just as two fans were handing Marlon and Jeb beers. Hocker wanted a beer and bought two, one for himself, and he gave one to Neusy.

A lone spotlight highlighted David as the crowd roared. He picked up his guitar. Then he pointed to his right, and Harold walked out on stage with a second spotlight on him. The crowd gave a less enthusiastic cheer. David started playing "Peaceful Easy Feeling." Then Harold played the rhythm on the bagpipes. Hocker could not look away. He liked it. Then, "Desperado" followed by "Witchy Woman."

Jeb and Marlon were each handed another beer by a person they just met.

From the stage, the song ended, and David spoke. "Thank you, Portland! You are amazing. Look at all of you. Thank you for coming out. It is an honor to open for the Doctor. I am a huge fan of his, so this is very special for me." Harold played near-impossible scales on the bagpipe, and then they were playing "Victim of Love." Neusy gave Jeb the eye of approval. A random fan handed Jeb another beer. Neusy wanted in on this and went behind the merch table with Marlon and Jeb.

Hocker, standing in front of the merch booth, had his fist in the air. His view was partially obstructed by Crow, who was now up on Sparrow's shoulders screaming with his fists in the air. The song ended, and Hocker bought a *Bagging With* T-shirt. Another half hour until the last song, "Tequila Sunrise." After, David said, "Thank you! We have to go; the Doctor will be out soon." The crowd was cheering and screaming. Hocker bought another shirt. The lights came on, and the screaming did not stop.

Somebody brought three beers over to the merch table. Neusy and Jeb clinked their bottles together, and the lights went back off. The only things illuminated on the stage were the guitar and the bagpipes. This made the crowd go insane. There was five minutes of people screaming in the dark room. Hocker bought a key chain from the girl in the mini skirt and smiled over at Jeb.

Then it happened. David and Harold walked on stage. David managed to calm the crowd down when he started to play the first few notes of "Hotel California." The El Diablo was rocking. Hocker chugged his beer and walked to the front near the stage. *This is incredible, how is this possible*, he was thinking. He put on one of his *Bagging With* shirts over the white T-shirt he was wearing. Then

David and Harold were jamming. People were screaming. David, up front by the crowd, his guitar over the first row as he was playing. Harold behind him, jumping up and down. Now Harold was taking the lead. Now David was jamming. Harold, then David, they traded leads for five minutes as the crowd was getting more intense. Harold, fueled by the crowd's noise, was moving back and forth, his head up and down. David, still up front. Harold was running back and forth, his head bobbing. Harold was about to take the lead—BAM, he crashed into the pillar, and David immediately ended the song as if on cue. The crowd roared, and the lights came on. Hocker went up on stage and helped one of the bouncers carry Harold off the stage.

The members of the band were all on the bus with the Doctor and missed the excitement. Jeb went out to get them and let them know it was time. The Doctor asked, "How is the crowd in there?"

"Interesting."

As they walked in the stage door, the band saw that the room was full. The Doctor said, "Yah! That is interesting." Then as he looked upon the stage, he added, "Und this is also interesting." Jeb looked at the MMM with the added toupee and a *Bagging With* T-shirt that Hocker put on the unit. The Doctor put on what he believed was the best show on the tour, playing the drums with his mind and guitar with his fingers. He was in control, and no one could envision the songs as he could. The audience thinned out as about half the *Bagging With* crowd left mid-way through the Doctor's set. No one much noticed that there was a mechanical drummer behind the kit. The show ended without another casualty of the pillar.

The Doctor was satisfied with the performance and needed to talk with Trenton Towers regarding tweaking the MMM and making it compatible with all the instruments. He gave some serious thought about touring without a band using these devices, all controlled by his mind. There will never be mistakes, all instruments in sync, and no rehearsing needed. He worked his way to the merch table and the meet and greet began as Hocker and Neusy started to break down the stage.

Neusy asked Hocker, "Where did you get the wig?"

"Triple has several. He doesn't want anyone to know this, but when I was sharing a room with him, I noticed in his suitcase there is a smaller case that has a half dozen wigs, all different lengths. He switches them up, making it look like his hair is growing, then cut shorter again."

"Hmm," said Neusy. "I never noticed."

They finished breaking down the stage, and after the meet and greet was over, Marlon broke down the merch table as Jeb settled up with the venue and got paid. They were loading out just as Cal arrived from his hotel and started up the bus. The band was milling about talking with fans left over until management chased them out.

Neusy, with his key in hand, was first to the trailer. He said to Jeb, who was behind him, "Did you remove the locks?"

"No, I did not. I do not know who is doing this, but these jokes are beginning to piss me off. Whoever they think they are, they are not funny. We will be using the new locks tonight."

Neusy pulled open the door to the dark trailer, flipped on the light switch, and there, hanging by one of the locks from the top of the trailer, was David from *Bagging With*. The lock had been pushed through both of his eye sockets.

The agents walked out to this scene, each carrying a *Bagging With* T-shirt. Sparrow said, "Shit… Everyone off of there. This trailer is now a crime scene, and no one goes anywhere till we are finished."

Cal, seeing the commotion in his side mirror, walked around back. "Boys, looks like we will not make it to Seattle in the morning as planned."

While they waited for CSI to arrive, the agents took statements. Once again, nothing. "This guy is a ghost," said Crow after an exhausting six hours of investigation. "Let them get going so they can make the next gig on time. Call in and get us flights up to Seattle. I want to poke around and ask the staff when they arrive later if they saw anything. These murders are making us look bad."

Cal walked up to Agent Sparrow. "Agent, you all left this on stage on the bass drum in San Diego. It is no one's hair that is part of the tour. I put it in this bag, careful not to touch it."

Sparrow and Crow looked at the unusual, kinked hair in the bag. Crow said, "We need to get this to the lab ASAP. Our first lead, maybe we can get our credit card limit increased."

Chapter 27

At 9:00 a.m., the agents cleared the bus to leave. Scaggz watched the action from atop the overpass. Jeb was standing on the step of the bus talking with Crow. "Jeb, you guys are cleared to leave; you should make it up there in time for your load-in. You have my number; call me if anything is not right."

"OK, you got it. We will do a better job of watching what is happening. I mean, we usually are pretty good at this. Neusy and Hocker are always watching the stage."

"OK, good, we will be up there by the time the doors are open," said Crow before he walked away.

Cal, who had been listening to the conversation, waited for Jeb to get back to his seat and yelled out, "Bro, I have been ready to go for hours, I drank three energy drinks and my coffee cup has not been empty since I arrived seven hours ago. Are we a bus?"

"Yes, we are a bus," said Jeb, and he got back to working the books from the show the night before. The next stop was Seattle. With the gas tank full, they would not have to stop for gas and should make the trip in three hours.

"HANG ON GUYS, WHOOOO! We are rolling!" shouted Cal. He started blasting his rock music very loud; he was trying to sing along, but he was terrible. Most of the guys were in the lounge except for the Doctor, Torsten, and Hocker, who had all went to sleep. Cal made it onto Interstate 5 North.

Triple T stood up; it was once again nap time. "Does he always have to shout like that?" he said.

"That's Cal Crabs, my friend," replied Neusy.

"I am feeling much better; I will have no problem tonight," continued Triple T. "That was difficult yesterday, but I'm much better now."

Neusy looked around and then mimicked the Doctor. "Yah, we will see when you are at soundcheck." Triple T laughed and disappeared into the bunks. After about an hour, almost everyone had to take care of their business. They would have to stop at the next truck stop. Cal pulled up the Truckers app on his cell phone and, with GPS, it showed there was one five miles ahead. When they arrived, anyone that was awake exited the bus and made their way to the restroom. Heinz finished last and came out and joined the rest sitting on a picnic bench, waiting.

"OK, are we all good now?" said Jeb.

"Yah, yah!" said Nathan.

"Alles gut!" said Heinz.

"I'm good," said Neusy.

"Alright, let's go!"

They got on the bus and proceeded to the on-ramp. Cal, being over-caffeinated, crossed over the freeway and entered the south on-ramp. He got spacey sometimes and was one of the reasons he had to give up smoking dope. After about twenty minutes, Jeb noticed a sign that said, Portland thirty-five miles. He thought, *Portland?*

"Hey, Cal, you're going the wrong way!"

Cal was blasting the stereo and couldn't hear. Jeb walked over to him and yelled, "Dude, you're going south, not north! You have to turn around!"

"Oh shit!" He exited at the next exit and got back on Interstate 5 North again. After thirty minutes, they had passed the truck stop that they were just at. *What a fucking waste of time*, thought Jeb as they continued north. About thirty minutes later, Jeb saw Marlon's cell phone on the table. He knew Marlon would take it to listen to tunes while he rested. He peeked behind the curtain to Marlon's bunk, but he wasn't there. Then it hit him, they left him behind at the truck stop. Jeb hurriedly walked over to Cal again.

"Hey, Cal, we have to go back to the truck stop!"

"What the fuck for?"

"We left Marlon behind!"

"What??"

"Left him in the shitter!"

Cal exited the freeway again and entered the southbound ramp back to the truck stop. Thirty-five minutes later, they arrived back at the truck stop. They could see Marlon standing by the picnic benches, very unhappy. Cal pulled the bus parallel to the curb and opened the door for him.

"Dudes! Why did you leave me? Was this a joke? It wasn't very funny!" cried Marlon.

"No, man, we just forgot you were taking a shit," replied Jeb. "Rule number one when leaving the bus: always take your phone."

"Man, I couldn't even call you! I left my phone on the bus… I thought I'd be stuck here forever!" cried Marlon.

"Exactly. Calm down! Take a few hits of weed and calm down," said Jeb.

After smoking a few hits of a joint, he got back on the bus. Cal entered the correct on-ramp going north to Seattle. Marlon sat at the table with Nathan, Jeb, Neusy, and Triple T, who had just woken up and sat at the table in his tight whites. Marlon kept whining; Jeb could not concentrate on his computer. "Shut the fuck up already. Make sure you always take your phone and you will never have a problem."

About halfway to Seattle, they hit stop-and-go traffic. "Hey, Jeb! You back there?" Cal called out.

"Yeah, Crabs, what do you want?"

"Come up here, dude, and I'll tell ya."

Jeb walked up front. "What is it?"

"Dude, I got take a piss; I want you to drive the bus while I use the head."

"What? I can't drive a bus."

"Sure you can; there's nothing to it."

"Dude, I don't know how to drive a bus."

"See here, these are how to use the air brakes. Press on this, it stops and goes, no problems. Over here is the gear shift. Use your mirrors and keep the trailer between the lines, OK? Alright, I'll get up, and you sit down," said Cal.

"I don't know about this!" said Jeb as he reluctantly sat in the barber's chair.

Cal ran past the lounge to the restroom. As he passed the guys in the lounge, he just said, "Hey, guys, I got to piss."

"What?" shouted Marlon. "Who is driving?" He went up to investigate. "Dude, I always wanted to drive a bus like this."

"Not happening," said Jeb, who was nervously looking into all the mirrors, handling the bus as best he could. The bus was huge, almost as wide as the lane, and he was towing the equipment trailer. If he were to brake, the trailer could sway and hit another vehicle. He managed to keep everything in order, and Cal returned to take over driving again.

Marlon, Neusy, Triple T, and Nathan played a poker game while Jeb went back to more business on his laptop. They were playing for almonds instead of money. They were about forty-five minutes from Seattle and cruising at about seventy mph.

Cal yelled back at Jeb, "Acorns! You back there?"

"What do you want now?" said Jeb.

"Come up here!"

Jeb stopped what he was doing on his laptop and went up to Cal once again.

"What do you want? I'm busy!"

"Dude, I have to piss again!"

"You just pissed less than an hour ago."

"Sorry man, I told you I had a lot, I mean a lot, of coffee today. Anyway, I need you to drive again."

"What? We're going seventy miles an hour! Why don't you pull over to pee? I can't drive this thing going seventy!"

"No, man! We can't stop. We'll be late for the load-in. Come, let's do it now!"

Cal stood up and pushed Jeb hard down into the barber's seat.

"Just hold the wheel steady and keep the accelerator down. Keep the speed at seventy. Always check those side mirrors and make sure the rear wheels are within the lines," said Cal.

"Fuck me, fuck me! Hurry up, asshole!" cried Jeb.

Cal walked past the guys playing poker; they looked at him walking down the hall. They could feel the bus was going fast. Triple T looked at the others and said, "Who the fuck is driving the bus now? I have never seen anything like this. I have toured for thirty-five years. This is fucked!"

Jeb did his best, and the bus stayed within the lines. Cal returned up front. Jeb started getting up, but Cal pushed him back down. "Not yet, I need to stretch." Cal began to stretch next to Jeb; he started doing aerobics and squatting, then jumping jacks, then both in one motion. Jeb was getting nervous and having a minor panic attack.

"OK, Crabs, get back in here; I am freaking out. Fifteen minutes is too long."

"OK, OK." They traded spots. Jeb went back to his table.

"Do you plan on doing that all tour?" asked Triple T.

"Shit, I hope not. It's a good thing the agents are not on board."

When they reached the Seattle city limits, everyone was excited. Cal made it with an hour and a half to spare. It was an important city in many ways. Jimi Hendrix, Bruce Lee, Soundgarden, Alice in Chains, Nirvana, and Pearl Jam were all part of its history. The Doctor was particularly interested in visiting Bruce Lee's grave, as he was also a martial arts practitioner and an avid fan. But even more so, he needed to see Jimi Hendrix's grave. He wanted to channel some of Jimi's energy for the evening by laying hands on his tombstone.

Another thing that Seattle is famous for is coffee, and Cal knew of a place. "Zeek's Coffee Palace is the next stop, boys," said Cal as he exited the interstate.

"Yeah, let's get some of that famous Seattle Joe," said Neusy.

"Und after the coffee, I must find the cemeteries where Bruce Lee und Jimi Hendrix are."

"Coffee time, guys!" Cal said as he parked his bus in the street next to the two-story parking structure that is Zeek's parking lot. "This is the Palace, all in-house roasting. And Zeek, he did it right. His search has been a lifetime adventure. He found the best coffee bean farms in Hawaii, Costa Rica, Colombia, and Kenya. He bought them all. Zeek is a buddy of mine from way back. His Dad put him through school and wanted him to be a lawyer, just like himself. He graduated law school, then passed the bar and worked for his dad for five years. He was always into the coffee. I mean, not just liking a great cup of coffee, he was obsessed. His house… He has several coffee makers of all kinds in every room. He is totally obsessed."

Marlon was listening intensely. "I could really go for a cup of coffee, Cal."

"Son, Zeek does not make a cup of coffee. He has perfected the art of the perfect pour. He won some crazy class action coffee suit many years ago and made millions. Left his dad's law firm and opened Zeek's. He now owns these coffee plantations around the world and brings beans here to Seattle and roasts them. Aaahh, gentlemen, follow me."

As soon as Cal opened the door, the smell of coffee filled the bus; even the guys in their bunks got up and followed Cal. Zeek's was not your average coffee shop. It was a three-story brick building that roasted four tons of coffee a day. The air all down the street smelled delicious. The boys were all sniffing the air as they walked.

They entered Zeek's, and from when they first walked in, they were in coffee heaven. To the right was a store that occupied half of the ground floor. The other half was the largest coffee house any of them had ever seen. The counter was forty yards long with twenty coffee serving stations, with three baristas operating from each station.

"Yah, in America, everything is much bigger, eh?" said the Doctor.

"Well, this is not a large coffee shop. This place is where the art is perfected. Zeek sends all of his baristas to Italy for a month to learn the barista's proper art. That word barista is thrown around so much here in the States. Everyone who works at every coffee shop seems to be called that."

"Yes, this is true," said Jeb.

Marlon added, "My wife is a barista for the local shop by my house. She makes a good cup of coffee, but at home, never will make me a cup."

"It's her job, idiot," said Hocker. "But it's coffee, just put it in the maker and turn it on."

Cal continued, "So, his employees that serve the coffee get this insane training in Italy, and when they return, he then presents them with their official certificate and name badge. The certificates are all framed and hung on the wall over there. Zeek despises the title barista. His employees here in the coffee shop are called Zeekristas. Look at their badges, they say *crowned Zeekrista* on them and the date they earned their certificate. He then trains them here for another month."

They all got in one of the twenty lines and looked around the room of what had to be over a hundred tables with couches in the lounge area. The place was loud. People talking, music playing, and names being called out with station numbers to pick up their coffee. Zeek walked out when he saw Cal and said, "Cal, you're in town; why didn't you call me? Good to see you, buddy!"

The two hugged, and Cal responded, "It has been a crazy tour so far, and we just got underway. I want to introduce to you the Doctor of Dynamics, Jurgen Weislangwolf, and his band and crew."

"Doctor, very nice to meet you. I am a huge fan… Huge. Please, guys, follow me. I have my best Zeekristas in the private tasting room next door. Come with me."

"Yah, I have lots of fans everywhere. We will follow you, but make it quick. I need to visit the Hendrix grave prior to the show. Jeb, you put Zeek on the guest list tonight, yah?"

Jeb looked at his phone. Now an hour and ten minutes until they were scheduled to load-in. He said, "OK, Zeek, you will have a pair of tickets at the gig later, but we really must hurry."

Zeek called another team of three away from the main counter and they all walked into the tasting room. The door opened, and they had to part a red curtain to enter. The room was a smaller version of the room that they were just in with four stations. The entire room was covered in tapestry and dimly lit with couches and recliners next to low coffee tables. They followed Zeek.

Zeek said to his employees, "Take care of these boys; they are my guests. Give them whatever they want."

They all gave their orders. Everything was served in gold cups and mugs. Even their takeaway cups were golden. Jeb said, "Everything to go, make it quick, guys, and if you need to go, do it here. We are challenged now for time since the Doctor wants to see those graves. We will not make any more stops. So, get it all out here."

One by one, their orders were ready. First, the Doctor with his quadruple espresso, then the Austrians who also ordered the same, except for Torsten, who wished for a tea and received a proprietary green tea from one of Zeek's plantations. Hocker asked for a large Caffè Americano, then decided to have two. Jeb and Neusy each received a cappuccino with their names spelled in the foam. Marlon watched all this and ordered a cappuccino and a quadruple espresso. He took pictures of his name in the foam as

Cal was handed his oversized coffee cup filled to the brim and three large coffees in a holder.

Triple T asked, "Don't you just have regular coffee?" The server informed him that Zeek's coffee is anything but regular coffee, but if you want a coffee with milk and sugar, then the Americano is what you want. Triple T ordered this.

Heinz, Marlon, and Torsten each needed to use the restroom. Jeb nervously looked at the time. Great, fifty-five minutes till load-in. They all said goodbye to Zeek and headed for the bus. Each was emitting a moaning sound as they sipped their coffee.

"MMM," said Hocker. "This shit is amazing!"

"Aaahh! That is good coffee," said the Doctor.

"OOOOHHHHH," moaned Marlon.

"Best coffee by far on the planet," assured Cal.

Neusy and Jeb gave each other the eye of approval. "Yeah, this is very good." The Austrians all agreed. Jeb looked around the room as they exited and realized why it was so loud. It wasn't the music or the names being called, there wasn't much talking going on; it was all of the patrons sipping their coffee, moaning, sighing, screeching, and crying at the taste. Jeb nodded at the room. Neusy shook his head to the right and then up in agreement.

Jeb was concerned about being late for the load-in and hoped that the Doctor would not waste too much time going to these cemeteries. "Hey, Jurgen, I hope you don't spend too much time with this stuff; we can't be late today with the load-in."

"Achhh, Jeb. You don't understand! I need to lay my hands on the tombstones of my idols und absorb the energy for tonight's performance, yah?"

Cal had already located the two cemeteries and was in route to the first one, which was on the opposite side of Seattle from the other one. Bruce Lee's gravesite was first, as it was closer, and then to Renton to Jimi Hendrix's gravesite.

Going to both places did waste about two hours, just as Jeb had anticipated. He called the Schooner Club and spoke to the manager. He received an earful, as this upset the timing of the entire evening. Jeb agreed on keeping the soundcheck short, which was a daily occurrence anyway. The rest of the band didn't seem to mind as everyone was pretty like-minded on visiting both gravesites. They all admired the greatest martial artist and the greatest guitarist of all time.

They took photos at Jimi Hendrix's site with the Doctor asking for ten minutes alone while the rest of the guys waited on the bus. The Doctor returned to the bus almost floating and proclaimed, "Yah, Jimi und I, we came up with this agreement. I felt the channeling of his inner spirit. This will be good!"

Jeb said, "Cal, hit it; we are now a bus. Remember the time."

"Yah, Jeb, you always ruin the moment."

"Whoohoo, is that a challenge? We are rolling. Hang on; this may get a little rough." The bus rolled out on the highway, almost hitting two parked cars and a dog crossing the street.

"Ach," said the Doctor, and he walked to his suite. About thirty minutes later, they were at Bruce Lee's gravesite.

Once again, they all took pictures, and after ten minutes, Jeb announced, "OK, we need to leave, let's go, guys, bus is leaving."

"Yah, once again, you ruin the mood."

"You are paying me to do a job; I am doing it. It's time to go, or no soundcheck and no checking the equipment."

They all returned to the bus, and the Doctor said, "Well, you can't threaten me with no soundcheck. I hate those, und better there is none."

Chapter 28

The agents vigorously interviewed all the people that were working at both sides of the club. Once again, nothing other than a dead, mutilated body. They were starting to be spread around everywhere.

They barely made their flight up to Seattle. They exited the airport and found a taxi to take to the Schooner Club. Crow said, "This is problematic; how can no one see this guy? What was that guy's name that used to work for the Doctor?"

Sparrow checked his notes. "Scaggz is what they called him."

"We should get a picture of him. We have nothing else to go on. At least it is something we can show to the office."

They arrived at the Schooner, but no bus. Sparrow checked his watch; they were running late again. At 4:00 p.m., Cal found the venue and parked around the corner, where Jeb said was reserved for them. Just as promised, the parking meters were covered with signs that said reserved.

Cal said, "Well, that was interesting. I will be around for an hour, then go to the hotel."

Jeb handed Cal the info for the hotel and said, "One room. There are showers in the club to use, so just go to your room, Crabs."

Jeb, Neusy, and Hocker exited the bus and walked toward the front door of the venue. The Schooner Club's tall two-story exterior looked like the front of a pirate ship. The bow extended three feet into the sidewalk, leaving only about two feet to the curb. There was a huge anchor mounted just above the entrance. The manager, Barnacle Bill, who looked like a crusty old pirate, greeted them as they walked in the door.

"Harr, maties! A bit late today, so we are not off to a good start."

"We are Jurgen Weislangwolf's crew. We are here to load-in."

"Harr, that'll be fine, mates; the stage door is over here." Barnacle Bill led them toward the side of the venue. The three scanned the venue. It certainly made them feel like they were in the old times, when pirates sailed the seas. Everything was dark, old, musty-smelling, wood décor with some old, tarnished, brass wall sconces here and there. The bar area had many incredible ancient relics, brass telescopes, and some sextants mounted around the alcohol shelf. The center of the building was open to the second story, where a railing and tables, along with ship sails, overlooked the stage. There were wooden statues of pirates all about the venue.

A giant ship's wheel was mounted next to the beer taps, which got the guys' attention. Jeb asked Barnacle Bill if they could get a beer before starting the load-in.

"Not so sure, matey! You are late, and now we are late."

"I promise that you have never seen a crew work like us. We are fast, and the Doctor does not do soundcheck; we will have you right back on schedule."

"OK, matey, one beer!"

"I'll have a Seattle Amber."

"That's not how we do it here, matey!"

"What? Huh?"

Barnacle Bill grabbed one of the eight handles on the ship's wheel and gave it a spin. RRRRRRRRRRRRPPPPPP. The wheel spun around. An arrow lit up with an electric sign just above the center position of the wheel. Each wheel handle was a different color. The green-colored handle pointed towards the arrow, and the electric sign lit up. Goblin Green IPA was written on it. "That's what you'll be having, matey!" Jeb was tripping out; he'd never seen that before. Each person would have whatever the wheel chose for them. Hocker had a Seattle Strongman's Ale, and Neusy got a Pirate's Bloody Pale Ale. How cool is that? What a concept.

They each chugged their beers as if perfectly rehearsed. Their empty glasses hit the bar in perfect timing. "Aahh, matey, I think we will work well together tonight."

The trio plus Marlon rolled everything in just as promised. It was not as easy as the night before. It was about two hundred feet down the sidewalk to the stage door. Jeb set up merch while the other three set up the stage. The agents were now positioning themselves in more of an official stance, one by each of the two doors. Barnacle Bill watched in amazement and spun the wheel three more times. When the boys finished, he gave them each a beer. He then spun it for Marlon after Marlon was sitting at the bar by himself, looking left out. Soundcheck with the band, minus the Doctor, was a quick song; then they were right back on schedule. Jeb walked up to Barnacle Bill and said, "The stage is all yours."

"You are a man of your word, matey!"

The evening's opening act was right on time at 5:30 p.m. and was the venue's house band, the Seattle Scallywags. They all wore pirate attire and sang songs about piracy, fishing, pillaging, and raping. All of the songs were sung in grunge style. The lead singer, Long John Silverstein, had a wooden leg. During the act, he would pull off the long thin part of the bottom of the leg. It was dual purpose: he had it hollowed out with finger holes and a mouthpiece installed. It was somewhere between a flute and a recorder. He called it his third leg, and he blew a mean flute. He would play balancing on his one leg. To release the leg, he developed a device that looks like a belt. However, it had a metal arm with a leather strap that went down the back of his leg. When he pulled the metal lever, the leg disengaged from his real leg and, with the belt, he would pull it in one motion to his mouth. The Seattle Scallywags set up their gear, and the doors opened on time.

The agents started to take more control, wanting all musicians to wait on the bus until showtime and not open the door until Jeb and Sparrow came around to fetch them. Jeb was a little more impressed that their talents seemed more than Blues Brothers look-a-likes.

It was a decent crowd tonight. The Seattle Scallywags had a fair amount of people that liked their music. Most were regulars of the club. "We want the Scallywags! We want the Scallywags!"

The band took the stage. Each person wore a various-colored long coat with wide straps over their shoulders and supported a cutlass on one hip or the other. Three guys wore black pirate hats with skulls and crossbones, and the drummer wore a red-and-blue headscarf with a gold earring on the left ear. The three frontmen each had a parrot sitting on their shoulder, and during musical pauses, the parrots would squawk a note and announce the next song in unison. It was pretty remarkable. Their music was primarily original and inspired by tales of the sea.

"Arrrrgh, good evening, maties!" said Long John Silverstein, the lead singer.

"WHOOOOOOO!"

"YEEEAAAAH!"

BLOW HO! A PIRATE'S LIFE FOR WEEE!
We'll blow you away with our cannons at bay
We'll pillage and rape your girls
We'll make you walk the plank today
And then rob the queen of her pearls
There's nothing like the pirate's life
We do what the fuck we please
We don't really care about taking a wife
We get plenty tang on the seas
Blow ho, blow ho, a pirate's life for we

The audience all knew the words. They pumped their fists and sang along. The parrots rocked back and forth. Long John Silverstein bent down and pulled the lever to remove his wooden leg's lower stem while balancing on one leg. He held the wooden rod with the twelve holes drilled in it up to his mouth and positioned himself in front of the mic. He gave a flute solo that was out of this world. The sound drove the parrots crazy, and they screeched along while the audience cheered him on!

"ARRGH, maties! You liked that one, eh?" He stood still, balancing on one leg. "Well, here's another you might remember!" He started the next song with solo flute, then stopped as the parrots squawked, "I do what I will," and then the electric guitar came in.

The sea is my home and I hate the land
Of the seas, I will sing with me and my band
Don't really care about whom I might kill
I sail on the sea and do what I will
I do what I will
I do what I will

The crowd knew this one as well. Silverstein put his wooden leg back together, and in the middle of the song, danced a pirate's jig, sometimes spinning in a circle on the stem of the wooden leg, like an ice skater's Salchow maneuver.

The band finished their last number, and Long John spoke to the crowd for the last time. "ARRGGGH!!! It's been a great time! We really enjoyed seeing all of you tonight! Now go get some more ale and drink hearty, me hearties."

In thirty minutes, it would be time for the Doctor to hit the stage. Jeb and Sparrow went to the bus to retrieve the band. The Doctor said, "Yes, I will stay here until showtime."

Sparrow said, "No sir, everyone inside now." They all followed. Even the Doctor went along with the program. The band was in the green room discussing the set before they went on. When the time came, the Doctor instructed Marlon to make the announcement, to which he did.

"Good evening, Seattle! Here is the moment that you have all been waiting for. Here he is, the man who needs no introduction but will get one anyway! The Doctor of Dynamics, my best friend and mentor, Jurgen Weislangwolf!"

"WWWAAAAAAAAAAAAHHHHH!!!!!"

"FUCK YEEEEAAAAH!!!"

"GUTEN TAG, SEATTLE!!!! How about some, 'Slap the Virgin?'"

"WWWAAAAAAHHHHHH!"

The guitar riff began; Nathan came in with the verse.

You don't want to share your pie
Do you wait for another guy?
Or save it
Wearing those tight jeans
It really makes me scream
I want it
Slap that virgin. Waaahh
No, no, no, you can't have me
No, no, no, you can't have me
Don't want your semen
Don't want your semen
Don't want your semen
Keep cryiiing!
"WAAAAAAHHHH!"

"IT'S GREAAAAAAT!"

Marlon joined Jeb at the merch table just as a fan brought over a couple of beers. Merch sales were going exceptionally well, which meant that they were getting fresh beers every twenty minutes. Each time a spin of the wheel, one song after another. the Doctor played one of his most intense shows, that later he will credit to his time at the graves. Marlon said, "He is on fire tonight."

"Yeah, he will say that it is the inspiration from his visit to the gravesites. He likes to play up this shit," said Jeb as he was handed another beer.

The agents kept their positions at the two doors while keeping an eye on the stage. The evening progressed with no incidents, which the murders were now referred to.

The show ended, and the Doctor said, "Thank you very much!" He took a bow, and as he walked away with the mic still active, the audience heard, "ACHHH, those birds, they pooped on my amp!"

Chapter 29

The boys said their goodbyes to Seattle right on time. Cal arrived, and they hit the road once more. "We are rolling!" shouted Cal. After two hours, they would reach the Canadian border. Soon they would be in Canada. Most of the boys have never visited Canada. They were expecting a giant national park filled with tall pines, redwoods, fresh air, animals, and tranquility.

Jeb was happy to be going into Canada and hopefully leaving the murders behind. He was bothered by the message written with a white grease pen that the Doctor thought was the bird's doing. Jeb had been thinking of this since he woke, using a white grease pen to write on the amp. Old school stage managers and stage techs would use these to write on the stage and equipment when they needed to mark instructions, such as "Don't touch!" or "Hands off!" and some used to mark positions for volume on amps to dial in quicker on set up. It was a strange device to use to write a message. And the message… What was the message all about? The agents talked it up that someone in the venue was playing a joke. They had the club locked down.

But the message bothered Jeb. It just said ***Deadweight*** with an arrow under it pointing to Triple T. It is true that Triple T is often behind the beat or sometimes in front of it. But it is so slight; no one noticed it other than the band and Jeb, having heard these songs hundreds of times with different bandmates. Was it someone working at the venue that noticed this? Someone having a little fun? Or was it referring to Triple T's actual weight, which could still be someone poking fun at the chubby drummer. But what Jeb could not get out of his mind was that it could be referring to actually lifting him from the bottom bunk to the top. If that was the case, this was not good. Would he be a target?

Sitting in the front lounge by himself, Jeb could not focus on his work. He managed to reconcile the books after the show and was pleased that the merch did well last night, as the tour needed extra cash. Neusy entered the lounge and put on a fresh pot of coffee. "Jeb, you want a refill?"

"Yes, that would be great."

From the front of the bus, Cal said, "When that is done, bro, my cup is getting low. Whooohooo! Canada today, boys."

Neusy waited for the coffee maker to finish, then poured himself a cup and topped off Jeb's mug. He poured the remainder into Cal's obnoxiously large cup. He sat across from Jeb. "That bullshit yesterday with the grease pen was fucked up. I don't want to alarm you, but I think it was a message from whoever is following us."

"You too? I can't stop thinking about it. What is his game? If it's to get into our heads, he has succeeded. I hope Tommy is not in trouble."

"Yes, hopefully just poking some fun at his physical appearance, or a message that, while he is not killing, he is still around."

"Did you tell the agents this?" asked Jeb.

"No, because they would have us up all night again, and we would leave late."

"OK. It would be nice to have them with us now, but they will be flying up to and throughout Canada. I can't chance them on the bus up there, with them not actually being part of the tour and not on our papers."

"It was the right call to keep them off the bus up there. Going across the border would have taken forever. We will have to always keep an eye on Tommy moving forward."

Jeb agreed, and the two sat and drank their coffee in silence until Cal informed them, "We are twenty minutes from the border. Go wake everyone up." Jeb went into the back and woke up all the guys.

He then knocked on the door to the rear lounge. The Doctor claimed this as his area long ago, so the rest of the guys had to cram into the one lounge up front. The band would jokingly call it the ICU, or Intensive Care Unit. Of course, this room was the most luxurious. It had an actual queen mattress and lovely wood paneling with brass wall lamps attached on both sides of the bed. A wooden nightstand stood on each side of the bed, and there was a small closet that he could hang some of his wardrobe. All over the bed, he had a collection of stuffed animals. There was a white tiger, a spotted orange giraffe, a fuzzy grey koala bear, a black-and-white emu with long legs, a green rubber crocodile, and a brown platypus. The platypus was his favorite. It was like God's mistake, a strange animal with a strange duck-billed mouth that had a certain grin about it. The ICU had a long window on each side of the room, which provided him private viewing of the beautiful landscapes he would be able to see along the road.

"Time to get up; we are almost at the border," said Jeb.

"Why?"

"We need to be ready; it will speed up the border crossing. Come up front."

"Yah, OK."

The traffic began to slow down. They were fifteen minutes from the border inspection. Jeb had warned Marlon to smoke up what he had and get rid of the rest before they got to the border. Marlon had other plans. He was not in favor of losing the weed. It is legal in both Washington and Canada, so what's the problem? He thought it better to hide his weed. But where? Jeb's computer bag, they won't look in there. And that is what he did.

Cal drove the bus to the designated parking as instructed by the Canadian border agent. The mood on the bus going through the border check was one of uncertainty. Half the guys were still trying to wake up and in a semi daze, while the others just nervously waited their turn. It could be quick or drawn out going through the border. Unfortunately, this would not be quick.

Cal opened the door, and the border agent stepped on. He said, "Who is the tour manager?"

Jeb stood up as Marlon said, "Can I go use the bathroom?"

The border agent said, "I am only talking to the tour manager. Do you have everyone's passports? We received your documents this morning." Jeb handed him the stack of passports. One by one, he looked through them and took roll call. When all were accounted for, he turned and said, "I will be right back; no one leaves the bus."

They waited twenty minutes and were instructed to exit the bus and stay in the waiting area inside the building. They walked single file into the building, where another agent showed them the waiting area. The room was about thirty feet by fifteen feet, with chairs lined up against the long wall opposite windows where they could look out at the bus. They watched as the border agents spent ten minutes inside the bus, and then watched as they opened the lower compartments under the bus where the luggage was stored. One by one, the border agents removed the suitcases and threw them on the sidewalk.

They watched the border agents try to open the locked trailer. They could not and came inside and asked Cal for the key. "I don't have the key. You will have to ask the tour manager."

"Who is the tour manager?" the border agent said authoritatively.

Jeb stepped forward. "I am, what's up?"

"We need you to open the trailer." Jeb followed the two men back out to the bus and the trailer, where he unlocked the two padlocks and then opened the doors. The border agents climbed up and over the cases loaded in the trailer, their flashlights out, opening boxes. One agent found the CDs and the other the T-shirts. They each brought out a sample and showed Jeb. "What is this? Why did you not declare that you have this merchandise?"

"You never asked me if we had merchandise. How am I supposed to know?"

"You need to declare everything that you have to sell. Now we have to go in and fill out the forms. Then you will pay the tax on all of it. When you return to the States, you can fill out additional forms upon exiting as to what was sold, then get a refund check mailed to you for the tax on the unsold units."

Jeb followed them inside to another border agent behind a counter. She handed him a form that asked the name of the tour and tour manager, address, and phone contact, and then asked the quantity of everything available to sell. Jeb read through it and completed the form as instructed, leaving out a few items not found, such as the DVDs and key chains. The border agent looked at the form and asked Jeb, "Where were the shirts manufactured?"

"How do I know where? They were printed in the US by our merchandise company."

"No, we need to know what country they were manufactured. That determines the tax you will pay."

Jeb said, "Great." He walked to the bus past the waiting room with all eyes on him. Neusy gave him the what's-up eyes, Jeb returned his this-is-bullshit look, and Neusy nodded in agreement. Jeb climbed into the open trailer and found the shirt the agent pulled sitting on the side. He read the label and brought the shirt inside, showed the border agent handling the taxes. "El Salvador," he said.

She punched that info into the computer and generated an invoice. Jeb looked at it and was surprised that it was only 392 Canadian dollars. Just enough for Canada to profit, but not enough to make the extra stop on both sides of the border while returning to the US. *Very smart*, he thought. With all the tours that zigzag across the border, it generates a nice extra income. He paid it with US dollars and was instructed to go back to the waiting area.

Neusy sighed when Jeb entered the room, and Jeb nodded. Yes, this sucks. An hour here already. Another twenty minutes, and the first agent returned to the room. He said, "Driver, I need you to drive the bus around the back; I will ride with you. First, the rest of you get your suitcases off the sidewalk and put them back on the bus, then return here and wait." They did what they were told and returned to the waiting area.

Another border agent that they had not yet seen walked into the room. "Tommy Thompson and Morton Flemming, please follow me."

Jeb responded, "We don't have a Morton; I think you got that wrong."

Hocker walked past Jeb and said, "That's me." The guys chuckled as they had no idea. They were each put into a room, and returned a half hour later.

The guys anxiously wanted to know what the heck just happened, as now they are two hours into the border crossing. Triple T explained that, while on another tour, he had drugs he did not declare—prescribed medications for his high blood pressure. "Bullshit," he said. "Now I am a person of interest every time that I come across the border. They asked if I had medication with me.

I told them I do, and I had to sign a form. You better all declare what you have, or we will be stuck here longer."

Marlon started to sweat and nervously moved about the room.

Hocker said, "I had an incident about five years ago driving across the border. I had beers and whiskey in my trunk, which he said was not that big of a deal, but the nine-inch knife under my seat now and always will flag me coming across the border as well. But they cleared me."

Another forty minutes later, Cal came back with yet another border agent. He had a strange look on his face. This new agent said, "Mr. Acorns, come with me." Jeb followed, and when he arrived in the small interrogation room, he saw his computer case on the table with a small bag of weed next to it and a little larger bag of weed next to that. "Have a seat."

"Wow, what is that? I did not bring either of those bags with me."

"Well, this is your computer case, right? It has your name on it." Jeb nodded. "The other was found by our dog in the back of the trailer in a box of what looked like extra cables. The box was a mess."

"Shit, now what? Am I arrested? I need to be able to complete this tour; they won't be able to continue without me."

"Relax, Mr. Acorns, you are lucky. It is a minimal amount of pot. You will have to sign a form, and we will take your picture. But you are fortunate you are coming into Canada through Washington, where it is legal on both sides of the border. Coming across here is just like taking alcohol and cigarettes across the border. We confiscate it. It's a little more severe, as it is a more controlled substance, but you are lucky you are not crossing elsewhere. You can take your case and return to the waiting room. I will call you when we are ready to take your picture and sign the form that says you were responsible for bringing this into Canada."

Jeb returned to the room and found Marlon outside, pacing. Neusy said, "Shit, bro, we thought you were going to jail when Cal told us about the weed."

"No, I got lucky, but that asshole outside put his weed into my case." Jeb nodded towards Marlon, who looked like he was crying. Neusy gave a double nod, one towards Marlon and the other looking Jeb right in the eyes.

Neusy informed the guys, "Jeb wants Marlon to sweat it out a little before he is let off the hook."

Jeb was called to a different counter that he was at earlier. They took his picture, and he signed the form. He emerged, shaking his head, and was back waiting in the waiting room after fifteen minutes. Jeb found Marlon still outside, now sitting on the curb with his face between his hands, sobbing, thinking Jeb had been arrested. Jeb said, "I am good; they said nothing would happen. I wasn't even flagged for next time." Marlon apologized four times and promised never to do that again.

After another thirty-five minutes, the first border agent told Cal, "You guys are cleared. Go get the bus and you guys can go. Enjoy your time in Canada. Tour manager, here are the passports."

After Cal returned with the bus, the band and crew got aboard. "Jeb, that wasted a lot of time. I am glad we left early. Are we a bus?"

Jeb accounted for everyone but Marlon. "No, we are not a bus. Does anyone know where that asshole Marlon is?"

Heinz motioned towards the window. "Here he comes now."

Cal opened the door, and Marlon stepped back inside. He seemed to be doing better. "Jeb, I am so sorry. It's all my fault. I am sorry, man. Please, nothing will happen again, I swear."

"Sit down; I am over it. Nothing happened, just a waste of time."

"I had a nice talk with this hippy guy; he gave me a hand-rolled cigarette, said that he is a big fan of the Doctor, it was cool," said Marlon.

The Doctor said, "Yes, you see, I have a lot of fans here in Canada."

Nobody was paying attention or cared as Marlon continued about the hand-rolled cigarette that was Scaggz' own personal tobacco blend.

Chapter 30

Cal Crabs pulled out of the parking lot and back onto the highway with everyone on the bus. The next stop: Vancouver. Only a little over an hour away, with no road hazards or lousy weather. The scenery changed, and no one except Triple T was in their bunks as they admired the beautiful scenery right outside the bus window. The Austrians enjoyed Canada's topography as it was very similar to their beautiful homeland.

The first stop needed to be a gas station. This would take a little while since it takes time to fill the large gas tank. It would also be the last time to get some snacks, drinks, cigarettes, condoms, or whatever, before getting on the road. Cal pulled into the nearest gas station that provided diesel fuel and stopped the bus near the gas pumps. There was a line of trucks waiting for the pumps. Cal parked in the far lane, which only had one truck waiting and one filling up. Cal opened the door for the boys, including the Doctor, who all got out and went into the convenience shop to get what they needed as he waited for his turn at the pump. After ten minutes, he got out, inserted his credit card into the gas pump, entered his pin, grabbed the pump handle, and inserted it into the gas tank receptacle.

Marlon was the first one in the store. He wanted to make sure he got his snacks, cigarettes, and drinks before anyone else. He trampled on Nathan and Torsten's feet as he raced into the front door.

"Quite rude of him!" said Heinz.

"Yah, sehr unhöflich und grob!" replied Torsten.

"Ein Lackel!" agreed Nathan.

Jeb, Neusy, and Hocker went to the beer section to see what kind of suds they could get.

"What do we have here? Pleasant River Mountain IPA," said Neusy.

"How about this one, Sweaty Goat's Ballsack Ale?" added Jeb.

"Nah, that sounds fucking disgusting!" said Hocker.

"But you like to eat Rocky Mountain oysters, don't you, Hocker?" asked Neusy.

"Yes, it's not gay to eat those. It's a delicacy, you know," replied Hocker.

"But these are just beer names; you're not eating balls," said Jeb.

"I'll pass. I will buy Uncle Earl's Pilsner. I think I like this one. I had an Uncle Earl, so it sounds safe," said Hocker.

"On your mom's side or your dad's side?" asked Neusy.

"Does it fucking matter?"

"I will get a sixer of this Johnny B. Goode IPA. It's 7.8%," said Jeb as Neusy grabbed a six-pack of Herr Roth's Double Hopped Lager, imported from Germany. As the three friends grabbed the beers they wanted, the Austrians looked in the snack aisle.

"I think I want some walnuts und cashews," said the Doctor.

"Yah, me too! Und some beef jerk off!" said Nathan.

"I think that's beef jerky. Und it's made from dead animals. Ahh, look, they have Austrian chocolate! I remember these with the little Mozart pictures when we were in Salzburg! How interesting that they have them here in Canada!" said the Doctor, grabbing a couple of packages. He often ate junk food and bought any food that had the word "ranch" on it. Ranch-flavored potato chips, ranch corn chips, vegan ranch pork rinds made from who knows what, ranch almonds, ranch walnuts, etc. Although he claimed he didn't like sweets as they are bad for one's health, he snuck many chocolate bars into his snack collection.

"I want to leave these things here und get some coffee," the Doctor told the clerk and went over to the coffee bar, smelling the separate pots of brewed coffee. He found one that smelled nice and poured himself a jumbo forty-two-ounce coffee.

Triple T got similar items as Marlon purchased: potato chips, mini frosted donuts, Twinkies, chocolate bars, beef jerky, and a six of Bud. He was the last one out of the store and last to the bus. The others were waiting on him.

They were all crammed into the front lounge, other than the Doctor, who was in the ICU. He didn't like to socialize with the band and crew too often, unless he felt sarcastic and wanted to ridicule someone. He often needed to sleep off the hangover from drinking several bottles of red wine after each show. The others often wondered what he did in his room all of the time. Could he be practicing guitar or writing music? Perhaps he was talking with his stuffed animal collection. They would joke, but no, he was always sleeping.

It was decided, being lunchtime, that they would all eat a nice meal on Jeb. He liked to do this periodically to treat the guys and unwind. Jeb pulled up restaurants on his phone, and he and Neusy decided on a restaurant nearby that had off-the-chart reviews.

The restaurant was called the Fair Game. Cal pulled into the parking lot and everyone exited the bus and made their way into the lobby. A hunter owned it and the place was decorated with full-sized deer, elk, bears, wolves, cougars, and bobcats standing in the middle, with trophy heads mounted on wooden plaques on the walls of raccoons, badgers, squirrels, and more bobcats, pumas, and smaller game. The group was in awe, looking at this collection of animals. It was like a natural history museum, but a restaurant that actually served almost everything you could see on the walls. The Doctor was the last one in the front door, and when he looked around and saw this display of animal murder, he was at a loss for words.

Finally, he spoke. "This is terrible! What kind of place is this? All of these poor, butchered animals, my little friends. What kind of people come to an awful place like this? Maybe I wait on the bus."

"Aaahh. Come on, Jurgen, don't be such a baby!" said Jeb as he nudged him.

The host looked like Daniel Boone, wearing tanned leather clothes with long fringe on the sleeves and a raccoon-skinned hat. "Good day, gentlemen! How many are you?"

"There are ten of us," exclaimed Jeb.

"Right this way." He led them from the main lobby to a large separate area with a long wooden table that could seat twelve. As they walked, the Doctor noticed a large map on the wall. It showed the locations from where each animal was shot and killed. He found that quite interesting, even though he hated the killing of animals.

They were seated at a beautiful twelve-foot-long wooden table made from local trees. The Doctor wanted to be sitting at the end of the table to be farthest away from the meat eaters. Surrounding the room on every wall were many different animal heads mounted on trophy plaques. Each plaque described the animal and where it came from.

A beautiful brunette wearing a tanned leather mini-skirt outfit came to the table. "Howdy! My name is Mirabelle! Here are your menus. I'll come back in a few minutes to take your orders. Can I get you anything to drink?"

"How about three pitchers of the Beaver Dam IPA. That should be enough to start with," said Hocker.

"I will have a glass of red wine, but bring the bottle," said the Doctor.

"You know what they say, red wine goes good with red meat," said Jeb. Neusy looked at Jeb and smiled.

"OK, I'll be right back with that," said Mirabelle.

Jeb thought it would be funny to call out some of the entrees off the menu to get a reaction from the Doctor. "Wow! Look at this, a skunk burger with Limburger cheese, arugula, and bacon. Or how about this French ratatouille with real rats. Or pasta à la squirrel with butternut squash."

"Achhh! Stop it, Acorns! That is nauseating!"

"I'll have a buffalo burger with duck fat fries and a side salad," said Jeb. Nuesy put two fingers in the air, indicating he too would eat what Jeb had just ordered.

"I'll just have a rib-eye steak, medium rare, with a baked potato and green beans," said Hocker.

"I'll have a ranch chicken sandwich with regular fries," said Marlon.

The Austrians were a bit more daring. "I'll have a black pepper rabbit with some duck fries," said Nathan.

"Give me the pulled mountain goat meat with mashed potatoes und gravy," said Torsten.

"I would like the shredded squirrel meat in the mustard sauce with lots of broccoli," said Heinz.

"Achhh! Give me the chef's salad, noooo bacon! Und give me an order of green beans. Please put ranch dressing on the green beans," said the Doctor.

"I'll have a raccoon-loaded baked potato with sour cream and chives and garlic toast," said Cal.

"Thank you, gentlemen! It won't be too long!"

Not twenty minutes had passed before the food was delivered. "Three more pitchers of beer, please!" said Hocker. "Let's switch to Logger's Lost Lager."

"Sure thing!" said Mirabelle.

All during the meal, the Doctor kept feeling that he was being watched. All those animal heads seemed to be watching him, staring at him. He was getting the creeps. "Just look at all of you eating the poor animals' flesh. It is revolting! Cannibals!"

"Actually, cannibals are people that eat people," said Marlon.

"Yah, well, you guys would probably eat people too!"

After the meal and feeling satisfied, the boys were ready to get back on the bus. A few needed to use the restroom as Jeb handled paying the bill. As they exited the building, the Doctor noticed the last animal head on the wall was a beaver. He wondered if he would see a real live one. They all entered the bus. Cal sat in the barber's chair and fired up the engine. Most of the guys feeling stuffed with beer and food retired to their bunks to recline.

The Doctor went to the ICU, mumbling something about beavers as he walked down the hall. Jeb and Neusy sat in the lounge waiting for the last few to return from the restroom and talked about Canada.

"What's it like in Canada?" asked Neusy.

"Well, everyone is kind of liberal and laid back. A lot of hippies and stoners. With pot legal in the entire country, many people smoke pot and get stoned all the time."

"Sounds like a place that Marlon is going to like."

"Man, I had to give that shit up. I couldn't keep things together," said Cal, interjecting into the conversation.

"I really need it, dude, to keep things together," said Marlon as he walked on the bus. "Wow, this is great; next to the restaurant was a dispensary. I was able to re-up. That same hippie guy from the border crossing was in there. He bought me a bag. He had all this to-go food from the restaurant, mostly raccoon, he told me."

"It made me a space case; I still lose my train of thought quite often," said Cal. Heinz and Torsten entered the bus, and with that, Cal took off.

The guys gathered in the lounge as Cal drove along. Marlon, in his stoned and relaxed sense of mind, asked, "Where is Tommy?"

"Oh shit!" said Jeb. "Hey, Cal, we have to stop and turn around!"

"What the fuck for?" was Cal's question.

"We left Tommy behind; he was taking a shit when we left."

"Oh fuck! Not again!" cried Cal as he exited the freeway and made a U-turn and entered the southbound on-ramp. And after twenty minutes, they were back at the restaurant with an angry Triple T standing on the curb, looking up at the bus's open door. He still had that look on his face like he was trying to force one out.

"What in the flying fuck is wrong with you?" cried Triple T.

"Sorry, dude, I guess I spaced," replied Cal.

"Well, don't let it happen again."

Chapter 31

With the workday just about to begin, the day has already been eventful. After a tough time at the border and the nightmare that Marlon caused, the bus pulled into downtown Vancouver. It wasn't as cold as was expected because of the Oceanic climate. Something about Canada awakens the senses of nature and beautiful surroundings. The lads had been anticipating a good time and a good show this evening.

Vancouver was a very important city in many ways. A major shipping port that provided many imported goods to Canada and famous cruise lines offering ocean travel. A multicultural hub, for sure. Many Chinese decorations about the city were still hanging from the Chinese New Year festival that had been active a month before. Vancouver also had other points of interest, like the Museum of Anthropology, the Vancouver Aquarium, and the Vancouver Museum of Art, all of which would be of interest to the Doctor and the rest of the group. None of which they now have time to explore.

The Doctor typically toured North America in the winter and spring to save money on lodging and travel expenses, as opposed to the summer touring season. This had a significant impact on the number of people that would come to this show. Many of Vancouver's famous events didn't happen until later on in the early or late summer.

The Celebration of Light Festival, a four-day event in July, would have provided large attendance to his shows. Or the Khatsahlano Music and Arts Festival later in mid-summer that featured forty plus bands would have been an excellent experience for the Doctor, giving the maximum crowd attendance possible. However, it was winter, and the attendance was expected to be lower than average.

The Doctor noticed a helicopter tour company before they arrived at the venue. He told Cal to stop the bus and he went into the office. Shortly after, he came out of the office and was back on the bus. "So, what's going on? You want to take a helicopter tour of the city? We really don't have the time," said Jeb.

"Nein, nein, I want to have a helicopter deliver me to the show tonight und drop me down to the door by wire."

"And how much does that cost?"

"$1,200."

"$1,200! Are you crazy? What a waste of money!"

"Yah, you have no imagination," said the Doctor, and he walked back to the ICU.

With the Doctor back on the bus, Cal navigated the streets of Vancouver and finally arrived at the venue, a converted theater called Theater One. The theater was an old movie theater with the seats removed and standing room only, except for the booths down the right side and the high top tables in the back. The floor, having been a theater, was inclined and had the reputation of being uncomfortable standing on it for long periods of time.

Cal parked his bus in the alley behind the theater as instructed and waited for the crew to load-in. He then took a taxi to the hotel with the Doctor, who would use the shower room to prepare for the show. Two rooms were all the tour had on this night. Tonight's show would only have twenty-six people in the audience, and that was a lot considering the pre-sale tickets were only at eight. The Doctor didn't mind playing for small crowds, and sometimes played at his best during these lightly attended venues. He wasn't happy about it, being he had scheduled the fantastic helicopter entrance.

The booking agent had promised that this venue would be packed with enthusiastic fans. They traveled all this way to play for twenty-six people. How disappointing. Jeb was feeling about the same, except from the business end of it. Eight pre-sale tickets sold. He didn't feel they would be selling much merchandise.

The Doctor, before he departed, instructed the band to make their way into the venue and get ready for his arrival at 9:00 p.m.

The band soundchecked as usual without the Doctor. It was quick yet productive.

Scaggz woke up in his van around the corner from the bus and could hear all. Still groggy from eating his triple raccoon meal, he missed being inside for the soundcheck; he would have to figure a way to take part at the future shows. As he was rounding the building on foot, a Ford van pulled up next to a parked Honda Accord with two occupants. The driver of the van opened his door and came around to the side window of the Honda. "Guys, we have a problem. I went to Scottie's house to pick him up and all hell was breaking loose. His wife went ballistic when he started to leave. They were yelling, and he said he would have to cancel for the night."

"Now we don't have a guitar player. How the hell are we supposed to play?" said the Honda driver. "Our one time that we open for a legend… I knew we should not have brought him into the band after Jimmy quit, but you swore your buddy was legit."

"Sorry man, this, though, is not my fault. Could we play without him?"

"Play without him? We are an eighties guitar cover band. How the hell are we going to play without a guitarist? We would be laughed off the stage."

Scaggz approached the two vehicles; the van driver said, "Go away, we don't have any money to give you. Go hang around that tour bus; maybe they will give you some money or food."

Scaggz initial instinct upon hearing that they thought he was homeless was to climb onto the roof of the Honda and kick this asshole in the mouth. He refrained and said, "Guys, I am free tonight. I was going to do something inside the theater, but it can wait for another night. I have played on the stage with some of the most famous guitarists. I toured the world many times over playing guitar with the Doctor. He taught me a lot and I would love to fill in for you guys. Just give me the set list. This will not be a problem."

The van driver said, "Give us a minute." He stuck his head through the driver's window of the Honda. After a minute, his head emerged from the car and he said, "OK, we don't have any other options. We will give you the set list. We have an amp for you, but no guitar; I hope you have an instrument."

"Yeah," said Scaggz. "My guitar and effects are in my van around the corner. Do you guys have a hotel? I want to shower and maybe shave off this new beard."

"No, we don't, but my apartment is close. You can go there and shower while we are setting up, but we need to do a soundcheck by 6:30, and we only get fifteen minutes max on the schedule. My name is Earl, I am the drummer; that is Larry behind the wheel, our bass player; and Martin in the passenger seat on keys and vocals. If you need something to wear on stage, right across the street from my apartment is a retro clothing store called Threads. We get all of our stage clothes there."

"Groovy. I'm Guitarman SJ," said Scaggz, and took the keys that Earl handed him, punched the address into his phone, and with that, he was off to prepare for the evening's gig. On the way to the apartment, he stopped at Threads and bought himself an outfit for the night.

At 6:30 p.m. on the dime, Scaggz returned to the venue. He once again was clean shaven. He was wearing a fluorescent yellow baseball cap backward with his hair tucked up inside. He had on red leopard-print spandex pants that he ripped in conspicuous places. He was also wearing a denim jacket, open with no shirt and the sleeves cut off. He had brought his powder blue Stratocaster with the custom pickups he invented himself. These are ultra-high-output, perfect for the evening's set list.

Scaggz handed Earl his keys and Earl said, "Wooow, I didn't recognize you. You look totally different. Here is the set list; we are playing these ten songs." They were all staring at the amount of hair revealed by the unbuttoned denim jacket.

Scaggz took the set list, read it over, and threw it in the trash. "No problems, I can play all these backward if needed. Can you guys play 'Slap the Virgin' by the Centipedes?"

What is he talking about? Earl thought. "Forwards will be fine. We are on in an hour, but we can't play the Centipedes song with the Doctor going on after us."

"We play it, or I walk," said Scaggz, and then he plugged in and they soundchecked with Van Halen's song "Running with the Devil." The guys in the band thought this guy was amazing. He played everything perfectly. Then they went into Deep Purple's

"Perfect Strangers." When the song was about to end, Scaggz went into another solo that caught the guys off guard, but they were able to compensate while he played a ten-minute solo that left the band speechless. Scaggz looked over at Earl and said, "I need an answer on the song I want to play."

Earl immediately said, "We are dropping 'Balls to the Wall' and adding 'Slap the Virgin,' guys." The guys didn't protest, and he revised the set list.

Neusy walked over to Jeb and said, "What do you think of that guy?"

"Well, yeah, pretty damn good. But weird clothes."

The doors opened, and the sparse crowd entered. Jeb said to Marlon, "We may have to buy our own beers tonight with this crowd." Marlon walked to the bar and returned with two beers that he talked one of the fans into buying for him. "Well, you are learning quite well, I must say."

"That crazy guitarist, he bought this for me, said when we are ready, he will buy us another round if I give him a shirt. So I said right on, bro!"

The agents had their own trouble. Their flight was canceled due to a mechanical problem with the plane. They were still in Seattle scrambling for another flight, which there were none. Not with any airline until after 10:30 p.m. Now they were contemplating flying directly to Kamloops, where the next show would be. Sitting in the waiting area of the canceled flight, Crow looked to his phone for options. "There is nothing until 10:48, which says here that we would get in at 11:37. Then go to the venue, get there after the show, and who knows, after they already leave."

"That's true," agreed Sparrow. "They do have a crazy schedule. Then they have that day off tomorrow. We are booked from Vancouver to Kamloops. We could just go to Kamloops."

"And what, hope nothing happens in Vancouver? How would we explain that we skipped going there?"

"Well, it's unforeseen circumstances. It is totally out of our control. We didn't break the airplane."

"OK, fuck it, let's book into Kamloops. It says here that the next flight to Kamloops is at 6:30 a.m. tomorrow. You go over to the counter there and see if they will switch our flight. I will get us a hotel room here outside the airport."

Twenty-five minutes later, they checked into their hotel and, being karaoke night in the lounge, they decided to investigate the possibilities there. The bar was in full swing for a Sunday night. They sat at the bar and ordered beers as the song "Ventura Highway" ended. The host said, "Hey, we have the Blues Brothers here in the house. Are you guys going to sing us a song?" and with that, the agents chugged their beers and walked out.

Almost showtime and Scaggz was tuning his guitar. He was wondering what these guys call themselves. But it didn't matter; these guys were simpletons, and this was a one-off gig for him. But damn, it was good to be going on stage again. The guys made their way to the stage. Scaggz plugged his guitar into the amp, and then, "Ladies and gentlemen, welcome to the stage, Dream Maker."

There was dead silence, no one applauded, and the keyboard intro to "Perfect Strangers" started. Then the guitar. This got the people's attention. The weird-looking guitarist was incredible. Song after song, they were on fire. Scaggz took the band to a level they'd never played before. Halfway through the set, he played a guitar solo that went from one end of the spectrum to the other. He played everything from the Doctor to classic songs of the seventies, and then slowed it down to the blues. Twenty minutes, this went on. The rest of the band was in awe. Who was this guy? *We have to get him to join the band.* They watched as Scaggz played behind his back, then with his teeth. He took off a shoe and played the guitar with the shoe and then with his bare foot.

Neusy looked at Jeb and noticed he was standing there with his mouth wide open. He looked at Neusy, and they agreed with a nod of their heads that this guy rocked. They continued to watch as Scaggz put his shoe back on and jumped off the stage. He was on his back on the floor. Then, with one movement, jumped up on his feet and leaped onto the stage. The twenty-six people in the audience were all watching to see what he would do next. Scaggz had their full attention and his disguise was perfect—no one recognized him.

When he finally finished, they only had time for one more song. The band seemed OK with the fact that they would only play about half of their set list. Scaggz played the intro to "Slap the Virgin." The audience once again roared as they thought this was all planned by the Doctor. What a show, too bad more people were not here to witness this.

Jeb said, "Oh shit! They are playing this as well." Neusy nodded, blinked twice, and shook his head at the stage. Jeb agreed with a nod of his head that it is lucky the Doctor was not there to see this.

Scaggz was on fire. Not only did he play the song exactly like the Doctor, but when the solo came, he also improvised the classic solo to a mind-bending level that seemed to hypnotize the audience. Even Hocker, who was standing up on the stage getting ready to prepare for the Doctor, seemed unable to move. Neusy looked around the room. Nothing, no one moving. What was happening? He looked over at Jeb, who nodded; he seemed OK and looked over at Marlon, who was asleep on the floor. They were both trying to figure out what was happening. Neusy walked over to Jeb. The two scanned the room, everyone just standing still. The bartender was shaking a drink for the entire solo, never breaking. The notes were flying off of Scaggz's guitar. Then Scaggz hit a footswitch and strummed his guitar. The guitar squealed, and the band stopped. Scaggz strummed his guitar again, and this time it was a deep, gut-wrenching sound. And with that, everyone came out of their hypnotized state. No one applauded; they were all trying to figure out what just happened. It seemed that they all urinated in their clothes. Hocker looked down at his pants; he ran full speed out the stage door to the bus to change.

Neusy said to Jeb, "Wow, I have never seen anything like that. Look at them all; they all have pissed themselves, except you and me."

"What was that? And who was that? Yeah, I am fine, dry pants," said Jeb.

"Yeah, me as well. I was following him in my mind as to what he was playing. Strange sequences and melodies."

"Yes, Neusy, I was following him as well. Playing in my mind what he was playing. That's what kept us from going into a trance."

Marlon was waking from the floor. "What did you guys do to me? Why was I on the floor?"

Neusy said, "Be happy you didn't piss your pants. The weed, with that crazy playing, caused you to go to sleep and spared you from the trance." Jeb nodded.

The bartender disappeared, as did everyone in the audience. There was a line to the restrooms with all twenty-six people waiting to dry their pants. One by one, people stood as close as they could to the electric hand dryer mounted on the wall next to the sinks as they tried to dry their pants. Some of the short guys stood on the waste can turned upside down to raise their crotches up to the hand dryer.

Hocker returned and prepared the stage while the opening band broke down their equipment. Earl said, "That was totally on the next level." The other guys agreed with him. "Where did he go? Where did Guitarman go? I never saw him leave."

Once everyone was dried off, Jeb called the Doctor. He informed him that the venue was ready and the band was waiting for him. It was time for the Doctor to fly to the venue. He had walked over to the helicopter tour company. Jeb announced to the audience, "Wow, that was intense, but now it is time for the Doctor. Everyone, go to the front and welcome him." The twenty-six people in the audience cheered and followed Jeb to the front.

The Doctor boarded the chopper; the pilot helped attach the harness and wire to lower him. They flew to the venue, and while the pilot hovered about 100 feet above, he lowered the Doctor to the street. The twenty-six people were cheering as he came down. Once on the ground, he detached the harness and made his way past the fans into the venue. They screamed, "Doctor, Doctor, Doctor," then followed him to the stage.

The Doctor played his regular show, and the audience ate it up once again. When he played "Slap the Virgin," they all covered their ears, fearing they would urinate again. Jeb and Neusy found this humorous. Marlon once again fell asleep.

After the show ended, there was a short meet and greet with a few fans. The Doctor was drunk and complained to Jeb about his dissatisfaction with the show's attendance, lack of merchandise sales, and general lack of income, along with the smell of urine in the club.

"Achhh! I can't believe this! This show was terrible! How much did we make in merch sales tonight?"

"We hardly made anything! It wasn't worth the stop, with the low pay and no merch sales."

"You see, this is what I mean! This place sucks! Why did you get us this place?"

"I didn't get us this place; Spud Berger booked it!"

"Yah, yah, your good friend!"

"He's not my friend; he's the only company that will take a risk booking your act. You're not as popular as you think!"

"You need to find another agent! This sucks! We are losing a lot of money. Und that nonsense with Marlon at the border, what a waste of time, und it could have been serious."

"I didn't know he was going to pull that shit; it's not my fault! Talk about wasting money, you're the one who wanted to fly to the venue tonight in a helicopter and be lowered down on a wire. That cost us $1,200, and we lost money tonight with everyone's salary and expenses for the bus."

"Achhh! It had to be done. It was spectacular! Plus, it was Canadian money!"

"Yeah, well, still expensive. Maybe if it was in the summer with a lot of people watching, but we only had twenty-six people tonight!"

"Yah, those twenty-six were screaming when I came down from the sky. When you speak to this Spud Berger, you must tell him I don't want to play in places that stink like piss!"

Chapter 32

Jeb was distraught with the Doctor after their conversation in Vancouver. He lay in his bunk and contemplated leaving the tour and going back home to continue to write his book of rad stories titled *Are We a Bus?* It was something that he had been working on for years with help from Neusy. The book told stories of his time on the road with the Doctor and other artists he worked with. He constantly was writing notes so he would remember. The border crossing on this tour would surely make it in his book. Neusy also had lots of stories of his time on the road, and the two decided that it would be entertaining to tell of these times.

The bus continued on the foggy road on its way to Kamloops. Here the guys would be able to have a day of rest. The next show would be in two days.

The Donner and Blitzen Inn would be where they would stay for a day. It was a couple of miles off the main highway, nestled amid the tall trees right outside of Kamloops. A single-story, multiple-building establishment, perfect for parking the bus, it seemed a cozy enough place to lodge for a night. But there would be one inconvenience for the group: the guys all had to share rooms, as usual, except for the Doctor, who always had his room or suite, if possible. Jeb decided to treat the band and crew to hotel rooms to relax on the day off. But they would have to shower in a separate facility next to the manager's office, which was about two hundred meters from where they would be sleeping.

The bus pulled into the parking lot close to the manager's office on the right end. The parking lot was filled with Harleys and bikers that were drinking and loudly carrying on. Jeb exited the bus with all eyes on him as he walked to the office to confirm arrival and get the room keys. He emerged minutes later and found that everyone, other than the Doctor, was gathered in the lounge. Jeb spoke to the crew.

"OK, here's the deal, there are only five rooms for us. And by the way, if anyone wants to take a shower, you have to walk back over here to the office. The showers are behind the office. There are only two showers. Nathan, Heinz, and Torsten, you're in room 113; there are two double beds, so two of you will have to share a bed. Here are your two keys. Tommy, Cal, and Marlon, you are in room 117; here are your two keys. It's the same deal. Hocker and Neusy will room with me; we are in room 121. Cal, you have room 122. The Doctor will be in room 124, if anyone cares," Jeb said with disgust. "First round on me, and I think you should take turns buying Cal a beer since he is doing a great job at keeping us safe. He has the night off, and we won't be traveling till noon. Make sure you all are on the bus by then."

"Well, hell yeah. Let's drink!" said Cal.

Neusy said, "We should all go put our shit in the rooms before we have too many beers, so we don't have to do it later. Then maybe meet back here, but first I am buying!"

"Wooohooo! Yeah, now we are rolling!" shouted Cal. They finished their beers and went to their rooms.

Jeb slid the Doctor's room key under his door in the back of the bus. He had not come out, and Jeb didn't care to speak with him. They exited the bus and walked to the right end of the parking lot. As they walked, they encountered the first group of bikers. About thirty bikers were talking and drinking; some were laughing loudly and being obnoxious.

"Who are you guys?" asked one tall biker.

"We are the Surgeons!" answered Jeb. "The band for the Doctor, Jurgen Weislangwolf."

"What kind of music do you guys play?" asked another biker.

"It's mostly rock music," answered Jeb.

"Jurgen Weislangwolf, I've heard of that guy, Billy."

"Yeah, he played in the Centipedes," said Biker Billy.

"Wow… Hey, do you have any free CDs or other free stuff?"

"Well, not right now; we have to get in our rooms. But if I come back out to the bus later, I'll have a look for a CD."

"All right, man… I'll remind you again later."

"I am sure you will," said Jeb.

The guys kept walking and encountered another group of bikers, a bit drunker than the first bikers.

"Heeey! What are yoooou guuuysss, some kind of rrrooock bannd?"

"They look like a band; they all have long hair, Rocky."

"Maybe they're fairies or fruit balls."

"We are the Surgeons; we play with the Doctor, Jurgen Weislangwolf."

"Who the fuck is that?"

"He is one of the most famous guitarists in the world."

"Famous, huh? How come I never heard of him?"

"Well, he is European, Austrian in fact. And these three guys here are from Austria."

"Hallo!" replied Heinz and Nathan.

"Have you ever heard the song, 'In Your Pants?'"

"Oh yeah! I remember that, from 1985, right?"

"Yeah, that's right. That was the Centipedes."

"Wow! That's a great song!"

"You got any free CDs?"

"Maybe later, we got to get in our rooms and then unwind a bit in the lounge."

"All right, we'll be seeing you."

There was another group of bikers off to the left. Jeb and the boys walked hurriedly past them to avoid any more conversations.

The guys each entered their rooms. After Jeb, Hocker, and Neusy made it into their room, Hocker opened a small ice chest and grabbed a beer. Jeb said, "I'm going for a walk. I don't know when I'll be back," and left the room. Jeb walked back past all of the groups of bikers. A couple of them reminded him about the CDs.

He just hurried by and said, "Yeah, yeah," to each one. He got by the tour bus and, as he passed it, he flipped the bird to the Doctor's room at the rear of the bus. He remembered seeing a roadside bar about two miles down the road and kept on walking in that direction.

Meanwhile, the Austrians, feeling unclean, wanted to have a shower. Nathan dug in his gunnysack for his shampoo, soap, and towel. Torsten had all of his bathroom items in a clear plastic zipper bag. Heinz kept his things in a black backpack. They all wore their winter jackets to battle the cold air and carried a bag of clothes.

"All right, men, let's go to the showers!" said Nathan.

"Einz, zwei, drei, vier!" And they marched out like soldiers.

They quickly passed the first group of bikers on the right. The second group of bikers stopped them.

"Hey, what do to guys play, anyway?"

"I am the singer und guitarist," said Nathan.

"Hey, do you have a guitar pick that I can have?"

"Maybe later!"

"What do you play?"

"I play the bass," replied Heinz.

"And you, Red?"

"I play the keyboards!"

"Can we have your guys' CD?"

"Later, later! We want to take showers now. You must talk with the tour manager," replied Torsten.

"OK, don't forget us."

The boys got past those guys, but there was the next group not twelve feet away. "Hey, you guys, I will race you to the showers," said Heinz.

"OK, then… On your Karl Marx, get set, go!" said Torsten.

They barreled past the last bikers to the showers behind the manager's office. They couldn't use the showers right away because they were both occupied, so they waited, but at least they had made it to the showers. After about five minutes, a blonde-haired girl exited one shower room wrapped in a blanket, and Torsten went in. Heinz and Nathan both said, "Guten Abend!" The girl smiled and quickly walked away.

Five minutes later, the second shower room door opened and a 6'6", 300-pound, red-bearded biker exited barechested. He was amazingly polite and said, "Excuse me," while he walked by. Heinz entered his stall, and Nathan waited outside. Heinz and Torsten both emerged from their shower rooms almost simultaneously, giving Nathan the choice of either stall. Nathan entered the left stall and began his shower. Heinz was now in a purple bathrobe under his jacket that he left open, and Torsten was in what looked like a yellow rainsuit, carrying his jacket. He was wearing a shower cap that enclosed his four-foot-long red hair.

"Hey, Torsten, I'll race you back to the room! I don't want to be bothered by them bikers!"

"OK, Heinz, let's go!"

The two ran like Olympic marathon runners as quickly as they could past the bikers. About halfway across the parking lot, Torsten's shower cap blew off his head and his four-foot-long red locks were whipping behind him as he ran. They made it across the parking lot and back to their room—what a relief.

When Nathan had emerged from the shower, he didn't see his friends waiting for him. He thought they must have played a trick on him and left him alone. Now he would have to pass all of the bikers by himself. He passed the first group of bikers unnoticed. *Good, that was easy.* He was in the midst of the second group of bikers when he heard, "Aaahh, which one are you?"

"I'm Nathan, the singer und guitarist."

"Do you have something for me? A CD or something?"

Nathan didn't have anything except his shower items. He looked around. "Ummmm, Ummmm." There on the ground, he saw Torsten's shower cap. He reached to pick it up.

"Here you are, it's the keyboardist's shower cap. You can ask him to autograph it for you later, yah?"

"Alright, cool!!" said the biker as Nathan handed the shower cap to him and hurried along.

He laughed to himself before he entered his room. "Hahaha! Wait till Torsten goes to shower next time. No shower cap! Play the tricks on me?"

All the while, Jeb had made his way to the bar that was two miles down the road. It was a typical log cabin building; a few locals were scattered about drinking, nothing special going on.

Jeb looked at the chalkboard with the list of beers. "Give me a Kamloops Golden Shower," the chalkboard noted that it was brewed locally and was similar to Molson Golden, "and a shot of Canadian Mist."

"Here you are," said the bartender. "I haven't seen you in here before. Are you traveling through?"

"Yeah, I'm the road manager with a rock band."

"Which band?"

"Well, the guitar player is Jurgen Weislangwolf. Some people call him the Doctor, and the band is called the Surgeons."

"Ohh, I've heard his name before. He's a great guitar player!"

"He's a great big dick too!" snipped Jeb.

"Huh?" said the bartender.

"Never mind, I'll have another shot!"

Meanwhile, the Doctor had awoken on the tour bus and stood up out of bed. He dressed in some casual attire and got ready to leave his room. Before he opened the door to leave, he saw his room key on the floor. He picked it up and walked out of his room into the sleeping area. Up ahead, he saw no one in the bus lounge. He wondered where everyone was. He grabbed his fanny pack and exited the bus. He walked into the manager's office and asked where his room was. The manager informed him it was on the other side of the parking lot. He left and walked outside. He saw the bikers, still there drinking, laughing, carrying on. He encountered the first group of bikers.

"Now, who are you? We haven't seen you before," asked one biker.

"I am the Doctor! I am Jurgen Weislangwolf."

"So, you're the man, Mr. Important."

"You sound strange; where are you from?"

"I am from Austria!"

"Ahh, that explains it. Hey, do you have a CD for me? The other guy said we could have a CD."

The Doctor looked in his fanny pack and found a CD. "Here you go, but only the one, OK? Und now I must go to my room. I am exhausted!"

The Doctor left and walked by the next group of bikers quickly. Then there were the last group of bikers. The same escapade happened. After going through the same thing with the group before, he gave one guy a CD and told them they had to share it amongst themselves, and he slithered away. He made his way to his room, opened the door, and slammed it shut quickly. A few moments later, a knock came on his door. He opened it to see who it was. It was one of the bikers from the third group that he passed.

"Yah, what do you want?"

"Hey man, this CD is like from three years ago. I've heard this album. Don't you have a new CD?"

The Doctor, looking baffled, thought for a minute. "There is a man named Jeb. He can find you a new one later. Guten Nacht!" and Jurgen closed the door.

Jeb was feeling better about all things Jurgen Weislangwolf related after his second beer and two shots. Time alone did wonders. He got up and said, "Goodnight, I have to walk back to the hotel." He paid his tab and walked towards the door. Jeb was not looking like the average patron at this country bar with his hair five inches past his shoulders. Although only on the road for two weeks, it showed on his face. His face had that road-worn, I-am-part-of-a-bigger-thing, touring-with-a-rock-band-sucks look. He was wearing one of the tour shirts under his jacket.

As he reached for the door to exit, he felt a hand on his shoulder. It was a soft touch, and this got his attention. He turned around and immediately smelled the perfume. He was looking directly into the eyes of Denise Dreckermund. Denise, at forty-seven, still had it. She was a groupie back in the day and still brought it with her blue eyes and long black hair. Denise, a long-time Centipedes fan, was always backstage at any Centipedes-related show in western Canada. She is well known in the Centipedes community. Jeb knew her from touring with the Doctor. Denise is known on the internet and social media as the woman with the Centipedes tattoo. Centipedes fans were constantly taking pictures with her and her tattoo.

Denise's tattoo was the Centipedes logo. It started on the front of her left shoulder and went over her shoulder and diagonally down her back, across her butt, then down the opposite leg, coming to an end on top of her right foot. The logo is an elongated centipede with the word Centipedes running through the center. She always wore clothes that revealed the tattoo in as many places as possible. She started jumping up and down in excitement. "Jeb, I didn't see you till you walked towards the door." She hugged him tightly.

"Denise, hello… What are you doing here?"

"I am so excited. I have taken the week off from work, and I am going to the next few shows. Kamloops, you're going to love the club. And guess what? I brought my needles!"

"Excellent, I could use your needles. Are you still living in Calgary?"

"Yes, but I am staying at this hotel up the street. I didn't want to go into their bar. There were a lot of bikers there."

"Yes, I am familiar with that place. We are there as well. I just had to get away. Are you going back? I could use a ride."

"Yes, but let me buy you a drink first." Jeb agreed, and they returned to where Jeb was sitting at the bar. Denise was OK in small doses, but she was always coming around looking for attention. The Doctor constantly invited her on the bus, where she stayed all night, partying and chatting with the guys. It would be nice, though. Jeb was thinking of having someone that can help out with a car for a few shows. Maybe they would eat better food, and she did bring the needles.

After answering all of Denise's questions as to how the tour was going, she said, "I heard that there was a murder at one of the shows."

"One? No, it's happened at multiple shows. We have a couple of FBI agents traveling with us now. But you must be very careful at the shows. Don't go anywhere alone."

"Wow, that's crazy, but it's so great to see you. A lot has happened over the last year in my life. I moved, started a new job as office manager—a nice change and making more a year. I was dating Jensen Slothman from the band Angel Dung. He just got divorced, and I am a big fan. It started out OK. I could never get him to come over to my new place. Then one day, he came by. He wouldn't let me kiss him; he only wanted to have sex with my knees. He wanted me to lay on my back with my legs in the air. I let him do that twice. He said he could not stop thinking of his ex. He just wanted me to lay on my back with my knees in the air. I couldn't take it and broke it off."

"Wow…that's a lot of info there, Denise. I don't know what to say." They finished their beers and headed back to the hotel. Denise was very excited that she would see the Doctor and the Surgeons.

Sparrow and Crow were at the Donner and Blitzen Inn when Jeb and Denise arrived. A drunken group of bikers had surrounded them. "The Blues Brovvers, sig us a sog," said one intoxicated biker while the other bikers cheered.

Sparrow was back to back with Crow and feeling uneasy. He said, "Guys, please, we had a long couple of days. We just want to get to our room."

The bikers were chanting, "Song, Song, Song."

Sparrow said to Crow in a whisper that Crow could not hear, "Let's run to the room."

"WHAT?" shouted Crow as Jeb walked up.

"Boys, what's up?"

"Are these guys wid thooo?"

"Yes," replied Jeb. "They are our opening band; we need them rested. I'll bring you guys some CDs after they get to their room." The agents saw their window and bolted to their room, and with a slam of the door, they were out of sight.

"Whooooo baby! Who arrre you?" said the drunk biker to Denise.

"Yeaaah, honey…givvvve us sommm hooony."

Jeb stood in front of her and said, "I'll tell you what, guys, be nice to her, and I'll give you guys shirts in the morning when I open the trailer." They agreed, and Jeb led Denise into the bar at the hotel.

"Denise…" said the Doctor as he saw them walk in.

"Herr Doctor," said Denise, trying to be cute. The band all surrounded her as she hugged them all. Marlon joined the hugs and was happy to hear that Denise also liked to smoke pot.

Neusy looked up, saw Jeb walk in, and gave him an upward head nod. Jeb gave Neusy a downward head nod and one to the right towards the door. Neusy smiled and understood that Jeb needed the time away and nodded in agreement. The two locked eyes, and Jeb raised an eyebrow at Denise. Neusy gave a return shrug of the shoulder as if saying, I know, but what can you do. The two were in perfect sync. Without the duo, with all that had happened, the tour would be finished. No one but the two realized this and started to converse less with the other guys on tour. Neusy brought Jeb a beer, and the two sat at a high-top table away from the other guys. "Feeling better?" asked Neusy.

"Yeah, ran into Denise when I was about to leave this bar I found up the street. She cornered me, and I had to spend a little time with her. Anyway, I got a ride back here. These bikers partying out there are going to be a problem."

"Yeah, I was trying to figure out what to do, other than moving to a new hotel."

"I've already promised enough merch to last weeks. It feels like I am buying our safety. I'm just hoping they are too drunk to remember in the morning that I was going to give them merch."

"We can leave early; Crabs only stayed here for a little bit. He will be fine to leave early."

"Might not be a bad idea; find a place to get laundry done. I'm running out of underwear," said Jeb.

"Yeah, I'm down to my last couple; I started wearing them for two days to make them last. I'm glad you walked in when you did. The Doctor was getting drunk and was more like the Dictator." Jeb appreciated the reference, and they drank their beers. "I'll look up a Wash and Fold and let everyone know that we are leaving early in the morning," said Neusy.

While the boys were inside enjoying their beers and winding down their evening, outside Scaggz was having some fun of his own. With two bikes already set on fire, he was about to ignite a row of a dozen more. He had watched what was going on from up top of the main building. Once Jeb and Denise went inside, he climbed down the drain spout and took out two of the largest and most drunk bikers using his powder blue Stratocaster like an ax that he had slung over his shoulder. BAM, one was out, then he turned and in one motion, BAM, the other. He climbed up the spout so fast he wasn't noticed.

Over to the other side of the building and down that spout— BAM, BAM, BAM—with the swipe of the Strat, he took out three of the second biker group. Back up on the roof before anyone saw him, he crawled to the rear of the building and slid down behind it. He walked to the side and BAM, BAM, then three steps to his right and BAM, BAM, BAM. He went around back and back up on the building, looking down.

The first group of bikers was looking around as they noticed their friends lying on the ground. They suspected the second group of bikers. This got the attention of the second group. They saw their brotherhood on the ground out cold and now suspected the first group had something to do with the bikers lying there motionless. The two groups of bikers started to get closer to each other, a couple of them with knives drawn.

The third group was very drunk and continued drinking. Scaggz was on the roof holding his guitar over his head with one hand and a rolled-up newspaper on fire in his other. He dropped it on two of the Harleys he had poured gasoline on prior to climbing up on the roof. All the bikers were now focused on him. He said, "Now that I got your attention, you will go inside and apologize to the people traveling on that bus."

Dead silence, then laughter. "Come down here, son. We have a nice little welcome for you." Scaggz disappeared. BAM, BAM, BAM, BAM—the back row of group three all down. Then back up on the roof.

"There he is," shouted one of the bikers in group one. "Shit, where did he go?" BAM, BAM, BAM, BAM. Ducking under the forearm of one of the bikers, he came up swinging—BAM, BAM, BAM—before he disappeared once again.

He appeared next to a row of twelve more Harleys with his guitar strung back over his shoulder. He lit another rolled-up newspaper while his other hand was pouring gasoline on the next set of bikes.

"Woooow!" shouted what appeared to be the leader of group one.

"Yeah, yeah… Wait…don't…" said another biker.

Scaggz emptied the gas can and was about to set fire to the bikes. "OK, OK… We will leave your friends alone. We were just having fun with them. They knew that. We will stop. Right boys?"

"Yes, please stop," came from group two.

The most anyone was able to say from group three was, "What the ffuuuuck. Yes, no morrrre."

Scaggz dropped the newspaper on the blacktop and said, "Now go in and apologize. Talk to Jeb and Neusy. When you come back out, you will not talk to them until they leave the hotel. Clear?"

"Yes," said the leaders of one and two; the group three representative just shook his head as he tripped on the curb.

"Oh shit," said Neusy as he saw the three bikers walk in.

Jeb turned and looked. "Now what?"

"We are looking for Jeb or Neusy, that you guys?" said number one.

"Yesss," said Jeb hesitantly.

Number one continued, "I just want to say that we are very, very sorry to have bothered you earlier. It was wrong, and we hope that you have a good tour."

"Yeah, sorry, we want to buy you a round of beers," said number two.

"Reah, wreee arrr ver sorry," mumbled number three's leader.

Neusy and Jeb were taken aback. "Well, thanks, guys, that was very nice of you, and yes, sure, we would love the drinks."

"Just do us a favor, keep that crazy guy in the weird eighties clothes away from us; he is nuts."

The bikers bought a round and left the bar. Neusy looked at Jeb and smiled. "Guy in eighties clothes?" They finished their drinks and, one by one, left the bar.

Denise said goodbye to the guys as they departed, but she was still in the bar when Neusy and Jeb headed out. They walked out of the bar together past group one, who all smiled and wished them a good night. Then group two, who did the same; one of the bikers handed Denise a flower off a nearby bush. When they passed group three, they could not understand what was said but figured it was along the same line. It turned out that Denise had the room right next to Neusy and Jeb. "I have my needles on me if you need it," said Denise.

"Yes, Denise, I do need it. My back is all tweaked, come on into our room," said Jeb.

"I could also use it, and my shoulders from the lifting are starting to bother me again," said Neusy.

Neusy opened the door and, as they walked in, they passed the bathroom. There stood Hocker in all his glory, the huge masculine physique, no shirt, and his beer belly hanging over the white towel that was wrapped around his waist. The open flap side of the towel exposed his rather small-looking penis with a triangular-shaped head that he aimed over the toilet.

"Gee, thanks fucker for letting Denise in while I'm pissing!" shouted Hocker at Neusy.

"Don't mention it, Hock!"

They chuckled as they passed by the bathroom, and Denise said, "I have some needles that might help with that." They all laughed again. As they got in the room, Denise added, "OK guys, take off your shirts and lay on the bed." They did as they were told, and Denise pulled a bag out of her purse. "Same place as last year, Jeb?"

"Yes, please." Denise inserted a half dozen acupuncture needles into Jeb's lower back. Then another half dozen into Neusy's shoulders.

Denise was married to a licensed Chinese acupuncturist and learned the trade after working as his assistant for eleven years when they were first married. One evening, she visited his office where he claimed he was working late and caught him cheating with one of his patients. He had two needles inserted into his abdomen, which he claimed gave him extra staying power. When Denise walked into the room, he jumped up. Denise pulled one of the needles out and stuck it into the tip of his erect penis. To this day, he pees in multiple directions, like a garden sprinkler.

Hocker emerged from the bathroom wearing his boxers. He looked at what was happening on the beds and said, "Great, can I get my nipples pierced?"

Chapter 33

Jeb woke and knocked on everyone's door. They were all awake and ready to go. The Doctor said, "I will be traveling with Denise." Jeb was happy to hear this. He was also glad that the group text Neusy had sent the night before to announce the earlier departure was read by the band and crew.

A few bikers were awake and standing outside; they watched as the band and crew entered the bus and drove away. Neusy said, "Cal, we are going to the Wash and Fold. Go to the venue; there is a Wash and Fold right around the corner." He then announced to the guys, "If you want your laundry done, put your clothes in a bag and put your name on it. We will have it washed and folded. They charge twenty a bag."

At 9:30 a.m., they parked behind Spirit Tavern. Neusy and Jeb handled the laundry detail and then went to breakfast while they waited. Hocker, Cal, and Marlon were already in the diner when they walked in. They sat in the same booth as them and ordered their breakfast while they had a production meeting. They discussed the remainder of the Canadian shows. Cal said, "I am concerned with the blizzard coming down tomorrow. We need to leave right after the show tonight to try and stay in front of it."

Jeb said, "Yes, what time are you thinking?"

"Right away, as soon as we can. 1:00, if we can. Hopefully you are all loaded out by then."

"OK," said Jeb. "Neusy, your group text worked well. Let everyone know that we will be leaving right after the gig tonight and that moving forward, you will be sending out the daily schedule by text. Let's see how this works. Marlon, I need you to be on your toes these next few days. The report I am getting is that the attendances are expected to be very good. Keep your eyes on the merch. I don't want to see anything disappear. Hocker, you're doing great. The Doctor complained that he did not have enough picks, so leave him a couple of extras on his amp. There are no hotel rooms today as the venue has a shower, except for you, Crabs."

After breakfast, Cal left to check into his hotel while the crew walked through town. They were getting strange looks from all that passed them. They thought nothing of it. They found a small department store and bought additional underwear, then returned to the Wash and Fold and picked up the laundry.

At 3:30 p.m., the scheduled load-in began. They were now dialed in with each other, working like a machine. Jeb now felt better than the day before, and he had the merch booth set up before soundcheck. The band came in and did the soundcheck in ten minutes. There were two openers on the bill: an acoustic guitarist singer-songwriter, and a local cover band.

The agents walked in, and Sparrow immediately walked over to Jeb. "Hey, thanks for helping out yesterday with the bikers. That was crazy. This morning they were a lot kinder to us."

"They bought us breakfast and took us to some waterfalls nearby. They were apologizing all morning," said Crow. "They just dropped us off here at the venue."

"OK, great! Did you hear that there is a blizzard coming in tonight? I would try and get the earliest flights that you can get."

"OK, we will check on this; I heard something of the snowstorm," said Sparrow.

The doors opened right on time, and by 8:00 p.m., the cover band was playing and finished right on time. Jeb was scanning the room. An average club, it was more like a local bar, with the stage on the far wall, a bar along the left side wall, and pool tables along the right sidewall. The decor was dimly lit with state-of-the-art LED stage lights and an average PA. The pool tables were lit bright, and Jeb knew the Doctor would complain about that later. He liked that there was a good-sized crowd. About two hundred, he guessed.

Marlon had the merch table under control. When it became busy, Jeb and Neusy went over to help. Neusy had to make sure that the Doctor's set up on stage was not only correct but working, which it was.

The singer-songwriter also started on time and played for forty minutes. They cleared the stage for the Doctor, whose time slot was at 10:00 p.m. At 10:30, the Doctor walked in with Denise. "Where the hell were you?" asked Jeb.

"Yah, I know you would say that. It is all OK; we had a nice day hiking und then dinner. I was able to shower in Denise's room."

Jeb signaled Neusy by putting his finger in the air so that Neusy could see him across the audience; Neusy turned on the Doctor's amp. The Surgeons took the stage, and the audience came to life. "YAH, Kamloops, who wants to 'Slap the Virgin?'" The audience cheered, and the Doctor started playing. Without speaking another word to the audience for the remainder of the show, he played his entire set list with no breaks.

The show ended early, and the meet and greet went for an hour. Hocker and Neusy had the stage broken down and loaded out. Now just the merch remained inside; easy night Jeb was thinking. The agents were also standing by the merch booth and signing an occasional autograph for fans of *The Blues Brothers*. The meet and greet was winding down when a waitress brought over a round of beers for the crew and the agents. She said, "This is from that guy over by the bar. The weird guy in the eighties clothes." They looked over but did not see the person she was referring to. "Oh, he must have left, but he said these two were for the Blues Brothers." They all took their beers and took a chug.

"Yum," said Hocker. "Nothing tastes as good as a free beer."

Jeb noticed something written on the label of Sparrow's and Crow's beers. "What does that say there on the back of your beer?"

Sparrow looked at his beer and read it out loud. "Missed you at the Vancouver show."

Then Crow read his. "You won't catch me if you don't show."

Chapter 34

The agents kept the band and crew for an hour, which was a waste of time as they knew nothing. Cal finally was able to get the bus moving to leave Kamloops and get on their way to Calgary. They left an hour later but still were ahead of the blizzard. The weather wasn't looking perfect, and the radio forecast mentioned a heavy snowstorm. Cal had already put the chains on the tires early in the morning and was prepared for slow driving.

"Are we a bus?"

Jeb scanned the bus, walked into the back, and came back out. "Yes, we are a bus, now let's get the fuck out of here."

"Whoohoo, we are rolling!"

Two hours after they departed, snow began to fall—just light snow. The first place that they would pass would be Banff National Forest. However, not much could be seen as the snow was now coming down heavier—what a disappointment to the guys not to see some of the national park. The trip to Calgary would normally take about seven hours from Kamloops, but Cal would have to reduce his speed drastically due to the falling snow.

Jeb, Neusy, Hocker, Heinz, and Nathan sat in the lounge drinking coffee. Heinz was steaming broccoli for his breakfast. "Oh God, do you have to have broccoli for breakfast too? It fucking stinks!" said Hocker.

"Yah, it smells awful, Heinz!" agreed Nathan.

Heinz paid no mind to them and continued making his breakfast.

"Open the windows, let some air in," said Jeb.

It was frigid air that came in. The guys would either have the smell or the cold. They thought it was better to be cold for a while. They all grabbed their jackets and put them on. After Heinz finished cooking, Jeb told him to pour the broccoli water from the steamer down the toilet so they wouldn't have to smell it. After the smell of the broccoli had dissipated, they closed the windows.

The Doctor woke and emerged from his room; he walked to the restroom. He came out and said, "I smell broccoli, is someone making broccoli? I love broccoli. Can I have some?"

"NOOO!" shouted Jeb, Hocker, and Neusy.

The Doctor turned toward the kitchen to find something to eat. He spotted a few almonds that were lying on the floor, probably from the poker game that some of the guys had the other night. He looked over his shoulder to see if anyone was watching him. When he saw that no one was, he reached down and quickly swooped up the almonds and popped them into his mouth. He continued to open cabinets and then looked in the refrigerator. He grabbed a package of white cheddar cheese and a loaf of pumpernickel bread and made himself a cheese sandwich. Slowly, Tommy emerged from his bunk in his tight whites and was standing over the Doctor's right shoulder. "Whatcha making there?"

"A white cheddar cheese on pumpernickel sandwich."

"Hey, that sounds pretty good. Can I have one?"

"Sure, you can have one if you make it yourself." The Doctor looked out the window and saw the snow pouring down. He was amazed at how beautifully white everything was outside, much whiter than Triple T's underwear.

"Achhh, this is just like my homeland, Austria. Why are we going so slow? What is the speed limit here?"

"It's fucking snowing, hard; we have to drive slow," said Jeb, annoyed. "Besides, Cal can barely see through the windshield. Do you want us to have an accident?"

"Can I drive the bus? I will show you how we drive in Austria."

"NO! Are you crazy? Of course, you can't drive the bus!" shouted Jeb.

"Listen to the way this guy talks to me. So rude! I think I will call him Rudie! He is our new Rudie. Go move some amps," said the Doctor with a smile on his face.

Jeb ignored the attempt at humor and said, "Well, all the work is done, and now it is nap time; see you guys later, I'm going to get some sleep."

"That's a good idea," Neusy replied. "I think I will follow you so I'm rested in Calgary."

With two hours until they would arrive in Calgary, Jeb made his way to his top bunk. After climbing up, he set the GPS on his phone and closed his eyes. The rolling of the bus, he found, was quite soothing, like a baby being rocked to sleep. When he awoke, he looked at his phone and realized that he slept for four hours. *How the hell did that happen? I must have been tired. Why are we still moving?* He opened up the GPS app on his phone and saw that they were two hours past Calgary heading towards Edmonton. "WHAT!" he screamed. He jumped down, put his shoes on, and ran upfront. The lounge was empty. Cal was driving as if in a hurry, squinting through the windshield with the tunes blasting. "Crabs, you fucking passed Calgary; look where we are!"

"OH SHIT!"

"Yeah, oh shit! What the hell were you doing?"

"I was driving; I just followed the highway north, I guess. I was listening to my music and zoned, sorry."

Cal exited at the next exit. The snow was deep, not plowed or compacted off the highway. He crossed over to the on-ramp to head south. He waited for a plow to go by in the opposite direction and crossed the freshly plowed road. He had to go slow to get over the mound of plowed snow. He inched forward and then nothing. Wheels were spinning, more gas, more wheels spinning. The bus was moving sideways. Then nothing.

"Come on, Crabs!"

"We are stuck, no way. I am getting out to look." Cal walked around the bus and then back in. He said, "We are stuck."

"Thanks for the update."

"I have to get us towed out." Cal called the roadside assistance that he uses while Jeb sat in the lounge.

"Well, they said about an hour."

"We'll never make this load-in on time!"

Jeb called the manager of the Stick and Puck Club in Calgary. Ex-hockey star Marin Pentlier managed the club. Jeb was looking forward to this show. "Marin, Jeb with the Doctor, here. Bad news: we are stuck in the snow, minimum three hours before we roll in."

"That's going to be tight; put you here about 5:30, doors at 6:30."

"Yes, Marin, I know, but there is nothing I can do. We are quick on load-in. Soundcheck is almost non-existent. You may have to push doors a little bit."

"My bartenders are not going to like that. They lose money when that happens. But nothing I can do about it. Just keep me informed."

Jeb got off the phone as Neusy entered the lounge. "Looks like we are a bit off course according to my phone," he said.

"We will be very late. I called the club. He is not happy."

"I'll do my best to get the guys moving once we get in."

"Just get the stage set up. I'll help. We could always move the merch in after doors," said Jeb.

"That sucks; I know how much you were looking forward to this club as you're a huge hockey fan."

They waited only forty minutes before the tow truck arrived: a heavy-duty tow truck capable of moving the large bus. After twenty-five minutes, Cal paid the $1,300 and they were back on the road. One by one, the band and crew awoke as they usually would be loading in at this time. As each one emerged from the back, it was the same conversation. Jeb finally stopped answering after the third time and let Marlon answer as he always wanted to seem important. Jeb called the club, gave the update, and then called once more when they were five minutes out.

At ten after five, they arrived at the Stick and Puck. Marin was waiting outside. "Thanks for the updates; my crew was getting nervous. I got two guys that can help with the load-in."

"Excellent!" said Jeb. "OK, guys, let's get this done." And they did. Twenty minutes to load everything in, including the merch. Jeb set up the merch, and Neusy had Marlon and Hocker work at warp speed. Marlon disappeared for a moment, then returned, ready to work. Neusy watched him, knowing he took a quick toke out back.

Chapter 35

Calgary was home to the Calgary Flames, the pride of Canada's hockey teams. Jeb, himself an avid hockey fan and amateur player, was overjoyed to be in Calgary. Maybe joy would overcome him and he could forget some of the nonsense that had occurred over the past few days. He was ecstatic to be inside the venue instead of being stuck on the side of the road and missing the gig.

Inside the venue were logos of every NHL team painted on the walls. Above the long wooden bar and the liquor shelf were framed photos of the greatest hockey players of all time. Wayne Gretsky, Bobby Orr, Gordie Howe, Mario Lemieux, Maurice Richard, Guy LaFleur, Terry Sawchuk, Bobby Hull, Patrick Roy, and Jaromir Jagr. Every photo was signed and dated. Jeb was in awe of the sight of these photos. There were also helmets, uniforms, sticks, pucks, and other paraphernalia of hockey attached to the walls or displayed in glass cases—a mini-museum of Jeb's favorite sport.

Inside of the venue was quite chilly; in fact, it was freezing. The floor of the venue was ice, just like a rink. The waitresses would skate around and serve the patrons, balancing their trays perfectly. Jeb told the guys to wear jackets during their performance, even the Surgeons; it was that cold inside the venue.

You could either wear ice skates or strap on ice cleats to enter the bar, so you didn't slip and fall on the ice floor. All guests upon entry also had to sign a waiver against slip-and-fall lawsuits. Since the boys did not have either, they had to rent ice paraphernalia. Jeb chose to wear ice skates, whereas Neusy, Marlon, and Hocker decided to strap on ice cleats they rented at the table near the entrance. The wooden stage was directly connected to a backdoor so the band would never have to step on the ice floor.

Jeb tested his skates. *Wow, they have decent skates here.* Bauer hockey skates, like he used at home. He skated to the bar area and back. Hocker stood there and was testing out his cleats. He was unsure of the whole ice thing and felt it safer if he stayed on stage. Jeb came full speed at Hocker and then stopped inches away, spraying Hocker with ice-snow from his waist on down. "What the fuck?" said Hocker while Neusy and Marlon laughed.

The wooden bar was also something of a novelty. The left corner of the bar was a section that extended back twelve feet toward the rear wall. At the end of this section of bar, there was a mini netted hockey goal. In the front of the bar laid a small, twelve-inch hockey stick and a tiny puck. Every fifteen minutes, one patron would be allowed to try and score a goal; if they made one, they would get a free beer.

The band was soundchecking a little before 6:00 p.m. Jeb was proud of his guys, and Marin was amazed. "Wow, you guys are good; I will say that. Beers on me when you guys are ready."

Jeb, Neusy, Marlon, and Hocker congregated in the merch booth and drank their perfectly chilled lagers. The merch booth was an actual booth recessed into the wall behind where the ice stopped. "Aaahh. The Canadians sure make some fine lagers," said Neusy.

"Yeaaah! It's a nice change to all of those bitter IPAs we're always drinking," said Jeb.

"Fucking A!" said Hocker.

It would be showtime soon. The Doctor was in the ICU, warming up on a Universe Guitar. The band was waiting on the bus as long as they could. It was super cold in the venue and they wanted to stay warm.

There would be no opening band. Neusy didn't need to worry about the opening band's backline equipment being in the way of his band's equipment. He comfortably drank his lager and waited for showtime.

The agents made it to Calgary and the venue. They walked into the Stick and Puck and were pleasantly surprised. "Wow!" said Crow. "This is pretty amazing."

They walked to the table and read the disclosures regarding the ice. When asked if it would be skates or cleats, Sparrow responded, "Cleats, of course, two sets."

"Well, actually, I would like skates," said Crow. "What type do you have?"

"Hockey or figure skates? Jackson or Bauer?" said the young lady in the winter jacket.

"I'll take a size ten of the Jackson." She handed him a pair of black Jackson figure skates. "Wow, this is great. Most skate rentals are garbage, but these are amazing."

Sparrow watched Crow put on his skates. "I had no idea you skated."

"I skated competitively from when I was a teen until I was twenty-three. I competed in eleven different states. I did OK, but it was more for fun. I wasn't good enough to get to the next level." Crow tied his skates, stood up, and walked onto the ice. He skated around the venue, then up to Jeb. "Hey, Jeb, how has it been? We were delayed a bit. Nice that you skate as well!"

"All OK, I guess. Nothing out of the ordinary. But to be honest, I don't know what we should be looking for other than someone messing with our equipment or stalking us."

"Yeah, just be vigilant. That guy in the eighties clothes?"

"The guitarist in Vancouver?"

"Let me know if you see him; we think he could be the guy. We will be stationed the same as before. I will be here on the ice and Sparrow backstage," said Crow. He skated away, making a toe loop and then landing an axel perfectly. Jeb was impressed and returned to the merch booth.

Scaggz burned his eighties clothes and found another clothing store that specialized in second-hand clothing. He found a snorkel parka with a hood that zipped all the way up, leaving only a small tunnel to see and breathe out of. *Perfect*, he thought. He zipped the snorkel up and left the store. He had only that small opening that he could see out.

He got back into his VW and could not drive with the hood zipped up; he could not see enough out the tiny slit. He unzipped the hood and drove his VW to the venue and found a parking spot in a nearby parking lot, far enough away not to be detected. He walked to the venue after zipping up his hood once again. After three days of not shaving, he had the beginnings of another beard. As he was walking, the whiskers were getting caught on the inside of the hood. It skewed the hood, along with his vision, and twice he walked into light poles. When he entered the venue, he chose the ice skates and skated around the venue, getting the layout. He spotted the agents and crew. The ice surface was large enough, and enough people were skating around, that he blended in. He skated to the bar, and then again to the side of the stage.

It was 9:00 p.m. The house was filled with about 250 people, estimated Jeb. The bar was filled from one end to the other. The people standing on the ice were anxiously waiting for the band to come on. The four waitresses were skating between the standing guests taking orders and delivering beers. The fans were mostly on skates, as this was Canada and people are born with skates on their feet. Jeb was watching the crowd. Nothing seemed out of the ordinary once he got past the fact that the concert was in an ice rink and the audience was skating around with beers in their hands, spilling everywhere.

Marlon was talking to a strange man wearing a snorkel; Neusy was watching the transaction. He had not seen one of these coats since he was a kid, vacationing in New York. The snorkel man bought two T-shirts and skated away. He returned with three beers, giving them to Marlon. Marlon distributed them to Jeb and Neusy. "Nice guy," said Marlon.

Hocker and the band were waiting on the bus. Jeb called Hocker on his cell phone. "Time to go on."

"Copy that," said Hocker, and he led the band into the stage door and onto the stage.

"Guten Tag, Calgary! It is cold in here, yah? It's time to rock with the Doctor! It reminds me of 'Polar Bear Days!'"

"WAAAAAAAHHH!!!!!"

"BRING IT!"

"ROCK WITH THE DOCTOR!!!! ROCK WITH THE DOCTOR!!!! ROCK WITH THE DOCTOR!!!!"

Nathan started the verse.

Walking upon the snow
I see your footprints go
Off in the distance

Look at your giant feet
Looking for seals to eat
Caught one in your glance
Vicious is your bite
It's hard to see you're white
Upon the tundra…
Deadly and huge are thee
Please stay away from me
Don't put me under….

The crowd loved the classic Centipedes song! Such a fitting song for the weather and the region it was being played in. The song finished, and the Doctor spoke once again.

"Would one of the pretty skating girls be kind enough to bring me a hot coffee? I am a bit cold up here."

A cute, skating waitress named Nancy skated back to the bar, got a coffee, set it on a tray, skated in and out of some patrons on the floor, and did a magnificent spinning axle right in front of the Doctor, holding the tray up high and not spilling a drop. When she came to a stop, she handed the Doctor his coffee.

"Ach! That was *wunderbar!* What is your name, my dear?"

"It's Nancy!"

"You are wunderbar! Danke!"

Nancy blushed and skated away to serve other customers.

Sparrow was on stage, watching the audience. He spotted Crow, watching people as he skated around doing various jumps and spins. Neither of them noticed the man in the snorkel parka as he followed Nancy to the bar and shadowed her the remainder of the evening.

When it was time for Nancy's break, she disappeared into the manager's office to warm up. With all eyes on the stage, no one noticed the waitress going on break with the man in the snorkel parka right behind her.

The Doctor played well; Scaggz enjoyed watching his ex-boss. With the show almost over, he returned his skates and left the venue. The Doctor ended the show with "Slap the Virgin," and the audience was screaming, "DOC-TOR! DOC-TOR! DOC-TOR!"

"Yah, now we must go. Danke Calgary!"

The lights came on, and the band walked out back. Hocker started breaking down the stage and Neusy braved the ice with his cleats to help him. Marlon and Jeb were selling lots of merch.

Hocker and Neusy finished breaking down the stage and loaded it out. The agents were now up front, returning their skates and cleats. There would be no meet and greet because of the cold and the ice. The Doctor did not want to be in the venue any more than he had to. So once the last of the merch was sold, Marlon and Jeb packed it up and loaded it out.

Jeb settled up with Marin, who was impressed that the evening went well after the late start. "You had me worried earlier, but you guys are professionals. Thanks for a great night." He handed Jeb an envelope with the cash settlement for the evening.

Jeb walked out to the bus; he was the last one. "Well, we have a couple of hours before Crabs comes back. I am going to rest. It's been a long day."

Someone pounded hard on the bus door. Neusy opened up, and Marin was standing there. "It's Nancy; she is in my office on my desk with two ice cleats stuck in her neck."

Chapter 36

"Where are the agents?" Neusy said.

Marin knew nothing of the agents. "What agents?"

"We have two FBI with us; they look like the Blues Brothers."

"I have seen these guys; didn't know they were with you. I will still have to call the police."

"Yes, yes, of course, just go find them. I'll get Jeb and we will come in." Neusy walked back to the bunks. Most of the guys were in their bunks, other than Marlon, Hocker, and Heinz, who was steaming broccoli. Neusy said, "Hey, Jeb." …. Nothing, he could hear that Jeb fell asleep. Again he called, "Jeb, wake up." … Nothing. He opened the curtain and shook Jeb. "Wake up; we have to go back inside."

Jeb jumped awake and hit his head on the top of his compartment. "What?"

"That waitress, the one that brought the coffee out, she is dead. We need to go in." Jeb climbed down and followed Neusy in.

Inside the venue, they had to put on the ice cleats to walk into the back office. Nancy laid there, her head nearly severed with the ice cleats. They weren't just in her neck, but looked like someone used them like a saw. The agents were in the room looking over the body. Sparrow said, "This one is a little more violent. I am guessing you two did not see anything?"

Neusy and Jeb shook their heads. Jeb said, "We are touring pros, not police or FBI; I have never seen this many dead people total in my life. I am sick, looking at this. So much blood."

"Well, when the neck is sliced open like this, that is what happens," said Crow.

The local Calgary Police entered the room, then a detective and crime scene officers. They collected samples, then fingerprinted Jeb and Neusy and ordered them to get the rest of the band and crew to be fingerprinted. Jeb brought them on the bus, which smelled like steamed broccoli. Crow said, "I have smelled dead bodies that don't smell this bad."

"Fuck, Heinz, open the damn windows when you do that shit," said Jeb.

The local police took fingerprints from everyone, and one by one, they went back to bed after convincing the officers and detective that they saw and knew nothing. Jeb said, "Guys, my crew and the band, they have no idea who did this or when it happened. These agents were here the whole time, and they did not see anything either."

"Is that everyone?" asked the detective.

"Where is the Doctor?" said Crow.

"Come on, he certainly didn't see anything."

"Go get him."

Jeb walked to the back and fetched the Doctor with the detective following. "What is this? I was sleeping. I don't like to be woken up!"

"We need to fingerprint you."

"You what? I don't know about this. Jeb, can't you do something?"

"No, they are insisting. Will we be cleared to leave after this? All of this is so unnecessary; we have been cleared from multiple crime scenes," said Jeb.

"No, I'll let you know when you can leave," said the detective.

"Yah, what is this? Black ink, you want me to put that on my fingers? This is just so primitive."

After listening to the Doctor complain for five minutes, everyone's fingerprints were collected. They waited, Cal returned, then they waited some more. Finally, at 4:00 a.m., they were allowed to leave. Cal said, "Maybe a heads up if there is another one, so I don't come here and have to wait like this. I know we are a bus now."

The drive to Edmonton took longer than usual due to the condition of the roads, and they arrived at the Old Vaudeville Theater after seven hours. It was a quaint auditorium, with dark wooden walls, plush red velvet curtains, brass wall sconces, and framed paintings of many famous Canadians. There was a giant moose head on the wall above to the left of the bar; ahead of it were two pool tables. Cal was exhausted and immediately went to check into his hotel room.

Jeb, Neusy, Marlon, and Hocker entered the venue, carrying some gear as always. Jeb began a conversation with the manager, Bobby Vinhauser. "Wow! You guys! I almost had to cancel the show. The police called me, and I had to agree to have a heavy police presence here in the venue! We have excellent pre-sale numbers, we are at 326, but I'm almost afraid to let it go on. You guys have a trail of death following you, I am hearing."

"Well, not our doing, I assure you," said Jeb. "Where can I set up my merch booth?"

"How about under the moose head on the back wall?"

"That should be fine," said Jeb.

"Marlon, Hocker, go grab some T-shirts and CD boxes out of the trailer. Neusy, go check out the stage."

Jeb scanned the area for his merch set up. He looked at the moose head. It would make a superior display.

Denise Dreckermund came bouncing in as if floating on air. She put her arms around Jeb and squeezed him tight. "Hi, Jeb, this is a nice venue. Sorry I missed the show yesterday; I didn't want to drive once the snow started. How was the show?"

"H, Denise. The show was good, but the after-show was not."

"I am here to help if you need; I'll go and sit over there in a booth if you need me." *Great*, thought Jeb.

The stage looked good to Neusy. It was twenty-eight feet wide, twenty feet deep, and four feet high with twenty-foot-long red-velvet curtains on both sides. Plenty of electrical outlets were flush with the stage's level. On both sides, outside the curtain, were the triple-stack PA speakers. It was very professional, and why shouldn't it be? It was an actual auditorium, not some cheesy local bar. Neusy went out to the equipment trailer to start wheeling in the cabinets. He would only need Hocker to help him lift the heavy stuff onto stage later, after Hocker helped Jeb bring in the lightweight merchandise. *Pussies!*

After the merch was loaded in, Hocker went up on stage to help Neusy set up. Denise walked over to Jeb. "I can help you hang the merch." Jeb let her hang up some posters and displays after he had the T-shirts hanging from the moose. "Tomorrow will be a good show. That venue always does well."

"I have never been to Regeena!" said Jeb.

"No, no, not Regeena, it's Regyyna, like vagina."

"OK, didn't know," Jeb chuckled. They finished setting up merch, and then Denise disappeared. A half hour later, soundcheck started early; Jeb once again was pleased.

The agents arrived and joined the party. "Hi, Jeb," said Crow.

"Hi, guys. It looks like you will have quite the gathering tonight. We just got off the phone with the locals. They are supplying six officers. We will have the place locked down."

"Well, good," said Jeb.

The agents took off to get a feel for the venue. All set up and an hour till doors, the down time was an opportunity for Jeb to leave and get something to eat. He thought about going up the street to the steakhouse he saw.

Neusy approached him and said, "I couldn't help but notice that there is a steakhouse within walking distance." Jeb just gave him the I-am-way-ahead-of-you look. "I had a feeling you were thinking the same."

They silently left and walked to the steakhouse, where the band was already enjoying dinner with Denise bouncing around the table from guy to guy, showing pictures on her phone. "Hi, guys," she said when she saw Jeb and Neusy. "I told the guys this place was here and they wanted to go."

The Doctor had also decided to go to the steakhouse and was with them. He had what looked like a hamburger, but must be a vegan burger. Neusy and Jeb gave each other looks of disgust as they walked to the bar away from the commotion of Denise. "I was hoping to avoid being with everyone," said Jeb.

"Yeah, me as well. But you know Denise, she always wants to be the center of attention." The bartender approached, and Neusy said, "Two lagers. Big mugs, if you have big mugs, and two menus. We are not in a big hurry but need to be back up the street in fifty minutes."

"Yes," said the bartender. "We have the Antler Dust Lager on special." They nodded their response. "I heard the Doctor is playing tonight. You guys are with him?"

"Yup," said Jeb.

"How is he? Is he nice? He is a great guitarist."

"Well, he is right over there eating something I would not."

"Excellent, I will say hello to him. Just order within the next fifteen minutes and you are fine. We are not that busy yet."

"Thanks," said Neusy. Then to Jeb, "I hope we have an easy night. No bullshit and no murders. Perhaps we should try and patrol the venues a little bit."

"I'm not putting myself in harm's way. I prefer just to do my job. I'm keeping an eye out. I think that if whoever is doing this wanted to hurt one of us, they would have. I do find it strange that there seems to have been someone always in the background and even helping us."

"Are you talking about Kamloops?"

"Yes, the hotel with the bikers. A guy in eighties clothes? The guitarist from Vancouver wore eighties clothes. Then the agents with the messages on their bottles. It had to be that guitarist. Marlon, he talked with that guy in Vancouver, the eighties-clothes guy. Marlon also talked to a guy near the border. Then he said he ran into that guy again. What about that strange guy last night with the weird hood?"

"The snorkel? Those are cool. But I see what you mean. I saw him bring beers to the booth."

"Yeah, I didn't say anything because it was dark, and I am not sure what I saw, but I thought for a second I saw Johnny Scaggz a few shows ago, still in the States."

"Scaggz. Ha! He is living off the grid, totally doing the hippie thing. He didn't come out this year. Remember last year he came around? It was cool to see him."

"I know, as I said, I think my eyes were playing tricks on me. I thought someone looked like him, but could not focus on who it was. Oh shit, Hocker just texted me. He wants to know where we are. Guess we don't get a little downtime."

Jeb texted Hocker their location while the volume at the table behind them grew. Denise's voice was at a high screaming level with lots of laughter. The Doctor suddenly got loud. "Yah, that is funny, Denise, you always have good stories. You are right; it is perfectly OK to drink a little wine before the show. Buuut, juuuusst not tooo muuuuch." They all touched glasses and took a sip of their drinks.

"Great, they will all be buzzing tonight," said Jeb as Hocker and Marlon walked in.

"Thanks for letting us know you were leaving," said Hocker.

"Have a beer and get over it."

The bartender took the orders as the boys had to listen to the commotion behind them. When their food arrived, they ate quickly and headed back to the venue. It wasn't the downtime that Jeb was hoping for.

The Doctor was feeling pretty good, still laughing with the Surgeons and Denise, when they left. "Yah boys, go in the venue; you must do work now. We will stay here und have another drink and listen to Denise some more." Jeb felt he should have just stayed in the venue. That was not worth it, although his ribeye was terrific.

Scaggz drove past the Old Vaudeville Theater and saw the six police cars parked in the parking lot. "Hmmmmm!" he said to himself. He found parking next to a steakhouse, about a block from the venue. He saw the Doctor and the Surgeons through the window. He did not want to wear the snorkel again, making him stand out after the last show. There he got away with it because of the ice. He put on his Jurgen Weislangwolf shirt that he purchased from Marlon in Calgary but did not have another coat. He also wore a black beanie that he had in the VW. In the dark venue, no one would recognize him, but he needed a coat.

Scaggz walked through the kitchen door of the steakhouse, and no one said anything to him. He learned that if he walked through an area with confidence like he was supposed to be there, very few people noticed or cared. He walked into the dining room, careful not to be seen. He eyed the table where the Doctor was having a good time. There, next to them but partially obstructed from their view, were their coats. He walked around the bar to the partition hiding the restrooms, and there were the coats on the wall waiting for him. He found a black winter coat, put it on, and continued out the front door past the hostess who said, "Thank you, sir, have a good evening."

Scaggz walked to the venue, then around back again and in the stage door. When Crow stopped him, he said, "Who are you? I am late for work." Crow let him in. Scaggz walked the club and watched the police. The audience was starting to fill in. He walked back behind the stage, and there was Crow again. "I have to run back to my car; I forgot something." He would show those agents and the police that he is quicker and more intelligent than they were. *Watch your temper tonight*, he told himself, *and stick to the plan. Wow, this coat sure is comfortable.*

The Doctor, along with Denise and the Surgeons, walked back to the venue. Denise insisted they watch the opening band. "They are fun; I have seen them many times."

The Doctor agreed. "Yes, we must see them if Denise says they are good."

They arrived at the venue but had trouble entering; the security guard said they needed a ticket. Denise finally convinced him that they were tonight's act after pulling up YouTube videos of other shows. Nathan was happy to be back at the venue, as he was freezing from walking back from the steakhouse without a coat.

Tonight's opening act would be very appealing to most of the lads on the bus. It would be appealing to almost any red-blooded man. It featured three vaudeville-type stage dancers dressed in red Royal Canadian Mounted Police uniform jackets and short red skirts with black fishnet stockings and garter belts. They all wore pink panties, and you could certainly see them when they kicked their legs up in the air.

They would dance and kick their legs up in the air just like the old chorus dancers of a century gone by. They were called Miss Mountie. The blonde was called Hally, the brunette was Ally, and the redhead was Sally.

Tonight, the band would not stay in the green room and wait to play at the appointed time. They would be active spectators of this extravagant show. Not only were these girls talented dancers, but they were gorgeous. Nathan looked with great intent. The

Doctor was enjoying the show; he thought the redhead was kind of cute. The dancing damsels also entranced Heinz and Torsten.

The girls' male counterparts were driving hard metallic rhythms. It was hard to believe that they could dance to those rhythms and hard, distorted guitar riffs. The band was immensely talented, and tight to boot. The harder the band played, the harder the girls danced with legs kicking high in the air and headbanging movements in between.

During the chorus, the girls sang.
You raise your glass or we'll kick your ass
Our legs you want to see
We'll kick them high up to your eyes
So drink and sing with me

The last song by Miss Mountie was like a Slayer number. The girls gave the most dynamic performance of the evening. The Doctor found it interesting that they could dance to the speed of the double bass drum and fast guitar rhythm. They were kicking and headbanging furiously to the rhythm.

Many men dreamed of spending the night with one of these hot vixens, but would they even last in bed with one of these energetic hotties? The song came to an abrupt end, and the girls were sweating bullets; their hair was drenched and hanging down straight past their shoulders. Short of breath, they began to speak to the crowd.

"Thanks so much, everyone!" said Sally.

"You've been a great audience!" said Ally.

"We hope to see you again!" said Hally.

After a twenty-minute intermission, Neusy checked on the gear. "Now, would you please welcome, the Doctor of Dynamics, Jurgen Weislangwolf!"

The Doctor, in good spirits, approached the microphone. "Achhh! Those girls were fantastic, yah?"

"YAAAAAHHH!"

"FUCKING EHHH RIGHT!"

"ENCOREEEEE!" WHOAAAAH!

"Well, we won't disappoint either. Here is 'Polar Bear Days!'"

The wah-wah pedal started the riff.

"Oh my god! 'Polar Bear Days!'" shouted a fan.

"That's my favorite song!" said his buddy.

Walking upon the snow

I see your footprints go
Off in the distance
Look at your giant feet
Looking for seals to eat
Caught one in your glance
Your camouflage is white
Vicious is your bite
Upon the tundra...
Deadly and huge are thee
Please stay away from me
Don't put me under....

Scaggz bought a ticket and walked in through the main entrance. Keeping out of sight from anyone that could possibly recognize him, he walked into the back by the stage, and then backstage, showing the security guard an old laminate tour pass. The security guard let him back and hated standing on the side of the stage where the Doctor's amp was blasting his inner ear.

Scaggz ducked into the Doctor's green room as he passed by. He grabbed two bananas and some peanuts. The next green room was also empty. Three women's costumes were hanging on a rack, and Scaggz grabbed three pink panties. He entered the Doctor's green room again and rummaged through all the guitar cases. He found five spare picks from a previous tour that had *The Doctor* in text on one side and an image of the Universe Guitar on the back.

He walked out and into the men's room and entered one of the stalls, pulling out a wireless mic receiver that he had designed. The receiver was coupled with a transmitter mounted in his VW. He exited the bathroom and made his way to the soundboard. The sound engineer was one he did not recognize and was more interested in his phone than the show. Scaggz ducked down in front and, when Nathan was not singing, pulled his input out and plugged it into his receiver. He then plugged his receiver into the mixing board before Nathan started singing once again. The bypass in the receiver would allow Nathan to sing as usual.

More challenging for Scaggz was to walk out the rear door again near Crow. He showed his old tour ID again to the security guard and was backstage, but instead of heading to the green rooms, he walked in the opposite direction to the rear door.

"YAAAAAAAAAAAAH!!!" screamed the Doctor and, feeling the effects of the wine, started playing 'Slap the Virgin,' pumping his fist in the air. The audience was screaming. Neusy gave Jeb the he-is-fucked-up look. Jeb gave Neusy a forward nod towards the Doctor and then down in agreement.

Jeb looked over at Marlon, who was enjoying a beer by the merch booth. "YAAAAAAAH!!!! I love it here in Edmonton. WHOOOO!"

Scaggz stopped for a moment to watch. Nathan was singing as usual; he was better at holding his liquor. Scaggz, the mastermind, was proud that his bypass receiver was working undetected. Nathan was now up front shaking his head. He screamed right before the solo into the mic, "LADIES AND GENTLEMEN, THE DOCTOR OF DYNAMICS."

The Doctor walked to the front of the stage and, with his head way back and the hair on his wig flying behind him, dropped to his knees and played the solo. WOW! The audience cherished the moment and let it be known. Jeb was embarrassed, and Neusy covered his eyes.

Scaggz walked to the back door to where Agent Crow was standing. "That's it, they have plenty of coverage, told me I can go home. Are you new here?"

Agent Crow opened the door for Scaggz and said, "No, I'm Agent Crow."

Scaggz hurried up the street to his VW and got in. He drove to the front of the venue and parked his vehicle in such a way so that he could drive away quickly. He waited for the song to stop and the Doctor to speak, and then turned on his transmitter. He plugged in his microphone and said to the quiet room, "Ladies and Gentlemen, let's hear it for the Doctor." Jeb was looking around the room, thinking that the sound engineer was cutting the show short. Neusy, too, was concerned and walked the room.

"At this time, a magic trick. Are you ready?" The audience cheered. "Agent Crow, reach into your jacket pocket, please." Scaggz turned off his transmitter and drove away. Crow reached into his pocket and pulled out three pink panties tied together with the Doctor's spare picks incorporated into the knots.

Chapter 37

After the show, since there were no murders and just a practical joke, the agents and the police interviewed a few fans near the stage. The security guard by the stage said he did not see anything and could barely think with the guitar's volume.

The meet and greet went well, and right on time, Cal arrived. "Bro, tell me we can leave on time. It is going to take us close to ten hours to get to Regeena."

"It's pronounced Regyyna, like vagina, is what I am told," said Jeb. "But as far as I know, we can leave on time, and I want to get the fuck out of here." Neusy and Hocker loaded out, and Jeb with Marlon finished the meet and greet. Business as normal. Jeb collected the guarantee and then loaded out the merch.

"Why are you in such a hurry?" asked the Doctor.

"Tight schedule tonight; we need to leave in a half hour."

"Yah, I will drive with Denise. She will let me drive. You will see. We will get there before the bus." No one cared.

"Are we a bus?"

"Crabs, my friend, go, we are good. The Doctor will get there on his own."

"Whooohoooo, we are rolling!"

The ride was uneventful, a stop for gas in the middle of the night while the guys were sleeping. Cal was driving with his tunes cranked. Life was good.

Jeb awoke first and walked up front and made coffee. "Jeb, fill me up, will you?" asked Cal. Jeb poured himself a cup and emptied the remainder into Cal's massive mug.

Jeb sat down and reconciled the books. Neusy awoke and joined Jeb. "What a night. There were 428 people, and merch was killer. We needed a night like that."

Neusy agreed. "Awesome! What have you heard about the show tonight in Regeena?"

From up front, Cal shouted, "Apparently, it's called Regyyna, like Vagina. Got that son? Just like vagina… Anymore coffee, Jeb?"

"OK, very interesting."

They arrived in Regina; the band and crew were all awake and in the front lounge. Lady Logger, a loud-mouthed, obnoxious woman, stood 6'2" with red hair and green eyes. She had freckles and a cleft chin. She had square shoulders, a large chest, square hips, was dressed in a red flannel shirt with the sleeves rolled up to her elbows, with brown work pants and mountain boots. She was a local that worked in the logging industry. Not very attractive, but she sure could swing an ax just as good as any man. She was a presence in the Moosehead Lodge and was waiting for an autograph when the bus drove up.

Like most Western Canadian bars, the Moosehead Lodge was made of local timbers cut down by the local logging company. The main features of this venue were the many moose heads that decorated the walls. At least fifteen moose heads, Jeb counted, just from looking around the room, all with large antlers. The stage was fifteen by twenty feet from what Neusy calculated; a decent size for the band's setup, but smaller than yesterday's show.

The tour bus pulled up to the doors early. Being a regular, Lady Logger informed Cal where he should park the bus behind the club in front of the stage doors. "Thank you."

"Can I get a prescription?" she asked.

Jeb, hearing this, told her, "The Doctor is not traveling with us. You can get the autograph tonight during the meet and greet." They all exited the bus; it was 11:30 a.m. so they still had time.

Lady Logger was able to get autographs from some of the Surgeons.

Jeb made it known that they needed to be back at 3:30 for load-in. They all went in different directions. The band, minus Heinz, went in one direction searching for food; Heinz stayed behind to steam broccoli. Marlon was off in search of a dispensary. Neusy stayed with Jeb and Hocker; they found a nearby sports bar for lunch.

At 3:30, Jeb, Marlon, Neusy, and Hocker entered the doors and were greeted by Bill. "Hey there, guys! I am the manager, welcome; let me open the double stage doors."

"Thanks a lot," said Jeb.

"Well, it's great to be here in Regeena! Glad you have a dispensary walking distance," said Marlon.

"No, no, not Regeena; it's Regyyna, like vagina."

"You're kidding me. Well, I do like a vagina," said Marlon.

Bill motioned at one of the bouncers sitting off to the side. "Hey, Freddy, what's the name of this town?"

"It's Regyyna!"

"Okaaaaay, Regina, like vagina. We get it now," said Jeb.

Neusy and Hocker started with the equipment while Marlon and Jeb started bringing in the merch. Jeb decided to set up in a little alcove just right of the entry door. He set up his portable table, and Marlon brought in the boxes of T-shirts, posters, picks, CDs, and DVDs. Neusy and Hocker continued with the gear, setting it on the stage. After everything was set up, it was time for the customary ritual of some brewskies.

"How about four Moosehead Lagers, Bill?"

"We are out, but their competition is a better beer: Wagging Moose Tail Pilsner."

"OK, we will try that. How are we looking for the show tonight?" asked Jeb.

"The usual, I would guess."

"What's the usual mean?"

"It will be good. We draw well."

At 4:30, Lady Logger barged in the front door. She sat at the far end of the bar, about fifteen feet from the guys, sitting at the left corner.

"Hey, Billy! Give me a twenty-two ouncer of that Wagging Moose Tail shit! I'm fucking thirsty! It's been a piss poor day!"

"We met her earlier when we arrived. What's her name?" asked Jeb.

"That's Lady Logger."

"She's pretty rough looking. She looks like she could beat up any dude. She gives me the chills. She wanted an autograph."

"She can! So watch yourselves with that one!"

"Hey Billy, who are these goofballs?" she said as she drank her beer.

"Oh, well, they're with the band that's playing here tonight."

"Yeaaah! I remember you," she said, looking at Jeb. "You wouldn't let me get the Doctor's fucking autograph."

"He was not here. Where is he, by the way? Anyone seen him?" said Jeb.

"Hey Hocker, is she a relative of yours?" said Neusy.

"Fuck you, asshole!"

"Hey Billy, give me another twenty-two ouncer!" demanded Lady Logger. "Hurry up!" BUURRRRP! "Hey, you guys want to play a game of darts?"

"No thanks, not right now," said Jeb.

"What's the matter, you afraid to lose to a woman?"

"No, we just have more work to do."

The guys finished their beers and said bye to Bill as they walked outside to search for the Doctor. They walked down the street and spotted Denise with the Doctor sitting in a pizza restaurant.

"Glad he made it," said Jeb sarcastically.

"Yeah, but his own funeral if he didn't; that was a bad decision. Let's head back to the venue," said Neusy, and the four turned around and headed back.

The venue had a bar that did not stay closed on a show night and was open when they returned. A few guys from the lumber mill came in and sat at the bar for a drink or two. Lady Logger was starting on her fourth twenty-two ouncer of Wagging Moose Tail Pilsner and was feeling no pain. Not everyone liked her. Most people didn't. She challenged everyone that walked in to a game of darts, but they all declined.

"What a bunch of fucking pussies! You're all afraid to lose to a woman! All right, who wants to see how many logs we can split in five minutes? I challenge anyone here."

A logger named Reilly O'Reilly answered her back, "Alright, I have a truckload of logs parked outside. I challenge you!"

"Let's go then!" said Lady Logger.

The two went outside. Reilly grabbed a small log while Lady Logger grabbed a larger log. They both grabbed an ax out of his truck bed and started hacking logs in half on the sidewalk in front of the venue. Bill walked outside and said, "Hey, you guys be sure to sweep up when you're done." After five minutes, Reilly split twenty logs and Lady Logger split twenty-four.

"Well, I guess you win, Lady Logger."

"You bet your ass I did! I'm thirsty; time for another beer. I won, you're buying."

"Let's sweep up this sawdust first."

"No, you sweep up all the sawdust; you lost!"

The band was soundchecking when everyone walked back in. Jeb loathed these types of venues that were open before the show. There always seemed to be a few on each tour. Locals drinking in their favorite bar while the guys worked to prepare for the show later in the evening.

The agent's plane was on time and they were tired and ready for a break when they walked in the venue. Road life was more difficult than they had prepared for and they had no patience when the patrons started laughing. They looked like they had been run through the wash a dozen times. Their suits were wrinkled and faces showed the late nights and long days filled with travel.

Lady Logger walked up to them and said, "The Blues Brothers. What's your deal here, guys?" They wanted no trouble with the large muscular woman standing in front of them. When they tried to walk around her, she said, "Hey, you can't talk to me?"

"Sparrow and Crow, FBI. We need to see the tour manager," said Sparrow. More laughter from the bar.

"Well, at least give me a fucking autograph so I can prove to people that I met the Blues Brothers."

Several autographs and photos later, they made it into the bar. Crow said to Jeb, "Rough crowd here tonight. We will be stationed as usual, in the back and the front. I will walk the Doctor in when the time comes."

"OK, sounds good," said Jeb.

"Jeb and Neusy, my boys," said Denise, bouncing in and hugging the pair. "The Doctor and I had a lovely time. We stopped and saw a moose. We ended up here in town at a pizza place. He said he was so glad he drove with me."

"That's great," said Neusy. He looked at Jeb and smiled. Jeb returned the can't-wait-to-get-out-of-Canada-in-the-morning look.

The time was 7:00 p.m. and the club was filled with a little over 200 people, primarily loggers and lumberjacks, with a few hockey fans. The drinks were flowing. "Hoo hah, hoo hah! Bring the Doctor, rah rah!" is what they chanted. Lady Logger joined in the chanting with some of her logging friends.

"Come on, where is this fucking Doctor?" yelled someone.

Their chanting was a bit premature because the band wouldn't play for another two hours. The noisy crowd continued to drink and get louder.

At last, the announcement came. Marlon would introduce the band. "And now, the moment you have all been waiting for! Here he is, the man that needs no introduction but will get one anyway. The Doctor of Dynamics! My best friend and mentor, Jurgen Weislangwolf!"

"WWWWAHHHHHHHAHAHAHAHAHAHHHH!!!!"

"Guten Abend, Reegeena!"

"Regyyna like vagina!" shouted the crowd in a lazy, laid-back tone.

"Ach, so sorry! Regyyna, guten Tag! Und now, here is an old Centipedes song, 'In Your Pants!'" The Doctor played the famous riff and Nathan began to sing.

I saw you walking toward me
With your jeans glued to your hips
I imagined what could be
I see your face you looked at me
And it seemed so did your tits
I want to get in your pants
Ohh baby, give it to me strong and hard

I'm in your pants

The band continued playing song after song, with the receptive crowd singing along and getting louder after every song. The chorus of voices singing along with Nathan elevated his performance. The Doctor, caught off guard by this, was constantly trying to get Nathan's attention to tell him to stop acting like an American hair metal singer; it was not the image he wanted. Nathan could not be bothered to look at the Doctor. He was focused on the audience, who was locked in on him as he moved his head around while jumping all over the stage. Having failed to get Nathan's attention, the Doctor turned his amp up louder to drown out the noise in the room.

A girl ran out of the women's room and up to the bartender. "Oh my God… There's something strange in the women's room!"

"Calm down, girlie! What is it?"

"There is a moose antler coming out of under a stall and blood all over the floor."

The bartender came out from behind the bar and followed the girl into the restroom. He saw the moose antler and blood coming from under the stall. He slowly approached the stall door and pulled it open.

Lady Logger was sitting and leaning backward in the toilet stall with a moose antler protruding from her vagina. She was undoubtedly dead. Bill was not a weak man, but he got sick to his stomach. He had never seen anything like this before. He grabbed his cell phone and called the locals. The policeman on the phone told him to seal off the club and not to let anyone out. Agents Sparrow and Crow noticed the commotion and entered the women's room. Bill exited the women's room and was stopped by the FBI agents. He told them he had to seal the club off and hurried away. Bill went to the front door bouncer and told him not to let anyone leave. He then found the other bouncer and told him not to let anyone out the back door. The band played on, unaware of what had happened. The audience had stopped singing along and focused back on the Doctor with his guitar being the loudest sound coming from the stage.

Agents Sparrow and Crow, standing over the body of Lady Logger, took pictures. "Fuck me! Again, how do we never see anything?" said Crow.

"In all my years, I've never seen anything like this."

"Gruesome, isn't it? It's a fucking moose antler!"

Sparrow noticed a small window in the back of the women's room was partially open. "Possibly the assailant escaped through there."

"Could be."

It was about midnight when the band stopped playing and said good night. The back door bouncer walked up the stage and told them that no one could leave the venue until the police arrived. The band looked puzzled and walked off to sit in the green room. At 12:15 a.m., two uniformed police officers arrived and met with Bill and began to ask him questions. Agents Sparrow and Crow were still in the women's room examining the crime scene when the police officers walked in. "Who are you guys?" asked one of the officers.

"I'm Agent Sparrow, and this is Agent Crow of the FBI."

"You have no authority here; this is Canada!"

"We have a special agreement with your government to cooperate in investigating these murders that began in the US."

Later in the venue, questioning the patrons, band, and staff, Agent Crow noticed that one of the moose heads on the wall to the right of the bar was missing an antler. They walked up to it, and it became more apparent as they approached. Written on the remaining antler were the words ***It's Regyyna, like Vagina***!

Chapter 38

Denise was sitting in a booth by herself, weeping. "How could this be happening to my band? They are simple people and would never hurt anyone." She took to social media and posted what had happened. The whole Centipedes community soon spread the word and were appalled. Social media was all buzzing with the happenings of Jurgen Weislangwolf's North American tour. Scaggz read this and was proud to be back on tour with people noticing his work.

All sorts of law enforcement were now in the venue. Another seven cars arrived to help with taking statements, and a detective was on the scene. He was talking with Sparrow and Crow. "Why did you guys not check in with the locals up here when you arrived? All this could have been avoided."

"We had it under control. This guy is in and out, and no one sees him; it would have happened with your guys in here as well," said Crow, carefully not mentioning the panties that were found in his pocket last night.

"It does not look like you had anything under control," said the detective.

"We don't know if this was the same guy that is following the tour. That woman was rude as hell to everyone. I could tell when I walked in here that no one liked her much," Sparrow said.

"Regardless, we have to assume it is the same guy, from what I learned about this tour. This tour should have been shut down and not allowed to continue through Canada. Now it's on my plate."

"Well, good luck! We were here the entire night. We were watching and didn't see anything."

"Nobody leaves. I am insisting that the entire tour stays through tomorrow until we can get this situation here under control."

"I'll tell them," said Crow. "Let us know if you need anything from us."

"I think we will be fine."

After Jeb learned that they would be delayed, he called Cal. "No rush, we are being detained, apparently, until at least sometime late in the day."

"What, again? This is getting out of control. My driving hours are all fucked up. It's a good thing that it is an off day before we have to be in Moorhead. I'm going back to sleep. Let me know when you have more info."

The detective canceled all after-show activity, so no meet and greet. Jeb was concerned that all the fans locked in the venue would be getting free autographs. It was a disaster. Many people knew Denise, and she was making introductions to the Doctor, who was more than happy to sign, liking the attention. The fact that no one paid for the access to him did not bother him. That is why he had Jeb—to make the tour successful.

Jeb sat in the back by the merch booth with Hocker and Neusy. Marlon was somewhere, but nowhere to be seen. "Well, Neusy, another clusterfuck. Look at him signing all that shit. He should be back here. People would just come over here as well, but we could control it. At least we would sell more merch. So now we are sitting here with our thumbs up our asses, waiting."

"How about a beer? I'm waiting for the coroner to arrive. I want to see how they remove that woman's body. I don't think a normal gurney will suffice," said Neusy.

"Good point." They could still get a beer from the bar and brought one back for Hocker, who was standing around waiting for instructions. They got questioned by the locals with the same answers: nothing had been seen, nothing heard, and nobody knew anything.

After another hour, the coroner showed up. Two men entered the restroom and then exited it and talked with the detective. The detective waved his hands around, and two of the officers followed the men back into the restroom. After a minute, one of the coroner's men walked out back and then back in with a second gurney.

Five minutes later, they wheeled Lady Logger out of the restroom strapped to both gurneys. It took all the men to wheel her out back. Neusy said, "Well, there you go. Not all that exciting."

They finished their beers. Now, a couple of hours after the show, Jeb wanted the guys to load-out the equipment while they were still with it and had the energy. "Where is Marlon?" he asked Neusy.

"I saw him a while ago talking with some guy up front. They seemed to be in serious conversation. Look, he is coming back here now with a beer."

Marlon, all excited, drinking the beer, said, "I just had an incredible conversation with this guy up front. He bought me a beer. He didn't look like a guy that toured, but he said he has been touring for the last twenty-five years. He gave me lots of advice. He said that soon I would be able to tour manage myself. He bought me a beer. Then the police called him to question him, and he was cleared to leave."

"You are really taking this free beer thing to another level. But I need you near the merch booth. That is what I'm paying you for. What did he look like?" asked Jeb.

"He wore a Jurgen Weislangwolf shirt. You know, the cool one with the Surgeons on the back and the Doctor on the front holding the Universe Guitar like a scalpel. That's my favorite shirt that we are selling. He had a baseball cap on that had some music festival's name on it. Short hair and clean shaven. Kind of a familiar face."

"Did he buy a shirt from you tonight?"

"I don't think so."

"So, where did he get that shirt? That's a new design that I came up with for this tour. He must have been at another show. OK, guys, start breaking down the stage. We have waited long enough."

Hocker and Neusy walked up on stage and started breaking it down. Jeb instructed Marlon to start loading out the merch. The detective stormed to the back where Jeb was standing and said, "Hey, did I say you could start messing with the stage?"

"It's getting late, and my guys cannot stay around all night and expect to load-out when you are finished. They will be too tired; they don't deserve to be punished like that. Look at the stage. The band was up there, and whoever did this was not on stage and not back here. If you want to look for clues, then go ahead. But we still have a job to do and have to move on to the next city."

"Well… Well… OK, I don't think that I will find any clues on the stage, so you have my permission to take that stuff outside."

"OK. Please tell security back there so that they don't mess with us. By the way, I think that one of your officers questioned the guy that did this and let him walk out. So he was right here under your nose."

"What? What are you talking about?"

"Just a guy that apparently has been at another show that none of us recognized. That would explain a lot. Talk with Marlon over there. He was talking to the guy."

The detective, with the agents, took Marlon into a booth and questioned him for an hour while Jeb loaded out all of the merch. A sketch artist was called in, and Marlon gave his description. He returned when Jeb had the last of the merchandise loaded up and said, "Wow, that was intense. Good thing I smoked some weed in the men's room. I had to describe that guy I was talking to. I could never do that straight."

Jeb wheeled out the last of the merchandise with his hand truck. When he returned, Marlon was sitting with Denise, and the two were taking selfies together. Marlon said, "Denise is going to post pictures on the Centipedes fan site. It should be cool!"

"I'll tell you what would be cool: if you helped Neusy up there."

Chapter 39

"How much longer do you need us here, wasting time like this? We are all on the bus, just waiting. We have a border crossing and then a show tomorrow night. But it's already noon. We have been here, as requested, all night and morning. You were done interviewing the concert-goers hours ago, and if we don't leave, I have to pay another day for our driver's hotel room," said Jeb to the detective.

"I guess it will be OK if you leave. Just make sure I can contact you."

"The FBI agents will be with us. They are riding back with us. You can get hold of us through them."

Jeb called Cal, and within a half hour, Cal was in the driver's seat. The agents appeared with Denise, laughing and taking pictures. They entered the bus. Jeb said to Denise, "We need to leave. Say your goodbyes quick." Twenty minutes later, Denise was still talking with the band, laughing and taking more pictures. Jeb instructed Cal to move the bus. Cal realized what Jeb was doing and shouted out, "Whooohoo, we are rolling, fellas."

"Yah, Jeb, you are always so rough," said the Doctor. Jeb ignored the comment and Neusy gave him the great-idea-to-rid-the-bus-of-Denise look.

Denise jumped up and ran to the front. Cal opened the door, and she was out. Jeb said, "Words do not work with her. Thanks, my friend, you knew exactly what I was doing."

"You bet, brother!" replied Cal. "I always got your back. Goodbye Regina, and goodbye to Canada! Are we a bus there, Jebster?"

"Yes, we are a bus."

"That's it! We are REALLY ROOOOLLLLIIINNNGGG! This will be a long day. Nine hours to Moorhead without stops, and we have the border and all the other bullshit stops you want me to make. We are crossing back at the Portal, North Dakota crossing. I hope all of their visas are in order," said Cal.

"Everything is fine. They already used the visas when they arrived from Austria. So all is good."

"I don't know. There is always something with you guys. Plus you have Sparrow and Crow riding back with you."

"Yes, but entering the US with FBI should not be a problem."

Jeb left Cal to do the driving and sat at his workstation. The Doctor, the agents, Neusy, and Marlon were still in the lounge while the others were in their bunks, resting after the long night. Neusy looked at Jeb, who started working, and said, "That was an interesting time here in Canada. This cannot continue." Jeb looked up with the you-got-that-right look, and Neusy continued, "Agents Sparrow and Crow, do you have any suspects? This is getting out of hand. Jeb, you should cancel the remaining dates."

The Doctor, who was sitting in the rear of the lounge, heard this. "Yah, we will not cancel the shows. We will lose too much money, und I cannot go home without this money. My women, they need to eat."

"Well, there you have it," said Jeb.

"You may be shut down if this guy is not caught and this continues. The practical jokes aside, the higher-ups might shut you down," added Crow.

"Can they do that?" asked the Doctor.

"I don't know. Let's hope for the best," said Jeb.

Three hours later they were at the border. Jeb woke up the guys who were sleeping. They did not get out on the Canadian side. Jeb decided the refund of a couple hundred in taxes that will arrive in two months was not worth the time and caused other expenses, such as paying Cal overtime. They made it to the US side and were instructed to park in the bus area. Jeb said, "OK, let me have all your passports. Marlon, I really hope you do not have any weed on you."

"Oh shit… I forgot, sorry," said Marlon.

"Yah, you see, this is once again no good," the Doctor added.

"Flush it!" said Neusy.

"Man, this is good shit. Maybe I will hide it in a guitar case," said Marlon.

"Fucking flush it!" said Jeb.

"If you don't flush it, I will drag you out of the bus myself and turn you in," said Hocker. "I am not going through this shit again. I want to go back to sleep."

Marlon did what he was told. When they heard the toilet flush, the Doctor said, "You are so violent, Hocker."

A border agent walked on the bus before Hocker could respond. Jeb handed him the passports. Same as the Canadian side, he called out for each member of the tour to raise their hand when their name was called. He then said, "You two, Blues Brothers, why are your passports not in the stack that the tour manager handed me?"

Crow replied, "Agents Sparrow and Crow, FBI." They both held up their badges on cue.

"OK, that's not getting you in. I need your passports."

"Here is mine," said Sparrow.

Crow reached in and out of all of his pockets but could not find his passport. He took everything out of his pockets, still nothing. "I misplaced mine. It's probably in my suitcase under the bus."

"Come with me," said the border agent. "Get your suitcase. The rest of you wait on the bus." Crow followed the agent off the bus. Jeb looked at Neusy and gave him a click of his head to the right. Neusy responded with eyebrows raised and a head shake.

After fifteen minutes, the border agent brought Crow back on the bus. Cal said, "Well, that wasn't too bad."

"I could not find my passport," exclaimed Crow. "Somehow, I misplaced it. He said being an FBI agent could be quicker, but they need proof that I am an American citizen. He said it could take hours as it has to go through a central contact point for this kind of issue. He can't just pick up a phone and get approval. There is a procedure."

Cal said, "We don't have time, and they won't let you in. We can either leave him here, Jeb, or get a hotel nearby, if there is one, and finish the drive in the morning. I am estimating another five to six hours. You guys are so lucky you have an off day today."

"Let's wait a little and see. We have not even been cleared ourselves."

The border agent returned with the passports and said, "I need all the Austrians to follow me."

They did as they were told. The Doctor was complaining, "This is so tiring! Why do they always do this coming into the US? In Europe, we do not have these types of problems."

"Sir, we need to process each of you. Please follow. It should not take too long."

"So," said Neusy, "here we are again, but heading back in."

"At least Marlon is not fucking us up again," said Hocker.

"They haven't asked me yet about what we have on board. They may still toss the bus." Then, to the agents, "We are clean, no weed."

"Hey," said Sparrow, "it's legal in Canada. That's all we know."

One by one, the Austrians returned. Nathan was first. "That was easy! They looked at my passport und my visa, und took my picture. Herr Doctor is with them now."

Soon they were all back on board, and so was the border agent. He said to Jeb, "Tour manager, any alcohol or tobacco on board that was purchased in Canada?"

Jeb looked at Neusy with the I-told-you-so look. "No, sir, nothing."

"So, if I were to open the cabinets and toss your bunks, I would not find anything?"

"Ummm," Jeb said and looked around the lounge to everyone shaking their heads. "No, sir, you would not find anything."

"OK, well, you are all cleared to enter. All the visas are in order, and you all may proceed. Except for you, Agent Crow. You may not enter the United States. My superior is submitting the form. I need you to come with me now. I will need your badge, and we will take your picture."

Cal interjected, "Agent, your buddy is knocking at the door," as he opened the bus door.

A second border agent stepped up on the bus and said, "Agent Mayfield, can I have a word with you?" The two agents stepped outside and walked in front of the bus.

The Doctor said, "What is it now?"

"I don't know," said Jeb.

"They are going at it pretty good," said Cal.

Five minutes later, Agent Mayfield stepped back on the bus. "Agent Crow, this is your lucky day. A US citizen coming back across the border had your passport and turned it in. He said that he was a fan of the Doctor and that you were at the same rest area as he was. He found your passport and saw you get on the bus, but it was driving away when he went out to give it to you."

"What rest area?" said Crow. "We didn't just stop anywhere."

"You must have. The guy checked out. He is a guy from California on a road trip. Nice guy, my partner said."

"Where is this guy? I want to thank him."

"He took off, said he was in a hurry to get to Moorhead. But now you are all good to go."

"Thank you, Agent Mayfield," said Jeb, and with that, Agent Mayfield walked off the bus.

"I must say that you are pretty lucky," said Jeb.

"What's the chance someone finds it and sees you in the distance like that?" said Neusy.

"We are rolling!" was heard from up front.

Crow, looking at his picture in his passport, said, "I guess I am. This is definitely my passport." He started to turn the pages and said, "Here is my stamp from Japan last year, and here is when Sparrow and I vacationed in Greece. So it is mine. Weird that I dropped it. It's usually right up here in my jacket pocket. Wait a second, what is this?" He turned the passport around so that Jeb and Sparrow could see the next page. In a dark marker written on that page, it said ***Remember Like a Vagina.***

Chapter 40

Jeb decided they would spend the night in Jamestown, ND, in a hotel parking lot about five hours from the border and two hours from Moorhead, MN.

The next day, they could relax a little due to Cal's determined driving the day before. They were all in good spirits. The Doctor was off walking, and with all the time they had to make it to the venue on time, they still left the hotel late. Jeb didn't say a word, as it would be pointless. Neusy saw Jeb's face when the Doctor entered the bus. He just gave Jeb the relax-don't-get-yourself-upset look. Jeb returned the I-need-a-beer-already look, and Neusy's eyes assured Jeb that soon a beer would be in his hand.

The Fargo-Moorhead area is mainly composed of Germanic and Scandinavian people. These two cities are a lot like twin cities, but not to be confused with the twin cities of Minneapolis and St. Paul.

Fargo carries a familiar name, as it was made famous by the film entitled *Fargo*. Based on a true story of a car executive who decided to have his wife kidnapped to extort money from his wealthy father-in-law, several murders were committed but eventually solved by a bright, pregnant, police chief. Neusy reflected on this as one murderer was killed, and the other was brought to justice. While the murders were continuing to happen on this tour, no one had been caught.

Cal, driving, was thinking that Fargo-Moorhead still had drive-in theaters. *Be fun to take the bus to one.* The bus pulled up to the venue, surprisingly at 3:00 p.m. right on time. Jeb now felt more relaxed after the late start. Neusy got to drink beers while not working. He was in a good mood. Hocker was not pleasant but did not have much to say, which Jeb took as him being content. Marlon managed to find someone to smoke a joint with him at the hotel. Cal had a room right in that hotel, and he felt energized. "Boys, like a clock today. Time for you guys to get to work."

Gorm Odinson wasn't a huge man but looked like someone you didn't want to fuck with. He was six feet tall, 190 pounds, with red hair, a medium-length beard, green eyes, and an animal cap of some animal's fur.

Tonight's venue was another Viking-themed bar: Odin's Lair. Gorm was outside waiting and instructed Cal as to where they had designated parking for the bus.

Neusy stood and said, "Let's make this quick. I read online that this place handcrafts some of the best Danish-style lagers and IPAs this side of Scandinavia. There are thirty handcrafted beers on tap. They even have a beer called Odin's Axe, which is eighteen percent alcohol."

"This will be a good day," said Hocker. "All of the beers are served in various-sized animal horns."

Marlon added, "I want one of those."

They followed Gorm into the club through the load-in, which was a garage door behind the stage. Hocker said, "Nice, easy load-in," and smiled. Neusy looked at Jeb to see if he saw the smile. Jeb shook his head, and the two chuckled.

Gorm showed them the club. The bar itself was about thirty feet long, a replica of a Viking dragon boat with shields hanging below bar level. There was a single mast in the middle of the ship, with a cross beam that the red-and-white sail hung down to the tops of the alcohol shelves. Upon the walls hung Viking weapons, axes and swords, and some Viking clothing. There were various wooden shields also hanging. And in glass cases, there were antique Viking helmets and a sword that once belonged to a famous Danish king. The stage was also a Viking dragon boat, about thirty feet wide, with a high-arched bow with a carved dragon on top. The red-and-white sail was suspended from the ceiling and came down to the ship's edge to conceal the band. It doubled as a curtain. The sail would be raised when the band started playing. Again, along the stage were many shields following the length of the ship.

The house PA system and the stage's floor monitors were the finest quality in the world. Neusy said, "Did you know that the Danish created the loudspeaker?"

"I did not know that," replied Marlon, "but this place is cool."

Gorm showed them the PA and said, "And these are some of the best money can buy. Each floor monitor can produce 1,000 watts of the purest, cleanest sound. The house PA, you see over there, is a towering, three-level, triple-wide arsenal of speakers on both sides of the stage, and when needed, can produce 15,000 watts, not that anyone would need that kind of volume."

Neusy said, "Jurgen Weislangwolf might appreciate it."

Gorm introduced them to Frode, who, at 6'5", weighed 280 pounds. He looked menacing with his long blonde hair in a ponytail, blue eyes, and furry sleeveless vest, but was one of the nicest bartenders in Minnesota.

There were two huge bouncers. "This is Knud," said Gorm. Knud was large. 6'9" of large that weighed 310 pounds, he had a thick brown long braided beard and brown locks hanging down in front of his left shoulder. "And this is Birger," who was even larger at 6'11". His 345 pounds were distributed perfectly proportionately. he was bald and had a long red beard that had four braids in it. These two guys made Arnold Schwarzenegger look tiny. Both of these guys were sitting on high stools at the long oak bar, and each rested their hand on a genuine Viking battle-ax. They shook hands with the crew.

"Let us know if you need anything," said Gorm.

"OK, thanks," said Jeb. "Guys, let's get to work. Make this load-in quick."

"Nice people here," said Neusy, and they walked back out the garage door.

"I should be able to get all sorts of free beer here," said Marlon.

Scaggz was driving his VW van about twenty car lengths behind the tour bus. He was very cautious not to be noticed by the FBI or Cal. But then again, he kept changing his appearance, and it would be difficult for anyone to recognize him. How would he dress for tonight's venue? He wasn't too concerned and thought he could adapt to any situation. He followed the bus around town until they parked in front of Odin's Lair. He parked at the corner where Odin's Lair was located. He sat and observed Jeb, Neusy, Hocker, and Marlon exit the bus and proceed into the venue. He continued to watch the bus and the venue. After ten minutes, he saw Neusy, Hocker, and Marlon come outside and go to the equipment trailer. They opened it and began to wheel out speaker cabinets and carry out the merch boxes. He wanted to peer in the doors of the venue to see what it was like. He climbed into the back of his VW van and started sifting through his clothes, but could not find the right disguise.

A man in a grey uniform walked by and Scaggz watched him go into businesses to read their electrical meters. He grabbed his blue Strat and stepped outside on the sidewalk and waited. As the electric meter man approached, he extended his blue guitar and asked, "Do you know anything about electric guitars?"

"Well, my son plays one, but—" BAM. "AAAAAAAHH!"

Scaggz undressed the unconscious man in the back of the VW and put on his grey uniform. He attached the man's name badge to the shirt pocket properly. He looked at the man, whose hair was almost the same color as his. He opened his shaving kit, removed his electric razor, and sheared all the hair off the unconscious man. He put it in his cereal bowl, then he opened his tool chest and took out a bottle of glue. He applied glue to his face and spread it around like shaving cream. Then he inserted his lower face into the bowl with the man's hair in it. The hair stuck all over his face. He grabbed the hairdryer that he had converted to work off of a car's battery through the cigarette lighter and turned it on his face to speed up the drying process of the glue. He looked in his compact mirror. "Not bad, pretty cool!" he said out loud. He gave himself a trim with a pair of scissors until he was satisfied with his new look. Now Scaggz had a medium-length beard. No one would recognize him.

What to do with this meter man? He started up the VW van and drove down the street. He drove past the tour bus and venue and kept on going. About a mile down the road, he found a schoolyard with no one there and moved to the far end of it. He got out of the van, slid open the side door, pulled out the unconscious man, and dragged him over to the playground area. Scaggz laid him on the small merry-go-round kiddy ride, gave it a spin with the man lying on it, and said, "See you!" Around and around went the man in his underwear.

Scaggz drove back to the venue and parked a block away. He got out and walked to the club. He looked in the door and, to the left, about fifteen feet away, he saw Jeb and Marlon setting up the merch booth on a sidewall. To his right, he saw Neusy and Hocker on the stage setting up the drums. The two bouncers, Knud and Birger, were near the stage, watching Neusy and Hocker set up. Gorm saw Scaggz standing in the doorway and approached him from the bar. "Can I help you?"

"Yes, I'm here to read your meter and check if any wiring looks unsafe. The routine inspection of the wires that we do once a year."

"Well, the meter is out that back door over there. As for our wiring, it's the best! It was a custom job by Viking Electrical Contractors a year ago."

"Yeah, well, I have to check anyway…it's my job, you know. Once a year to make sure your patrons are safe."

"OK, have at it!"

Everything was perfect. Scaggz could move around freely, after all, he was now a city electric company worker doing an inspection. Looking about the venue and seeing all of the Viking memorabilia, he came up with his next brainstorm. He would come back as Hrothgar the Great since the electric meter man already had been seen.

He was thinking of stealing some clothes and apparel off the wall, but they might be missed. There must be a second-hand store, or even a costume shop. He was liking his glued-on beard and thought that would accent things nicely. He proceeded to leave the venue and told Gorm, "Everything checked out. That is some pretty nice wiring. You will have a nice show tonight." He walked back to the van, changed into some more comfortable clothes, and sat watching the tour bus from down the block.

Jeb and his crew were back on the bus. Scaggz could hear the bus engine fire up, and then it pulled away from the curb and down the street. He started his engine and slowly tailed them through the town. They made a turn here, a turn there. They went fifteen minutes out from the center of town. He saw the tour bus pull into a parking lot next to a decent-looking hotel. Scaggz decided to park at a public park across the street and pulled into the parking area.

As he watched, he saw the band and crew exit the bus and enter the hotel. He saw the Doctor exit the bus last. "There you are, my old friend! I will see you later tonight." He drove away to find a store to get the clothes for tonight. He found a costume shop that had Viking apparel. The rental was not expensive because there were many Viking festivals and events throughout the year, and it was quite common to rent Viking clothes.

He went inside, found something suitable, paid the proprietor twenty dollars, and left. He made it back to the public park and, as he parked his VW, he heard CACUGA! CHUM! BANG! BANG! BINGANGGGG!*That's not good!* It sounded like he threw a rod in his engine. *Fuck! I can't fix this. I don't have enough for a repair job either.* He sat there, hopelessly thinking what his next move would be. *How can I follow the bus now?*

He saw Cal come out of the hotel and walk over to the main door. He saw Cal punch his code in the keypad and enter the bus. Cal disappeared into the bus. He had to find out what that code was. He went back to his tool chest and removed a cylindrical tube. Then he pulled on one end, and it telescoped out into three sections. He created this telescope from tubular metal used in the lighting scaffolds in the larger stages that he worked on. He peered through his telescope out of his VW van towards the bus. A few minutes later, Cal came outside again, closed the main door, and faced the keypad. He focused on the keypad. What is he doing now? Cal punched in a code; Scaggz got it, 567477. One of the lower cargo bay doors opened. That's it!

He quickly changed into his Viking clothes and waited for Cal to get his suitcase out of the bay and go into the hotel. Then Scaggz hurried across the street, looked around, and entered the code on the keypad. The bay opened. Once it was fully extended, he punched in the code again and jumped inside the cargo bay before it closed all the way. Now inside, he lit his cigarette lighter and found the emergency release lever that he could let himself out with.

Torsten was very enthusiastic about playing in this venue. When Jeb returned to the bus after the load-in, he told Torsten how incredible this place was.

"Are you going to wear your horned helmet again tonight, Torsten?" asked Marlon.

"You know it, little man!" replied Torsten.

"Maybe you can speak Danish with some of those guys that work in the bar?"

"What makes you think that they can speak Danish?"

"Well, just by the names. They don't sound normal. Grom, Frode, Knud, and Birger."

"Hahaha! Yes, those are real ancient Viking names. Maybe they can speak Danish."

"The two bouncers are HUGE! They were even carrying battle-axes."

"Really?"

"Yeah, really!"

Everyone was in their hotel rooms. The contract at this club supplied the rooms, which was unusual to have this many rooms in a contract. But the hotel and the club were owned by the same person. Jeb would take whatever he could, and it helped the guys rest. They had an hour before they needed to be back at the venue. The agents had their room supplied by the FBI and rested, as neither of them could sleep on the bus while moving.

Nathan was slipping into tight-fitting jeans and a black, sleeveless shirt. Torsten had on his brown leather armored vest and grey stretchy pants. Both stood side by side in their room in front of a mirror mounted on the wall. Later at the club, Torsten would put on his Viking horned helmet that his grandfather had given him.

Heinz had some fresh carrot and celery sticks and decided on a quick jog. He put on his green sweatshirt and sweatpants. "I'll see you guys later. I'm going for a jog." Nathan and Torsten didn't care as long as Heinz was not steaming broccoli in their room.

"Don't be late! We have to be at the venue in an hour," said Torsten.

Cal laid on his bed reading a MAD magazine. It was getting close to leaving time. Jeb sent a text to everyone that it was time to head out to the bus. Cal got up off his bed, went to the toilet, grabbed his jacket, and went out to the bus. Entering the bus, he started the engine. Scaggz was getting anxious to leave. He was relieved to hear the bus engine fire up. All of the guys eventually were out of their rooms and on the bus. The Doctor was the last on the bus. Everyone was there now, everyone except Heinz. "Where the hell is Heinz?" asked Jeb.

"He went for a jog!" said Torsten.

"What? We have to leave! What a fuck head!" said Jeb.

"Well, I guess he will see the text und jog over to the club, yah?" said Nathan.

"I must talk with Heinz later; exercises must be done earlier in the day, not before showtime!" said the Doctor.

"Fuck it, let's go, Cal!" yelled Jeb.

"Don't worry! I can cover his parts on the keyboards. I have two hands, you know," said Torsten.

Cal pulled out of the hotel parking lot and they were on their way to the venue once again. Cal parked in front of the club, and everyone exited the bus. Torsten left first, wearing his Viking helmet. He was feeling good about tonight. There was already a long line of people outside the venue waiting for the doors to open. Many people shouted and screamed when the Doctor exited the bus.

"WHHHOOOO!!! It's the Doctor!"

"Can we have a prescription?"

"In your Pants! Bitchy Wife! YEAAAHH!!!"

"Why are the Blues Brothers on the bus?"

Jeb hurried them along in through the front doors and past Knud and Birger. They made their way to the green room in the back of the large room. Cal remained on the bus and continued reading his MAD magazine. They would spend the night in their comfortable hotel rooms and leave in the morning.

While walking inside toward the green room, Torsten was distracted by all of the ancient relics he saw on display. Torsten was fascinated by what he saw. A lot of the clothes, shields, and helmets were authentic, not just copies. He saw King Hrothgar's sword in the glass case on the sidewall. *Wow! It was the king's sword. How did these guys get that?* Feeling a little thirsty, he stopped at the bar. There he met Frode, the bartender. Frode said hello in English.

Torsten replied, "Hej." (Hello.)

"God aften." (Good Evening.)

"Kan du tale dansk?" (Can you speak Danish?)

"Ja lidt." (A little.)

"Hej kan jeg få en pils?" (Hey, can I get a lager?)

"Jamen, prøv denne." (Sure, here you are.)

"Mmmmm! Velsmagende! Nå, jeg må være klar til showet. Farvel!" (Mmmmm! Delicious! I have to get ready for the show.)

"Hav et godt show!" (Have a good show!)

Frode had handed Torsten a lager in an animal horn. *Wow!* Torsten thought. *That was cool.* He hadn't spoken in his father's tongue in many years. It's always German or English. He sipped his fine lager out of his animal horn and made his way to the green room to join the others.

Scaggz was listening to the crowd outside. They sounded excited about the show. It was time to get out of the cargo bay and stand in line. He shimmied over to the emergency lever and pulled on it. He gently pushed on one of the cargo bay doors and slightly opened it enough to slide out onto the sidewalk. He looked around to see if anyone was watching him. There wasn't. He gently closed the bay door and walked towards the back of the line. As he stood in line, he noticed the tall guy in front of him had his show tickets sticking out of his back pocket. Scaggz gently lifted one of the tickets out of the guy's pocket and put it in his own pocket. Now he was all set to go in.

Meanwhile, Jeb was at the merch booth with Marlon. "That fucking Heinz! He always has to exercise at the worst times."

"Why don't you text him again?"

"Yes, good idea, Marlon. For once, you are growing a little piece of your brain."

"Gee, thanks!"

About ten minutes later, Jeb got a phone call. It was Heinz. "Where the fuck are you? We are on in thirty minutes."

"Man, I just came to."

"Just came to? What the fuck does that mean?"

"I don't know… I was running in this field und I wasn't looking where I was going…und I fell into a manhole."

"You fell into a manhole… Are you kidding me? Where is this manhole?"

"You know where is the movie theater?"

"No!"

"It's by a Mobil station!"

"OK! I'm going to call the police to get you out."

Jeb called the police, but they said they were busy with the many burglaries that had been called in. They didn't have any extra officers to assist a minor problem like a guy in a manhole. Jeb called the fire department. The fire department operator said a five-alarm fire had been called in and that they could not assist Heinz until after. Jeb was furious.

Jeb asked Neusy, who was standing nearby, to help. "I need you to go outside and find out where the movie theater is that is next to a Mobil station. Look for a field next to it and look for a manhole. Try to get Heinz the fuck out of the manhole and get him back here for the show. We don't have much time."

"OK, boss!"

Neusy asked Birger by the front door if he knew where the theater was. Birger told him to make a left out of the venue, walk a block and turn left on Vahalla Blvd and you should see it. He jogged to the field next to the theater in five minutes, located the manhole, and shined the light from his cell phone down the hole. Heinz was about about seven feet down, leaning sideways against the inner wall.

"Heinz, can you stand and reach for my hand?"

"Nein! There are some metal bars around my legs. Rebar."

"Wait a minute, let me think."

He had an idea and called Jeb. "I found him. I cannot get him out of the manhole. He is down too far to pull him up, some storm sewer, but he is about eight feet down. I have no rope or ladder."

"Fuck me! Fuck, always some bullshit! Do you have any ideas?"

"Yeah, a pretty good one. Ask the sound engineer to send me his best wireless setup for the bass and a wireless earphone head monitor. Have Marlon run it over here with Heinz's bass. There is a lot of room down there. He should be able to play in the sewer."

"That's pretty fucking out there, Neusy! But it just might work. How far are you from the club?"

"About two blocks."

"How many feet is that?"

"About 1,200 feet."

"OK, I'll ask the sound man."

The sound man told Jeb that his best wireless setup could transmit clearly about 1,200 feet, maybe a little farther. That would just get the job done. Jeb collected the components from the sound man, got the bass from the green room, and gave them to Marlon. Birger told Marlon how to go, and he was off. Jeb delayed announcing the Doctor until Neusy called him and told him they were set up and ready. Marlon found the field next to the theater and saw Neusy in the middle of it. "Dude! Heinz, are you OK?" asked Marlon.

"Yah, I think so, but I can't get out!" replied Heinz from down in the hole. Marlon was digging the echo.

"Don't worry, I'm going to hand you down your bass. We have it connected to a wireless transmitter," said Neusy. "You have to wear these wireless headphones."

"OK… I got it. Danke!"

"OK, Heinz, play a few notes."

Suddenly, everyone heard thunderous bass booming out of the PA speakers in the venue, but no one was on stage. The crowd started getting excited. "YAAAHH!!!! BRING ON THE DOCTOR!!!" The sound engineer thought everything must be in order and he lowered the volume fader for the bass channel on his mixing console.

Neusy called Jeb and told him they were ready to go. Jeb texted Hocker in the green room and told him to come out and make the announcement. The agents were in position: Crow guarding the back and Sparrow up front. Nothing would get past them tonight.

Hocker went out. "Good evening, Moorhead!"

"YAAAAHHHH!"

"BRING ON THE DOCTOR!!"

"I hope while I am in your town, I can get a little more head." Hocker was smiling, thinking he was the first to say such a thing.

"BRINNG OUT THE DOCTORRRR!!!!"

"Hey, bartender, can I get more head on my beer? Hahaha."

"BRING ON THE DOCTOR!!"

"YOU'RE A FUCKING IDIOT."

"OK, OK… Here is the man you've all been waiting for. If it weren't for this man, I wouldn't get a paycheck, so thanks for buying a ticket and maybe a T-shirt later. Here he is, the Doctor!"

The Doctor came out blazing, then noticed that the bass was lagging. Nobody told him that Heinz was stuck in a hole. The Doctor was looking around the stage. No Heinz! The Doctor looked over at Hocker, who gave him the thumbs up. The Doctor stopped playing, and the band stopped playing. Heinz continued to play and then noticed the band had stopped and followed suit.

The Doctor called through the PA, "Jeb, where is Heinz?"

Jeb walked up on stage. "He is not here."

"Yah, that much I can see."

"He fell into a manhole, and Neusy brought him a wireless and an in-ear monitor so he can hear what the band is playing."

"Yah, that is most unusual. He is playing behind in the song."

"It's probably the lag time. Between hearing in the monitors and his playing coming through the PA."

"Yah, that is for sure, a lag time. He needs to fix that."

Jeb walked over to the mic and said, "Heinz, can you hear me? Slap the bass if you can." B-BA-BOOM came thundering out of the PA.

"Fuck that. 'Slap the Virgin!'" someone up front in the audience yelled, and the audience erupted in a cheer.

"Good Heinz, listen, you are coming in a little behind the band through the PA. You will have to compensate. Can you do this? Give me another slap." B-BA-BA-BOOM. "Excellent. OK, guys, he is ready."

The Doctor stepped up to the mic and said, "Yah, so unprofessional. Here we go again." He started playing, and right on cue, Heinz was there. The Doctor became motivated and played one song after the next with Heinz right there with him.

Scaggz stood in the back. *This is going to be so fantastic tonight. Ha, these agents have no clue. Heinz is right on. Very talented. I must tell him this.*

"Yah," said the Doctor. "Now it's time for you to 'Slap the Virgin.'" The audience went crazy. The Doctor found the night inspirational with the ships, the audience's enthusiasm, and Heinz being able to pull off the best bass he has played on the entire tour from a remote location.

The agents were scanning the room as the show was almost over. Nothing was going on. Crow texted Sparrow, *Keep yourself sharp that guy said he was heading to Moorhead.*

What guy? Sparrow texted back.

The guy with my passport.

The show ended, and the Doctor started his meet and greet. Jeb called Neusy. "All OK over there?"

"Yeah, Heinz is wondering why it has been hours and no one has come to rescue him."

"I don't know, I will call again, but I need you to come back and help Hocker. He is up there, not so happy. I don't want him breaking anything."

"Right on, Jeb, on my way."

Neusy said to Heinz down in the sewer, "Heinz, I have to go and work. Hang tight, and I am sure they will be here soon. I'll come back as soon as I am finished."

"Neusy, thank you." And with that, Neusy left Heinz in the sewer in the dark with only his bass and phone to keep him company. Neusy got a bad feeling as he walked back to the club, leaving Heinz all alone in the sewer. He arrived at the club, and the site was spectacular. The meet and greet was the busiest he had seen. People were lined up around the venue to meet the Doctor. Jeb must be pleased. The Doctor was signing and taking pictures with the fans.

Agent Sparrow was now standing next to Jeb. "Nice to see an evening going well. Nothing even close to being any trouble tonight. I think our positioning has scared him off."

"No trouble, other than the bass player down the street in a hole."

"Oh shit, that's right," said Sparrow. "Where is he?"

"Neusy knows where he is. He spent the whole show there."

"I need to go there now," said Sparrow.

"Take Neusy, he will show you, but I need him back here after."

Sparrow told Crow what he was thinking, and the two of them left the venue with Neusy. Hocker kicked over one of the mic stands when he saw Neusy go again. "Fucking amateurs," he said.

Chapter 41

Heinz was playing solitaire on his phone to pass the time. *Why is it taking so long?* He checked his phone for messages. There were none. Out of one of the connecting storm pipes came a voice. "Jimmy?"

"About time," said Heinz. "I thought you forgot about me."

"Are you kidding? This is my plan," said Scaggz as he entered the collection basin that Heinz was in.

"It's good to see you, Johnny," said Heinz to Scaggz. "You have them going crazy, and those agents are clueless. Brilliant to call in all those burglaries tonight."

"Yes, it's good to talk to you, Jimmy. I kept seeing you from a distance, afraid you would break character, but you were perfect. Damn, for an hour I called in those burglaries. Kept the locals busy."

"I learned it all from you. Mom always said you had the perfect mind. You can always visualize something before it happens. I miss her, Johnny."

"I miss her too, but now we have to go before they come back. It's about three hundred feet, and we can come up a block away. Follow me."

The two brothers crawled through the storm pipe until they arrived at the next collection basin. Scaggz had a ladder in place so the two would be able to exit, and they did. "This way. I don't have my van, it's broke, but I have a better plan. Did you prick your finger and leave a couple of drops behind for the agents?"

"Yes, of course, that's what you told me to do."

The two walked back to the hotel and across the street to where Scaggz had his VW parked.

"What's wrong with the van? I can have a look. Fifteen years of working at the garage taught me some things."

"It will make us stand out too much. It's hidden now. So tell me, the Doctor has no idea that you are my brother, right?"

"No way, it was perfect. He has no idea. Your friend in Germany made me the passport to be undetectable, just like you said. I hooked up with Torsten at the open mic night, just like you said. Everything went perfect."

"Your playing was superb. What was it, fourteen years ago I brought you in for the audition?"

"Yeah, close to fifteen. That asshole, the Doctor, remember what he said? He called me a hack and a poser. He deserves all this shit that is falling on him now."

"The name you chose was perfect, Heinz Beckenschultz. Those two years of German did you well. They could not tell your German was not natural?"

"It's funny, when I speak with them, we speak English a lot. I had to put effort into sounding like them. Those idiot crew members couldn't tell."

They arrived at the van and Scaggs said, "Now we must wait until they leave. They will go to Chicago in the morning, I am assuming, since they are all in hotel rooms."

"What do you mean there is no one in the hole?" shouted Crow.

When the agents arrived at the manhole, the fire department and the police were already there. The agents showed their badges and were allowed to enter the roped-off area.

"That's what I am telling you," said a fireman climbing out of the basin. "Just some equipment. Looks like a transmitter of some type, and a set of headphones plugged into some device, and also a bass guitar."

"This is impossible," said Sparrow.

"He was here when I left maybe twenty-five minutes ago," said Neusy.

"Well, no one here now. We did find a little blood. Looks like whoever was in there cut themselves, not too bad from what I can see."

The agents went down into the manhole and took pictures. Nothing abnormal other than a couple of drops of blood. Neusy grabbed the equipment and they exited the manhole.

"Well, I guess he somehow freed himself," said Crow.

"It could have been worse. I am just glad we didn't find another body," replied Sparrow.

They returned to the venue. The meet and greet was almost finished. Hocker, dragging the last of the equipment off the stage, looked over at Neusy and spit. Neusy walked up on the stage. "Don't be like that, big guy. I could not help it. It was not my choice not to be here."

"I fucking know that, but it still pisses me off to have to do this all by myself. Did they get Heinz out?"

"No, he wasn't there. He must have gotten himself out. Let me help you with that," said Neusy. He lifted one of the amps and helped Hocker out of the building.

The following day, according to Jeb's text, they would be leaving at 8:00 a.m. Cal was first on the bus and started it up. Then the crew walked out together, refreshed, as they slept in a bed and got an early morning shower. "You must be happy," said Neusy. "That meet and greet was sick."

"Yeah, we did well," Jeb said. "It bothers me that Heinz never checked in with me. Hopefully he is on the bus."

The four of them arrived at the bus. "Good morning, boys," said Cal as he drank coffee from his oversized cup.

"Good morning," said Jeb. "Nice day, we should make good time."

"I believe you are correct!"

The crew entered the bus and went to their bunks to put their shower bags away. Jeb came out with a piece of paper with the words, ***It's all over when the bass stops playing. He was a hack so I hacked him and put him out of his misery.*** Handwritten, as if by a child.

"We got a problem," said Jeb.

After another two days in Moorhead and a search that engulfed the entire city, the tour was canceled. Not by the Doctor, but by the FBI.

"Yah, we can still play. Torsten, he can play the bass parts on the keyboards," the Doctor pleaded.

"They won't let you continue," said Crow. "I just got off the phone with my supervisor, and they pulled your visa."

"What does that mean?"

"You no longer can work here in the US on this tour. You have to return to Austria."

"Well, my ladies will not be happy."

"We searched with the local police and FBI, two dozen law enforcement officers and nothing. I am afraid it does not look good. The note mentioned he hacked Heinz, and with this psycho, that is entirely possible," said Sparrow. "They searched the sewer plant, dredged the pools, nothing. He is gone. I am sorry, guys."

An hour later, Jeb announced, "I got you all booked back to Austria from Chicago and us back home as well. Two extra nights hotel here, this was quite expensive. But in the morning, we leave at five."

The following morning at five, they were all on the bus emptying their bunks as the bus departed. The agents stayed behind to continue to work the case.

"Yah, you know this sucks!" said the Doctor.

Neusy added, "If only I stayed there, Hocker, you could have loaded that out. We would still have Heinz."

"Fuck you, this is not on me," said Hocker.

"Guys, listen, it's not on anyone. We have to deal with this, and hopefully next year tour again," said Jeb.

"Yah, we must tour again."

Marlon, showing his phone, said, "Look, I took a couple of pictures with Sparrow and Crow. I will post these."

Nathan was lying on one of the benches in the lounge and sighed. "Yah, again, I do not get any women." Torsten was making tea and wearing his Viking helmet.

"Boys, this is going to be a ride. We are about ten hours from the airport in Chicago. So we will make only one stop if you want to make those flights tonight," said Cal. He then put on his music.

"Neusy, thanks for a great tour, actually all you guys. Hocker, steady as usual, and Marlon, next time out, are you up for it?" Jeb asked.

"Hell yes! I am in."

"I know it's early in the morning," said Neusy, "but we still have some beers they gave us to go at the club. One more for the road, guys?"

"You were reading my mind," said Jeb.

"Fuck yes," replied Hocker.

"I could go for one," added Marlon.

The bus was moving along to send the guys home. They could not finish what they began, but as usual, they remained a precision unit, one that will indeed tour again. "Cheers, boys, to a tour that we managed to survive," said Jeb, and they all drank their beer.

"This is not so comfortable down here. I was much more comfortable in my bunk as Heinz," Jimmy Scaggz said.

"No, it's not, but we will survive. We have food and water, and these guys up there need a proper send-off," said Scaggz. "What did you do with your Heinz passport?"

"It is in my bunk. They will find it when they do their final sweep. I made sure to put the bloody fingerprints on it like you said."

Epilogue

The Doctor and the Surgeons arrived at O'hare Airport and discovered that their flight had been delayed. There was no reason that the Doctor's suitcase, containing many of his guitar effects, was not under the bus. He had seen Jeb put it under there the night before. While waiting at the airport with Torsten and Nathan, the doctor contemplated what he would tell his women when he arrived back home. He had a little money from the tour. Certainly not enough to afford the lifestyle that they are all used to.

Torsten did not mind as much regarding the money. Touring with the Doctor never made him much money. He accepted just to tour North America and it was more like a vacation for him.

He was a very talented musician and got more offers than he had time to take on the workload. It was nice that he could pick and choose which tours he took part in. Many bands hired him, making money on the tours to carry him for the year. He had been getting away from the metal bands and had played at various sporting events as the keyboard/organist. He also had accepted a tour with a gospel band, which he found attractive. His loss, heading home, was that he would not experience the interesting cities and people he always met along the way.

Nathan had to take a leave of absence from his job as a music teacher. Not going home with the full salary of the tour was a problem. He did not often tour or have the offers that Torsten received. He would have to beg to get his job back early as the school hired a temporary replacement. He didn't realize that, while he was flying back home, the school signed a contract with the replacement teacher and had no intention of breaking that contract, as these teachers are in demand.

Once Nathan returned home, he found work for the next five weeks as a singing tour guide for one of the resorts in the Austrian Alps. He was issued the official uniform of the resort and had to wear Austrian lederhosen for nine hours a day and went home every evening with chafed inner thighs. After five weeks and seven tubes of relief cream, he was welcomed back into the school.

Once home, the Doctor had to answer to his live-in girlfriend Beatrice Fanning, or Bea, as he called her. Together they had eleven children. Bea was born in England. She met the Doctor at the age of twenty-three and moved to Austria. This was twenty-eight years ago.

The Doctor would get an earful every day regarding why they did not have enough money for simple things like ketchup or hot sauce. Luckily, he saved the day when he produced a handful of ketchup packets he took from the airport.

He spent the next few months planning his next year's worth of tours. Working with many booking agents in different countries was challenging. It's a good thing that Jeb kept this on track. He would start the touring in India. He had never been and looked forward to making the most of his time there.

He picked up one-off gigs at various clubs in Austria, bringing his acoustic guitar to fill in the gaps in his finances.

Hocker Flemming counted on the income from this tour to take him through the next six months. Upon returning home, he had enough to last three weeks. He worked for local bars, booking bands and helping them set up their gear. Three days a week was not enough to pay his rent.

His landlord locked him out of his apartment, threatening to sell his belongings if he did not catch up on the rent. After sleeping in the bar for a week, he convinced his landlord to let him back in the apartment as he just landed a second job at the tobacco store up the street and would have the back rent and any rent moving forward on time.

Marlon Jiggs went back to work at the music store and could not stop talking about the tour. Sales decreased in the first two weeks he was back. He was ordered to take a week off after customers complained that he was following them around repeating the same stories all day.

Now at home, Marlon missed the life on the road he now craved. Since returning, his wife's voice made him yearn to be back on the road. He could not understand why he was sad and panic ridden when he left home. He now spent his day smoking weed and checking his messages every fifteen minutes to see if the call to go back on the road had come.

Tommy Thompson was on his flight home to northern California. The flight was not full, and he had an empty seat next to him. He was hoping that when the Doctor next toured, he would already have another tour and decline. He put on his alarm collar and set the alarm on his phone. He fell asleep thinking how nice his bed would be once at home.

He was violently awoken in Des Moines with guns pointed at him. They were screaming something about a collar around his neck. He could see that passengers on the plane had already exited when the taser hit him and he was out again. The police put him in handcuffs when the alarm on the phone went off and his collar zapped him awake right before he was tased a second time.

Jeb and Neusy spent the first week after the shortened tour on a pub crawl. They did the preliminary work for the next tour by visiting nineteen breweries in a week. Drinking some of the best beer California had to offer, the pair searched for a new booking agent for the Doctor. They made call after call but were unsuccessful in their efforts. Spud Burger remained the lone booking agent willing to book the Doctor in North America.

They decided that was that and spent the remainder of their time between beer tasting, lounging at pools from the different hotels they were staying at, and discussing their experience on the road while working on their book. They had enough material from this tour to not only complete their current book, but start a second follow-up book.

They were lucky enough to get the first book published. Their stories seemed to be an interesting, behind the scenes look at the touring scene that most people were curious about. After a few months, they, too, were ready to get back at it and start touring again. The prospect of touring India with the Doctor was looking like a reality, and there was a lot for them to do on the production side.

The murders were something they would have to deal with next time out. Would it continue, or was that it? What happened to

Heinz? His body or pieces were never found. Who was behind all of it and why?

Scaggz and his brother Jimmy (Heinz Bechenshultz) spent the following months in the mountains in southern California. Scaggz, too, was getting close to completing his book: a cookbook called *The Guide To Neighborhood Critters.*

Scaggz had formulated new recipes that he wanted to try, and these would complete his cookbook. Unfortunately, the California mountain beaver was highly elusive. He spent days searching for and tracking this rodent while Jimmy stayed at camp. Jimmy, never a big camper, refused to sleep in the tent and spent his days in the VW, which he repaired once they left the storage bay of the bus. Scaggz finished his book without the recipe for the California mountain beaver. He included the spice recipe as an alternative option to the one in his book for the common rat.

After two hours under the bus, Scaggz could no longer listen to Jimmy complain about how uncomfortable this was while a bunk was more comfortable up top with his name on it. When the bus finally made its one stop at a truck stop, they opened the bay door and snuck away undetected with the Doctor's effect suitcase. They managed to hitchhike back to Moorhead.

While Jimmy repaired the van, Scaggz watched the agents, who were still at the venue. He walked into the front entrance in his meter-reading uniform and explained to security that he needed to shut the power off for a few minutes while his co-workers were repairing the area. An hour later, the power was still out. The agents found the electrical panel but no sight of the meter guy. Agent Sparrow slid the main breaker, and the lights to the venue were back on. Crow was first to see it, then Sparrow. Written on the wall next to the meter was a message for them. ***Agents, this was fun. I hope to see you next tour!***

Once Jimmy repaired the van, he found Scaggz and the two drove back to California. Scaggz was hoping for an announcement that the Doctor would be touring again. After a couple of months, Scaggz was sleeping when his phone buzzed with a message that the Doctor had announced a pending tour of India. In his excitement, he jumped out of his sleeping bag, ripped a hole in his tent, and landed outside on something that made a squooshing sound. He shined the light from his phone on what he just landed on and was looking in the eyes of a flattened California mountain beaver.

Agents Sparrow and Crow finished up business in Moorhead. They reported into their field office and decided that they deserved a vacation. They both had their passports; it was agreed on Cabo San Lucas for a three-night deal that Crow found after searching on his phone.

They stepped off the plane in Cabo, and just as the resort promised, their private driver was waiting for them. *This is more like it*, they thought. They arrived at their resort, checked in, and, after purchasing sunblock, were at the private beach, each with a glass in their hand that had an umbrella sticking out of it.

Agent Crow's phone rang, and he sat up. He motioned what number was calling him to Sparrow. Sparrow said, "Put it on speaker. I want to hear this."

Agent Crow set his phone down and answered, "Crow here."

"Agent Crow, this is Jesse White over here at the forensic lab. We got some results back for you on that hair you sent in."

"OK, great, I have you on speaker with Agent Sparrow sitting next to me. What did you find out?"

"Hi, Agent Sparrow. Well, the hair is human, but we do not have a match, nothing in our database as to whom it belongs to. But there was something else. We ran a complete makeup of the hair."

"What else?" asked Agent Sparrow. "What do you mean?"

"Well, it's different than I have ever seen. It seems there is a microscopic similarity to a cheetah, but very small. It had me baffled. Something unique. But then there was something else. I had to run it past the scientists upstairs, and they all looked at it, and not one of them had seen it before. They could not pinpoint it. No one has ever seen anything like it. But the consensus was that there is also something else in there, although just a tiny amount. They unanimously agree that it is a sasquatch."

"WHAT?" said the agents.

"Yes, and there is something else. The sasquatch has a defect. It would not have grown to full size. Like a smaller version, almost a dwarf."

"Is this for real?" asked Agent Crow.

"Yes, Agent, it is. I will email you the report, but wanted to reach out because of the uniqueness of the issue."

"Thank you, Jesse. I appreciate it."

"OK, Agents, good luck." Jesse White hung up.

The agents sat there, not moving for ten minutes. Agent Sparrow finally spoke. "Does the field office get a copy of this?"

"I don't know."

"Don't say a word to them about this."

"Agreed."

"White," said Jesse as he picked up his phone. "Yes, I read the script verbatim. That sure was the easiest $200 I have ever made. The next time you want to play a joke on an agent, look me up," and he hung up once again.

Follow Johnny Scaggz as he continues his pursuit of the Doctor in the follow-up release *Parody of Himself* scheduled for release in the first half of 2022.

www.ingramcontent.com/pod-product-compliance
Lightning Source LLC
Chambersburg PA
CBHW061323190726
48288CB00002B/628